DIVINE AKBAR AND HOLY INDIA

I0593008

Farzana Moon

Hamilton Books
A member of
The Rowman & Littlefield Publishing Group
Lanham · Boulder · New York · Toronto · Plymouth, UK

British Library Cataloging in Publication Information Available

Library of Congress Control Number: 2011931495
ISBN: 978-0-7618-5639-9 (paperback : alk. paper)
eISBN: 978-0-7618-5640-5

For dear Nathan,
My computer-angel and savior

Table of Contents

Preface

Third in the series of the Moghuls this book is written to honor Akbar much in the likeness of Shakespeare since he is remembered as the Shakespeare of India, besides being known simply as Great Akbar. Akbar's life itself created several *plays* on the stage of Hindustan, offering its audience the jewels of love, harmony and understanding. Streets of India *paved with gold* as deemed by foreign merchants became Akbar's theatres, inviting preachers of diverse faiths to hold open discussions in his royal court. As a great patron of religious tolerance, he employed learned scholars to translate Holy Scriptures into Persian, including Mahabharata. Jesuits as well as pundits, and spiritual leaders of diverse sects and religions flocked to his court for knowledge and patronage. He welcomed the pearls of wisdom from Gita, Torah, Bible and Quran, practicing the art of unity in the ocean of diversity. His edict of tolerance extended as far as building churches in Agra and Delhi, granting Christians the freedom to proselytize. Akbar's successor is his son prince Salim styled as Jahangir to become the fourth emperor of Hindustan. *The Moghul Hedonist* follows the fourth emperor to Kashmir four times during his reign, while his empress Nur Jahan rules the emperor and his empire.

1

Hira of Amber

Allah is the Light of the heavens and the earth. The similitude of His light is as a lustrous niche, wherein is a lamp. The lamp is in a glass. The glass as if it were a glittering star. It is lit from a blessed tree—an olive—neither of the east nor of the west; whose oil will well-nigh glow forth though fire touched it not. Light upon light! Allah guides to His light whomsoever He wills. And Allah sets forth parables to men, and Allah knows all things full well.

— Quran

I am the lover, trying to find my beloved in the loveless soul of holy Hind! Beloved, not the Lover—Akbar thought as he kept riding his horse, named Harian.

Akbar—the third Moghul emperor of India was on his way to wed the princess of Amber. This young emperor of India, oblivious to his twenty-one springs of youth, was a unique bridegroom. Unique in respect to this auspicious event that for the first time a Muslim monarch was going to wed his Hindu bride at the home of her parents!

Brides, brides, I learn more from my wives than from any sage, scholar or theologian! Each new bride of mine is a holy book, entrusted unto my hands with the sacred thread of wedlock. They are goddesses, goddesses all, houris indeed! Their minds the holy temples, their hearts the sacred mosques and in their souls live the holies of the holy. The sacred shrines from continents all, in their bodies and souls! Churches as well as synagogues; monasteries as well as mandars; and mosques of such sublime purity in their souls that no mortal sight can violate their sacredness within, and mine too—within and without! Are we all not holy? Akbar was thinking.

Salima! My own dear soul! My true beloved! I would not have married another if she could have— Are jealousy and hatred not holy, in a woman's heart, in the heart of my Salima? As sacred as love and purity, it seems to me. Did I not marry Hind as my intriguing bride? The corrupted bride of holiness in this holy land! Am I not to wed religions as my future brides, to seek Truth, God, Essence—or to seek oblivion?

Akbar donned in pure silks the color of the sky, with a matching turban slashed with pearls, seemed oblivious to his might and wealth, a part of which followed him, like a shadow from some divine munificence. He kept riding silently, his nut-colored complexion glowing with the fire of youth and exuberance. The divine munificence which followed him, were actually the emperor's chosen friends—the rajas, the nabobs, the courtiers, the soldiers and the scholars, not to mention the poets, the musicians and the theologians. Following this cavalcade were one hundred elephants decked with velvets and brocades. The wedding procession was moving slowly toward the palace of the raja, the Bihari Mall of Amber. The path was wide and unpaved with a scanty verdure against the array of tamarind groves in the distance.

Aziz Koka—Akbar's foster-brother was riding beside the emperor, unable to cross the breach of etiquette in breaking silence, until addressed by the emperor himself. Right now, while riding silently, Akbar's thoughts were slipping away from Salima to his accession. To insurrections and to the warring spirituality in his soul and psyche!

Akbar was still a young prince, the master of thirteen turbulent seasons as his entire legacy, when the sudden death of his father—emperor Humayun, had fettered him to the throne as the third Moghul emperor of Hindustan. Profoundly saddened by the unexpected death of his father, Akbar had been more baffled than shocked.

Whether life is nourished on its breath alone, or whether it is fed by the choicest of morsels in death in this simmering cauldron of life and death, who knows!

The inception of such Sufic thoughts was the first ones in Akbar's life, right after the death of his father. Self-taught by his propensity toward spirituality, he was to hold both life and death sacred as some holy rituals to celebrate the living and dying in one's soul, as much as in the actual process of life and death. The death of his father, whom he had loved more than he loved his mother, had carved a deep rent of grief in his young heart. And he was granted no respite to close this rent, but was plunged headlong into the warfare of survival for the fittest.

Akbar, though young and inexperienced at the time of his father's sudden death, was jolted out of his grief into the harsh realities of the world, where power was the key to unlock the Pandora box in this gilded cage of Hind. There and then, he had made a resolve that rule he would by the commandments of his compassion, not ever to be ruled by the dictates of the brutal world crashing within and without, everywhere, to maim and destroy nobleness in men and nature alike.

Akbar was truly the child of Hind. The first of the Moghul heirs to be born at Umarkot while his father was preparing for exile—his empire of Hind usurped by Sher Shah Suri. When emperor Humayun fled to Persia to seek aid from Shah Tahmasp, Akbar was still a babe of few months old, captured by his uncle Askeri, and taken to Kabul. When emperor Humayun had returned to Kabul as a conqueror, and was reunited with his son, he had appointed noble tutors to instruct Akbar in arts and sciences, in religion, philosophy and literature. But the royal heir was more interested in studying nature than in reading books. While still in Kabul, emperor Humayun was embroiled in several warring expeditions. During those bitter times in intrigues and rebellions, Akbar's studies were sorely neglected, much to the delight of his young heart. His love for hunting and exploring was cultivated by him, where nature was the book of art to him and nature alone its author and mentor. He had remained illiterate in a literal sense of the word that he could not read, didn't wish to acquire such a mode of learning, but was enriched by the knowledge of his inner-being. Seeking *truth* within his soul and psyche, nourishing his love for books, where words were alive with the resonance of a sound, not dead under the curse of speechless form or thought. Regardless of time and place his hunger for knowledge was satisfied by his court readers whenever he desired.

A bibliophile who doesn't like to read, yet he can, he can, if he wishes to, and can write too! Yes, I can, I can read and write both, making my will my command—mine and the emperor's. Akbar was thinking about the time when he had read ghazals with his mentor Abdul Latif and had recited the odes of Hafiz. His sharp Moghul features with a small nose, on the left of which glistened rather a large, black mole, were proclaiming him every inch the emperor of Hind, as he kept on riding nonchalantly.

"Your Majesty, I hope you don't attract enemies by marrying the Princess of Amber in conformity with the Hindu customs. Muslims are quick to raise the sword of heresy against their Muslim brothers, and to brand them as infidels with their pious zeal." Aziz Koka ventured a statement, rather than addressing the emperor directly.

"Between you and me runs a stream of milk, Aziz." Akbar commented in reference to Aziz being his foster brother. "But try not to cross it on the breach of etiquette. Religion is a beautiful deformity in the souls of us all, and everyone is heathen in the eyes of someone." He murmured.

The emperor was the master of his solitude once again, spurring his horse ahead of all, and plunging his thoughts into the sea of not too-distant memories.

Akbar was in Punjab with Biram Khan as his guardian before the death of his father. They were on a campaign to fight Sikandar Shah, when the news of emperor Humayun's sudden death had reached Akbar. And he was proclaimed the emperor of Hindustan, his coronation being staged by Biram Khan in an unfinished garden, in the town of Kalanaur. Akbar was then barely fourteen, already married to his cousin, Princess Ruqaiya, and drugged with the wine of youth and conquests.

To Akbar, at that precarious age and time, wars were *hunting expeditions.* He did not know then, that this coined expression of his would be his talisman for life, to hunt down his foes in the ever-warring domains of Hind. At the time of Akbar's accession, his half-brother, Muhammed Hakim, was two years old, and was the nominal governor of Kabul under the guardianship of Munim Khan.

After emperor Humayun's death, several claimants to the throne of Agra and Delhi had surfaced, the rebellions erupting forth from Kabul to Badakhshan, from Hind to Sindh. Biram Khan, appointed as Akbar's guardian during Humayun's lifetime, had taken full command of the tragic situation after the emperor's death. Working toward the interests of the young monarch apparently, yet giving vent to his cruel impulses in such a crafty way, where Akbar's kindnesses could never penetrate! Akbar had great respect for his guardian, Biram Khan, and loved him more than he was capable of loving any man. But young as he was, Akbar had fallen in love with beautiful Salima Sultan—Biram Khan's betroth. Late emperor himself had sanctioned this betrothal with a further promise that the couple was to be married shortly after the campaign of Punjab.

The Punjab was not the only state where the clouds of rebellions had surged and billowed, but Agra and Delhi were the seats of contention also. Also, Humayun's cousin, Sulaiman Mirza, who was the governor of Badakhshan, had risen against Munim Khan to capture Kabul. Fortunately, Munim Khan had resisted the attack, and the government of Kabul was left intact under the nominal command of two year old Muhammed Hakim. Hemu, a Hindu aspirant to the throne of kingship, had captured Agra, and had defeated Terdi Beg at Delhi. The Punjab campaign was left under the care of Khwaja Khizr, the husband of Akbar's aunt, Gulbadan Begum, and Akbar along with Biram Khan had marched eastward to chastise Hemu. Reaching Sirhind, Biram Khan, without the consent of Akbar, had had Terdi Beg murdered on the charges of treason.

Akbar, pressed by the urgency of his need to defeat Hemu, had no time to check Biram Khan's cruelties or indiscretions. And together, at the head of a large army, both Akbar and Biram Khan had marched on, succeeding in defeating Hemu at the battle of Panipat. Hemu, defeated and injured, both in body and soul, was brought before Akbar as a prisoner of war. Biram Khan, standing next to Akbar, had requested the young emperor to strike off the enemy's head. But Akbar had desisted, stating that his personal ethics did not permit him to strike an injured person, no matter a foe. Biram Khan then, without waiting for any command from Akbar, had struck off Hemu's head with his sword.

Akbar had regained his lost kingdoms, and had returned to Delhi as the young emperor of Hindustan. Biram Khan's indiscretions were turning Akbar's heart against his vizier, but he was quick to blame his own self that his secret love for Salima was the cause of this bitterness against his guardian. To deny— rather to appease this terrible passion, Akbar was infatuated with another beautiful lady, Suriya, and had married her without delay or ceremony.

Before marching back to Punjab campaign, Akbar had ordered his engineer, Qasim Khan, to begin the construction of a large fort at Agra. The young bride, Suriya, was left behind as the emperor had marched forth toward Punjab. But Biram Khan's betroth had traveled with the Imperial cavalcade as a privileged bride-to-be. The marriage of Biram and Salima was solemnized after the conquest of Punjab, as promised by Akbar's late father, emperor Humayun.

In Punjab, Khwaja Khizr had been unable to defeat Sikandar Shah. Sikandar Shah, though besieged in the fortress of Mankot, had no intentions of surrendering. Upon the arrival of Akbar with his royal standards, sweeping along the kingdoms in quick victories, Sikandar Shah had finally surrendered. Akbar, in his love for compassion and magnanimity, had pardoned Sikandar Shah. Bestowing upon him the jagirs of Bihar and Kharid where he could live like a lord, if not like a king. That was the time when Biram and Salima were married in fulfillment of Akbar's promise in honoring his late father's wishes. But then, Akbar had grown so wretchedly unhappy at heart, that he had contracted another impromptu marriage for himself with Mahmooda Begum, much in opposition to Biram Khan's arguments. Biram Khan had opposed this marriage on the grounds that Mahmooda Begum's aunt was married to Prince Kamran, known as the wicked brother of Humayun. Prince Kamran had imprisoned Akbar thrice when he was just a child, Biram Khan had reminded the young Emperor.

Returning to Agra, Akbar had ordered large houses to be built surrounded by attractive gardens. He had also sent messages to Kabul, commanding all the ladies of Humayun's harem to return to Hindustan. Especially his mother, Hamida Banu, Known as Miryam Makani, meaning literally, the sister of Virgin Mary!

Following the conquest of Punjab and Biram Khan's marriage to Salima, Akbar had learned to live with his sole love for knowledge. *Living like a martyr*, he would think, *with denial and suffering as his great passion.* Much were changing on the map of Hindustan, while Akbar reigned from his capitol at Agra. The Afghans in the eastern provinces had twice rebelled, but was defeated by his loyal general, Ali Quli, near Lucknow. The emperor's other generals had secured foothold in Rajputana by conquering Ajmer and the forts in Jodhpur and Gwalior. As Akbar was adding new kingdoms to his empire in Hind, his claim to the throne of Kabul, Kandahar and Badakhshan, was exposed to the temptations of foreign monarchs. Shah Tahmasp of Iran, learning of Akbar's warring campaigns all over Hindustan, had taken the opportunity in conquering Kandahar. *Kandahar! Which was dearly won by Humayun after his return from Persia, leading to his final conquest of Kabul.*

Akbar was not only fighting battles within his heart and soul and inside the heart of Hind, but over the legacy of his rule in Kabul, Kandahar and Badakhshan.

Biram Khan had acquired the audacity of making important decisions without the consent of the emperor. He was maintaining his palace like a king's, and depriving Akbar of the royal funds which were *his* rightful share, by the very virtue of his being the sole emperor of Hind. Akbar had been kind to Biram Khan, bestowing upon him many treasures after a son was born to him by Salima whom the emperor himself had named Abdur Rahim. Akbar's memory-book of retribution was filled to the brim when Biram had had Takht Mal executed on the charges of treason, while the emperor was in Lahore on a hunting excursion. Biram Khan had fallen from the emperor's grace!

Akbar's thoughts were a strange mixture of relief and sadness, as they followed Biram Khan down the road to death. Biram Khan had received several warnings from the emperor as to his unseemly conduct. But Biram Khan had condoned all warnings of the emperor, feeling smug and confident in his heart that as Akbar had bestowed upon him the title of *Khan Baba*—father, no harm would ever come to him from the emperor. Exhausting his store of warnings and reprimands, Akbar had then dismissed Biram Khan from his governorship of the Punjab. Sending him a missive, both kind and stern!

> *Khan Baba, salaam! Accept my loving message. May it be known to you that on account of certain important matters I have come to Delhi. As I hear that you intend coming to wait on me, I am sending Tarsun Beg to inform you that I am not happy with you on account of certain grievances that I have against you. My heart does not allow that you should at this time come to see me. You should remain where you are and attend to the business at hand. If need be I myself will go to Agra, but before I do so, it is desirable that you should retire to Gwalior and those parts and come to me only when I summon you. I write this to assure you that even if there be a misunderstanding between father and son, it need not lead to bitterness. In spite of all my grievances and the injuries and improprieties that I have suffered at your hands, I even now have regard and affection for you, and as usual I call you and look upon you as Khan Baba. Nevertheless, a meeting between us at present is out of question. I accede to your request to allow you to go on a pilgrimage to the sacred shrines. You may proceed on the pilgrimage, and send someone to take charge of your cash and affects at Sirhind and Lahore. Emperor Jalaluddin Muhammed Akbar.*

Biram Khan, instead of seeking the emperor's favor, had resorted to rebellion. He was defeated and brought before Akbar as a traitor with a handkerchief tied around his neck as a token of shame and repentance. Akbar had pardoned him and had received him with kindness, had untied the handkerchief with his own hands, and had presented to him his royal robe. Biram Khan was then sent on a pilgrimage to Mecca with a promise from the emperor that the revenues from his jagir would be transmitted to his family by the emperor's royal agents. During this holy journey toward Mecca, Biram Khan had just reached Patan in Gujrat, when he was slain by a band of Afghans.

Salima Sultan was widowed when her son was only two years old!

Salima. Akbar's heart, even now, was somersaulting as he kept riding.

This memory tinged with grief and regret was luring Akbar's thoughts back to the joys and sadness' of the past. His wedlock with the beloved widow, Salima Sultan!

Akbar's grief at the unfortunate death of Biram Khan, though genuine, was corrupted by his longing to woo the love of his life! And woo he did, for two long years till the heartless beloved consented to marry the emperor. Salima had brought her grief as a dowry from her late husband, blaming Akbar for the death of Biram Khan. Hating the emperor! The young emperor, barely nineteen then, had suffered all, pouring love in return for hatred. Her hatred for the emperor had abated slowly, against the ocean of Akbar's love for both herself and her son. Akbar had adopted Abdur Rahim.

Still a childless emperor, a lover despised. Akbar's thoughts were gallivanting. *Accursed in love, if love be the curse of my youth, the folly of my young wisdom! Another curse! Another folly! Still! I am the emperor. Still under the curse of the intriguing wretches—my childhood friends, mentors and guardians!*

His thoughts were racing after that ambitious Mahum Anaga and her intriguing son, Adham, but the emperor didn't wish to think about any intrigues on this auspicious day of his wedding with the Princess of Amber. Instead, his thoughts were flying to Mankot, where he had the one and only spiritual experience of a lifetime, which had changed him from the lover of beauty to the lover of truth.

During one of his campaigns against Adali, Akbar had defeated his enemy, and the fortress of Mankot was surrendered to him. On his way to Lahore, wearing the laurels of victory over his shoulders, hatred awaiting him in the eyes of his beloved bride, Akbar was overwhelmed with disgust for life. Pressed by his need for solitude he had raced his horse ahead of his cavalcade, commanding over his shoulders at his valets and attendants not to follow him!

Finding a secluded spot in the grove of tamarind trees, Akbar had dismounted from his steed, and had flung himself to the ground. A string of wordless prayers had died on his lips as he had lain there communing with his God in the silence of his soul and psyche. Some dazzling glare of light behind the closed shutters of his eyes had encompassed his spirit, burning and consuming. His very soul had floated away, drifting, being consumed in mists and clouds, the *light*. His tear-streaked eyes had been wide open, beholding nothing in nature, but awe, silence and reverence in life—to life! He had then mounted his horse, and had returned to his companions, to the flood of humanity, to *light*.

Quest for truth! Akbar could hear music in the wind, becoming aware of the precincts of Sambhar. Sambhar, where his bride-to-be waited for the emperor with loving tenderness, Akbar was hoping.

Actually, the music had begun to ripple forth from the ranks of Akbar's wedding procession. The royal musicians were striking bridal tunes on their lutes and flutes! Shahnai accompanying the notes with a dulcet wooing! A sea of colors in silks, velvets and brocades, was drifting jubilantly toward the palace of Raja Bihari Mall.

The large, brick stone palace of Bihari Mall was lit up to such exquisite refulgence with *deutis* and candles that from the marble halls to the wide columns in front, it appeared to glow like a bride. A myriad of flames from gold candelabras were Akbar's companions as he sat on the red velvet couch as the honored bridegroom.

This spacious room where the emperor sat enjoying the wedding rituals was housing about one hundred chosen guests invited by the father of the bride. The colorful silks, velvets and brocades on men and women, and fiery jewels on their royal persons were creating fantastic shadows on the marble floor which was left uncarpeted. With the exception of the emperor, all guests were seated on the floor with brocaded pillows as their seats or couches to recline upon. In the middle of the room was an oval, Persian carpet where the Hindu priest sat facing the sculptured gods and goddesses. The priest was chanting mantras, and feeding the rigol of fire in brass urn with oils, spices and perfumes. The wide mantelpiece, against which Akbar sat on his velvet couch fringed with gold along with his friends and courtiers, was cluttered with candelabras and floral arrangements. Right across from the emperor, on the farthest side near the bronzed portals, were a group of musicians over the carpeted stage.

Akbar, seated there on his cushioned retreat, was trying to sketch the portrait of his bride-to-be in his head. He had yet not caught a glimpse of the Princess of Amber. To the parents of the bride, he had presented the gifts in gold, and jewels most precious, and the silks and brocades of finest quality.

Hira, Hira! Akbar's thoughts were repeating the name of his bride-to-be, as if the sweetness in murmuring sounds could paint her picture on the window of his mind. *Rajkumar Hira Kunwari*, he repeated her full name in his head, but liking only the sound of Hira, meaning literally, diamond.

Akbar was being royally entertained by Bihari Mall, and he in return, was showering his host with the light of his royal wit and laughter. The emperor was talking with Raja's son, Bhagwan Das, and with Man Singh, the adopted son of Bhagwan Das. He was impressed by the pleasant manners of these young men which could render them suitable as his royal viziers.

Aziz Koka seated by the emperor was thinking about Adham Khan's false sense of pride and power after he had been assigned a high post in the imperial army by the kindness of the emperor. Adham Khan had taken it for granted that he would always be favored by the emperor, simply, because he was the son of Mahum Anaga, Akbar's childhood nurse. Akbar, at the time of his accession, had appointed Adham Khan a general of small battalion. Then he was sent by the emperor to Malwa to defeat Baz Bahadur, who had not offered his submission to the emperor.

Adham Khan had defeated Baz Bahadur, and had conquered Malwa. And then, along with the bigoted mullah, Pir Muhammed, had run a blood-bath over the heads of the vanquished prisoners, including women and the children. Akbar had no knowledge of these cruelties, but was informed of Adham's victory and of his neglect by not sending the choicest of treasures and elephants to the emperor, as enforced by the law of the empire. Also, he had withheld more than what was his share, including the musicians and the dancing girls. The most beautiful of these dancing girls, Rupmati, had defied Adham's claim over her by taking poison and ending her life.

Akbar, upon learning of Adham Khan's deceit, had marched to Malwa to chastise the bold thief, personally. As the emperor had reached Malwa, Adham Khan had prostrated himself before the young emperor most humbly. Pleading forgiveness for his neglect, and offering most of the treasures which were the emperor's due claim and share, as him being the sovereign of Hindustan! Akbar had chosen two beautiful girls for the care of his harem, leaving them under the guidance of Mahum Anaga while journeying back toward Agra. As soon as the emperor was on the road, Adham khan had had those two girls murdered, fearing, lest they inform the emperor of his atrocities during the war. The atrocities, which were no more to be concealed after this heinous crime! Incensed as Akbar was, he was pressed more by the urgent demands to chastise such another general as Ali Quli. By the time Akbar could turn his attention to Adham Khan, Mahum Anaga had interceded, pleading for the life of her son.

Aziz Koka's thoughts now were circling around Shamsuddin—the husband of Akbar's other childhood nurse, Jiji Anaga. Akbar had made Shamsuddin the governor of Punjab after the death of Biram Khan.

Adham Khan is envious of Shamsuddin, coveting that position, and plotting murder! Aziz Koka's thoughts themselves were aghast and shuddering. Before he could check his thoughts, he found Akbar's gaze fixed to him.

"Your Majesty, Adham Khan is not to be trusted. He is at Agra and plotting mischief under the skirt of his doting mother." Aziz Koka murmured.

"Don't be such a simpering fool, Aziz! Didn't I tell you not to talk about impending evils on this auspicious eve of my wedding?" Akbar chided.

"I crave your pardon, Your Majesty." Aziz Koka contrived a chastened look. "May the emperor have many auspicious days and evenings at Agra, where the Princess of Amber will grace the chambers of his seraglio? Veiled and secluded, and protected from all eyes under the blessings of Muslim laws and Muslim traditions."

"The emperor is not so bigoted as to lend piety to false interpretations of the Islamic laws!" Akbar laughed. "Islam indeed! And Muslims most besotted! Nowhere in the Quran is mentioned that the women should be veiled, or secluded behind four walls. I should know, for I know Quran by heart, and can recite it in one day and night without ever missing a word of it. By veiling my brides, I am simply obeying the wishes of my late father. When he returned to Hind, he issued a *Farman* to such affect. Veiling and secluding the royal ladies! His Farman just some tender babe out of the kernel of his love and jealousy for his beloved wife, Mah Chuchak Begum! Mah Chuchak Begum, my step-mother, she has chosen to stay in Kabul, if you don't know. To rule over Kabul and over my half-brother, not from behind a veil, but in a veil of treacheries and infidelities, I hear." He paused. "No, I am not merely obeying the wishes of my late father, but adapting to the diversity of culture and tradition in Hind. Great Ranis and Maharanis of traditional Hindu families wear veils, and stay secluded in their own haven of palaces. Next time the emperor argues about the culture and religion, in conformity or in contrast with, he will be branded with lies by the mullahs that he is adopting Hindu customs."

"If mullahs ever challenge your faith, Your Majesty, you can always visit the tomb of Shaikh Chishti, and pray that their souls be cleansed." Aziz Koka intoned softly. More baffled than pacified!

"How little men know of their hearts, less so of their sovereigns who are close to them as brothers." Akbar murmured gently. "The emperor prays only to God, Aziz, the One and Only God of all gods. Shaikh Chishti was a pious and humble man, tolerant toward all creeds, kind and affectionate toward both Hindus and Muslims. I revere him for his piety and for his creed of tolerance. I revere that holy ground which is blessed with his *presence.* Somehow, his sacred tomb draws me closer to God, to the God of all gods! God's presence is felt more keenly over there. The nearness of God! All gods live there, I feel at times. Men with fear in their hearts and love in their souls visit that shrine. Another reason that I visit that shrine is to pay homage to the grave of Nizam, the water-carrier, who saved the life of my father, once. Yet, I do pray in my heart to God at the tomb of Shaikh Chishti. Not to the saint, but to God alone! I pray that I might be blessed with sons. My own sons and daughters!"

"You will have many sons, Your Majesty!" Aziz Koka prophesied histrionically. "The mullahs are already waiting, anxiously for the arrival of the Princess of Amber at Agra, with much agog and interest. Foretelling fortunes! Prophesying that once the Princess comes to Agra and is converted to Islam and wedded again in conformity with the Islamic ceremonial rites, she will beget sons, many, many sons!"

"Islamic rites, yes! But the emperor has no intention of converting his bride to Islam. She is free to practice her religion in my harem, to pray to her gods in anyway she wishes." Akbar intoned firmly. "Gods are no commodity to be bartered in exchange for holy, matrimonial vows. The emperor believes in absolute tolerance for all religions, for all his subjects, in his vast empire of Hind. To practice religion in one's home, in one's country, on this vast, vast earth with diverse faiths and creeds must not be a privilege but a birthright. A necessity, for the dignity of mankind! If all of us could do so, without offending the beliefs of others?" He concluded rather sadly.

Aziz Koka was stricken dumb. Todar Mall was smiling to himself, his gaze seeking the attention of Birbal seated opposite him. The priest was chanting sonorously. The garlanded gods and goddesses were immersed waist-high in fresh petals of red roses and yellow marigolds. Todar Mall was catching and holding the emperor's gaze in his own with the devotion of a loyal subject.

"Your Majesty, may I be as bold as to touch on this subject of religion with a small piece of news?" Todar mall began reluctantly. "Weddings are for gaiety and laughter. But, since Your Majesty has entrusted me with the duty to report all information in my knowledge without delay, I feel I can take the liberty to relate this episode. Even now, that is, though Your Majesty is about to be wedded soon."

"Since the Princess of Amber makes the emperor wait like a slave, I shall remain so, burdened by the pressing reports or canards, whichever come my way." Akbar laughed suddenly.

"Your Majesty, Mulla Pir Muhammed in Altar is judging everyone on the basis of religion. Recently, the father of Hemu was brought to him as a captive. The Mulla commanded the old man to become a Muslim, or to face death. The father of Hemu replied: *I have worshipped my gods for eighty years, why should I change at this time, and why should I, merely from fear of my life, and without understanding it, come into your way of worship?* The Mulla then put him to death with one blow of his saber."

"May all the bigots rot in hell?" Akbar exclaimed. "Make sure, Todar Mall, Mulla doesn't escape the wrath of the emperor in this world first." Akbar paused, lowering his voice. "Am I going to be surrounded by bigots all my life? What comfort are pious and holy men who pretend to be so in name alone? Staining their hands with blood and corrupting their souls with the rivers of lies, deceit, injustice and intolerance!" He murmured. "Yes, they will be around! But the emperor shall watch them like a hawk, snatching corruptions out of their souls as if driving away some evil spirits. Pious demons and unholy saints all! The emperor forbids the enslavement of the prisoners of war and of their forcible conversion to Islam. This is my Farman and is to be proclaimed all over Hind after my wedding celebrations. And whoever dares disobey the emperor, does so on the peril of his life." His eyes were spilling commands.

Akbar was trying to find a reprieve, to assuage his anger and anguish. His anger, which had flared up in him with volcanic haste, paralyzing his restraint and sense of propriety! Finding Man Singh and Bhagwan Das close by, the emperor ventured to soothe his senses with diversions kindly and congenial.

"Bhagwan Das and Man Singh, would you accompany the emperor on his journey to Agra? You may join the Imperial services, or find something suitable for your talents!" Akbar inquired kindly.

"Your Majesty, Your Majesty." Both the son and the grandson of Bihari Mall bowed simultaneously. "Our pleasure, Your Majesty, entirely!"

"My gallant courtiers." Akbar laughed in return, shifting his attention to Birbal. "My most beloved poet, amuse the emperor with a funny couplet or two. Better yet, let me hunt for amusement on the rungs of my ignorance. Is there anything on which the light of the sun or moon can never fall? No, do not answer yet." He commanded. "What is your answer to this riddle, Todar Mall?"

"The floor of my cellar, Your Majesty!" Todar Mall smiled.

"Leave the cellar door open and the light would enter." Akbar retorted, directing his query to Aziz Koka.

"The bed of a river, Your Majesty." Aziz Koka murmured punctiliously.

"If the river dries up, the bed would be exposed to light." Akbar countered. "Anyone, with the exception of Birbal, is welcome to solve this riddle."

A group of courtiers seated close to the emperor, were intent on solving this riddle with some answers subtle or profound. So were Man Singh and Bhagwan Das, laboring their young minds, but the emperor had ceased to seek an answer, it seemed.

Akbar's gaze was intently fixed to one young musician on the stage who had begun to strike beautiful notes on his veena! The emperor could distinguish the simple notes, sa, re, ga, ma, pa, dha, ni, sa, but beyond that simplicity were some sounds sweet and unutterable.

The young musician had begun to sing!

Akbar's very soul was melting in some ocean of song and music. *The low moan of a cataract! The song of the nightingale! The jingle of bells in the wind! The lapping of waves in the ocean! The awesome murmur of remote thunder! All, not chasing each other, but drifting, yielding, mating and surrendering, to each other and all.* Akbar thought that this music had cast a spell on him alone, and in order to break away from that spell, his gaze was returning to Birbal.

"Your turn, Birbal. You may solve the riddle now." Akbar murmured.

"Darkness, Your Majesty." Was Birbal's laconic response!

"Yes." Akbar murmured again. "The wisdom is the light in darkness, which few dare claim even in jest." He commented.

Akbar had ceased to think, drunk with the wine-bliss in this voice. Suddenly, the words were leaping like fire from the musician's throat, scorching the very air, destroying everything that was music and beauty.

The songs were silent!

The chanting of the priest, the only voice in this song-hush, was drowned into a volley of applause. The lord of the song and music had risen to his feet, curtsying and smiling. Akbar's gaze was returning to Birbal again, his eyes kindled to some flames of pain and bewilderment.

"Who is this mortal god?" Akbar appeared to groan than exclaim. "Who would dare silence the holy gods of the Hindus, if all men could but sing like him? What is his name, Birbal?"

"His name is Tansen, Your Majesty." Was Birbal's quick response! "His real name is Ramtanu Pandy of Saint Haridas, a Bhakti Saint. His family converted to Islam, so he is a Muslim from the race of the Rajputs, also a disciple of Saint Sheikh. His patron was Ram Chandra of Gwalior. Now he resides at Amber, and is much beloved by Bihari Mall. He is the greatest of singers and musicians in all Hind."

"No words can ever describe the greatness of his voice, so holy and awesome! All praises melt before the magic in his voice like unsung prayers." Akbar murmured to himself. "He shall be my royal musician at Agra, and no patronage will be denied him in the flourishing art of music and song. He would shine like the finest of jewels in the Moghul court of my poets, scholars, philosophers and theologians—"

The emperor was in for another pleasant shock. His gaze was arrested to the lovely vision from the heavens itself, Akbar's very thoughts were proclaiming. The Princess of Amber was being swept into the room, led by her father, toward the altar of the gods and the goddesses. A goddess herself! Akbar's thoughts were delirious with joy. The bejeweled princess was donned in red sari, shimmering with silver stars down to her feet. The red tilak on her forehead, and the red sandoor in her hair with the silken glow of rose petals, were drugging Akbar's senses to swoon. He had eased himself out of his seat, his gaze following the lovely princess.

Smitten with the charms of her beauty, more bewildered than bewitched, Akbar was being escorted by the bride's father to join in the wedding ceremonies. The emperor was drifting toward the altar of the deities where his goddess stood like a white flame.

One white flame amidst the blaze of sunsets! When the stars bow low to gather sunshine in their eyes, just before the darkness could swallow the king of the heavens! Akbar's thoughts were giddy and poetic.

A silk cord was tied to the wrist of the princess at one end, and the other end claiming the emperor's wrist, as an emblem of everlasting commitment to happiness. The first three times, the bride was to lead the groom around the rigol of fire, while the priest invoked prayers and blessings for conjugal affinity of the royal couple. The last four rounds were to be led by the groom, while the holy vows to solemnize the marriage were to be repeated aloud by both the bride and the groom.

If I could just hold her into my arms now! Our holy passion, feeding this holy fire with our kisses—kisses divine. Such royal impropriety! Would the priest toss us alive into this circle of fire, while the pious guests would sit mute and scandalized. Akbar was thinking. *Hira, Hira could I kiss her, my starry beloved.*

The priest was chanting and feeding the fire with clarified butter. The emperor and the princess were completing the seventh round, their wrists still tied with a single silk cord. They were taking seven steps together, and repeating their marriage vows. The emperor was now garlanded like the gods, and the princess like the goddesses. The priest was sprinkling rose petals over the royal couple.

The newly-weds were now exchanging garlands, showered afresh by rose-petals from the ecstatic guests. Heedless to the litany of the priest, Akbar managed to steal sunshine out of his bride's eyes, and whispered ardently.

"You belong to the sun, the moon and the stars, my love, but all the heavenly orbs have gathered in my soul to greet you." Akbar's endearments were swallowed by the sea of cheers and felicitations rising upon the lips of the guests. "A diamond from the sky you are to me, my Hira!"

2

The Royal Brides

Emperor Akbar though protected by the harem walls, was, in fact, danger-
ously besieged by his lovely wives. All exclaiming in horror and fright at the
emperor's caprice in exposing himself to danger!

To needless danger! Was the general verdict of the royal wives!

Why did the emperor chastise the marauders himself?

*Were the emperor's viziers not able and valiant to crush the petty rebel-
lions?*

*Were the emperor's soldiers not ready to prove themselves worthy in subdu-
ing such a rebellion?*

*Why did the emperor confront those brutal rebels without even a thought of
protecting himself from their shower of arrows?*

What if the emperor was mortally wounded?

Akbar had just returned to Agra from his expedition at Sakit. But the news
of his victory and wild escapade in that small town had reached the harem ladies
much earlier even before he himself had stepped into his palace. Several sad-
happy months had elapsed since Akbar had returned to Agra with his bride of
Amber, his heart still exploring the shrine of love in the holiness of her soul.
During all those sad-happy months, he had communed with sages, the hermits
and the Sannyasis. Also, indulging in his all-time love for hunting! In fact, *hunting* was all that had fitted in his plans that particular day, which had led him
toward the small town of Sakit.

While the emperor was riding jauntily toward Sakit along with his courtiers,
a Brahman by the name of Hapa had approached the emperor, requesting an
urgent interview. Hapa had a grievous complaint against the marauders from
eight villages, who had formed a large group under the name of Athgarha. They
had murdered Hapa's son, and had plundered his home. Escaping unavenged,
now they were on a spree to wreak havoc in the neighboring villages with their
plundering and pillaging.

The hunting trip was abandoned, and the emperor's small band of two hundred soldiers, along with two hundred elephants had marched toward the village

surrendering your will to the Will of one God alone, then you might be absolved of all fears. Fearing neither pain, nor sorrow! Neither grief nor adversity! Yet, how difficult each Faith is? Shattering each hope, each belief and each inspiration to the very face of tragedies."

"Is Allah benevolent to women, or just to men?" Suriya Begum chanted.

"More benevolent than the Allah of the Jews, or of the Christians!" Akbar retorted brightly. "The Quran grants equality to women, and absolves them from sin in the Garden of Eden. Equality, by revealing that Eve was not fashioned out of the rib of Adam, but created from the same blood clot which had given life to Adam. Absolution from sin, by revealing that Eve was neither beguiled by the serpent, nor did she beguile Adam, both ate of the fruit from the tree of Knowledge in the Garden of Eden of their own free wills. Muslim women have the right to own property, to engage in business, to divorce their husbands. You all are free to divorce the emperor! But dare not be tempted to do so, for his wrath would turn you all into pillars of salt." He got to his feet.

"Better to be turned into a pillar of salt than to die on a funeral pyre—all that butter churning one's bones to soft pulp. Hira says she will burn herself to death if the emperor—" Mahmooda Begum cried happily.

"Dies! If the emperor dies!" Akbar snatched the word *dies* from the happy pause of his ever-chirping wife. "No, my lovely bird, I don't want my beautiful wives to die on the funeral pyres. Instead, they should marry rajas, nabobs, or viziers in memory of their kind emperor. Death would have to wait though, for a long, long time to come, to me. Not before, if God willing, I can bring the cream of this earth's surface under my sway, and fulfill the desires of the sorrowful of the seven climes. Right now, the emperor needs rest before commencing the duties of his court. So, my lovely birds, leave the emperor alone to his sweet rest and sweet reveries. Salima, be kind as to stay with the emperor a moment longer." He commanded, as Salima was the first one in an act of haste to obey the emperor. "Why this coldness? This indifference, this cruelty, my love! My very own true love!" Akbar looked into her eyes after his other wives were gone.

"The eternal fire of puja in Hira's room leaves me cold, Your Majesty." Salima murmured. "She worships the Hindu gods!"

"And I worship the holy shrine in your cold, cold heart. Loving the fires of hell in my soul in the name of true love!" Akbar laughed.

"This epigram alone, Your Majesty, warms my heart that the emperor still proclaims to love!" Salima's eyes were lit up with the stars of mockery.

"Proclaims!" Akbar exclaimed. "Do the oceans not love their depths? Do I not cling to the deeps in your soul like an ocean churning with desire? Engrave these words in your pretty head, my love that your wit doesn't abide well at the altar of my love. Not at the altar of such a love as mine! You can forbid the emperor to see his other wives, and his joy would abound at the mere glimpse of warmth in your beautiful eyes."

"How can I forbid, Your Majesty?" Salima's lips curled into another mockery of a smile. "How can, when I can't return the love your passion demands."

"Demands!" Another exclamation broke through Akbar's lips. "No, my beauty, the emperor only begs and pleads. Love can never force but yield, even to its harsh pleas, in love, silencing all torments. Yes, torments, where love sits like a bleeding rose on the bed of thorns, its tender soul torn and wounded with longings inconsolable!" His thoughts were truncated by the rude assault of noise in his palace.

The emperor was in an act of clasping her into his arms, when a fresh assault of noise lashed at his awareness. As a man pressed by fate, he snatched his scimitar from the couch, racing toward the portals to meet the challenge of these rude warnings. Before he could reach the harem gates, his path was crossed by his devoted eunuch, Bahlul.

"Your Majesty, don't step out, not like this, Your Majesty, your life is—" Bahlul was pleading like a fool.

"Speak, you cowering wretch! What is the meaning of this commotion? And don't block the emperor's way, lest he flays you alive." Akbar commanded impatiently.

"Your Majesty, Atka Khan—Shamsuddin, Munim Khan and Shihabuddin. They, they were in the hall, discussing some business. Adham Khan, with two others stabbed Atka Khan. He, Atka Khan ran, is dead, in the courtyard." Bahlul could not finish, for Akbar marched past him with the fury of a hurricane.

At the foot of the staircase Akbar confronted Adham Khan who stood there in a daze, unblinking. Reading the edict of death in the emperor's eyes, his hand was reaching forth to grab the emperor's hand.

"Adham, you child of perdition! Why have you killed my Atka Khan?" Akbar thundered, dealing him a violent blow in the face with his bare hands.

"Asaf Khan." Akbar thundered again. "Bind this murderer in chains, and fling him down from the top of the highest parapet in my palace." He began to pace.

Akbar kept pacing in utter oblivion to his rage and grief. Against the mists of his cankerous despair, he didn't even notice the unconscious Adham Khan being dragged away by Asaf Khan and the others. He was pacing, his thoughts merging with time and silence. The merging of time with silence seemed like a flash, as Asaf Khan returned, panting and flustered.

"Your Majesty, your command is fulfilled." Asaf Khan breathed low.

"Is he dead?" Akbar inquired, without ceasing to pace.

"No, Your Majesty." Asaf Khan responded tonelessly.

"Then fling him down again and again and again, till his wretched soul breaks free from the fetters of life. And report his death to the emperor promptly." Akbar commanded. A sea of anguish in his heart throbbing and churning!

The emperor was rarely angry, but on those rare occasions when he was, all dreaded the fury of his anger. He was contemplating now, utterly and fiercely in combat with his own self, within and beyond. Right now the demon of his rage was fleeing. And before he could pursue it to the nether voids, Asaf Khan returned.

"Your Majesty, Adham Khan is dead." Asaf Khan announced solemnly.

"Arrange his funeral with all due rites and ceremony." Akbar paused amidst the ritual of his pacing. "And let this be a lesson to you all that the emperor would tolerate no murder, cruelty or aggression, either on the streets of Hind, or in the homes of his subjects, and certainly not in his palace. And each crime would carry its weight of evil in the scale of justice and just punishment."

Mounting the marble steps under some spell of utter despair, he could barely notice Hamida Banu Begum standing there on the damasked landing. As soon as Akbar plodded closer, he was swept into her arms in one eager embrace.

"My son, my son! Your Majesty." Hamida Banu Begum murmured.

"Mamma, Miryam Makani. Dear, dear Mamma!" Akbar murmured back. "No need to address me as *Your Majesty*, Mamma. *My son* sounds so sweet that it leaves me with a sense of longing to be a child once again." He stood facing her.

"My son, my son." Hamida Banu Begum lamented in response.

"Dear Mamma—" Akbar sighed. "What would the emperor say to Mahum Anaga, his childhood nurse? What would he say, dear Mamma, that he killed her son! A thousand pities that Mahum Anaga should suffer thus! I grieve more for her than for Adham Khan. Ah, my Atka Khan, murdered. The murderer and the murdered! Ah, well, God's will and justice. Who can conceive the inconceivable?"

"I pray for you, my son, that no grief may ever cross your path." Hamida Banu Begum consoled feebly. "Adham Khan came to the very doors of the harem to attack you—the emperor!" An imperceptible shudder passed through her delicate frame. "Bahlul would not let him in, I was informed. Bahlul, your dear, devoted servant. He ordered Adham Khan to stay down the hall, I heard him! He was telling Adham Khan that the emperor is sleeping, and that he—Adham Khan was disturbing the emperor's sleep. May no evil ever cross your path, my son! May God Almighty always be with you, and may you remain in His protection, always!"

"Evil, it will cross my path, Mamma. Evil crosses the path of every man, it will always follow—man, from one end of the earth to the other, on each and every path." Akbar demurred. "God forgive me, I have paid the ransom of cruelty with cruelty. The blood of a murdered victim weeps for justice, and justice without compassion knows no mercy, but vengeance. How can the wombs of gentle mothers give birth to sons so brutal? I would ponder on that, in my sleep, Mamma." He plodded down the hall.

The Agra palace with its vast gardens appeared to be robed in mourning shades of the twilight. Only light-shadows from Imperial workshops in the background were piercing the gloom and the stillness of the early dusk. The early dusk with its unwaning intensity was bright, keeping the artists and the artisans immersed in the pleasure-inventions of their creations, both superb and nonpareil.

But inside the palace were light and music. The candles were burning vividly. *Diwan-i-Khas* was the most spacious of all the chambers in this palace, where Akbar was seated on his gold throne under an ornate alcove. He was receiving embassies, listening to the proposals, and sealing the fates of the warring lords with decisions formidable and with Farmans unchallenged. He was wearing blue silks this evening, his pallor the color of flames from the candles, absorbing glow from pearls in his turban and around his neck. Since the shocking events, the murder of Atka Khan and the tragic end of Adham Khan, Akbar had spent the entire afternoon in profound contemplations.

Is creation not the part of each created? The Creator living in each cell, breathing in each fiber, dying in each particle, re-living in each vein of cosmic revelation! In each man, beast, plant and nature, in galaxies and continents, in the ever-dying, ever-resurrecting throb of life. In the cycle of birth, death, renewal and surcease!

Are kings, monarchs, emperors, not the divine vassals of one God? The emperors; the mortal gods themselves, showering commands kind or unjust and exacting justice out of the penal servitude of their wills and whims! Men have learned from the very gods! Yes, the gods. The gods themselves fighting the war of supremacy, subjugating races, creeds and kingdoms! Gods, raining showers of punishments on mankind! Lowering down the rods of vengeance, brandishing the weapons of cruelty? Gods, inflicting grief, misery and despair! Thundering down their commands, enveloping all into the storm-clouds of fires, floods, murrains, hurricanes! Gods, demanding surrender, obedience, reverence, absolute devotion and subservience. Oh, the ransom of life, with toil and grief, with blind faith and lame suffering. Gods, warring—always engaged in the battles of jealousy and vengeance, of justice and injustice, of mercy and unkindness, of wrath and compassion. Ravishing the very kernels of man's intellect with laws holy, with commandments divine and with parables sacrosanct! Akbar had thought.

Why are men branded with such names in religions as pagans, as Jews, Muslims and Christians, as Hindus and Buddhists? Do gods speak in different tongues to different Faiths? Were pagan gods of the Greeks not holy and of the Romans not divine? The gods of the Caesars, now dead inside the irreverent oceans of time! Where did the pagans go? Were they hounded by the believers, or charmed by them into believing that their gods were dead? Ah, the infidels, the believers of one God? Christians call Muslims, the infidels and Muslims call Christians, kafirs! Yet, the gods of the pagans live in the hearts of all Muslims and the Christians, in their rituals and customs, in deifications. Akbar's opiate senses had sought the comfort of his bed.

The first godless man on earth, did he not sense fear, seeking refuge in prayer, worshipping the unknown God of all gods? Was not the first child born from the womb of Eve, the unwedded bride of Adam? With the boon of a miracle, the virgin mother, the virgin birth, the virgin child? Was not the first man in his grave of death and doubt, born again as the ultimate believer of resurrection in life or death!

When did the gods come? How did the legends begin? The Egyptians, the Sumerians, the Sabaeans. Was not the Garden of Eden in men's hearts when they walked on the face of the stark wilderness, this wild, awful land, so vast and terrible? Did man not see evil in the eye of death, famine and disease? Did he not discover goodness in warmth and sunshine? All inconceivable, all unutterable, all unapproachable!

Is sin born out of evil, and purity from good? Is evil darkness and goodness light? Forces of nature belong to God, do they, and to His designs of mercy, wrath and compassion? Are those forces in conformity with Nature? Could they be divined? Could His mercy be implored? Could His wrath be appeased with prayers and supplications? Sin gave birth to perdition, and perdition reared the babes of fear and guilt, both seeking the throne of justice and contrition. The birth of a conscience! The death of a soul! Akbar's subconscious thoughts had been loud while he had slept.

Was the soul born first, or did the conscience, or? Was conscience the devil despised by God, thrown out of its abode of fire into the river of lightning, possessing the mind of man, to torment his soul forever? Is soul the light, or is it darkness, or both? Light giving refuge to darkness in its bountiful purity of light, or darkness holding a candle of purity to lend light to light! Ignorance is the answer! Understanding, a puzzle! Wisdom, an enigma! Enlightenment, the truth! How does one get enlightened, by not knowing and knowing! Akbar's thoughts had retreated into the past.

The emperor was back in time, when his father was alive. Akbar was just a lad of thirteen then, campaigning in the Punjab against Sikandar Shah. Also entrusted with authority to chastise Abul Maali—the general favored by emperor Humayun, who had begun to assume the air of power, and was bloated with pride and arrogance. Emperor Humayun was dead. His son, Akbar, had ascended the throne of Hind. Akbar was incensed by Abul Maali's pride and arrogance, and had dispatched him to Mecca on a pilgrimage. Now Abul Maali was returning to Hind. Neither humble, nor contrite, but swollen with deceit, rising in arms against Akbar, and scattering kernels of sedition and anarchy! From this real-life dream, Akbar had been startled to awakening. He was not suspended in the time past, but in the time to come, which had to be reckoned with.

Seated on his gold throne now, Akbar was re-living that dream. After awakening to the world of reality, Akbar had bathed, and had robed himself meticulously as was his wont. Then, he had summoned Mahum Anaga, and had told her gently of her son's crime and of the punishment inflicted upon him.

Your Majesty has done well. Mahum Anaga had responded. Against the weight of her shock, she must have thought that her son was not dead, but imprisoned. Akbar was thinking, his gaze sweeping over the illustrious guests in Diwan-i-Khas. The monarch of Persia, Shah Tahmasp, had sent his cousin, Said Baig, as an ambassador. Said Baig had brought before Akbar rich gifts from the Persian monarch, including the Iraqi, Turki and Arabian steeds. The Shah of Persia had also entrusted Said Baig with a letter of condolence over the death of Humayun, and of felicitations on Akbar's accession to the throne of Hind. This letter was undelivered, but Akbar knew its import.

Munim Khan, who was appointed the governor of Kabul under the nominal command of Hakim Mirza, had just returned to Agra. He was the one, now, recounting the events of his journey and defeat by the hands of Mah Chuchak. By Munim Khan's account, it was becoming painfully clear to Akbar that Mah Chuchak was assuming the power of sovereignty herself. After Humayun's death, she had taken three consorts. Then she had had them murdered in the brutal struggle for power. Now, she had chosen Haider Qasim as her latest consort. Keeping Haider Qasim by her side, she had opposed the entry of Munim Khan who was sent to Kabul by the emperor's orders. Munim Khan had not even entered Kabul when Mah Chuchak, suspecting evil designs, had marched as far as Jalalabad herself at the head of a large army. She had succeeded in defeating Munim Khan. Sulaiman Mirza, Akbar's kind and ever-plotting uncle, taking advantage of this scandalous event, was trying to annex Kabul to his beloved territory of Badakhshan.

My step-mother, my father's most beloved wife, a harlot of greed and power! A harlot indeed! Akbar was thinking, summoning Said Baig to present his embassy.

"Your Majesty." Said Baig paused, bowing his head respectfully. "The Shah of Persia sends you greetings and his deepest condolences on the demise of your father, the emperor Humayun. And, the Shah of Persia congratulates you on your accession."

"Irony of fates! Condolences and felicitations!" Akbar exclaimed. "Both complement and negate each other. Both sad and ineffable! Both somber and unutterable! Sorrow precedes joy, and joy in turn flees farther from grief. Fleeting sorrow, some say. A joy most cowardly! Both floating parallel, never mating, forever racing in the never-ending race of a conquest! Destroying only their surge in an act of self-annihilation! No need to unfold that missive, young lord! The emperor can't read."

"Your Majesty." Said Baig stood there nonplused.

"It seems you are struck by the rod of lightning. Though lightning never strikes my palace, Said Baig! God favors the emperor, so have no fear. Ah, lightning, even if it did fall on my palace roof, it would strike only the proud and the ignorant, or the wicked. And wicked, you are not! The emperor can tell by the halo of sincerity suspended over your head. Your words are sincere, and the light of intelligence in your eyes belies ignorance." Akbar's bantering tones were both kind and caustic. "Wickedness is a vice, and ignorance more wicked than the white lies in truth. But illiteracy, ah! Illiteracy is a blessing for the ones who can read the souls of men! For, they don't have to trust the scroll of lies, upon which men have scribbled out their vices and conceits under the veil of worthy boasts. Yes, those conceited thoughts, giving vent to black lies, which remain concealed to all, but to the eye of great perception. The emperor has a grand library of twenty-four thousand books, and he reveres each volume equally. Hungering for words and ideas! Searching the essence of thought somewhere in there, the speechless meaning of each *thought*, not the *word!* Though, those words are hymns of holiness to me, my holy friends, keeping me company silently and unobtrusively. Speaking to me only when I command?" He paused. "Well, enough of pedantry! Tell your happy monarch that the emperor thanks him most warmly, for gifts and greetings, for all the gifts. Especially, for the handsome horses! I love horses more than elephants and elephants, more than all the treasures in the world, even all the treasures this holy land of Hind can offer me." He clapped his hands as a royal signal for all, to present their proposals or complaints.

Todar Mall was the first one to step forward, offering a lengthy *kornish.*

"Your Majesty, Pir Muhammed, by Your Majesty's orders, was severely reprimanded and stripped off of all his titles. From his acts of cruelties, though, he had abstained, but only for a brief interval of time. A few days short of a month, he was back on his trail of zeal and rampage. He had succeeded in burning quite a few villages in Malwa. His pretext for such an act was that an underground faction, comprised mainly of Hindus, was plotting to murder Muslim families in those villages. While, in truth, his intention was to plunder the homes of the rich Hindus to gain booties in gold and jewels! After the plunderings, his camels laden with rich booty, he was struggling to get away, when he and his men were attacked by the two chiefs of Malwa from the towns of Asir and Burhanpur. Baz Bahadur had also joined these two brave chiefs. Pir Muhammed and his band of marauders were defeated, fleeing pell-mell toward Mandu. Pir Muhammed had managed to reach the bank of Narbada at night. As he was plunging his horse into the waters of Narbada in blind haste, neglecting to notice his camel with the burden of jewels right behind him, he was met with an unfortunate accident. The camel colliding with his horse had bounded forward with a sudden rage, grabbing the beast's neck in its fierce jaws, and chewing on it without mercy. Pir Muhammed was thrown off balance, his horse groaning, and he himself being swallowed by the bloated waves. His treasures were perished along with his body, for no one was able to recover his remains. To end this comic tragedy, Your Majesty, now Baz Bahadur is claiming Malwa his dearly conquered jagir." Todar Mall concluded solemnly.

"Baz Bahadur may live to regret his claim, but Pir Muhammed, yes! His liquid grave would sink deeper yet into the fires of hell when the cries of the orphans and the widows would rise above the agony-clamor of the underworld!" Akbar murmured under his breath, his gaze turning to Birbal. "Is Narbada not a holy river of the Hindus, Birbal? Though Ganga and Jamna are known to be the holiest of all?" He asked abruptly.

"Yes, Your Majesty." Birbal began thoughtfully. "The rocks in the riverbed of Narbada reveal the third eye of Shiva. It sprouts into three lines in the semblance of lingams. The representations of which are worshipped in all the temples in Hind. God Shiva lives in the stones of Narbada, people say. And it is a holy river indeed."

"No holiness will ever wash the sins of our zealous Pir, though. The very earth despised him on which he walked." Akbar contrived a smile.

"May I recite a song to Narbada River, Your Majesty?" Appealed Birbal.

"More pleasant the songs, when accursed truths hound the living and the dead. Proceed, my beloved poet." Akbar murmured genially.

"Then hear my praise
O holy Narbada."

Birbal paused. "Pardon, Your Majesty. My memory is missing a quatrain in between.

"Proceed, just the same." Akbar commanded. "You are the poet! You may construe a few lines of your own if you wish."

"You cleanse the earth
Of its impurities
The devoted call you Surasa
The holy soul
You leap through the earth
Like a dancing deer
The devout call you Rewa
The leaping one
But Shiva called you
Delight
And laughing
Named you Narbada."

Birbal recited quickly lest he forget.

"Divine, divine! *Delight! And laughing*! Exquisite words to lend a sense of living to the river Narbada." Akbar applauded. "*Divine, divine*, my grandfather used to say after hearing Kabir recite his poems in the Moghul court! Kabir, who was inspired to write, *O, seeker, find God in the breath of all breathing.*"

The entire chamber was flooded with a thunderous applause from all. More so to please the emperor, than to praise the flawless recitation of Birbal!

"Abdullah Khan, you are to command five thousand soldiers. Choose the same amount of horses, and fifty elephants. Begin your preparations right away, and march to Malwa early at dawn. Baz Bahadur must be reminded that Malwa is the conquered domain of the Moghul Empire." Akbar commanded suddenly. "Take the place of Lucifer, as Pir Muhammed had proved to be. And be a Gabriel to the victims of Malwa. And don't return to Agra until the laurels of victory are yours to claim. You would be excused from the duties of the court till that time."

"Your Majesty, You are very generous in trusting me with this campaign." Abdullah Khan retraced his steps, bowing and curtsying.

"Your Majesty, as you are already informed of Sharfuddin Husain's sudden departure from Agra—his departure, since his father's return to your court, I am spared of the need to repeat those lengthy details." Man Singh was the next to present his report. "He was last seen in Jalaur, joined by Abul Maali upon Maali's return from Mecca. Together, they had plotted to capture the Punjab, but failing in such an attempt, they were compelled to flee toward Narnaul. There they had succeeded in plundering a small booty of treasures from one Imperial convoy. The Imperialists had routed them with such heavy assaults then, that they had no choice left but to retreat toward Daharsu. Now, they are hiding somewhere in Jhunjhun in the Jaipur Division of Rajasthan." He smiled.

"Splendid! Now the emperor doesn't have to cancel his hunting trip to the jungles of Mathura." Akbar commented thoughtfully.

"Hunting! Your Majesty." Was Man Singh's puzzled response.

"Yes, my loyal general. The emperor doesn't go to war, but hunting. And if wars fall on his way, he will hunt down enemy just the same. I may pardon Abul Maali, but Sharfuddin, no! He is priggish and arrogant, much-too conceited to obey even God's edicts, save alone the emperor's commands. I will personally chastise him. Squeeze the rebellion out of his very bones. Hound him down clear to the nether lands of perdition where he is destined to flee. Yes, Man Singh, we would chase those allies of affliction to the very ends of the earth. Get ready the royal troops, the best horses, the war elephants. We will go hunting, on expedition, to war! A wise monarch should ever be intent on conquest; otherwise his neighbors rise in arms against him." Akbar concluded.

"Your Majesty, the brother of Miryam Makani, Khwaja Muazzam—" Aziz Koka was the next one commencing incoherently.

"I know who Khwaja Muazzam is, my fool of a foster brother!" Akbar declared rather chidingly. "Khwaja Muazzam, my contentious uncle; spoiled and protected by the love of my dear, dear mother. To what heights of absurdity he has risen lately, so as to invoke your concern and sympathy? You are sympathetic! I guess. I can tell by the turbulent waves in your eyes. Not to mention, your incoherence! And your incoherence is a positive proof, that your sympathies are unbalanced." He added kindly.

"None other than a domestic squabble, Your Majesty!" Aziz Koka's lips relaxed into one feeble smile. "Khwaja Muazzam is in a violent mood these days. He is mistreating his wife, Zuhra Agha, threatening to kill her, if she as much as dare whisper a complaint against him to Miryam Makani, or to the emperor. Zuhra Agha is the daughter of Fatima. Fatima, she herself requested me to appeal to you, Your Majesty. To save her daughter from those brutal threats followed by abuse and violence—" His speech was arrested by the sudden blaze of anger in the emperor's eyes.

"An insufferable outrage!" Akbar murmured. "Wife battering is the most heinous of crimes in the eyes of the emperor. And it must be dealt with royal punishments by the royal hands of the emperor himself. I will visit him with such intent at the first opportunity, before I go *hunting*. No kin of mine is exempt from the rod of just punishments if they choose to polish the craft of cruelty and injustice." His eyes were cradling Aziz Koka in their fiery blaze. "Warn Muazzam Khan, Aziz. Better yet, tell him that this is emperor's Farman *not to excel in his violent moods, and to stay away from Zuhra Agha.*" He commanded. "Fatima, isn't she the match-maker? A worthy lady with great accomplishments! I will speak to her myself, and allay her fears."

Mukhdum-ul-Mulk, in turn, approached the emperor burdened with pride and prejudice. He seemed to be carrying a load of self-righteousness over his shoulders.

"Your Majesty, I will be brief since Your Majesty looks tired." Mukhdum-ul-Mulk commenced most piously.

"My presumptuous ulema, the emperor is not in the least tired. He is but awakening to the vigor of intrigue and rebellion, this very moment?" Akbar flashed him a piercing look. "And as to being brief, brevity will sit better on your brow than the crescent of zeal or false humility, which you always wear without even knowing that you do. Must you arch your brows when you speak?" He chided.

"Pardon me, Your Majesty." Was Mukhdum-ul-Mulk's quick response! "A major issue has been brought to our notice lately, to us ulemas, Your Majesty. A large majority of Hindus are stealing into the holy shrines without paying the pilgrim tax. The royal treasuries will suffer immensely, if—"

"If!" Akbar snatched this word out of his ulema's lips with the whip of a thunder. "If, the most hated of words in the vocabulary of mankind! A pilgrim tax, ah, the pilgrim tax! Why was the emperor not informed that such a tax is still being extorted? Oh, the sons of greed!" He exclaimed. "Are not all the muddied fields on this earth, God's land—all? All the holy lands and Hind the holiest of the holy! Its each river sacred, each pasture hallowed, each hill the altar of all faiths. And we all its pilgrims! Do we all pay taxes to God for the benefit of praying at the altar of His heaven? Are we seeking knowledge through His wisdom, while letting our ignorance blight us with bigotry, injustice and intolerance? I, the emperor of Hind, abolish this pilgrim tax. No man in this holy land of Hind will suffer the indignity of such a tax, as long as the emperor is alive." He let his gaze sweep over all searchingly. "Do we have any more claims, proposals? Or issues of the rich and the avaricious, from rebels and the cut-throats? Well, the poor and defenseless will speak one day! And the world will be a better place, if it can lend sight to the blind, and *wisdom* to the sightless." Since no one spoke, he got to his feet, his gaze resting on Munim Khan.

"Kabul is in no danger of melting under the rueful intrigues of Mah Chuchak Begum, Munim Khan, be assured." Akbar's sole attention was fixed to Munim Khan. "Just send instructions to Masum Khan that he should keep a close watch over all the events, and that he must send all reports to the emperor. Masum Khan is a trustworthy general. He guards the citadel of Kabul like a hawk."

The emperor walking through the files of his guests and courtiers was smiling and exchanging amenities. The drums had begun to beat in the music gallery to announce the dismissal of the court. The beating of the drums was just a formality, while the emperor getting to his feet was a royal signal itself, that the court was adjourned till the next meeting. This was also a signal that no one was to follow the emperor wherever he chose to go. With the exception of his guards, watching the emperor from a safe distance!

Akbar was floating through the sea of colorful robes and plumed turbans, down into the marble halls leading toward the private gardens. He was heading straight for the gilded portals, which would transport him into the sanctuary of his royal gardens. Once he was outside his palace, Akbar could drink deep of the night air, his gaze also drinking the beauty of his garden. The stars in his eyes were absorbing light from the lamps hung high on the golden posts. He was admiring the variety and abundance of flowers in his garden, inhaling their scent and innocence with a longing akin to love and passion.

Flowers care not whether it is day or night, for they know no dearth of light in their fragrant little lives. One thoughtless epigram was chirping in Akbar's mind.

He was turning wistfully toward the flowerbeds of saffron. The saffron bulbs, he had imported from Kashmir, to be planted in his garden at Agra. Now, he could see the full-grown clusters with a myriad of blooms. The saffron blooms were lilac-tinted, silken and argent, beckoning him closer, almost challenging him to feel their blushing cheeks. A sudden downpour of thoughts was intruding upon the emperor's solitude. His thoughts were summoning Atka Khan and Adham Khan and tearing open their shrouds of death.

Death is a pilgrimage to afterlife, from whence we shall return to life, together, peaceful! Absolved of all passions terrible, except of the passion to love!

*Mah Chuchak, the beloved wife of my father, as much loved as Salima, by me! Am I comparing Salima with—could Salima after my, death—*Akbar's thoughts were aghast at this comparison unvoiced.

Pity, that my father didn't know the soul of Mah Chuchak! Do I know Salima's? Yes, I do! Her soul is cold and chaste as a mountain-lily, the volcano of love buried deep inside the glacier of her soul, simmering, simmering. Never bubbling, never exploding! Not ever corrupting the shrine of silence on her lips.

The pale, flickering shadows in the distance from his one hundred royal workshops were welcoming Akbar to their warm hearths. Reaching the arena of his Imperial workshops, the emperor was watching his men making shoes, or weaving shawls, or dying cloths in several hues of textures rough or delicate. Involuntarily, his feet were carrying him into the workshop of one of his goldsmiths.

"What new marvel of gems you are creating this evening, Amrat?" Akbar smiled.

"A curious necklace, Your Majesty!" Amrat returned the smile.

"Exquisite. More charming than the handiwork of nature with its wealth of flowers!" Akbar couldn't take his eyes off the necklace with gold flowers. "Feed these buds of roses with blue diamonds, and add a circlet of sapphires at the fringe of the lotus bloom. Yes, then this necklace would be fit for an empress." He commented. "Feel your genius, Amrat, expand it, and experience the joy and ecstasy. As soon as you are satisfied with your creation of art, send this necklace to the emperor."

"Your Majesty," Amrat stood there overwhelmed by the emperor's praise.

The emperor was leaving. Acknowledging Amrat's awkward curtsy and smiling.

Salima, Salima, this necklace is fit for an empress. For Her, for my Beloved!

The emperor was window-shopping in the bazaar of his Imperial workshops. He was entering one shop where gunnery and cannon were designed and perfected.

"Your Majesty." Husein's hammer was left poised in mid-air in an act of beating the thin metal into perfect contours.

"Don't mind the emperor, and no need to curtsy." Akbar whisked past him toward Ustad Kabir. "Ustad Kabir, You should design cannons with a lighter metal, and with several parts to assemble and disassemble when needed. So that it can be transported conveniently on long marches. Rather than this monstrous thing rumbling on the dusty roads of Hind without proving its worth?" Akbar suggested, turning his attention to Husein quickly. "These guns here, Husein! They can be joined together, at least seventeen of them. Yes, it can be done, and they can be fired simultaneously with only one match. I will teach you how to implement this design, Husein. Remind me tomorrow, and we will work together." Akbar was leaving this workshop.

The emperor was walking away hurriedly, as if exhilarated beyond measure by the prospect of inventing new guns and cannons. His thoughts were creating and recreating images, yet he was becoming aware of a subtle presence behind him. Looking over his shoulders, he could detect a shadow sweeping past the other shops, and melting into the flood of moonlight in the distance. Whirling on his feet, his hand reaching down to his jeweled hilt, he was chasing the shadow. A lady donned in chiffon sari, the color of the night sky, was fleeing in utmost haste. The pipal trees were scattering a carpet of moonlit lace over the path, where her steps were falling light and quicksilver.

"Cease your flight, pretty maiden." Akbar reached closer. "The night spirits might devour you, if you do not heed the voice of authority." He was right beside her now. His very eyes were compelling her to abandon her attempt in fleeing.

The lady had no choice but to halt, coming face-to-face with the emperor, fear shining in her bright eyes. The moonlit night was revealing her white, slightly oval face with the glow of its charm and beauty.

"What brings you into the hamlet of these Imperial workshops? No one is allowed to trespass here! Not even the princes, unless they are granted permission by the emperor himself." Akbar murmured, rather than queried.

"I—my brother works here and I, quite often visit him. When—" The lady, though flustered and incoherent, was watching the emperor quite admiringly.

"Do you know, dear child, who you are speaking with!" Akbar was consumed by the volcano of his desires.

"Yes, Your Majesty." The lady murmured. "You are the emperor of Hind!"

"No, the slave of your beauty, my innocent flower!" Akbar murmured back. "What is your name?" He asked softly.

"Nighat." The lady could barely murmur.

"Nighat! How sweetly it melts on the emperor's lips." Akbar's lips were tasting the wine-song of his agony and restraint. "And your brother, what is his name?"

"Amrat." Another lone murmur escaped Nighat's lips.

Akbar tore his gaze away, summoning one of his night guards out of the shadows.

"Daulat Khurd, escort this lady to her home. She shouldn't walk unattended at this hour on the streets of Agra." Akbar instructed his guard.

The emperor then turned to his heels abruptly and resumed his walk. He was drifting toward the palace in some dream-haze, his steps slow and ponderous.

She will be my bride. Akbar was thinking. His agony of the spirit was playing harlot with his mute suffering, awakening it to wounded throbs. *A miracle divine! She has—the eyes of Salima, the lips of Hira, and the body of a Nereid. Some water-lily with the glow of silk under a moonlit night! The purity of snows on the highest peaks of Himalayas can't be compared with her slender neck. Ah, her ivory throat, and her smooth, bare arms! Ah, the fool, the madman, the emperor.*

The emperor must speak with Fatima, after all! Soon! Tonight! This very moment! Yes, he must speak, in an effort, not to alleviate Fatima's fears concerning her daughter, but to assuage his agony! Oh, this separation from my starry beloved! The miracle of night, she was? Separation, for just this one night! Tomorrow, she shall be my bride. Akbar didn't even realize that he was mounting the steps leading toward the front entrance of his palace. The gilded portals were thrown open at the approach of the emperor, but he seemed oblivious to all.

"Summon Fatima to the presence of the emperor." Akbar commanded!

In utter obedience to the emperor's command, the door-keeper was lost beyond the damasked walls of the marble hall.

The emperor had begun to pace, the gold sconces his lone companions as he kept pacing. His feet were coming to a slow halt before one Moghul painting, and before he could resume his pacing, he espied Fatima lumbering toward him.

"Fatima, the emperor wishes to entrust you with a happy task. I met a lady outside the hamlet of my Imperial workshops. Her name is Nighat. Her brother, Amrat, works as a goldsmith at one of the workshops. Tomorrow, if not this very evening, find out where this lady lives. Approach her parents with all due courtesy and deliver my message, that the emperor requests the hand of their daughter in marriage. And when you return with glad tidings, the emperor would reward you generously." Akbar intoned firmly. "And, yes, remind the emperor tomorrow about your grievance. And be assured, just punishments would fall on the head of Muazzam Khan tomorrow."

The emperor was already scaling the flight of his marble staircase with a quiet exigency. He was not seeking the warmth-refuge of his harem, but the cold, cold sanctuary of his private chambers.

Once in his damasked room of gilt and ivory, Akbar resumed the ritual of his pacing. He was in love! *Salima, his true Beloved.* She was forgotten in the deluge of sweet pain all this time, in this overwhelming storm of love and passion. No, his love for the *other* was lust and desire, one insane thought was cleaving through Akbar's agony with the noble madness of its own.

Lust and desire, why should the emperor—Akbar's pacing was truncated. His next impulse was to fling himself upon his royal bed. The tormented spirit inside him could not be consoled until its desire-need was fulfilled, completely and absolutely.

Nighat. What, if she is betrothed? Does the emperor care if she is betrothed, or if she is in love with another? No! By the divine right of my will, by the law and virtue of my love, torment and suffering, she will be my bride! This is a Farman from the very deeps in my soul and psyche. Yes, a Farman! And no man, noble or corrupt, dare violate its sanctity. Akbar's suffered thoughts were yielding to sleep. They were more savage in their dream-rest than when shooting lethal arrows in their wakefulness.

3

The Moon Lady

Akbar was standing in his Imperial library, drinking wine out of his jeweled goblet. In fact, he was waiting for the arrival of Nighat, expecting her to walk right into his arms before the morning hours were dissolved into the golden pools of noon. His thoughts had named her, the Moon Lady, his starry-bride.

Life is a dream—all a dream! Even waking up is a dream. A delusion! A dream-reality, sleeping in the hour of awakening! What hour? Ah, the illusion supreme. Akbar was waiting for the beat of the morning drums, when he was to appear at the east window in due conformity with *jharoka.* Jharoka—a ceremonial rite, when the emperor had to appear at the window of his balcony in confirmation to the needs of his subjects, that the emperor is in good health to defend his empire with the best of his abilities.

The emperor is in love! Yes and no? Akbar's mind was commencing the rite of introspection. *Yes and no? Yes, for he loved all beautiful ladies, beauty in all forms. And no, for he could not love another, but Salima!* Akbar's heart was throbbing with the violence of a need supreme. *This need could not be subjugated! It could not be crushed or destroyed, lest his youth and virility perish along with it? No, he could not immolate his need at the altar of impotence and renunciation.*

The emperor was leaving his library of gilt and damask at the first beat of the drums. The marble balcony with its facade of red sandstone was stealing light from sunshine. Akbar stood there in majestic silence, his royal form bathed in sunlight, a kind smile playing upon his lips gracefully. And then he turned to leave, one light of a promise shining in his eyes that he was to receive his subjects in Diwan-i-Am.

Once again, the beat of drums from the music gallery, was announcing the approach of the emperor. But, before he could even reach the spacious parlor at the end of the staircase, he was delayed by the hurried approach of Aziz Koka.

"Your Majesty, Khwaja Muazzam is raving mad, with threats and jealousies. A messenger arrived from Delhi, early this morning. Zuhra Agha herself has requested, sent pleas. Muazzam Khan has hit her thrice in the face, her lips bleeding, her one eye black and blue, her cheek bruised and swollen—" Aziz Koka gasped for breath.

"This son of Iblis, though my own uncle, would taste the wrath of his nephew. The emperor would chastise him personally. Right now!" Akbar hummed more royal oaths under his breath. "Instruct Todar Mall and Mukhdum-ul-Mulk to preside in my absence, with my explicit permission, and command, to act justly and kindly in the court of Diwan-i-Am. And summon twenty of my strong, trustworthy men. And get ready the swiftest of horses, the best of Iraqi and Arabian! The emperor is going hunting! To *hunt*, to shoot his uncle inside his jungle of malefic moods! Unpardonable!"

Akbar himself had taken two quick leaps to reach the front portals, when Fatima huddled in green silks, was plodding forward to meet the emperor.

"Ah, Fatima!" Akbar exclaimed. "Is the emperor's bride ready to be fetched to his palace at Agra?" He demanded.

"Your Majesty." Fatima murmured tremulously. "Your Majesty. The lady—she is married to Abdul Wasi."

"The emperor cares not if she is married, widowed, or divorced!" Akbar thundered. "Request, or even command some pious mullah to accompany you. Begin with a divorce. Then she would be a married lady no more! Free to marry the emperor, till the emperor's own death proclaims her a widow. Fetch her to my palace before I return, lest the emperor orders the death of all husbands on his way back from Delhi to Agra!" He stormed out of his palace like a man possessed.

Akbar's caparisoned horse, with twenty other mounts leagues behind, was emulating the speed of Pegasus. His heart was raging and thundering. Rage at his uncle's unpardonable act of cruelty in striking a woman—a wife. Rage at his implacability in wishing, rather dying to wed the *love* of his one night's vision?

And the emperor claims to rule with justice! Justice, from man to man, with man to God. Love knows no pity, no mercy, no reason, no justice, but the noble pain of despair and longings. Akbar's thoughts were tracing the cruelties and stupidities of his uncle, to the time when his mother was married to emperor Humayun.

Khwaja Muazzam, who had assumed the role of a pugnacious lord since his sister was married to my father. Akbar's thoughts were unleashing a string of memories. *Khwaja Muazzam, whom my father pardoned, when he pleaded innocence for the death of Khwaja Rashidi! He was the murderer, though! I myself have pardoned him several times. Didn't he threaten Abdullah Khan, that he would murder him? When brought before me, confessing falsely and unashamedly, that he had issued no such threat? Were the tears of contrition in his eyes false? My uncle, an evil brute!*

Zuhra Agha, who had feared death the most, was visited by this black visitor too soon. Khwaja Muazzam, upon discovering that his wife had secretly appealed to the emperor, was quick to stab her to death. Watching his wife bleed to death, he had begun raving like a lunatic, repeating to himself that Miryam Makani would intercede on his behalf, and that the emperor would spare his life.

He was pacing in circles, fatigue and delirium spinning his head and making his legs weak and wobbly, when the emperor had stormed into this room. The emperor's very gaze brandishing the whip of nemesis!

"This foul reptile! Bind his hands and feet to his neck, and toss him into the waters of Jamna till his sins are purged, and till his soul is free to join the silence-torment of his murdered wife." Akbar commanded. "And report his death to the emperor."

"Your Majesty, Your Majesty." Khwaja Muazzam's pleas were not to be heard by the emperor. He had left this chamber of horror.

The emperor had emerged forth into the open courtyard like a man bereaved and bereaving. He had begun to pace while Khwaja Muazzam was being hauled into a carriage. He was screaming with all his might for mercy and forgiveness.

These inhuman cries are violating the purity in sunshine! They are disturbing the calm of the clear, blue skies. Some sort of singeing mists were drifting in Akbar's thoughts. He was aware of Aziz Koka who had been following him for some time now, trying to solicit the emperor's attention.

"Your Majesty." Aziz Koka ventured forth. "Miryam Makani would be sorely grieved, when she learns about the death of her brother. May I plead on her behalf, there is still time! Spare the life of Khwaja Muazzam, Your Majesty. Only command and I myself would jump into the waters of Jamna to save him from this horrible death!"

"Cruelty demands vengeance! And vengeance sanctions not pity, but chastisement." Akbar's feet came to a slow halt. "Your sympathies are unbalanced, didn't I tell you, Aziz? God grants life, and God takes life. The emperor's will or commands are nothing, Aziz, but the mere slaves of God's mighty commands. God's will, it can neither be averted, nor challenged! With my meager sense of truth and justice, in my rage, I have condemned my uncle to death. And if God, in his Great Mercy, spares the life of this murderer, then the emperor will banish his rage, and surrender to the will of God."

The silence in sunshine was splintered by the rumbling noise of the carriage wheels, rolling mercilessly on the cobbled path. It was the same carriage in which the murderer had been transported to meet death in the holy waters of Jamna. A flustered servant was racing toward the emperor, and falling at his feet in one jumble of a curtsy.

"Your Majesty, we plunged Khwaja Muazzam into the waters of Jamna three times, but he would not die, still living." The servant muttered.

"Plunged, but not drowned." Akbar murmured in response. "The holy waters of Jamna reject this sinner, Aziz. His countless sins cannot be purged thus! Jamna refuses to accept this murderer inside the deeps of its mercy, this heathen, this cut-throat. Send this Lucifer uncle of mine into the prison of Gwalior fort, Aziz. And the emperor condemns him to the torment in life, for life!" He commanded, turning away and whistling for his horse, Harian.

The long, slanting shadows of the late afternoon were entering the temples of Agra, as Akbar kept riding toward his palace. *The saddest of all deaths!* He was thinking and shuddering inwardly. *To murder a woman, the most heinous of all crimes! Yes, this is the most vile and savage act of cowardice on any man's part. What vice, what animal hunger, what corrupt passions enslave men to such a degree of abject violence that they violate the sanctity of womanhood?* His thoughts had grown dull.

Wives, sacred all, and the emperor has ordered! What? The annulment of a marriage! Do I not stand charged— am I not about to violate the sanctity of a woman? A bewitching woman, a lovely wife, a charming lady, my moon-bride!

The emperor was stung by the abrupt assault of his psyche. He had seen providence face-to-face, this very day. When he was playing the part of a sovereign as the protector of life, God had already taken this life in His safe-keeping from the pain and suffering in life. And when he had judged life as a ransom for life, God had granted this life reprieve, condemning it to the servitude in life. So that it could taste its sins to the last, bitter, bitter dregs of its absolute misery and despair.

Death, not life, is sacred. Yes, I will recant my decision, or command. No divorce! No marriage! Yet, God most Great and Glorious! Grant me this joy just once, my Moon Lady and I will not ever ask for another boon! Nor will I ever be a slave to my passions, this slave requests but—

The dream-haze in Akbar's eyes was replaced by wonder and disbelief, as soon as he stepped into his parlor. The very walls of the palace appeared to sing the hymns of joy to him. The large couch smothered with silks, was hosting both Fatima and Nighat.

"Your Majesty, Abdul Wasi agreed to divorce his wife, and it is done." Fatima murmured happily.

Akbar was standing there in some sort of trance, barely heeding Fatima's words, his gaze devouring his beloved. His voice was clear as he turned to command his guard.

"Khan Alam, summon Mukhdum-ul-Mulk to the emperor's presence. The emperor is to be wedded, this very moment." Akbar's command had the dint of a request.

The marriage ceremony was performed in haste, much to the chagrin of Mukhdum-ul-Mulk whose pious zeal was dictating that the emperor should not marry this woman. Two guards had served as witnesses. Fatima had also stayed to serve as a third witness, and to fawn upon the emperor. After this brief ceremony, Akbar had ordered his guards to inform the royal cooks that the emperor would dine in his chamber.

The private chamber of the emperor in gilt and ivory was resplendent with gold candelabras, casting soft shadows on the much-desired bride. Akbar was sipping his wine wistfully, his gaze warm and admiring. He was seated at one end of the large table, and Nighat at the other. This table spread before, or rather between them, was serving a royal feast for two, though it could feed two dozen more from its bounteous variety, if more were invited. The emperor was still feasting on the beauty of his bride. But he replaced his goblet on the table, and asked quite winsomely.

"What are you thinking, Love?"

"I am wondering, Your Majesty. Well, I was thinking, why were all these dishes of food wrapped in colorful napkins? And, you had to do all the unwrapping!" Nighat asked innocently, her sing-song voice music to the emperor's ears.

"Your thoughts, my starry love, have evoked no bridal dreams, but just curiosity." Akbar laughed. "These napkins are seals against the danger of poisoning, my innocent flower. Each color of the napkin a final proof from each royal cook, that this food has been tasted by them before being served to the emperor. Though, least they know! That right this minute, the emperor is being poisoned by your beauty." He murmured ardently.

"God forbid, Your Majesty." Nighat murmured back, lowering her eyes.

"God forbid that I be poisoned! Or, God forbid, that your beauty should tempt me thus?" Akbar laughed again.

"God forbid that the emperor's wisdom should ever fail him in detecting the poison of treachery." A tremor of mirth broke forth on Nighat's lips. "I have heard that the emperor is wise!" The musical notes in her eyes were teasing the emperor.

"And yet, I have proved myself a fool! And your beauty alone claims the throne of wisdom!" Akbar declared passionately. "And yet again, I would rather be a fool to claim beauty as my sweet legacy, than an emperor in possession of many mindless kingdoms, all without a soul." He eased himself out of his seat slowly. "Yet, this fool has wronged you. Pleading neither mercy, nor forgiveness! Neither feeling contrite, nor remorseful! Only madly and insanely in love! "Were you—" He dared not violate the sanctity of her soul by asking *if she was in love with her husband.* "Was your husband kind to you?" He held out his hands to her, and lifted her to her feet.

"Men are incapable of kindness, Your Majesty." Nighat murmured.

"You are right, love, and the emperor is no exception. Though, I am ready to fall into a pit of shame, dragging all the rest of mankind with me." Akbar kissed her hands reverently. "My dearest, say *no* to the emperor with your eyes alone, and he would not ever desecrate the temple of your soul."

Since sweet surrender was the only answer brimming with love in Nighat's eyes, Akbar sealed her lips with his own. He was crushing her warm, yielding body into one eager, maddening embrace. Kissing, kissing, and kissing!

Forty days of wedded joys and forty nights of sheer agony and rapture, had kept Akbar prisoner to the charms of Nighat. Precisely forty days, for then Mahum Anaga had died. And forty more days, Akbar had quelled the rebellion of Abul Maali and Sharfuddin Husain. Abul Maali had escaped the Imperialists, and had fled to Kabul. There, he had found a happy refuge, and the latest news was that he was plotting with Mah Chuchak to invade Punjab.

Abdullah Khan had defected, and was plotting rebellion in Malwa. More and more reports of plots and intrigues were reaching the emperor day after day, whether he was already on campaigns, or busy in managing the state affairs at Agra. Ali Kuli and his brother, Bahadur Khan, and the Uzbek rebels, Ibrahim Khan and Sikander khan were plotting rebellions in the eastern provinces of the

Punjab. The time was ripe now, and the emperor had made his decision as to chastising his foes and scattering them all in one single blow. *Or with blows after blows in rapid succession, even if it took him a lifetime to instill reason and discipline into the besotted heads of all miscreants.*

Such were Akbar's thoughts, as he sat on his gold throne in Diwan-i-Khas. Today was his birthday. He was twenty-two year old. Today was Mahum Anaga's first death anniversary also, so the emperor was donned in garbs of mourning than of rejoicing. Today, in memory of his affection toward his childhood nurse, he had forbidden all birthday celebrations. Permitting only the sanction of the annual ritual, the weighing of the emperor against gold! This ritual was performed early in the morning and Akbar had distributed that gold amongst the poor and the Brahmans. He had then shaved his head in conformity with the tradition of pilgrims at Mecca, offering prayer and sacrifice to Allah.

Akbar sat listening to his courtiers, his expression neither sad nor mournful. Right this moment, his thoughts were sending bouquets of love to his five-month pregnant wife Nighat with a sense of relief and gratitude. Especially grateful since Nighat had completely recovered from her illness of two, long weeks!

Nighat, poor, suffered soul, my moon-bride just the same! Such moods! It seems, Salima is schooling her in the art of intemperance? Or rather, instructing her to hate the emperor as much as—Salima, Beloved. One impudent thought was whistling in Akbar's head, as he sat receiving a trail of embassies.

Salima. Can any lover be as besotted as the emperor himself? Akbar's thoughts were hovering over the son of Salima. *I already have a son, Abdur Rahim, the tender sapling. The son of my beloved Salima, almost seven, almost my son! Why do I need more sons?* His thoughts were quiet at the approach of Munim Khan.

"Your Majesty." Munim Khan intoned histrionically. "The news from Kabul is dripping blood. Tied in rags of murder and violence!"

"Not with the blood of my half-brother, I hope! He is my only royal vassal, close to my heart and soul. I wish him to remain as the sovereign of Kabul, to rule and to protect this kingdom of my father." Akbar commented thoughtfully.

"No, not Hakim Mirza, Your Majesty! He is enjoying good health, and is much in control of his affairs at Kabul. Too much in command, I should say. Considering, that he is barely a lad of ten?" Munim Khan, in his effort at haste, blundered quite profusely.

"Abul Maali, Your Majesty, after fleeing from Hind as a fugitive and assassin, was favored much by Mah Chuchak Begum in Kabul. There was no end to her favors! She even married her daughter, Fakhru-Nissa, to him. But he wanted more than favors and alliances, I have heard. One day, under the spell of ambition and jealousy, he broke open the doors of harem, entered Mah Chuchak Begum's apartment, and stabbed her to death. Killing also, Haider Qasim! Soon, a turbulent revolt broke forth in the palace, everyone wanting the blood of Abul Maali. Abul Maali was quick to befriend Hakim Mirza, bringing him forward, and proclaiming him as the true sovereign of Kabul. This way, he had succeeded in quelling the revolt. Hakim Mirza, though apparently obeying Abul Maali's orders, had sent a secret missive to Sulaiman Mirza in Badakhshan, asking for help against the murderer of his mother. Sulaiman Mirza had then marched on Kabul. Hakim Mirza was still pretending to obey Abul Maali's commands—had even accompanied him to the battlefield. But as soon as he had espied the troops of Sulaiman Mirza, he had deserted Abul Maali on the bridge over the Ghorband. Abul Maali was captured by Sulaiman Mirza himself, and left to the mercy of Hakim Mirza. Hakim Mirza issued the orders that Abul Maali be strangled to death, and his orders were quickly obeyed. Now Hakim Mirza is married to one of Sulaiman Mirza's daughters. Sulaiman Mirza has gone back to Badakhshan, though many of his men are appointed as viziers in the major towns of Kabul, keeping him informed of all events, and encouraging him to annex the kingdom of Kabul to his small one of Badakhshan."

"Kabul belongs to no one, but to Babur, my late grandfather!" Akbar declared! "Kabul was Babur's first love, his first bride of conquest. He loved and ruled it with the wild abandon of a lover. He cherished its memory after conquering Hind, and longed to return to Kabul, to his love. Alas, that he returned only after death. But now, Babur is back in Kabul, united with his love! He would possess it, always, ruling forever, from under the beloved bosom of Kabul, upto the lovely sky over his peace-filled grave—" His eyes were gathering rills of memories. "My father lost Kabul several times, but forever succeeded in winning it back, even from the treacherous hold of his wicked brothers. And now, his son Akbar, would neither lose Kabul, nor share it with any Badakhshani kin or satraps, no matter how kind and generous! Ah, happy fools that men are! The slaves of greed and ambition! The children of vainglory! They all will fall under the sway of the emperor, sooner or later? Sooner, I hope. Ah, but I do pity the slain Begum. My father loved her the most! He would not have wished that she meet her death so tragically. What deceptions corrupt our hearts? What tragedies lurk in our souls unchecked? Could we ever tell? Would we ever know? Even at the portals of death, beyond the confines of darkness."

"Your Majesty." Asaf Khan stepped forward. "Abdunnabi's reports are brought to my attention, just recently, Your Majesty. The arrears show a remarkable change since the past few years. Quite a few Hindus in the Punjab are not paying jizya. The funds in the royal treasuries are being depleted. The treasury will suffer much worse, if—"

"Ah, that hated word again!" Akbar interrupted quite genially. "And jizya, the most hated of all the words in the continent of Hind. Jizya, isn't it the most hated of all taxes, levied on non-Muslims, to feed the greed-piety of all Muslims who don't know what Islam is? Pity, that the emperor is not quick in learning the follies of this age and time! He is too busy in quelling rebellions, and warring with his thoughts to crush the spirit of unrest and anarchy in his empire. Pity, that he is not shattering the minds of his subjects with the bullets of *reason*! Though, I believe myself to be the disciple of my own *reason*! Some people's wants are greater than the needs of the others. Those wants more terrible than the agony and despair of the needy! But the emperor's wants are simple. He needs not riches, only peace, justice and equality. And the gold-nuggets of toler-ance! Tolerance toward all, for all, for all the subjects in his empire, regardless of their race, creed or religion! Didn't I forbid jizya? If that didn't make a dent over the heads of the zealots, then I forbid it again as the most solemn of my Farmans. I abolish jizya, on this day, fifteen of March, Year 1564. Proclaim this Farman all over the empire of Hind that from this day on, all men, poor or rich, Believer or non-Believer would erase this hated name, jizya, from the books of their memories."

"Your Majesty, if I may be permitted to speak?" Abdunnabi hastened for-ward.

"Yes, my learned ulema, you may voice your dissent. For, dissent is shining in your eyes. And the emperor can read your face like a book, though its words are as unintelligible to him as the voiceless words printed on a page." Akbar assented.

"Your Majesty, this tax is the emblem of Islam." Abdunnabi began with a smoldering zeal. "It has been the legacy of all Muslims, centuries old tradition. It has been collected since—"

"The emperor knows, since when this tax has been levied, and why it was exacted, not collected!" Akbar stalled Abdunnabi's zeal with an impatient wave of his arm. "This hated practice of levying such a tax is more than eight-hundred years old, since the Arab conquest of Sindh by Muhammed bin Qasim. An un-fair practice indeed, which has nothing to do with Islam, but with zeal, bigotry and intolerance! Those pious sons of greed had hoped that under the burden of such tax, their subjects would embrace Islam. They were the victims of their age and time, thinking themselves superior, while groveling into the mire of their false piety. And gloating over their power to rule and subjugate, tarnishing their souls with the brand of vice and cruelty. Do you challenge the emperor's Far-man, my revered ulema?" He asked softly.

"No, Your Majesty." Was Abdunnabi's flustered response! "It's just, that the jewels in your royal treasury would not withstand the expense of the Impe-rial army."

"Yet, most precious of all the jewels is the jewel of *reason*, and man's self-dignity rests on this jewel alone." Akbar responded kindly. "The emperor changes old traditions, not just for the sake of change, but for the needs of the changing world, and for his inner need to offer love, peace and freedom to all who fight for his cause. Yes, who fight for his cause, not in the name of God, but in the name of *reason!* For, God, in any language or in any religion, never told man to burden mankind with tax and tyranny. In the very face of our pride we forget that we should rule in the name of justice, seeking only God's love, mercy and compassion. And the emperor doesn't want to forget that, striving to remind his own self and his subjects that justice alone would conquer all."

"Yet, Your Majesty. If I may be as bold as to say, that the essence of justice changes in the face of each god, for Hindus." Abdunnabi was unable to check his surge of bigotry. "But for Muslims, justice is a true reflection of Islam, from

the eyes of one God alone. And that God is Allah, the Great and the Glorious."
He commented piously.

"And, the Merciful! Did you forget that, Abdunnabi?" Akbar laughed suddenly. "Ah, the ninety-nine names of Allah! The emperor himself recites all the ninety-nine, glorious names of Allah before sunrise, in his heart, if not on his rosary. God, since ages past, has manifested Himself in nature and in men's hearts. In many forms and shapes! And in visions most illusive and ineffable. And in names most beautiful and unutterable, the same God speaking through many tongues, revealing His essence as One and All. Hindus, my besotted scholar, have such a God as One-without-the-other. One Essence beyond shape, one form beyond comprehension! One essence nameless and one form indescribable! Allah, with ninety-nine, beautiful names! Is He not the same by any name? Don't the Muslims praise Him by the oft-repeated, oft-exalted names such as: the Creator, the Producer, and the Fashioner? Do Hindus not pray to the same God, when they invoke Brahma as the Creator, Vishnu as the Preserver, and Shiva as the destroyer? Is Creator not the same as Brahma? Is Producer not the same as Vishnu, the Preserver, who produces and preserves? Is Fashioner not the same as Shiva, the Destroyer, who fashions and destroys in order to create and preserve? Oh, the emperor digresses! Tempt him not into this ocean of theology, for he would forever wade into its muddied waters, without ever reaching the shore of enlightenment! Or, ever attaining the wealth of knowledge! Neglecting too, the wealth of land in this world where kingdoms upon kingdoms are falling into the pit of anarchy and ignorance." He let his gaze sweep over the ulemas. "Unsheathe your arguments, you all! Come forward, and the emperor would welcome you with kindness. Though, he is skilled in deflecting the munitions of zeal."

Since no learned ulema dared brand the emperor's liberal views with the stamp of blasphemy, Akbar returned his gaze to Abdunnabi.

"Your Majesty, my love for you makes me bold to say, that such a talk, such sanctions to the Hindus, may alienate the emperor from his Muslim subjects. May–besides Islam—" Abdunnabi appeared to fall into a pit of his confusion.

"Islam, my devoted ulema, is very simple. It is corrupted by the zeal of the ignorant, by mullahs and zealots alike. Didn't Prophet Muhammad himself say? *I have been sent to make things easy, and not to make them difficult.*" Akbar intoned merrily. "Does the virtue of tolerance condemn one into the rivers of heresy? Nurturing the seeds of tolerance! Is that some sort of abominable sin to damn the emperor into the hoary fires of hell? Speak, speak, my poets, friends, ulemas, and my courtiers! What horror has seized you all in the grip of dull inertia?" He demanded.

"Your Majesty, this sense of tolerance is fodder for the enemy, to malign the emperor—"

"Your Majesty, evil tongues may discredit the emperor's—"

"Your Majesty, people distort the meanings of—"

"Your Majesty, many tongues will utter lies to weaken the power of—"

Many voices were melting in low murmurs, as the emperor listened patiently.

"No harm would ever come to the emperor in his pursuit of religious tolerance! For, his laws and edicts are just, as true as any pennants of truth over the holy words of the Quran." Akbar commented. "Truth tempts lies, so that it can conquer untruth with the sword of reason, not with the dagger of ignorance. The Present holds us prisoner in its harsh climes of intrigues and insurrections. We wade and founder in the diversity of faiths and creeds. We stray and stagger in the munificence of riches and knowledge. What choices do we have? Either, we should look into the eyes of the future, holding the light of peace and prosperity? Or, we can fall back into the pit of the past, sinking deeper into its turbulent waters, where the unjust laws and the intolerant views still embrace darkness? Future, I say, stands before us like a rock. A solid rock, heavy and colossal! We are constantly banging our heads against its impervious walls, blindly and willfully. Not ever noticing its countless million rents and crevices in the face of time and assault. For, if we did notice, our sightless minds would discover comforting homes behind those walls. Astonishing as it may seem, we can discover comforting homes in the *future-walls* of our minds. Where our thoughts would grow larger and vaster, each thought greeting the next, and each thought embracing each and all, each thought expanding and palpitating. Each fiber in our soul and psyche reflecting oceans, galaxies and continents of wisdom, the splintering of rocks against the sea of knowledge! If we only looked, if we could only see the silent abyss in this *future-rock*, inside our soul." His tone was splintering fears and doubts within his soul. "Let us adjourn this court on the note of splendid hopes, not with the ropes of jaded fears. And remember jizya is the misinterpretation of the tax levied over non-Muslim Arabs as an expense toward protecting their caravans from marauders."

The emperor seemed to have forgotten that there were more embassies to be received. But the punctilious page was quick to announce the last one, before the emperor could rise to his feet.

"Your Majesty." Man Singh spoke without hesitation. "Malwa has been the victim of unrest under the rule of all its governors, so far. Now Abdullah Khan is wearing the mantle of revolt. He is assuming the power of a king, and defying the authority of the Imperial rule. Also, he is despoiling the peace and property of the villagers in his ambition to conquer small villages." He concluded quickly.

"Malwa is no worse the victim of all those inveterate rebels, whom the emperor has had no chance to chastise. Once they taste the whip of the emperor's authority, they would be molded into the disciples of discipline!" Akbar declared quite genially. "The emperor enjoys hunting, it is fortunate! And he will be going hunting quite often, all his life, it seems, to hunt and breed new disciples of discipline. Well, my real hunting expedition is in the forest of Narwar, and then I will march straight to Malwa."

"Your Majesty, Abdullah Khan has gone as far as Mandu and is residing there most splendidly." Man Singh was quick to inform the emperor.

"Mandu, it is then, my prudent general. And order the Imperial troops to prepare for a long, long journey." Akbar murmured. "The army should be exercised in warfare, lest from want of training they become self-indulgent." He got to his feet.

The sunlit parlor with gleaming marbles and silk friezes, was the abode that Akbar had chosen to spend this afternoon with his wives, and with the ladies of his late father's harem. Amongst the motley of royal gathering, this particular afternoon, was Akbar's Aunt, Gulbadan Begum. Gulbadan Begum had just joined Salima, their love for poetry drawing them together like two conspiring poets. Right now, his attention was absorbed by his mother's words of caution and advice.

"My son, wisdom and discretion are the most prized weapons of war. Think, and think twice before exposing yourself to valorous deeds," Hamida Banu Begum was saying. "Employ wise and learned men to rule all the kingdoms, small or large. Guide them toward truth and righteousness. Lead them on the path to loyalty and devotion. You are the emperor, and you must guide them toward the right path. You have the wisdom to make them noble and truthful, and honest and just."

"Dear Mamma, how should I guide, or even claim to guide men, before I myself am guided!" Akbar exclaimed suddenly.

"You need guidance from your mother, Your Majesty!" Hamida Banu Begum rebuked with a dint of tenderness. "May I caution you, Your Majesty, on the rungs of great misfortunes? The misfortunes which befall emperors if they do not discover that their whims and faults are their greatest of enemies?"

"Now, Miryam Makani! My dear Mamma. This caution, if it lacks wit, is not for the emperor." Akbar laughed. "As to the misfortunes! A great misfortune, indeed, when my subjects dare not tell me of my faults, but sing praises of my false virtues."

"The ambitious who praise, are more dangerous than the fools who flatter, for the fools' only ambition is to gain riches, not sovereignty." Hamida Banu Begum chided. "Laugh as you will, my son, and tease your mother to your heart's content! But, do not alienate the ulemas by changing age-old edicts. Your new Farmans must seek their support and judgment. You are blessed with the gift of wisdom from God, use it wisely!"

"Music and laughter are the gifts from God too, Mamma!" Akbar declared evasively. "The gifts, which all of us can enjoy without paying the ransom with toil and suffering." He laughed, summoning his wine-bearer to replenish his cup!

"These gifts will not benefit you, Your Majesty, when the ulemas choose to pronounce you heretic! If they are already not doing so behind your back, professing to have perfect knowledge and understanding of Islam?" Hamida Banu Begum murmured low.

"Shallow knowledge, dear Mamma! Their knowledge, shallow and muddied." Akbar murmured back. "*Knowledge is not understanding*, Mamma! Didn't you tell me this, yourself? Your son never forgets, nor does he cease to reflect upon it. To climb the rungs of *understanding* is like taking a leap in the air, and trying to fly without wings. While knowledge, one can gather, and absorb, on every little step on the path of one's slow ascent, until one reaches the last rung! Then, one knows not which way to turn? The only way to keep going farther, lies in the fact that one has to plunge oneself downward into the very mud from where the ascent begins. Humbled thus, then, one can begin exploring the path of *understanding*. Aspiring to soar without the weight of knowledge and without the shackles of pride! And with the humility of ignorance, which is the very first step outside the door to wisdom." He smiled. "Harem politics, Mamma, it's dangerous. How the emperor's Farmans reach my harem, even before they escape the emperor's lips, is beyond the power of his perception?" His eyes were turning to Salima. "All court proceedings, including the royal gossip, reach the harem doors, except the groans in the emperor's heart and soul." He returned his gaze to his mother.

"Such mystic knowledge, my son, my dull senses can never grasp." Hamida Banu Begum murmured again. "Since you know, all talk reaches here, tell me what they mean when they say, Believer, non-Believer? I know what the words mean, but not the way the ulemas imply! I don't understand."

"Believers, dear Mamma, are the non-believers who shamelessly drag people into the marshes of their non-beliefs." Akbar's Sufic thoughts were kindled to mischief. "And I wish, the ulemas thought this way." His eyes were seeking the company of Salima. "Don't you hear the groans in the emperor's soul, my cruel Salima?"

"Yes, Your Majesty, the groans of hunger, from your stomach!" Salima complied most sweetly. "You should have breakfast, every morning, then eat all day, as we all do till dinner, and after dinner, and into the late hours of the night."

"Your wit, dear Salima, sits heavy on the emperor's soul, not in his stomach." Akbar demurred. "My hungers, as you know, never crave food, but the morsels of contemplation, if it be a morning. During the day, even that hunger is gone, only my mind thirsts, draining the cups of beauty from nature, or quenching its thirst from the coffer-flagons of duties. The bitter, bitter draughts, with a promise of joy and sport on the way! What hungers and thirsts, all kindling into appetites for books, and—" He was draining his cup once again, and holding it out to his wine-bearer for replenishing.

"Wine must be the sweetest of all your appetites, Your Majesty." Was Salima's flustered murmur of a comment!

"Wine has been the curse of our family, drowning our young men into the rivers of misfortunes." Hamida Banu Begum intoned, shuddering inwardly. "I hope, Your Majesty, that you will stay temperate in your drinking. And when sons are born to you, you would restrain them from this indulgence! How tempting and unfortunate this habit is?"

"War and treachery, not wine, have been the cause of the Moghul misfortunes, Miryam Makani." Gulbadan Begum was allaying the fears of Hamida Banu Begum. "My dear, dear brother was killed by the treachery of our foster-brother. I can never forget that woeful day." She sighed. Sadness alighting in her eyes in one poetic gleam!

"In wars, men both noble and wicked are tempted by the sword of treachery." Akbar thought aloud. "But, when this sword of treachery touches the hem of a noble soul, it becomes more savage than a hurricane. That is when vice and wickedness flourish and rule over the land and the sea." He added thoughtfully.

"This talk of war makes me sad, Your Majesty." Hira Begum protested. "The subject of wine is pleasant, sweet and smooth! No danger, that this talk can chill us in fear and sadness." Her gaze was inciting other wives to rebellion, as planned beforehand.

"Yes, Your Majesty, wine is good. We should all drink wine, and sing couplets." Ruqaiya Begum was the first one to jump into this surge of pre-plotted mischief.

"Yes, Your Majesty, the wine is sweet and good. We have never tasted it, though! Can we?" Mahmooda Begum couldn't be left behind.

A chorus of mirthful demands was followed by all, with the exception of Hamida Banu Begum and Gulbadan Begum. *Oh, this raillery, charged with impudence! Such rudeness and impropriety*! Both these ladies were thinking.

"Sweet rebellion and sweet rebels, inside the very palace of the emperor's harem!" Akbar exclaimed happily. "What need of wine, my loves, when you all—nay, when all the women in the world are made of wine and honey! Wine in their eyes, and honey on their lips. If wine touched your lips, my sweets, the honey on them would taste only bitterness." He got to his feet laughingly.

"How times change, and how ideas churn and push the very thoughts to the edge of impropriety!" Hamida Banu Begum joined her son in his mirth.

"Dear Mamma." Akbar turned to her quickly. "Your son is going hunting, to war, at the first bright streak of dawn! Watch his wives most tenderly, lest they drown themselves into the rivers of wine."

Akbar was hugging all his wives with the exception of one cruel one, his beloved Salima. Talking with them gaily, and then sweeping Nighat into his arms most tenderly.

"Keep our royal babe warm and healthy, my Moon Lady. A royal heir to my throne, the emperor hopes." Akbar was turning toward Salima. "The emperor is going on dangerous expeditions, Salima, and needs the prayers of all his wives. But their evil ways may block his passage back to Agra. Alas, only my Salima would lead the emperor to the very gates of hell." He murmured to the icy gleam in her eyes.

"To heaven, I hope, Your Majesty, if the heavenly womb of Nighat doesn't distract me from my prayers, to my God." Salima murmured back.

"Sweet insurrection from the sweet lips of love, or hatred!" Akbar murmured inaudibly. "She also prays to your God, my love, and without the eternal fire of puja, which you find insufferable in Hira's chamber. Nighat will keep you warm with her dear, dear presence. And when I return from Mandu, I wish you cured of all chills, if not of your hatreds and jealousies." He folded her into his arms in one eager embrace.

Akbar was drifting past all in some stupor of rage and agony. His feet were carrying him toward the sanctuary of his library, where his solitude alone could assuage the pain of his loneliness.

Can one taste hatred? I have tasted it times and times again. In her eyes! Inside her soul! On her lips! Yet, I will taste it in her body, this very night! Yes, and cherish this hatred too, in the sinews of my wild dreams, where wars play not harlot with kingdoms, until they are subjugated and compelled to yield under the magic and witchcraft of human passions, terrible and fathomless— Akbar's thoughts were murmuring inanities, his feet encompassing the floor of his vast, quiet library.

4

A Great Hunt

The clear lakes with a wealth of weeping willows were sprinkled with the scintillating dusk-haze from the trees, as the Imperial cavalcade kept marching on the road toward Lawani. Lawani—a small town where Abdullah Khan had finally fled after learning about the approach of the Imperial march toward Mandu.

Akbar, with his usual sense of adventure, was riding ahead of his cavalry in some sort of relentless mood. Almost two weeks were swallowed up by the rush and caprice of time in an effort to cross Chambal River, for its waters was swollen by the downpour from monsoon rains. Finally, the emperor had reached Narwar in time to indulge in his favorite sport of hunting. After the hunt, the Imperialists had resumed their march, but this march from Narwar to Surangpur was no less difficult, the monsoon rains still pelting them with the fury of their own. But, Akbar had felt refreshed after this Great Hunt, riding eighty miles non-stop, and reaching Surangpur in one day. Next morning, Akbar had reached the city of Dhar via Ujjain. At Dhar, the emperor was informed that Abdullah Khan had fled from Mandu, and was hiding in the lower defiles of Lawani.

Am I the hunter or the hunted? The deceiver or the deceived! Akbar's thoughts were flying back to Agra, where his heart lay torn inside the very cups of Salima's eyes.

The eyes of my beloved Salima! The most beautiful eyes the emperor has ever seen? How many times I have drowned myself in them? Yet, this sort of drowning, is that not a ritual in loving and living? And being cast ashore from the lovely depths of those eyes, a suffering most intolerable! How many times— Akbar kept riding.

His thoughts were entering the dark alleys of pride, and the intolerance of his ulemas.

False is pride? False the atom of wisdom, which cannot tame the weeds of discord, cruelty, intolerance, watching silently the destruction of everything that life holds sacred? Life and death, both living and dying in the pulse of timelessness, both stirring and kindling the flames of false pride!

Is life itself a battleground? An utter chaos, where some sort of bloody peace is whirling like a hurricane to attain conformity through greed, hatred, ignorance, in the battlefield of slaughter, bloodshed, devastation.

Sin awakens where virtue sleeps! Evil breathes where goodness rests! Misery abounds where joy prospers? The blind, avenging winds of peace, devour chaos into non-conformity, from whence the bliss in Whole labors for the miracle of birth and rebirth, from the fibres of peace-chaos into nothingness once again, from the beginning of time to the end of timelessness.

The emperor's thoughts were floating back to the jungles of Narwar. After the Great Hunt, he had rested in the pleasant gardens of Kakrali. The same gardens now were flowering in his mind like a colorful tapestry.

"On our way back to Agra, remind the emperor to stop at Kakrali, Munim Khan. I want to choose a splendid spot, and order a hunting lodge to be built for the convenience of our next hunts." Akbar appeared to reminisce aloud.

"Your Majesty." Was Munim Khan's startled response! "We need a rest house on this very spot, Your Majesty! You have not slept since the last couple of days, but for three hours." He breathed happily, noticing the emperor's bright and carefree expression.

"Sleep, my brave warrior, is the luxury of the idle and the godless!" Akbar declared warmly. "Sleep, although, it does bring health to the body! Yet, as life is the greatest of gifts from God, it should be spent in wakefulness. And yet again, sleep and food are means of the renewal of strength in seeking to do the will of God, and yet the miserable man, from folly, regards those means as an end."

"I am neither idle, nor godless, Your Majesty, but I need plenty of food and sleep in order to function properly, both mentally and physically. Pretty soon, I would need both food and sleep, lest I fall into the folly of gluttony and imprudence." Munim Khan ventured forth thoughtlessly.

"Plenty of both nurture the dearth of spiritual hungers, unfortunately." Akbar murmured to himself. "You are neither idle, nor godless, the emperor knows and agrees. A man of your valor and energy rests but little in his sleep, and thinks himself a glutton with the share of a child's portion. Sleep is the shadow of our wakefulness, awakening while we sleep, and sleep-walking after we awaken. Hunger is the companion of our body and soul, hungering forever for food, and for something other than food? These hungers silenced when visited by solitude, and clamoring, when the baser needs of our flesh drug our solitary contemplations to sleep. One can tame both these hungers with the morsels of noble thoughts. But first, one has to understand one's needs and appetites. Practice and perseverance! Discipline and restraint! What wondrous tools in the living tomb of life, if man can but learn to use them."

"Your Majesty, how does one employ these tools, when one is wearied with hunger and fatigue?" Was Munim Khan's befuddled inquiry! "I mean, when one is embarked on a long, long journey? When distances stretch farther and farther from one's destination? When one's body demands food and rest!"

"These tools, Munim, are our thoughts and experiences. The best way to handle these tools is to feel, touch and acknowledge their being, or existence, if you will! Let us begin with the practice of handling these tools, right now." Akbar began thoughtfully. "Our stay in Malwa was prolonged. Rain slapping our faces, muddied roads unwelcoming and swollen rivers detaining us with the churning fury of their own. But we did overcome all obstacles. We crossed the river Chambal, enjoyed hunting in Narwar. We reached our destination in Mandu, now another destination is luring us toward Lawani. In this journey alone, we have learned much and have gathered much experience! Much more, by sharing our fortunes and adversities alike! Much more, than any book of knowledge could teach or expound, or even hold in words these changing vistas on the way? The sounds and the sights! The caprice of the lands and the seas! The habits of the people and their reservoir of tales unforgotten and unforgettable! The stories that they tell are not a separate entity, but a part of *whole* in them. They are living and re-living the lives of their ancestors in the richness of their souls. Tell me, Munim, did you hear any strange stories concerning Malwa, when we were in Malwa?"

"None, Your Majesty. Only a few comments, here and there!" Was Munim Khan's puzzled response! "Only, that the peasants around there, even the grain dealers, are never without arms. And that the people, both high and low, give opium to their children, up to the age of three years." His thoughts were laconic and unrevealing.

"Is that all, Munim, and the land itself told you nothing, no stories?" Akbar prodded, his gaze fixed to the heliotrope sky.

"Much have been on my mind, Your Majesty, the war and the killing of our foes!" Munim Khan's response was but a whisper in the wind.

"Engrave these words of mine in the book of your knowledge, Munim. Do not be hasty in killing the sons of men, who are fruit-bearing plants and the sublime foundation of God." Akbar commanded. "And next time you open this book of knowledge, try to retrieve at least one story out of its rusty pages, for the emperor delights in hearing about the lands he has journeyed through, and about the people he has met. Disuse of memory is dangerous to the law and order in living. A mere slip in recollection and one may fall into the dungeons of misery and despair."

"I suddenly remember one story, Your Majesty, if I may recount? But I am afraid, you have already heard it." Munim Khan appealed quickly.

"If the emperor has heard it, he will command you to silence!" Akbar's tone was brandishing the whip of an ultimate command.

"Yes, Your Majesty, I will begin without delay." Munim Khan obeyed. "The peasant who sold us the fodder for our horses told me this story. There was a prince named, Bhoja, born in the town of Malwa, centuries ago. At the time of his birth, the astrologers foretold that the life of this prince would hold a great threat to the reigning monarch in Malwa. The reigning monarch was Raja Munja, who fearing that this prince would pose a great threat to his glorious reign, ordered this child-prince to be murdered. But one sage took pity on this prince, saved him from the edict of death, and concealed him in his home. Bhoja was eight years old, when the sage drew his own chart of astrology, and proved the predictions of the other astrologers as miscalculations. He told the young prince about the gross errors of the astrologers at the time of his birth. And he informed him that his stars foretold wisdom and prosperity, not evil and treachery. Then he announced to the prince that he was taking the results of his calculations to Raja Munja in his effort to right the wrong which had been done to this prince of illustrious birth. The sage had taken Bhoja into confidence, for the prince had shown signs of wisdom since his early age. Bhoja was moved to tears by the kindness of this sage. Entreating the sage to deliver a letter to Raja Munja, which he himself was going to write! While the sage was preparing for his journey, Bhoja was able to finish his letter. This is what he wrote. *How doth darkness of soul in a man cast him out of the light of wisdom, and in unholy machinations stain his hands in the blood of the innocent! No monarch in his senses thinks to carry with him to the grave his kingdoms and treasures, but thou by slaying me, seemest to imagine that his treasures perpetually endure and that he himself is beyond the reach of harm.* Raja Munja, upon receiving the missive was filled with remorse and contrition. Bhoja was brought to the palace, and reared as a princely scholar to the best of his wisdom and understanding. He succeeded to the throne after Raja Munja's death, and ruled Malwa with honor and justice."

"Splendid!" Akbar echoed his praise aloud. "Have you experienced the might of this nameless tool, Munim? Have you felt its power, its texture, and its smoothness? The distance to our destination is almost effaced. It is not moving farther, but racing closer. It is beckoning us to wage war and to receive the trophies of conquest."

The deep, crimson haze of dawn was enveloping the town of Lawani in the mantle of foreboding, as the Imperial troops kept marching forward. Akbar was riding ahead with merely a group of three hundred soldiers. And the emperor was the first one to espy the enemy. They were laying in ambush down the slope of a garden near one small village called the, Bagh. The drummers had begun to beat their drums, and the trumpeters were blowing on their horns under some spell of frenzy and exhilaration. Akbar was riding ahead, his eyes shining with a challenge, and his hand reaching down to his jeweled hilt to unsheathe his sword.

"Your Majesty, it is not safe to ride alone! Abdullah Khan is waiting for such a chance." One Imperial guard leaped forward, breaking his crescent-shaped formation.

"Get behind me, you craven fool!" Akbar thundered.

"Your Majesty. Wait, till the rest of the cavalry joins us." Munim Khan pleaded.

"Charge! With valor and without delay!" Akbar commanded.

"Your Majesty, Abdullah Khan is with several thousands of his army! While we have only three hundred with us, right now!" Munim Khan grunted his plea.

Akbar was heedless to all pleas. One young officer from the cavalry, swifter than the rest had galloped forth, confronting the emperor. He had succeeded in seizing the reins of the emperor's horse, while pleading with the emperor not to endanger his life!

"You will taste the whip of obedience yet, you impudent wretch! Begone, begone." Akbar wrenched free the reins of his horse, and charged ahead.

The three hundred of the emperor's cavalry had followed the emperor, along with the impudent wretch of an officer. They had circled the enemy like a wall of vengeance, hailing a shower of arrows, and baring their swords with the valor of the Moghuls.

The crimson streaks of dawn were long past swallowed, now pale haze of the evening consuming the light of the day. The fighting had yet not ceased on this battlefield of great slaughter. Abdullah Khan, seeing the emperor himself fighting like a war-lord was quickly disheartened. His soldiers too, witnessing the valor and the prowess of the emperor were seized with a panic akin to chaos and confusion. Mindless of the hail of arrows they were driven straight into the arms of the flashing swords, as if lured to welcome death by the hands of the Moghuls. Most of them were brave though, fighting to the end, caring not if they were injured or unhorsed.

The tamarind groves down yonder, further flanked by weeping willows at the borders of the silvery lakes were offering kind refuge to the vanquished. The drums and the trumpets were sounding the victory songs. But Akbar was listening to the groans of the night from the very lips of the dead and the dying.

The hopes of the wounded are dying on their lips, and their torments unwilling to welcome peace in death. Akbar was thinking.

"No need to pursue the sightless rebels, this night." Akbar announced. "A time for feasting and a time for celebration! We would chase the rebels early at dawn. Attend to the wounded, while the cooks prepare the food." He let his horse canter toward the encampment in the distance.

A few, cold stars in clusters of light were scattered over the sky, lowering beams of peace over the royal encampment. Akbar's damasked tent was lined with velvet and brocade. One flaming torch on a lofty mast was erected at the gate of his tent. He was wide awake and enjoying the company of his few companions, but was becoming aware of their fatigue and drowsiness.

Their minds and bodies require more rest and sleep than the emperor's.

"If there are no more sweet couplets to delight the emperor, and no glad tidings, you all may repair to rest." Akbar smiled. "But before you seek comfort in your rich tents, the emperor wishes to know more about the rumors of treachery in Khandesh. Is Mubarak Shah pretending to seek our alliance, while plotting treason?" He asked.

"Those rumors are proved to be false, Your Majesty." Aziz Koka responded. "Mubarak Shah, though he rules Khandesh most possessively, is devoted to the emperor's cause. He is desirous of seeking alliance it is true, by marrying his daughter to you, Your Majesty, as a further proof of his loyalty and devotion." He concluded quickly.

"This happy alliance, the emperor intends not to postpone." Akbar laughed suddenly. "Dispatch a kind missive to Mubarak Shah, my good brother that the emperor wishes to marry the Khandesh princess after his victorious return to Agra, or before!" His gaze was turning to Birbal. "Are you going to pen some couplets for the emperor's wedding, my wise poet and my valorous knight?" His gaze was teasing and holding Birbal prisoner.

"For sure, Your Majesty, for sure. I will, I will! In my sleep, I might write a whole diwan!" Birbal elicited one brave smile.

"In my sleep, I write not noble couplets, but suffer the heresy of dreaming lurid dreams!" Akbar declared aloud. "But when I wake up from this glorious death in sleep, I offer thanks to Almighty God for this renewal in life, where I can at least attempt to act kindly and justly." He claimed his goblet and began to sip his wine slowly.

"Your Majesty." Todar Mall procured a dish of kabobs, and offered it to the emperor. "Meat has not tempted your palate, this evening, Your Majesty. And you have eaten, but very little." His eyelids were heavy and drooping.

"The emperor has had no savory preference for meat since his childhood, my droopy lord! Besides, it is not right that a man should make his stomach the grave of animals." Akbar got to his feet laughingly. "The emperor himself will escort you all to your sleepy abodes. Yes, your sleepy abodes which are nothing but the sleepless temples inside the bosom of the wakeful nights!" He was outside his tent, looking at stars.

"Your Majesty, Your Majesty! No need, no need—" Several protests exploded.

"Your Majesty, you should not expose yourself to danger, as you did this evening, on the battlefield? Without the reinforcements! Your guards are sleeping, no one to—" Bhagwan Das' protest was silenced by Akbar's abrupt exclamation.

"Danger is the daughter of *fear*, and *fear* the misbegotten son of the weak and cowardly." Akbar was awed by the starry night lit by the globe of full moon. "Men who fear their *great destiny* are crushed only by the weight of their cowardliness." He bent down, and drew a line in the dust with the tip of his index finger. "A riddle in the night!" He sprang up quickly. "Make this line shorter! But don't, by any means, erase any part of it. Once, that you have accomplished that, you will all sleep better."

A wall of silence met the emperor's challenge. The emperor was looking at the moon again, and wondering. *Is the moon mocking the challenger and the challenged alike*? His gaze was returning to the earth, falling on Birbal.

"Birbal, come forward. Dissolve this puzzle inside the well of your wisdom by your ingenuity alone." Akbar commanded. "You scarcely breathed a word all evening. But now, you must breathe wisdom. Relieve all your friends from the burden of this challenge, for they must snatch a few hours of sleep before dawn. And you must, too!"

"Your Majesty." Birbal obeyed. Right beside that line, he drew a longer one.

"A miracle in the night!" Akbar applauded. "Birbal, your wisdom makes the emperor more aware of his ignorance. His ignorance, indeed!" He clapped his hands. "Now, farewell and good night. And may you dream of joy and hope, and of valor and wisdom." He sauntered past the wall of silence.

The emperor's feet were coming to a slow halt before the flaming torch, where it stood burning on its lofty mast like an eternal flame. He was retracing his steps. Inside the comfort of his royal tent, Akbar was accosting sleep. His heart was longing for the nearness of Salima, but his thoughts were grazing on the love-pastures in Khandesh.

Fate, destiny, are they not just words? Without cause, without substance, without meaning! Could they be the flimsy threads of one's imagination? No, a thousand times, no! Fates are real. They could neither be averted, nor challenged. Neither subdued, nor defied? Each man follows his destiny to the utter failure of his efforts, or to the utmost success in his life.

The brief hours of the night flanked by the morning sunshine were once again fading into the haze of a glorious sunset. The emperor, donned in gleaming armor with gold helmet gracing his head was almost concealed against the standards of red and yellow. They appeared to follow him like the shadows, much like the haze and glow in sunset which looked the same as day before yesterday.

The crimson sun itself murders the days! A myriad of its scimitar-shafts cleaving through the bowels of the earth, quenching its thirst for life, and filling its bowl of fire with life-blood! The sun itself trembling on the verge of death and dissipation! Blood! Crimson haze, blood everywhere! A red haze, the volcano of death, life dying at the altar of darkness! Haze, oblivion, surcease! Haze swallowing haze. Blood curdling in the bosom of the earth! Pallid cheeks of the night yearning for rest and oblivion! Dark sleep dreaming to churn the skies to pearly whiteness at the wake of dawn! Akbar was riding without haste, his thoughts exigent and crowding.

Another Dawn! Another day! Another Light! Another fire in the sun! The blood of life coursing through the very veins of the night in sleep! Resurrecting shadows, bringing shades to life in the death of another day? More shades and shadows sweeping over the world like the wild, restless spirits in semblance of thoughts. The thought-spirits unafraid, undying—inconsolable! The blood-red eyes of dawn again. Mocking the pearly whiteness in the skies! Holding open the portals of heaven, where the sun-king will sit on his gold throne, contemplating the aura of its smoldering power over life, death and resurrection. Ah, the virgin dawns and the ravished nights! The labor-consummation of strange wedlocks! The sweet, mysterious hymns from the very throats of the larks and the nightingales!

The Imperial cavalcade was entering the town of Champaner. Akbar, with his keen sense of direction and perspicacity was leading his army toward the very sight where Abdullah Khan might be hiding. Abdullah Khan's small band of army was suddenly overtaken by the Imperialists. This fray had lasted but a few minutes, the slaughter of the rebellious foes more swift than the day before.

The losses on their side were pitiful, the death-toll numbering to more than nine hundred. Abdullah Khan, with defeat leering him in the face had no choice but to flee again. *This time, he was fleeing with a numbered few. Cursing his ambition and stupidity!*

Akbar once again was commanding his soldiers not to pursue the fallen rebel. Suddenly, his heart was a river of compassion! He was overwhelmed by this inner deluge, throbbing in waves upon waves of mercy and forgiveness.

Oh, this woeful night! Akbar was thinking, his gaze falling on Abdunnabi, who was riding toward him post-haste.

"Your Majesty." Abdunnabi pulled the reins on his steed a little distance from the emperor. "In your kindness and compassion, I know, you have issued this command! But Abdullah Khan is an inveterate rebel! He doesn't deserve your compassion, Your Majesty." His very eyes were breathing fire and zeal. "Even Allah doesn't show compassion to the cowards. Abdullah Khan shows no mercy to anyone? He is a coward, fleeing for his life, never stopping to think that the lives of his followers are perishing at the cost of his foolishness. Let me, Your Majesty follow this fool of a rebel. He deserves my compassion, for I will slay him and end his misery."

"Compassion, my good fool, is to show mercy to the unmerciful." Akbar thundered without rage. "Merry-making tonight, and tomorrow we repair to Mandu. We will hunt there, and hunt no more for wars!"

Akbar, the night rider, was on a lonely spree till the royal tents were pitched. He could feel the vacuum of his innate need, longing for true love, searching *truth* in love. *Truth in love! Some rude lust for beauty! Some appetites nameless! Oh, this love, hungering and thirsting for love— my passion unrequited, my desire undying. Weight of Desire is like gold! Of no value, but worth many a suffering! The prison of suffering! Ah, but the golden abode! My beautiful cage!*

The journey from Champaner to Mandu was sprinkled with songs and jubilations, with a promise of swift and safe return to Agra. But the emperor had found Mandu more delightful than before, and had decided to delay his return back to Agra. Besides, Mubarak Shah had journeyed from Khandesh to Mandu along with the beautiful princess, Farida Mubarak. Her marriage with Akbar was solemnized with twin celebrations, for the emperor had received happy news from Agra the same day, even before the wedding ceremonies had begun. Nighat Begum had blessed the emperor with two sons.

The bride of my love and caprice! The only bride who has given me the treasures of the world! Two sons, my own sons, my very own sons! Akbar had been ecstatic.

This time and illusion! Chasing and fleeing, making days harlots of the nights! And nights, lusts of the days!

Akbar this particular evening was seated on a throne in his gilded tent on the plains of Mandu. Mubarak Shah was the honored guest in this royal tent, assigned a seat next to Akbar as being the new father-in-law of the emperor. The emperor was laughing and expounding under some spell of carefree abandon.

"A sovereign should abstain from four things!" Akbar was saying. "An excessive devotion to hunting, which should be the first one. Then incessant play and the third one, a state of inebriation night and day! And the last one, the constant intercourse with women." He elicited one mock sigh. "If your daughter were not endowed with bewitching charms, Mubarak, the emperor would be sitting in Agra! Ruling wisely, attending to the matters of his state, and not indulging in the pleasures of hunting.

"Your Majesty, your wisdom has the power to rule anywhere regardless of your absence or presence in any particular place! Mandu or Agra, names matter not, as long as you are the sole sovereign of Hind." Mubarak Shah retorted happily. "Keeping in mind the chaos and devastation in wars, and the misery and the hopelessness!"

"From the abode of ruin we escape, and to the garden of bliss we return!" Akbar laughed. "And as for misery and hopelessness in wars we can always buy hope with the jewel of wisdom. And can sell despair to the wretched horde of humanity who dare not earn even a dirham. And, who like to wallow in hopelessness at the expense of their misery! Those miserable wretches always longing for more crumbs of misery to feed their rueful appetites! An even barter for those in the bazaar of plenty and dearth! Oh, this inebriated night! The emperor wishes to drink no more. My plans for a palace and a hunting lodge at Kakrali are finalized in my head. You would be entrusted with the execution of these plans, Mubarak. I would send my architect, Qasim Khan, as soon as I reach Agra. Next time I visit I wish to enjoy hawking in the meadows of Kakrali, while finding rest and comfort in my palace. Encourage the viziers and the grandees to build large mansions in this city, with beautiful gardens all around. Kakrali would be named, Nagarchain, which means, the city of repose. We would play polo at night. I love to watch those luminous polo balls, floating around like the burning coals, as if by the sheer witchery of the polo players. Ah, the play of darkness in the light-fire of that small ball which allows us to play polo at night!"

"Your Majesty, may we play polo, tonight?" Munim Khan's abrupt plea was brimming with the sense of nostalgia.

"Not tonight, my valiant soldier, not tonight." Akbar murmured. "Not before we reach Agra, and not until Qasim Khan erects a palace here for the emperor, and that is when we return for hunting."

"Your Majesty, that is a long, long wait." Munim Khan protested. "You have ordered Qasim Khan to build a palace at Fathpur-Sikri! And he is so engrossed in the ecstasy of his unfinished plan that he possibly can't design another one here, just in time for your next visit." He was feigning despair, if not disappointment.

"He will be buried alive in his unadorned monuments, if he doesn't obey the emperor with the urgency of his genius." Akbar resorted to raillery. "The emperor has no dearth of architects at Agra. And he would have beautiful palaces all over Hind, in no time. And gardens too, and hunting resorts. The people of Hind would live in better homes too, no fakirs on the streets with a brood of deformed, misshapen children—" His gaze was turning to his court historian. "Write this Farman of the emperor most precisely, Inayat, and let it be proclaimed all over the empire of Hind. No boy under the age of eighteen is permitted to marry, and no girl under the age of sixteen." He announced. "The emperor plans to build schools for children, in every village. The children must learn to feed their minds with the wisdom of the ages lost and living, and then they would grow up to be the pillars and prosperity of Hind. A large school close to my palace at Agra too for all the children of the royal household and for my sons, the precious twins, Hasan and Husain! The lovely, precious names! If I had daughters, I would have named them, Hasina and Hamida."

A mysterious sense of foreboding was chilling Akbar's thoughts. He was descending his throne slowly and thoughtfully. His gaze settling on Munim Khan!

"The emperor has assigned four thousand skilled masons to Qasim Khan, and he will assign a thousand many times over to all the architects, who are willing to work for the emperor." Akbar was trying to banish his sense of foreboding. "Don't feel disappointed, Munim. Soon, we would reside in our newly-built hunting lodge, and play polo all night, much too soon, perhaps." He turned to Mubarak Shah, abruptly. "The emperor would lend you the services of Mirza Ghiyas, Mubarak. He is one of my devoted architects, and is adding final touches to the mausoleum of my father." Akbar's attention was shifted to Birbal. "Sadness follows the emperor at his heels, while his noble poet basks in the glitter of mirth." Akbar beckoned Birbal to follow him.

The path was lit by torches on the lofty masts, but the torch-bearers were scurrying ahead of the poet and the emperor to light the way.

"Your Majesty. What sadness?" Was Birbal's merry exclamation!

"A sadness of the kind which splinters joy into a thousand pieces! And then glues them together at the peril of suffering once again. A mere whim! Fate's caprice!" Akbar murmured, more to himself, than to the merry response of his poet-companion.

"Your Majesty, Fate has nothing in common with caprice. Fate breathes the odor of certainty, while caprice trembles at the gate of uncertainty." Birbal murmured back.

"Then arrest this caprice inside the prison of fate with your wisdom, my night scholar, and cheer the emperor with your wit alone." Akbar commanded amusedly. "The emperor is surrounded by heathens, though they appear before him wearing the masks of the ulemas, pundits or mullahs! And how the emperor dreams of befriending some pious man, noble in spirit! And with a soul as great as the great oceans which have the power to melt snows over the Himalayas into clear, bubbling streams of peace and purity."

"Your Majesty!" A low exclamation was Birbal's only response.

"Madness in the night! Darkness indeed!" Akbar chanted to himself.

"Your Majesty, could madness consume sadness, if it was mad enough to swallow such an unsavory morsel." Birbal attempted a merry stab at his wit to cheer the emperor.

"Of course!" Akbar laughed without joy. "Unsavory morsels are the best, when madness craves for nothing but pain and darkness." His thoughts were straying into the realms unknown. "Imagine yourself at a gathering, Birbal, watching a group of four men, and thinking to yourself that the one over there looks modest, and the other, shameless. The one a coward, and the other, heroic! Have you ever done that, judging people and making assumptions quite arbitrarily?" He asked, as if questioning his own self.

"Quite often, Your Majesty." Birbal confessed. "Not in a gathering, but in the privacy of my home, I watch and ponder. Especially when inspiration strikes me to construe weak rime and dull verse!"

"How is that?" Akbar inquired with a mingling of interest and curiosity.

"I watch my servant, Your majesty. A woman of middle age and middle height! She has the habit of intruding right at the moment, when the height of absurdity in my head is at its peak, the culminating point in inspiration, my—"

"Your!" Akbar interrupted with impatience. "Your head is gathering absurdities right now, it seems! And stupidities are swimming in your thoughts. What inanities?" He was quick to divine Birbal's witless attempt to cheer him. "The emperor is talking about four people with different characters, and you are chortling about a mediocre woman mired in the pool of her middle age and middle height!"

"She represents all four persons in one, Your Majesty." Birbal insisted.

"How so, my absurd poet and scholar?" Akbar challenged.

"Your Majesty, I have studied the character of my servant thoroughly. "When she stays in the house of her in-laws, out of modesty, she doesn't even open her mouth. So, she is modest. And when she sings obscene songs at the weddings, she doesn't feel any shame at being tawdry or explicit. So, she is shameless. When she is with her husband, she won't even dare step out of the house at night, telling him that she is afraid. So, she is cowardly. But if she takes a fancy to some man, she goes fearlessly to meet her lover in the middle of the night. So, she is brave and heroic." Birbal concluded jovially.

"Your subtle wit, Birbal, can tear open the fists of wisdom with its clenched teeth." Akbar was disappearing behind the silken folds of his tent.

Wisdom is like the pearls scattered inside the minds of the fools! The fools, who view them as pebbles within the mirrors of their hearts, while the wise seal them in the caskets of their souls. Inside the purity of their souls, they are kept well-preserved, retrieved at the mere whim of a revelation, shining forth with twice the lustre of the treasures preserved, and revealing the very kingdoms in heavens. Akbar was inside his tent, watching Farida robed in ripples of silks and laces, resting there, soft and seductive.

"My lotus of Khandesh! How you keep floating forever in the pool of love inside the emperor's foolish heart." Akbar was floating toward Farida like the lord of mirth.

The emperor was the lover incarnate! Making love to Salima in the body of Farida? He was dreaming dreams about Agra in his wakefulness, while summoning sleep at his bedside. His ravished bride had fallen asleep right into his arms.

The meridian sun with its rays of gold was heralding the victorious return of the emperor to Delhi. Agra was still forty miles ahead, and stretching farther against the fury of the dust and the heat. Akbar was becoming aware of his surroundings now, the city of Delhi washed clean of its mist-haze. His gaze was arrested to the elephants carved out of stone at the Gates of Delhi, and now exquisite carvings on the buildings were alluring his attention. So engrossed was he in admiring the peacocks carved out of red sandstone, that he had slackened the pace of his horse to a slow canter. These peacocks were embedded on the facade of a college dedicated to Mahum Anaga, and the memory of his childhood nurse was alighting in his mind with all its sadness and tragedy.

Suddenly, an arrow was seen flying down from the roof of this college. So swift and sudden was its aim that it had landed on the right shoulder-blade of the emperor with the violence of a bullet. In a flash, the Imperial guards had made a circle around the emperor, a few of them rushing to his side to assist him. But the emperor had plucked out this arrow from his shoulder with one impatient flick of his left hand, commanding his guards to keep their distance, and refusing to accept any help from them.

The Moghul soldiers had already surrounded the college like a wall of steel, a large group of them rushing inside to catch the daring assassin. The ones who were outside the building, and had caught the glimpse of the culprit on the top of the college roof were firing their guesswork in a volley of exclamations.

"Isn't that Qatlaq Faulad?"

"Yes, I believe he is the one! Wasn't he the slave of the arch rebel, Sharfuddin?"

"Abul Maali must be ordering from his grave! He was the one, who sent this slave to Sharfuddin—"

"Abdul Wasi seems to be the possible culprit behind all this—"

"Treason, traitor—murderer—" All sounds were hushed as Qatlaq Faulad was dragged out of college into the open. He was shivering and whimpering.

"Cut this son of perdition to pieces! This will serve as a lesson to all, that no one dare attack the emperor, ever again!" Akbar thundered. "No need to fit those pieces into the peace-comfort of a grave, and then continue your journey."

"Your Majesty! Pray to God that He may protect you from all wounds or injuries." Abdunnabi ventured a small comment.

"When I pray to God, I pray that I be protected from mullahs, not from the wounds!" Akbar spurred his horse, breaking away from the shield of his Imperial guards.

Akbar's horse was flying on the road toward Agra, pain shooting from his shoulders. His royal physicians were racing after him, shooting their pleas for ministering his wound. But the emperor was heeding none, charging all to silence with more of his thunderous commands.

Dusk and pallor were greeting the Imperial cavalcade to Agra in some sort of funereal hush. Akbar's steed seemed to know the mood of the emperor, its horse-sense guiding him toward home swiftly. The emperor was riding with the burden of longings and forebodings over his shoulders, not to mention the throbbing wound.

Can the heart of this beast know the pain of the emperor? Its whinnying makes me surmise that he understands the emperor's moods? And yet do I understand my vile moods of rage and torment. A rash act of rage! A rage, where vengeance strikes like the stealthy murrain! Compassion is noble, and forgiveness sublime! Do I consider my actions kind and considerate? How ignorance, not cruelty, has ruled my judgment! Do I understand the worth of justice and kindness? Or, even the value of pity?

The haze and dusk were deepening into a curtain of soft, bleak shadows as Akbar entered his Agra Fort. He was alighting from his horse amidst the sounding of the drums and the trumpets. A mingling of perfumes from jasmine and tuberoses were greeting him home with the scent of nostalgia. But, for some strange, astonishing reason, this scent of nostalgia was gathering the odor of doom and misfortune. The palace doors, under their tapering domes of trabeate style were flung open at the second beating of the drums. The first one to greet the emperor was Hakim Mirri—one of the royal physicians.

"Your Majesty." Hakim Mirri was curtsying low. "Pardon me, Your Majesty. I am the messenger of sorrow. But this tragedy weighs heavy on the whole palace. Your sons, Your Majesty, they died, in their—" His voice was choked on the word *infancy*.

The light of joy in Akbar's eyes was replaced by such an intensity of pain that it appeared to speak with the tongue of grief. He could not fathom the assault of his grief, and walked past the astonied physician without a word.

A hurricane of grief was swept over Akbar's senses, with the hunger-violence of all hopes blasted and memories scorched.

Each time, you wed a princess, you hope for a son with the savage longings of a human animal to beget heirs and rulers, to protect your fortunes and kingdoms! And now, your hopes are burnt to cinders, inside the little graves of your first-born sons.

He was transported into realms beyond the portals of grief, facing a wall of grief again, as he crossed the marble hall and stepped into another damasked parlor. Ruqaiya Begum, Suriya Begum, Mahmooda Begum, Salima Begum, Hira Begum, Nighat Begum, all the emperor's wives were there, along with the Begums from his father's harem.

A low sob from Nighat sent the emperor flying to her side. He swept Nighat into his arms, caressing her warmly and tenderly.

"Rest, my loves, rest and sleep. The emperor himself needs rest and—" Akbar released Nighat. He was plodding toward the marble staircase.

"Your Majesty." Hakim Mirri was attempting to follow the emperor. "Comfort your heart, Your Majesty. God is merciful. You will have many sons."

"Do not mock grief, Hakim." Akbar's response was hollow, an echo from some well of his inner silence. "Has grief ever touched you? Or, has it left any scars to remind you that the anguish can only be felt if your heart were warm and compassionate!" He was seeking the sanctuary of his private chamber.

Yes, the Merciful God has punished me for my sins, for being a slave to the lusts in my heart and to the agonies in my soul. Akbar flung himself on his gilded bed. *Yes, God is punishing me for my sins, for marrying Salima, for marrying Nighat. One widowed, and the other divorced, two precious, precious pearls of my youth and folly, two priceless jewels of my love and lust.* Two big tears were glistening on his cheeks like the offerings of his shame and vulnerability. *My two sons, whom I couldn't even see! My wives, whom I couldn't comfort—Salima, Salima.*

Nothing lives forever, but nothing in nothingness. Akbar's opiate thoughts were murmuring. *Grief shall fade from the footprints of joy. Joy will rest at the door of grief.* Pain and misery were weaving their webs inside the sinews of his dreams. *Hopes cannot break the windows of despair, but with the fists of their own hopelessness.* Some sort of hysterical mirth was knocking at the doors of his dream-agony. *Mirth enters the door of sadness from the front, and leaves through the back door, into the dark jungle of everlasting torments.* One last reed-thought was suspended in his dreams, offering him the comfort of sleep from the jungle of everlasting torments.

5

Lions of Chitor

Akbar, wearing a coat-of-mail wrought with gleaming studs, and his favorite gun Sangram slung at his waist was inspecting *sabats* near his encampment at Chitor. Not far from the sloping hills could be seen a white stone column in the shape of a pyramid. It was thirty-five feet in height and crowned with a huge lamp. Akbar in his carefree stroll was passing right under the light of this lamp, his gold helmet kindling to the pale luminescence of its own, and swallowing light. His gaze was reaching out to the sun in its chariot of light and death.

How strange the sun is, this evening? A revolving mirror, consuming many rainbowed suns in its reflecting orb, emitting white light of the heavens, not the pale splendor of the earthly sun.

The emperor was drifting toward his gallery on the hillock nearby, a white stone structure of the same height as the pyramidal column left behind. This gallery was erected by the emperor's orders at the beginning of the siege. He had chosen this spot, so that he could watch the enemy's moves. While the pyramid's top could only be reached by a spiral staircase, the gallery was designed to hold straight columns and a small staircase, its narrow steps leading into a spacious chamber. This chamber had windows on all sides, admitting view from the hills, forts and the vistas, and revealing the intricate web of nature's own reckless handiwork.

Immersed deep in thoughts, Akbar had mounted the steps of his gallery, and was now mingling with his soldiers and generals with the ease of a mighty monarch. But his thoughts were poking one large rent within him which had grown like an abscessed wound after the death of his twin sons. This wound had nothing to do with his grief long past dispelled, but with the inexorability of his longing to have sons and daughters. Another of his longing was to find a friend, with whom he could commune without the barrage of zeal and bigotry.

While conversing with his generals, Akbar could see the impregnable fort of Chitor resting on a table shaped rock, elevated half a thousand feet high, escarped on all sides, and guarded by deep ravines and jagged buttresses. To Akbar, it appeared like an eagle's eyrie crested by fort grit. The dark clouds swollen with rain were hovering over the west of the horizon, carrying beams of lightning in their bosoms.

Akbar's thoughts were retreating back in time over the whirlwinds of intrigue and rebellion in his empire. Ali Quli and his brother Bahadur Khan, joined by Sikandar Shah had rebelled, claiming Juanpur as their dearly won kingdom, but were defeated and captured. Munim Khan had interceded for the much-penitent wretches, and the emperor had forgiven them with the magnanimity of a victorious lord.

The victorious emperor had returned to Agra once again, finding his half brother, Hakim Mirza as a refugee escaping the warring turmoils in Kabul. Hakim Mirza had informed the emperor that Sulaiman Mirza was advancing with a large body of force to invade Kabul. Akbar had furnished his half brother with grand array of troops as requested by him to guard the kingdom of Kabul. Not long after Hakim Mirza's departure, Akbar had learned that his governor, Masum Khan, had repelled the attack on Kabul, and that Sulaiman Mirza had retreated back to Badakhshan. Meanwhile Hakim Mirza, instead of proceeding to Kabul, was on the verge of invading Punjab with the emperor's cavalry of grand troops. The emperor had left Agra once more, marching toward Lahore to chastise his half brother. Hakim Mirza, upon learning of the emperor's approach was quick to abandon his plan to capture Lahore, and had made a swift retreat back to Kabul. Akbar had forgiven his half brother since he had sent a missive of apologies brimming with oaths of loyalty and contrition.

While journeying back to Agra, Akbar was informed of more plots and insurrections. Ali Quli and Bahadur Khan had rebelled too soon, their rebellions quelled and forgiveness granted, once again. Twice forgiven, their jagirs were restored too, by the kind intercession of Munim Khan. Too soon, did they rise in rebellion again, the third time in a row. Akbar, by now, had lost patience with these intriguing rebels and had marched from Agra nonstop for one whole day and night. He had then crossed the swollen Ganges on his elephant named, Bulsandar, and had reached Sakrawal.

The rebels were camping in the town of Sakrawal near the province of Allahabad. They were spending the night in drunken revelry, until someone amidst them had cried.

O all ye doomed ones, know that His Majesty, the emperor has crossed the Ganges with an innumerable host to destroy you. He is already here.

The rebels were caught unawares, slaughtered by the imperialists. Ali Quli was unhorsed, hugging his wounded arms and pleading mercy.

I am a great man, if you take me alive to the emperor, he will reward you. Ali Quli was trampled to death under the feet of an elephant driven by one mahout.

Bahadur Khan was captured alive, and brought to the emperor.

Praise be to God, that He has preserved me once more to see Your Majesty's countenance. Bahadur Khan had cried. But his head was severed with one blow of the captor's sword, before he could plead mercy from the emperor.

The heads of both Ali Quli and Bahadur Khan were stuffed with sweet-scented herbs, and paraded before the public on the streets of Agra, Delhi and Multan as tokens of warning for future rebels. After this victory, the emperor was on the road to Agra. Munim Khan was entrusted with the governments of Benares, Juanpur, Ghazipur and Zamaniya, as far as the ferry of Chausa. He was also instructed to guard and to protect the eastern frontier of the empire as far as the borders of Bengal.

The tomb of Muinaldin Chishti in Ajmer had become the emperor's sanctuary, whenever he could afford to visit this sacred shrine. He had discovered the tomb of this saint during one of his hunting expeditions, moved by the songs of the minstrels singing all the way toward this holy tomb. Finding also, a friend in this tomb, the dead saint, with whom he could commune in silence before making any decisions.

Udai Singh, the Rana of Chitor, had professed his allegiance to the emperor, sending his son, Sakat, to the Moghul court. But he himself had never come to the court at Agra, to pay homage to the emperor, or to confirm his allegiance. Akbar was about to march to Malwa, when he had commented to Sakat, more in jest, than as a warning, though putting to test the weak allegiance of Udai Singh.

The emperor is going hunting again, Sakat, and you are to accompany him. Your father, he never came to my court to pay his allegiance. The emperor dislikes dilatoriness on the part of his loyal subjects, and he might order your father to appear in person! And that is, at the court in Agra, after I return from this hunting expedition.

This expedition had proven to be the longest the emperor had yet undertaken, and still it was stretching the boundaries of time to their furthest limits. Sakat, mistaking the emperor's jest as a threat, had fled to Chitor, telling his father that the emperor was planning to attack the fortress of Chitor. The emperor, condoning the flight of Sakat, had marched forth toward Malwa. He had reached as far as Supar when the news were brought to him that Udai Singh was devastating the country surrounding the fort of Chitor. Udai Singh after learning that the emperor was marching toward Chitor had left the fortress of Chitor along with his son Sakat.

He had appointed Patta and Jai Mall as the generals, entrusting them with eight thousand Rajput warriors to defend the fortress of Chitor. The forty thousand peasants in Chitor, bound by the pact of honor were also there to support the soldiers and the generals. Udai Singh then, along with his son, had journeyed past the acacia hills, and had entrenched himself in the district of Girwa, hoping to find this place a safe refuge from the much-dreaded attack and captivity.

The emperor himself had undertaken the task of besieging this impregnable fort of Chitor. He had assayed the surroundings of the fort with the eye of an explorer, and it had cost his engineers the labor of one whole month to prepare for the final siege. The skirmishes between both sides were rampant, while the Imperialists were gaining time to dig the mines, and to invest hills with trenches and batteries for future assaults.

Akbar was not conversing with his generals anymore, his gaze keen and searching as if expecting some bold Rajput who would dare crawl out of the shadows of the dusk to shoot arrows at the Imperialists. His thoughts were following his gaze, halting on the steps of two weeks hence when he was inspecting a battery in one projection of the hill not far from the fortress, where the Rajputs had entrenched themselves to repel all attacks from the Imperialists. This battery was maintained by the Rajputs, at all times, with a lively fire of matchlock and artillery, intended to be used against the Moghuls, if they were to come close to shatter the defenses of the fortress.

While Akbar had ventured to have a close look at this battery, not knowing that his soldiers had followed him, a cannon ball had struck the ground a few paces away from him with the noise of a thunderbolt. Astonishingly enough, the emperor had remained unscathed, but twenty of his soldiers were instantly killed in this sudden blast. The very next day, when Akbar accompanied by Alam Khan, was inspecting the mines, a bullet from the enemy's side had pierced his coat-of-mail, grazing his tunic of silk which he wore under his armor. Once again, the emperor was not injured.

How passing strange! What capricious stroke of tragedy and fortune? Twice in a row, I have evaded the blows of death. Or, have been spared, what divine munificence?

Akbar's gaze was reaching out to the Chitori fort now, as he stood wondering.

This bewitching fort! The miracle of beauty and ugliness! It still stands unmoved, defying both time and assault, while men and beasts fall at its feet like chaff? Its magic walls, and battlements designed by the hands of witchcraft.

The cold, cold hearths in stone, the emperor's reward for ruling and fighting! An orgy of ruin, death, devastation! A needless struggle to conquer and to subjugate! Yes, men live in the hearts of wars, and wars live in their hearts. They fear and respect power! Men like to rule and to be ruled. They need a subtle transformation within, from the beast of prey to a civilized beast. Attaining this change, only, if herded together into ranks of order, discipline, obedience. But who are the rulers, and who must be ruled? Some lone shepherd to lead the straying herd on a path to homeward journey! Akbar's thoughts were stumbling over the paths of his strategic journeys.

The emperor's first decisive act to win this fort was, when he had ordered a raid through cannon-shots, not far from the Lakutah gate, but those shots had made not even a dent on this impregnable fort. The second incontestable attack on the fort had taken affect right after the emperor's master-gunner Kabir Khan had announced, that the two mines and several sabats were in readiness to be tested. Akbar had advised that each mine should be furnished with a separate fuse, but Kabir Khan had convinced the emperor that with one fuse, both the mines would explode simultaneously.

When the attack was launched, only one mine had exploded, tearing the bastion of the fort to pieces, and hurling its defenders down the slopes. The Imperialist had rushed toward the fortress. Then the second mine had exploded suddenly, engulfing both the Moghuls and the Rajputs in a whirlwind of powdery clouds.

The emperor had lost the cream of his infantry in that battle. Amongst many dead were Barha and Jamaluddin, the emperor's two most devoted and faithful soldiers. The fort of Chitor had suffered its third heavy assault by the Imperialists this very day; Akbar's thoughts were surfacing over the waters of the *present*. The breast-works of the Rajputs were shaken, exposing more than one breach on the walls, from where the Moghuls could gain entry into this fort. The sabats had to be rested with the promise of resuming their work the next morning, considering that after hours of maneuvering, only a few breaches were exposed in the walls, each breach the size of a bullet-hole.

And these breaches could be sealed by the Rajputs, overnight. Akbar's thoughts were journeying beyond the defenses of this fortress. He could see the town of Banas behind this fortress, its wild gorges coiling around it like the serpents at rest, and its stately castles looming tall and lofty. This fortress itself was balanced on a chain of mountains, as if fashioned by the hands of the Titans, its fortifications crested with double ramparts. Akbar's gaze was following the ascent of this fort, then getting lost in its seven, successive gateways, hewn out of solid rocks in circumvallation.

The Rampol gate was the most inaccessible of all, Akbar was informed, but he had not seen it. The next unapproachable one was the Surajpol gate on the east, also concealed from the emperor's sight right now, from where he stood watching. He could see the Lakutah gate on the north, his gaze as well his mind's sight leaving this fortress, and seeking the Sun gate to visit the city right behind this fortress. This city with its springs and citadels, with its shrines and palaces, could be seen unwinding beyond thought or imagination. Inside the heart of this city was Nolakha Bandar, a great citadel with lofty towers and drooping archways. Farther down the rock-hewn roads and alleyways were the nine story palaces of Rana Khumba.

Akbar's mind-sight was closing the gates of its exploration, while his gaze was straining to catch one ghost of a man. From the shadowy veil of dusk, he could espy one man lurking near the Lakutah gate. This man was edging closer to the larger breach, which the Imperialists had succeeded in making with the labor of their half day's work. He was dressed in coat-of-mail, wrought with gleaming studs, just like the emperor' own armor gracing his royal person.

He doesn't have my gun—my beautiful sangram? Akbar was thinking. So absorbed was he in his intense scrutiny, that he didn't feel the presence of Bhagwan Das right behind him. Bhagwan Das was changing his position, stepping beside the emperor, and tracing the emperor's gaze with warm intensity in his own eyes.

"Another horde of seditious Rajputs, I reckon! Attempting to repair the breach, before we could invade these sedition-mongers! If these slithering rebels are a source of annoyance to you, Your Majesty, permit me! I am ready to launch another attack this very evening." Bhagwan Das commented, as if to himself.

"No, my valorous friend. You have tasted no grain of rest since last night." Akbar intoned gently. "But this night has rewarded us with the gift of a new sabat. Do you know that the sabat which we have fashioned together is so wide that ten horsemen abreast could ride along it? And its height alone can lend one elephant an easy passage under it, even if its mahout chooses to raise his spear above his head! And this same sabat would mark the road to victory for us, to-morrow. No, no need for a night assault. Generally, the great seditions do not annoy the emperor, but serve as great challenges. Only the petty rebellions move me toward the ocean of rage indescribable."

My guards, are they watching this night-rider with much interest and curi-osity? The emperor should hope so. Akbar was thinking. *Yes, watching and measuring each move of this proud son of the Sun, as these Rajputs claim and profess, to be born as the children of the Sun?* His thoughts were gathering sad-ness.

Bhagwan Das was standing beside the emperor in mute recollections of his own. He was watching apprehensively, not the Rajput, but the clouds which were gathering in clusters over the sky in black, menacing shrouds. The master-gunner Kabir Khan had also joined the emperor, slipping quietly beside him to his left. His heart could sense the emperor's sadness, but he was imputing it, rightfully so, to the cause of recent tragedies by his folly in connecting the two mines with one fuse. His guilt had begun to throb inside him and he was strug-gling to voice his apology.

"Pardon me, Your Majesty. If I had enough intelligence to heed your ad-vice, all those deaths could have been avoided." Kabir Khan blurted out quickly.

"No blame rests on you, Kabir." Akbar murmured. "The fault is mine, I should have commanded, not advised! What a pity? Out of tragedies, legends are born."

"No, Your Majesty, the fault is mine, entirely!" Kabir Khan confessed.

"Faults, O Kabir, nurture great misfortunes if repeated too often—" Akbar's quick response was left unfinished by a sudden explosion of gunshot in the air!

This single shot was, perhaps, fired accidentally by the night-rider, for he looked alarmed and searching the darkness with his eyes alone, while remaining astride his horse. Suddenly, the man and the beast were sketched in there against the shadow of the wall like a lone silhouette. Akbar raised his gun, his unerring aim blasting through the air like a whistle of doom, and landing on the night-rider with the swiftness of lightning. The silhouette was seen shuddering on the wall. The Rajput was slumping over his beast in one ungainly heap. A band of other Rajputs was appearing on this quiet scene of doom, whisking away the wounded man in utmost hush.

"Your Majesty, that was Jai Mall! You have killed him, the Lion of Chitor. Yes, I recognized him!" Bhagwan Das exclaimed. "Yes, Your Majesty, you have killed him, just like, as you killed Ismail, the other night. Remember, how you brought him down, when he wounded our soldiers? The one who struck Jalal Khan in the ear! But now, with Jai Mall fallen, Chitor is ours." He con-cluded exultantly.

"Yes, I fear I have killed him. The Lion of Chitor! A valorous foe! The most brave of all Rajputs. Much valor did he show all these months, and such a valor like his should be remembered and honored." Akbar murmured low.

"If he indeed be Jai Mall, then he may rot in his grave!" Abdunnabi shot a curse from the other end of the gallery. He was watching the ominous sky with dread.

"All men do—rot in their graves." Akbar turned around slowly. His gaze was sweeping over all with a quiet intensity, before it rested on Abdunnabi. "Yes, we all would rot in our graves, the virtuous and the sinners alike, both the heathen and God-fearing, but our flesh would always taste sweet to the worms."

Suddenly there was a firework of lightning. A shower of dazzling light was consumed by torrents of rain. Watching the sky raging and storming thus, Bhagwan Das' heart was trembling and constricting. It was reminding him of the first night of siege, when he had thought that the Sun, being the chief deity of Chitor, had not welcomed the Moghuls, revealing its anger in shafts of thunder and lightning. He had thought of warning the emperor then, but knowing the emperor's contempt for superstition, he had kept his ill-omened thoughts to himself. He didn't know then that the hearts of many pious Muslims on that first night of siege were also troubled by the violence of that storm. But now he could see naked fear shining in the eyes of many of his Muslim colleagues and he could not help but exclaim.

"The voice of Indra!" Bhagwan Das laughed.

"Bhagwan Das, order the night watch to stay alert and never leave their posts. The Rajputs might strike at any hour." Akbar's eyes were lit up with a gleam of challenge. "Might as well make the storm-clouds our bed pillows! We can snatch thunderbolts from the sky, and roll them back to shoot the stars of fate which are yet to be seen! We will all take turns in staying awake, and this gallery is a perfect place to keep watch on the enemy." He intoned rather gently.

"Your Majesty, a great majority of us, including the soldiers, would like to retire to our tents." Abdunnabi's voice was tremulous. "Even the satan himself would dare not stay in the open on a night like this!"

"A few of us, who live in the stream of minority, can fight the waves of adversity and rise above the ocean of mediocrity." Akbar's eyes were lit up with the glow of mockery. "The ones, who aspire to be a part of the *great majority*, wade forever inside the little pools of their fears. They are better suited to join the congregation of the dead, than to suffer the honor of living, in living and struggling."

The storm had abated as quickly as it had begun, leaving behind the scent of fecundity from the hills and the plains. Akbar was the true night watcher in a sense that he could summon wakeful hours of the day to his side, and make them his night companions. He was seated in his white gallery, keeping vigil, while a host of his generals were either sleeping, or suffering the pangs of sleep. The emperor needed no company, for his thoughts themselves were crowding around him like the best of friends.

Each day awakening with the splinter of hopes, doubts, uncertainties. Neither victories, nor kingdoms can satisfy the hunger in my soul, but a crumb of knowledge from the feast of understanding, that too, from the very hands of God's love, mercy and compassion. Akbar's thoughts were summoning, not Birbal but the *other* poet to his side.

The name of this other poet was Faizi, whose fame had reached the emperor during his long journey from Agra to Chitor. And he had dispatched Aziz Koka with urgent orders to fetch this poet to Chitor. Right this moment, the emperor's very thoughts were wandering in some wistful surge to greet this famous poet.

Faizi was the son of Shaikh Mubarak, whose descent could be traced to an Arab dervish in Yemen, who himself was the claimant of illustrious ancestry back to the courts of Persian kings and viziers. Faizi had amassed such skill and knowledge in rhyme and prosody, in history and philosophy, in prose composition, and in the composition of enigmas, that no man of any learning could be found in the whole of Hind to match his fertile genius. Shaikh Mubarak himself was blessed with brilliant gifts in learning. He had studied in Ahmadabad, and had then settled in Agra. Two sons were born to him there at Agra. His first-born was named Abdul Faiz, born in Year 1547, who later chose the pen-name of Faizi during his scholarly pursuits. The second son was born in Year 1551, named Abul Fazl. Shaikh Mubarak, of being noble and liberal disposition, had exposed his sons to knowledge in all faiths since their early schooling. Later, the learned father and the two scholarly sons were branded as heretics by the Sunni theologians.

Mukhdum-ul-Mulk had been appointed as the chief of ulemas by Akbar's father, and since then he had been after the Mubarak family to persecute them. After the accession of Akbar, Mukhdum-ul-Mulk had sought the young emperor's attention to chastise the *heretical* family of Shaikh Mubarak, but without success. Resorting to deceit and stratagem, and even obtaining arrest warrants for them, and concealing this fact from the emperor. The Mubarak family had to flee for their lives, hiding themselves in remote villages, until the matter was brought to the emperor's attention.

By then, Akbar had learned much about the Mubarak family, and about the devious designs of his ulemas. And when the fame of Faizi had reached him, he himself had issued a warrant, summoning the poet to his presence, even at the very battle-front in Chitor. He had thought of this plan so that he could expose his ulemas to their deceit and wickedness. Not even hinting to any of his courtiers, that the emperor meant to honor Faizi as a friend, not to receive him as a heretic!

Abdunnabi, with his deep scorn for the Mubarak family, had refused Faizi the ownership of a land, requested by him in recompense for his talents. He thought that the emperor had no knowledge of this, and was happy that the summons for Faizi's arrest would prove to be the doom of his family.

The summons for arrest was conveyed through the ulemas, but Aziz Koka was instructed to fetch Faizi before the emperor with all due honor and courtesy.

The emperor, while entertaining these thoughts, had no knowledge that Aziz Koka was delayed in his plans to reach the poet's residence on time. The soldiers under the false assumption of an arrest-warrant had reached there first, obeying the emperor's orders without delay. They had treated the poet roughly, literally, throwing him on a horse, to be conducted to Chitor as a prisoner. But Aziz Koka, arriving on this scene had rescued the poet from the indignity of such circumstances.

Akbar's thoughts were shifting from Faizi to his younger brother, Abul Fazl, whose scholarly fame was the envy of the bigots in his court. Before he could pursue his thoughts, Abdunnabi's eyes smoldering with the coals of zeal were claiming his attention.

"Your Majesty, this sky, even in its silence portends ill-omens, for the armies on either side." Abdunnabi began reluctantly. "Rajputs would not dare engage in a fight, this next morning, and we shouldn't either.

"Look not at the sky, and no evil will lower its shafts on you." Akbar intoned softly. "Fear of evil compels men to lose many worthy wars, even in their souls. They know not that one has to lose many battles, before one can win a war." His gaze was falling on Mukhdum-ul-Mulk. "What do you predict, my wise ulema? Are the Rajputs going to wage war on us, soon, this very morning which is not far away?"

"Rajputs, Your Majesty, they are a proud race. And Patta is still alive, their second Lion of Chitor! Under his banner, they might?" Mukhdum-ul-Mulk responded doubtfully. "Yet if they feel threatened, fearing defeat, if Jai Mall is really dead, they might resort to johar." He murmured without conviction.

"Ah, the johar! The rite of burning their women before they come out naked with their swords drawn to efface the ignominy of defeat! Exposing their own selves to be slaughtered like the lambs of piety?" One ripple of cynicism escaped Akbar's lips. "This rite doesn't sit wisely on the proud shoulders of the Rajputs, but they are valorous, and I do admire their valor. And yet, there are men and women more valorous than the Rajputs. I forget, yes, Rani Durgawati, that was her name. She fought against Asaf Khan, our brave general. I admire her courage the most, and no Rajput could ever match her valorous spirit. Didn't she fight like a queen on the current of a gentle breeze, but with the tyranny of wisdom as her shield? And when both abandoned her, she took her life to escape the disgrace of captivity, not the ignominy of a defeat! Such women should live inside the bowers of song and poetry." His gaze was holding Birbal captive. "What is your verdict on Rajputs, my wise poet?"

"My verdict is simple, Your Majesty, based on the tradition, that they are a heroic race." Birbal responded eagerly. "Tradition says that the Rajputs sprang from the family of the Sun called Suryavansa, through Rams, the king of Audh. In order of descent from Ikshwaku, the grandson of the Sun! Also, from the family of the moon called Chandravansa. Through Buddha under the reign of Mercury, and from the fire race called Agnikul. They are the descendants of Agastya, the holy fire which blazes on Mount Abu—" His thoughts were cut short by sudden noise of hoof-beats.

Two night-riders were approaching close to the stone gallery, Faizi and Aziz Koka, their bold approach holding the caprice of the rain and the wind in abeyance. The companions of the emperor were awakening.

Akbar's eyes were lit up with the light of joy and anticipation. His gaze was accosting the welcome intruders with keen interest. By fixing his attention solely on Faizi and Aziz Koka, he had missed the expression of gloating in Abdunnabi and Mukhdum-ul-Mulk's eyes. They were sure that Faizi was being conducted to the emperor for reprisal and imprisonment.

Aziz Koka was presenting Faizi before the emperor in conformity with the royal customs of the court, with all due honors and courtesy. Faizi, in return, was bowing before the emperor most gracefully. His handsome features were pale and luminescent.

Akbar was acknowledging the curtsies of both men with smiles fond and wistful, the intensity in his eyes warm and kindling. The hearts of Abdunnabi and Mukhdum-ul-Mulk were constricted with fears and forebodings. They could see Faizi standing there, not as a prisoner, but as a royal subject favored by the emperor.

"I present before you, Your Majesty, the honorable son of Shaikh Mubarak, the poet Faizi. His fame stands nonpareil from the kingdoms in Hind to the borders of Persia—" Aziz Koka was saying.

"Another ill omen—" Abdunnabi could not help but murmur under his breath.

Akbar didn't miss this comment, but he couldn't see the fright and dejection written all over the faces of both his ulemas, for his gaze was arrested to the young poet.

"Welcome, Faizi, to our realm of war and intrigue." Akbar bestowed a smile on the poet. "The emperor is surrounded by superstitious brutes, and he welcomes you with great joy. Your youth compliments your age, but you look like a man endowed with the poetry of reason. Come, sit by the emperor. We will talk all night, and welcome dawn with the songs of knowledge and understanding." He waved to Aziz Koka, who was quick to procure rich cushions for the poet to sit at the emperor's feet.

"Your Majesty." Faizi bowed again. "Thank you for your gracious welcome to an impoverished poet, who is still groping for the rungs of reason. May I recite a verse, Your Majesty? This was written a long time back when I learned of your kindness and generosity to all, who sought your favor and guidance."

"A welcome reprieve!" Akbar murmured. "My soul hungers for poetry. You may recite verses all night, and the emperor alone would be your devoted audience."

"Your most grateful subject, Your Majesty." Faizi murmured in return.
"The royal divan and the dervish's carpet
The nine heavens revolve for his purpose
The seven stars travel for his work
By wisdom, he is the age's provider
By vigilance, the world's watchman

His love and hate, in the banquet and the battle
Are brimming cups of wine and blood
The Khaqan—Great Khan of China fears his wrath
Caesar is disturbed by his frown
Heaven in glory, earth in stability
Lord of universal Reason, Jalaluddin
Essence of sunlight and shadow of God
Pearl of crown and throne is, Akbar Shah
May this old world be renewed by him
May his star be the sun's rays."
He recited with the skill of a poetaster.

"A handsome poet with a flattering tongue, and with eyes like Solomon's, is welcome inside my heart." Akbar laughed. "You would be the brightest of jewels in my court at Agra! You are welcome to look at another of my jewels, seated right here, shining in the night like a ruby." He flashed a smile at Birbal before returning his gaze to Faizi. "Yes, I would name him Ruby, and you would be my Emerald. Don't ask me, why, but the emperor likes emeralds the most, and the pearls?"

The night was edging closer to dawn, as the emperor sat conversing with his poets. The rest were slumbering, or just awakening to the horror of imminent danger to their lives, it seemed. Faizi was talking about his brother, but Akbar's thoughts were already befriending that recluse of a scholar.

Abul Fazl could be my life-long companion, accompanying me in my search for truth, knowledge and understanding, always.

A puppet in God's hands is more alive than a free-willed man-animal, pulled by the reins of his baser needs.

The emperor was informed of how Faizi was arrested and thrown on a horse to be carried off as a prisoner. This information had not escaped the lips of the poet, but was offered by Aziz Koka, intended solely for the emperor's ears. He had deemed it necessary to inform the emperor of the simmering hatred in the hearts of the ulemas, which had resulted in instructing the soldiers to deal with the poet roughly.

Fanaticism is the fire from the ever-kindling fuel of hatred! It smolders forever, rushing forth to consume all who are lovers of truth and seekers of understanding.

"Faizi, I hear, you are a scholar of Sanskrit, and you can write both in Persian and Arabic." Akbar commented with a kind indulgence. "Is your brother endowed with such talents, and with much more, of which the emperor has no knowledge?"

"Abul Fazl, Your Majesty. He is a child prodigy." Faizi responded with a quick animation. "A year old, and he could talk fluently. Barely five and he could read and write with the intelligence of an adult. To him, Arabic, Persian, Sanskrit, are languages of the cradle. By twenty, he had devoured all the books on religion, literature, philosophy and theology. His spiritual training was undertaken by my father, but he had explored knowledge on his own, being a vora-

cious reader. Learning about the religions of the world with such gluttony, that
his mind was distracted, and he would care neither for food, nor for sleep, for
days on stretch. My father said, Abul was wading through the ocean of lies and
truths, seeking some pearl of wisdom, which might offer him solace from confusion and bewilderment, the state that he was in, then!"

"And, has he found, this pearl of wisdom?" Akbar asked.

"He is searching, Your Majesty." Faizi began fervently. "Before Abul became the slave of his solitude, he sought the company of the ascetics. His heart
always yearning for the sages of Mongolia and for the hermits of Lebanon! He
wished to commune with the lamas of Tibet and with the padres of Portugal. He
enjoyed reading the holy books of the Hindus, and studied Zendavesta with the
priests of the Parses."

"Is he still the slave of his solitude?" Akbar commented, rather than queried.

"Your Majesty." Faizi murmured. "Besides shunning his childhood friends,
he is inexpressibly happy now, with his Hindu, Persian and Kashmiri wives."

"Wives." Akbar thought aloud. "Does he have any children?"

"Not yet, Your Majesty." Faizi's gaze was following the emperor's, where
it seemed arrested to the pulchritude in the sky. A red glow from some unseen
flames was coloring the marble hearth of a sky in opaline colors. The poet was
awed and silent.

"Faizi, have you heard about Shaikh Salim, the sage who guards the tomb
of Muinaldin Chishti in Ajmer?" Akbar asked abruptly.

"Yes, Your Majesty." Faizi's tone was soft and reminiscent. "The sage and
the saint, both are revered by all creeds. All who pray at the tomb of Chishti,
they say, receive his blessings. Their prayers are answered and their wishes fulfilled."

"All, wishes and the prayers!" Akbar murmured to himself. "How imperfect
is our vision, which deems the beauty in heavens peace-loving?"

Another red glow from the north was draining color from the cheeks of
dawn. The sky was being painted afresh, the crimson streaks with the tongues of
fire licking its pallor. Akbar was closing his eyes, holding this painted canvas of
a sky as some corrupted form of a dream-illusion behind the closed shutters of
his eyes. Slowly and dreamily, his eyes were opening with a sense of rude
awakening.

"What betokens this red glow in the north?" Akbar exclaimed.

"Be on your guard, Your Majesty. It's the johar, the Rajputs are burning
their women." Bhagwan Das was leaping to his feet.

"Oh, the beautiful ladies dying on their funeral pyres of sandal wood! Can
they inhale the perfumes of fragrant oils with their sweet senses?" Faizi murmured.

"Valor, madness and insanity are going to play harlots in the hills of Chitor,
this morning!" Akbar got to his feet without haste.

All the men in this white gallery had stumbled to their feet in some stupor
of shock and disbelief. Their eyes were glued to the north in stupefaction.

"To pay homage to the ashes, we must walk over the live pyres of the Rajput men. The only way to gain entry into this impregnable fort!" Akbar's very gaze was flashing commands. "Aziz Koka, get Faizi a suit of armor, before his poetic spirit is wounded in the breast." His gaze was shifting to Bhagwan Das. "Command the army to stay alert at their posts, Bhagwan Das. All man and beast in readiness! Patta's fate would be similar to Jai Mall, or worse." He whisked past all, abandoning the white gallery of his vigil.

The red-rimmed eyes of dawn were shedding off their gloom. The hills of Chitor were donned in the white mantle of haze, while the Moghuls were wending their way down the rugged hills in files of cantering floats. Both the man and the beast appeared to be charged with the power of invulnerability, as the flood of their army kept carving its way toward the fort of Chitor.

Three hundred war elephants with swords in their tusks, were padding ahead of the infantry. Akbar was leading his army down the rugged slopes, from where the mighty fortress itself could be seen looming above like a giant eagle. The emperor was mounted on his favorite elephant which he had named Asman Shakoh, meaning literally, high as heaven. His gold helmet and his armor wrought in gleaming studs were lending him the aura of power and invulnerability. The Imperial troops were entering the streets of Chitor without encountering any opposition on the way.

Suddenly, from the very womb of emptiness, and out on the deserted streets were appearing the ghosts of the Rajputs. The real men-ghosts, naked to the waist, with swords drawn in their hands, and milling around on all sides to confront the Moghuls. In a flash, they were pouncing on the Moghuls like the self-ignited cannon-bolts. The quick blows of their swords were clashing with the swords in the tusks of the elephants, and they were embracing the agony of death with no fear to guard their madness.

Leaving behind the tapestry of the slain and the wounded, the Imperialists were advancing closer to the Rampol gate. They were a few leagues away from the Rana's palace, from where this palace could be seen ebbing and spiraling in its grandeur of domes and turrets. Behind the Rampol gate, the peasants had joined the diminished horde of the Rajputs, and their combined forces were confronting the Imperialists.

It seemed that the judgment day had arrived with its final promise of ruin and devastation. Akbar, oblivious to the carnage and bloodshed all around him, was fighting like a man possessed by his inner need to greet the standards of victory. A volcano of rage was burning in his thoughts, kindled by the very hands of fate and held in abeyance. This rage was against the idiocy of men, against the Rajputs, who could burn their women in their mad anticipation to be slaughtered like the beasts themselves. *Destiny itself is wreaking vengeance on these savage men. Yes, destiny is raining blows of insults on the very heads of these murderers, for killing their wives, sisters, daughters. Hundreds of women consumed by the flames of stupidity!*

Akbar's rage was blinded by its kindling of fire and impatience, as he noticed a fresh surge of peasants emerging forth from the Govind temple to attack the Moghuls.

"These men are coming out on the streets like the locusts, and without a king." Akbar shouted over his shoulders.

The emperor was confronted with a stray elephant to his right, whose Moghul mahout was missing. This elephant was being attacked by another assailant, so the emperor was aiming to slay this wretch who was bent on injuring the riderless beast. One Rajput close by, witnessing the unerring aim of the emperor, had struck his dagger into the trunk of the elephant, shouting hysterically.

"Let this be my greeting to the emperor." This mad wretch was trampled under foot by the injured elephant, before the emperor himself could silence this outrage.

"Does anyone know the name of this brave lunatic?" Akbar asked.

"Aisardas Chohan, Your Majesty." Bhagwan Das offered quickly.

"The last of the brave warriors, perhaps!" Akbar was not heeding the response of his general. His gaze was fixed to one of his other favorite elephants named, Siam.

Siam was holding out toward the emperor, the limp body of Patta, who was just trampled by the same elephant while attacking this ferocious beast.

The last of the brave warriors, indeed! No peace is offered to the dead or living, except to the sages who care for nothing on this earth or in heavens beyond, discovering bliss and oblivion in their non-being.

Reaching close to the fort, Akbar had alighted from his elephant, not knowing that he was literally walking over the ashes of the dead queens on his way to the fortress.

Wives and mothers, sisters and daughters, and the prettiest of God's creatures on earth, have immolated their lives to the pride in life, and to the honor in death.

A large booty of treasures was found in the fortress during a thorough search by the Imperialists for any miscreant who could still be hiding in its dark chambers. Jewels and silks, the silks embroidered with gold and silver, and exquisite articles of decorative art studded with precious gems, were a few of the many more treasures to be recovered later. But the emperor had shown no interest in the treasures. Overwhelmed with fatigue and sorrow, he had sought refuge in sleep. And deep within his psyche was a strange murmur, he could neither silence, nor ignore.

The city of desolation in my heart.

Three days after the victory of the Moghuls, Chitor was still the city of desolation in Akbar's heart. His gaze was reaching down the verdant hills below, but his thoughts were hugging his decision which he had made the night after his victory. He had decided to go on a pilgrimage to Ajmer, on foot, before returning to Agra.

A perfect day for a pilgrimage and a journey homeward!

The emperor was dressed like a pilgrim, wearing a blue, woolen robe of the Sufis. He was carrying a staff in his hand, and a dry gourd was slung over his shoulders to serve as a drinking cup, so that he could quench his thirst during the heat of the day.

This valley of death is raising empty cries through the lips of the kettle-drums. The emperor's gaze was shifting to his soldiers down there in the valley, who were intent on practicing their skills on the naqqaras—the great kettle-drums, which were a part of the booty from the fortress of Chitor. These drums were the prized possession of Udai Singh, who had flown to hiding down the acacia hills.

These drums, the emblem of Rana's rule and sovereignty over Chitor! He has lost all. No Rajputs left alive to defend his fortress. The Unseen, Unapproachable God of my Faith, has bestowed upon me the laurels of victory, but I need to do penance within the sight of some holy man. I want to hear the voice of Reason through the very lips of holiness. Akbar was thinking.

Holy men have perfect ways to reach the throne of God, such ways unknown to ordinary mortals like me. Suddenly, the emperor had begun to descend the rugged steps, followed by Faizi, Aziz Koka and Bhagwan Das.

My Other Supreme, no distances long or endless could ever separate her from me. Akbar's heart was longing for the nearness of Salima. *Can one atone one's sins, purge all follies, and know the bliss in love?*

The emperor was walking ahead of all, with the lamps of holiness shining in his eyes and inside his heart. His steps were light and swift, carrying him further toward his white gallery, which he had designed himself. The white gallery opposite was holding one lamp on a high mast, bright and blazing against the gold-haze of sunshine.

Akbar's diya, Akbar's diya. Akbar's poets and generals behind him were expressing their delight at this lamp erected high on a tall mast, as if heeding its mockery and challenge. Diya, meaning literally in Hindi, the lamp. And since Akbar had designed it, they were naming it, Akbar's diya.

"Your Majesty, do you really wish to walk all the way from here to Ajmer?" Aziz Koka asked as he had a couple of times before.

"Has the emperor ever lied to you before?" Akbar laughed.

"No, Your Majesty, but such a long way! Such a long, long time, when—" Aziz Koka could not continue, for Akbar's eyes were flashing rebuke.

"Time breaks all boundaries of time, and retires into timelessness, when one is doing penance." Akbar commented.

"Penance, Your Majesty! Penance, for victory! Victory is no sin!" Was Aziz Koka's baffled comment!

"Yet, great victors live in the glory of their ignorance that they sinned not while waging wars! Carrying the burden of death on their shoulders, and the weight of ambition in their hearts?" Akbar commented again.

"Sin and corruption, Your Majesty, all rest on the enemy's head." Aziz Koka began all flustered. "The Rajputs were the ones who incited us to lay

siege, compelled us to wage this war, and the other wars sprouting all over the—
"

"Talk not of war, kind brother." Akbar interrupted impatiently. "Or, I might, sooner than anticipated, gather this whole world into my arms with the fury of a storm, in my effort to bring a long-lasting peace on this earth. Some sort of peace, in the likeness of calm, sunny day after the violence of a storm from the flashing eye of thunder."

"Your Majesty!" Bhagwan Das quickly leaped to the emperor's side. "If men had wisdom, they would escape this thunder of retribution."

"If men could only have one little grain of understanding and if only they could experience the fear of God in their hearts." Akbar murmured to himself. "Experience of countless years in living, and nothing could teach man the art of wisdom. If inspiration comes not from God to light the way to understanding, we learn nothing, but the charms of our conceit. And yet, by the reason of our mortal ignorance, we can neither know God, nor understand His ways in terms of judgment or retribution."

"The mighty have fallen." Bhagwan Das murmured back. "Jai Mall and Patta, the most valorous of all the Rajputs."

"Yes, the mighty and the valorous." Akbar's feet were coming to a slow halt before the white gallery. "For the valor of these soldiers, the emperor is going to order two statues to be carved out of solid rock, one of Jai Mall, and the other of Patta, both riding the stone elephants. These statues would be erected on either side of the gate of Delhi, not very far from the fort of Agra."

"Your Majesty." Faizi stepped closer. "I penned this verse last night in honor of your victory. And to pay homage to the emperor who has received me with kindness and generosity. And, well, to pay homage to this lamp, Akbar's diya."

"Go on, Faizi. Recite your poem, and may you live in the bounties of my favors, always." Akbar smiled. "This lamp would shed its light on the whole world till eternity. Yet, my lamp of life would dim, and fade, in a few years."

"Your Majesty." Faizi murmured, reciting dreamily.
"Hail to thee to whom is committed reason's exaltation
The kingly revolution of the universe is for thee
Like thee, the earth had no garden
Like thee, heaven's vault no lamp
Creative ocean rolled away many a wave
Till it cast ashore a pearl like thee
Fate's pencil drew many a sketch
Till she made a portrait like thee
The world's book is but an illusion to thee
Heaven's volume but an analysis of thee."

"Divine verse and divine praise!" Akbar exclaimed. "Our God is a jealous God, Faizi, always remember this! He is both merciful and wrathful. It would be better if no one invoked His anger by singing praises to mortal men, even if they be emperors. And yet, in His mercy, He is most kind, most benevolent. Your genius belongs to Him alone."

A lone man riding on the steed of wind had caught the emperor's attention. Birbal had emerged forth from the very fabric of the hills, it seemed.

"Your Majesty, Your Majesty." Birbal alighted from his horse hastily. "Shaikh Salim's courier just arrived from Ajmer. The Pir, I mean the Shaikh had a wonderful dream, months ago. He dreamt, or rather heard commandments from the very lips of Muinaldin Chishti. Muinaldin Chishti was commanding that if Your Majesty was coming to pray to God, then you should come riding. But if the emperor was coming to seek the saint's intercession in prayer and penance, then he must sweat and slither all the way, wearing blisters on his feet as mark of his devotion."

"Your mad wit alone has broken the emperor's resolve." Akbar laughed, stealing a mischievous look at Aziz Koka. "If the court poets turn dull and lose their rime of intellect, then the emperor must gallop ahead of them. Fighting off the demons of stupidity before them in the fashion of Great Hunt! Ah, the ages past and forgotten! Go, my prudent rebel, fetch the emperor's horse. Pegasus itself would fly me to Ajmer, if I wished. And as for that reed of a dream, be assured, I pray only to God. But I revere the Shaikh for his piety, and for his tolerance. And for his kindness and affection toward all Hindus and Muslims alike! And I would very much like to meet him."

Measure of love is longer than the centuries, before time on earth, beyond the confines of time? In continents far and wide! The emperor was becoming aware of the hamlets on the left, the city of Ajmer sprawled before his sight like a dream-shadow with its high domes and cupolas. Akbar was alighting from his horse, casting off his shoes, and feeling the pillow of earth under his feet with a sigh of relief. The soldiers had begun to beat the naqqara drums, announcing the arrival of the emperor in Ajmer.

Akbar seemed oblivious to the pomp and pageantry of his retinue. His gaze was arrested to a group of minstrels who were singing songs with the accompaniment of flutes and cymbals. He was so enchanted by this symphony of song and music that he didn't even know that he was standing inside the enclosure of the shrine.

A few devotees were seated there with their heads bowed, as if immersed in a sea of prayers behind the closed shutters of their eyes. Shaikh Salim was seated not far from the devotees, his meditative posture barely touching the small rug under him, and his expression peaceful and soothing. By the glow of warmth on his features and by the look of tenderness in his eyes, Akbar could tell that this man could be no other, but the holy Shaikh himself. And by Akbar's royal demeanor, Shaikh Salim could not doubt as to the identity of the emperor, whose fame had reached him much earlier than he himself could visit this humble abode. The eyes of both the sage and the emperor were locked together, warmth flowing from one to the other in speechless communion. Shaikh Salim had eased himself up, and was now curtsying before the emperor.

"Your Majesty, you would be blessed with a son, with many more sons and daughters." Shaikh Salim's tone was smooth and tender. "The glory of Hind would lie at your feet, and the men of learning would gather at your door to claim the virtue of your wisdom. Kindness would walk on the right side of the emperor, and compassion on his left. His path would be strewn with pearls of devotion from the men of all Faith."

"Oracles speak through your lips, holy Shaikh!" Akbar exclaimed abruptly. "You have divined my inmost prayers, yet you know not that love sits foremost in the emperor's heart, and in his thoughts. All glories melt before the inexorability in love to attain—" He paused as if divining the thoughts of this sage. "And yet, one's religion is one's love supreme, when this love raises no barriers before race, creed, faith or belief. And even the shadow of such a love has the power to melt all barriers to insignificance." His gaze was arrested to the red strings tied to the marble screen.

These strings were the ceremonial offerings of the pilgrims, as the emblems of their prayers to the revered saint. When their prayers were answered, they would return to claim these strings, making room for the countless others who needed to seek the blessings of this saint. Akbar knew the significance of these strings, but he was turning his back on all, on the holy man too!

"Your Majesty, would you accept the offering of simple food before you leave?" Shaikh Salim requested softly.

"Your kindness lends me a feast to my thoughts." Akbar turned back slowly. "My offering to this shrine would be grand and opulent, and I hope that Muinaldin Chishti would accept it." He smiled. "No one can tell from outside that the shrine of this saint is so bright and exquisite. After I return to Agra, I would order my architects to design a tall gate, which will lend grandeur to this shrine." He turned to leave, smiling.

Oblivious to the flight of time, the emperor had reached Agra under some spell of enchantment. *Ah, the scent of home and passion! The warmth of love and nearness! Ah, dreams of the past, often lost and then resurrected! Wars and victories, all illusions!*

All the emperor's wives were there, Ruqaiya, Suriya, Mahmooda, Salima, Hira, Nighat, and Farida. All were talking at once, with tears of joy in their eyes, and songs of greetings on their lips. With the exception of Salima, of course, whose eyes were serene like the blue lakes under a moonlit night.

Though Akbar was gathering joy and warmth from his young wives, his thoughts were following the cold, stabbing stars in Salima's eyes. He was leaving the others, drifting closer to his supremely *other*, his very thoughts were mocking. Akbar clutched Salima by the waist under the spell of some wild impulse, whispering into her ear.

"My love! Oh, my love supreme, you shall welcome the emperor with the blight of your kisses cold and shuddering. And you would cry for mercy, against the agony of my passion blind and terrible."

6

The Rite of Suttee

Akbar was pacing in his library inside his newly built palace at Agra, his thoughts wild and turbulent. He had recently prohibited the rite of suttee, the burning of widows on the pyres of their deceased husbands. But this particular afternoon, Akbar was informed that one Rajput princess whose husband had just died, did not wish to commit suttee. And that her son and her uncle were forcing her to end her life by burning herself on the pyre of her deceased husband! After learning about such news he had mounted on his steed like a war-lord, reaching there on time, and literally snatching her out of the flames. Her son and uncle were ordered to be flogged and imprisoned. The princess was brought to Agra, and granted safety under the care of the ladies of the harem.

What reek of vanity breathes through the ashes of these men? Strange! Passing strange, that these men scorched by their prides, and delivered free by the hands of death, should seek deliverance still, through the sacrifice of their wives?

Six years had flitted past since Akbar's victory at Chitor, and his thoughts for some inexplicable reason were bent on jogging back. But he was keeping them in abeyance in anticipation of receiving Faizi's brother, Abul Fazl and one learned Ulema by the name of Baduani. His thoughts now were greeting Fath Ullah, who had joined his court most recently. Fath Ullah was thoroughly versed in geomancy, geometry, astrology, astronomy, philosophy, and arithmetic. He was proficient in Arabic, with a perfect understanding of talismans and incantations as a supplemental knowledge to dabble with mysticism. He had written a book on rhetoric, and was working on the interpretation of the Quran. Mahyarji, a Parsee priest, had also joined Akbar's court, participating in the open discussions of theology, along with the Brahman priests, Puru, Debi, and Khatam.

Shortly after Akbar's return to Agra, Shaikh Salim from Ajmer had prophesied that the emperor would be blessed with three sons in a short period of time. Shaikh Salim's prophecies were blossomed when Hira Begum and Farida Begum had conceived simultaneously. In honor of Shaikh Salim's prophecy, Akbar had sent Hira Begum to the hermitage in Ajmer, just a few weeks before her delivery. Akbar had named his first-born son, Salim, thus honoring further this saint and friend, Shaikh Salim. Another name that he had bestowed on his son was, Shaikhu Baba, also in honor of Shaikh Salim, for the emperor had grown to love this saint as his own father. Baba, meaning literally, father, and Akbar was wont to address Shaikh Salim as Shaikhu Baba, now choosing the same expression as a nickname for his royal son.

Shaikhu Baba! You are the heir to my throne. Akbar had exclaimed.

A week after the birth of prince Salim, Farida Begum had given birth to a princess. Akbar had named his daughter, Khanam, his joy exceeding far beyond the limits of his hope and tenderness. Soon after the birth of the prince and the princess, Salima Begum had conceived. She too was sent to the hermitage in Ajmer, a few weeks before her delivery. This time, Akbar had suffered the torments of fear and separation, but his love for his Beloved had conquered his agony of the spirit, in knowing that she was safe near the holy shrine of Muinuldin Chishti. Prince Salim was a year old, when Salima had given birth to a son, named by Akbar, Murad, meaning literally, Hope.

Salima's hatred for the emperor would surface in her eyes now and then, clouding the joys of the present along with the sadness of the past. But Akbar had learned to live with the whim and caprice of his Beloved. Two more brides were added to his harem during the turbulent years of wars and intrigues. Raja of Bikaner had sought Akbar's alliance, by offering his brother's daughter Usha in marriage to the emperor. At the same time, the ruler of Jeselmir had offered his daughter Jagruti in marriage to the emperor.

Shaikh Salim had become Akbar's closest of friends, and through him the emperor's patronage was extended to another saint in Ajmer by the name of Shaikh Daniyal, also a devotee of the saint Muinaldin Chishti. A son was born to Usha Begum in the hermitage of Shaikh Daniyal and Akbar had named his third son, Daniyal. Akbar had to drink hemlock from the lovely eyes of his Beloved, whose hatred for the emperor could not be concealed at that time of rejoicing.

To the temples of her soul, I cannot reach, where all doors are barred, all windows shut. Akbar's thoughts were one poetic surge, his feet too coming to an abrupt halt at the appearance of servants, carrying the emperor's feast. Akbar had forgotten, that an hour ago he had ordered his meal of the day to be served to him in his library. After the ritual of serving was completed, Akbar dismissed his servants, commencing his own ritual of eating, but his thoughts were inhaling the dust of wars and intrigues.

Prince Salim and princess Khanam were yet not born, when Akbar was compelled to chastise Surjan Hada in the fort of Ranthambor. He had refused to accept the suzerainty of Akbar, entrenching himself in his fort in Rajputana. Akbar had then marched from Agra and reaching Rajputana had ordered a swift assault of cannon-balls over the fort of Ranthambor. The Raja was quick to sue for peace, hastening to the emperor's camp along with his two sons, and surrendering the gold and silver keys of the fort Ranthambor to the emperor. Akbar in return had bestowed upon Rana the governments of Garha and Katanga. His sons too were employed in the Moghul army as the royal imperialists. The fort of Ranthambhor was in Akbar's possession, and he had won his enemy as a friend, a strong ally for his peaceful rule in Hindustan.

Amidst the festivities at the births of prince Salim and princess Khanam, the news had reached Akbar that raja Ram Chand of Kalinjar had submitted, whose fort had been under siege by the imperialists for a long time. This happy news was slashed by petty rebellions in Malwa and Orissa. Sulaiman Karrani had raised his standard of rebellion, refusing to accept the suzerainty of the emperor. He had marched to Orissa and by the sheer force of his evil plots, had murdered the raja, and had slain his rival, Ibrahim.

At the same time, Malwa was being raided by the rebellious Mirzas, Akbar's cousins. The emperor had sent his commander, Sadiq Khan, to chase the Mirzas out of Malwa. They were chased out, much too swiftly, from Ujjain to Mandu, but they had fled to Gujrat, and it was rumored that they were plotting to seize the forts of Surat and Champaner. At that time Akbar had been so happy celebrating the births of his son and daughter that nothing could move him to hunting expeditions. Instead, he had decided to move his capital to Sikri, ordering grand palaces to be built for him, surrounded by vast gardens. Sikri was to be the capital of his empire with new schools, luxuriant baths and colorful bazaars. All the nawabs, viziers and courtiers were also ordered to build their palaces at Sikri, where the emperor was to move after his palace was completed.

After the birth of prince Murad, Akbar was on the road to warring campaigns once again, his hunting expeditions. He had marched toward Mewar. Barely had he reached Nagar, that the raja of Bikaner, Rai Kaflan, had come to offer his submission, also offering the hand of his daughter in marriage to the emperor. Raja of Jeselmir had followed suit, submitting and offering his brother—Rawal Hai's daughter in marriage to the emperor. With the exception of Udai Singh, all the rulers in Rajasthan had submitted to the emperor. Not to stain his bridal joys with the blood of an enemy, Akbar had postponed his confrontation with Udai Singh, and had returned to Agra with his Rajput brides. This time, Akbar had stayed in Agra the longest ever, celebrating two joyous occasions at one and the same time. One was the birth of his third son, Daniyal, and the second, the completion of a grand palace in his new capital at Sikri.

This palace at Sikri had become Akbar's most favorite of retreats. From there, he could visit Ajmer, and could pray at the tomb of Muinaldin Chishti before embarking on his hunting expeditions. It was here in Sikri at his new palace that he had improved upon the revenue from the khalisa lands, the lands reserved for the state. His next hunting expedition was toward Gujrat, more so to chastise his cousins, the Mirzas, than to punish the petty contenders. Those petty contenders were Itamid Khan and Ikhtiyarul Mulk, both of whom were claiming Gujrat as their sole possession.

Akbar had left Sikri at the head of a grand army, equipped with musketry, cannon and elephants. On his way toward Gujrat, he had learned that Sulaiman Karrani, who had proclaimed himself to be the sovereign of Orissa, Bihar and Bengal, had died. Learning also, that his step-brother, Hakim Mirza, was planning to invade Punjab! Akbar had then sent Munim Khan to subjugate Bengal.

Birbal was sent to Nagarkot, where the emperor's governor, Quli Khan, was stationed to rule and protect Punjab. Nothing could deter the emperor from his plan of conquering Gujrat. As soon as the emperor had reached Ahmadabad, the people of the town had surrendered without resistance.

Leaving Aziz Koka as the governor of Ahmadabad, Akbar had proceeded toward the port of Cambay. Reaching there, he had convened an opulent durbar in his royal encampment, receiving embassies from Iran, Turan, Syria and Turkey. His next stop was at Baroda, where Man Singh had requested the privilege of leading the royal van to crush the boast of Mirza, who had dared rebel against the emperor on these sea ports. The battle was fought at Sarnal, on the opposite side of Mahindri River. The Moghuls were victorious, but Bhagwan Das' foster brother, Bhupat, was killed in the first melee of the battle. Hussain Mirza had fled. Next, the imperialists had marched on to Surat, where the enemy's garrison had summoned some Portuguese to assist them. But the Portuguese, awed by the might of the Moghuls, had assumed the guise of harmless traders.

Akbar's thoughts were quite exhausted by the time he finished his meal. They had found a dwelling place in the cloaks of the Goanese Christians, whose embassies he had received at the port of Surat. Amongst those embassies, one was from Antonio Cabral, whose well-mannered speech had impressed the emperor. Yet Goanese Christians were deemed dangerous on the ports of Cambay. They were constrained to return to Goa, but Akbar had commanded them to send Christian priests to his court.

The emperor had ordered sacred Hindu texts to be translated from Sanskrit to Persian. Lilavati, Ramayana, Mahabharata and Atharva Veda were already in the process of being translated. Akbar had also ordered the history of Kashmir to be translated into Persian, for the songs of its beauty sung by Sulaiman Mirza through letters had tempted the emperor to visit this rich paradise on earth, when the time could afford him such a luxury. His thoughts were retreating back to the conquest of Surat, and farther back to Ahmadabad. Ahmadabad, which was lost once, and won twice.

After the conquests of Surat and Ahmadabad, Akbar had moved to his capital at Sikri, naming it Fathehpur Sikri, meaning, victorious city of Sikri. All his hunting campaigns were commenced from there, and he had always returned as a victor during the past six years of joys and tribulations. Before moving to Fatehpur Sikri, the emperor's wife, Hira Begum, along with her son, prince Salim, had journeyed to Amber. She was going to attend the mourning ceremony of her foster brother, Bhupat, who had died in the battle at Sarnal. Upon her return, the circumcision ceremony for all the three sons of the emperor was marked with grand festivities. These festivities were further enhanced by the celebrations for the emperor's birthday. He had turned thirty-one, and was weighed against gold, silver and precious jewels, all of which were distributed amongst the poor, the needy and the religious men.

Mirzas were on their rebellious sprees once again. Ibrahim Mirza had joined Hussain Mirza and Shah Mirza, and together, they were besieging the town of Patan. Akbar had marched from Sikri. No sooner had he reached Pattan, when he was informed, that the Mirzas were challenging Aziz Koka at Ahmadabad. Akbar had then marched toward the city of Ahmadabad. A fierce battle was fought and Moghuls had claimed the victory once again. Ibrahim Mirza was badly wounded, but was carried to a safe place by one of his faithful slaves. Shah Mirza had fled, but Husain Mirza was brought before emperor as a captive, murmuring in delirium when prodded by Birbal.

The salt of the lord of the faith and of the world has taken me.

Akbar was saddened by the condition of Husain Mirza, ordering that he should be left under the charge of Ria Singh. The emperor's kindness was about to be extended to the other prisoners, when a surprise attack by Ikhtiyarul Mulk was announced. Another battle was commenced in which Ikhtiyarul Mulk was slain. Akbar's foster brother, Saif Khan, was also killed.

Akbar's thoughts were caught inside the wonder of a few imponderables. The emperor had miraculously escaped injuries in this battle at Ahmadabad. Three consecutive times, to be precise! Once, when a foe had aimed his sword at the head of the emperor's horse, and the emperor had swiftly run his spear into the body of the rude assailant. Then another foe had aimed his sword at the emperor's thigh, but the emperor had parried the blow, and the assailant had fled as if pursued by the very eyes of death. Then a third foe had attacked the emperor with his lance. But the emperor's guard, Gujar, was quick to wound him, before the emperor himself could chastise this rude rebel.

By God's will—is the emperor invincible!

The emperor's next hunting expedition was to Bengal. He had taken prince Salim with him, joking with his viziers, that the emperor wished to expose his child prince to the art and danger of wars. But then, he had left the consolidation of Bengal under the command of Todar Mall, and had returned to Sikri.

Fatehpur Sikri after the first conquest of Gujrat.

Mounted on a war-horse with henna-stained mane and tail, the emperor had raised his spear before him, while riding forth jauntily. His royal guards were riding behind him, their lances adorned with golden apples. In the rear, the royal band had continued striking the tunes of victory.

Salima, Beloved! I have alienated my Beloved from me, eternally and absolutely alienated, by marrying others? I have alienated the only woman I love, my Beloved I would always love, the only Soul of my soul, I would not ever cease loving. Akbar's thoughts were murmuring a prayer.

The emperor was seeking the gilded walls of his harem!

The rectangular chamber with damasked walls and Persian rugs was ringing with laughter. Akbar had stepped into this chamber of royal intrigue, without being royally announced. Bahlul, guarding the harem doors, was left speechless by the unexpected arrival of the emperor, and could not announce the approach of the royal host.

Prince Salim, prince Murad and prince Daniyal, in the company of their sister, princess Khanam, were being entertained by the royal ayah. She was a young girl of robust health, bejeweled and garlanded from head to toe. She was pirouetting on her toes, dressed as the goddess Lakshami, showering wealth from her smiles. Jouhar, the ewer-bearer was standing behind the princes, watching this dance with much amusement and concentration. Emperor's wives were seated in a wide circle, on the thick Persian rug with gold medallions. They were leaning against the velvety cushions at their backs, playing cards, and laughing and gossiping with wild abandon.

Akbar stood hugging the princess, prince Salim was offering his curtsy. He had just learned kornish from his tutor, Qutbuddin Khan, and was proud to parade his skill in curtsying before the emperor. Prince Murad, a year younger than prince Salim, was trying his best to imitate his older brother, but was stumbling in his act of raising his right arm over his head. Prince Daniyal, barely two years old, was just clapping his hands.

"It is time that you went to Abdunnabi's school in Fathehpur Sikri, my young stars." Akbar commented with a wistful intensity.

"Your Majesty, I already know Hindi, Arabic and Persian alphabets." Prince Salim boasted. "I can recite the invocation from the Quran, Your Majesty. Mir Haravi taught me: In the name of Allah, the Gracious, the Merciful."

"Excellent, my charming prince." Akbar laughed. "Your studies are just beginning, Shaikhu Baba! You would study theology as well as history. And philosophy, geography and mathematics, not under the tutelage of Mir Haravi or Qutbuddin Khan, but in the school of Abdunnabi at Fatehpur Sikri." His gaze was turning to prince Murad. "And what has my young hermit learned from Faizi?"

"Persian alphabet, Your Majesty." Prince Murad responded bashfully.

"I shouldn't have appointed Faizi as your tutor, my son." Akbar laughed again. "He is in the habit of reciting divine verses to his young wards. Yes, the emperor can read them in the poetry of your eyes, my prince."

"No, Your Majesty!" Prince Murad protested suddenly. "He reads those only to princess Khanam." His bright eyes were teasing his sister.

"Ah, my princess!" Akbar lifted princess Khanam into his arms. "By the glow of sun-beams in your eyes, my sweet, I can tell, that you would rather learn archery and horse-riding, than master the art of versifying. No verses for my beautiful princess! Leave them to the dream-poet, your brother. And that is Murad, if you didn't know, my love." He kissed her cheeks laughingly.

"Your Majesty." Princess Khanam chirped happily. "Abdur Rahim teaches me songs and games."

"Abdur Rahim." Akbar's gaze was searching him and he found him concealed behind Hamida Banu Begum. He smiled at him, Khanam still cradled into his arms.

He is only seventeen, and as tall as his late father, close to six feet—Biram Khan would have been proud. Akbar was thinking.

"Your Majesty, let my grandchildren enjoy their tender years with laughter on their lips and sunshine in their eyes." Hamida Banu Begum shot this comment. "It is not time yet to burden them with studies and schools."

"Even the emperor must pay heed to his mother." Akbar commented back. He lowered his daughter down to the carpet. "Alas, that in the first flush of youth our inestimable lives are unworthily spent. Let us hope that in future they may virtuously terminate. Dear Mamma, the early lessons of life begin in the womb of a mother. Then, why not let the children commence their studies as soon as they are born?" He lowered himself beside his mother, laughing.

"They do, they do, commence their studies, on their own!" Hamida Banu Begum exclaimed happily. "And without the aid of tutors and schools! Mother Nature is their tutor, and the presence of their mothers, their heart-warming schools. Prince Salim has learned enough, at his age, that is! And prince Murad knows too much, though he is the quiet one. And princess Khanam, my sweet blossom! She probably knows more than the combined wealth of knowledge of our two princes? Daniyal, well, he is a little saint, learning most profoundly from the manners of his sister and brothers. The name of God is on the lips of our children, and they will remain obedient to His will. And God's will is to let them play as befitting all children, not burying them inside the books."

"What royal philosophy, Miryam Makani! If it was up to the royal grand-mother, all the emperor's children would stay illiterate." Akbar laughed. "Al-though temporal and spiritual prosperity is based on the due worship of God, the welfare of children first lies in obedience to their fathers. They should learn to think and act at an early age. Especially, the children of the emperor!"

"Such heavy burdens, and thoughts, Your Majesty!" Hamida Banu Begum smiled. "Children studying history, philosophy, geography, mathematics and theology! What good is thought, and what its worth, if it steals laughter from the eyes of a child?"

"Thought!" Akbar exclaimed with a sudden animation. "Nature's greatest miracle is thought! From the seed unknown, a thought grows tall and mighty. Blooming and flourishing into that exquisite flower of perfection, which some cherish with love, and some abandon it to wilt. They are the ones who neglect the hungers and thirsts of its soul, while the thought lies there abandoned and rejected. And the ones who cherish it, ah, they feed it with the nectar of action, and nurture it with the labor of their hands."

"First, thought, now labor, Your Majesty?" Gulbadan Begum couldn't help but exclaim. "Yet, thoughts need not the labor of any hands, Your Majesty, if they alight like the divine miracles?" She challenged. Her agate eyes bright and intense.

"Ah, my sweet aunt!" Akbar responded joyfully. "A poetess and a philoso-pher, much the same, that's what you are! I meant metaphorically, my dear aunt, metaphorically. I should have said labor of the minds in acquiring knowledge. First, one should labor for one's own edification, and then turn to the acquisition of knowledge in the hope of lighting the lamp of wisdom. If one can blow out the flame of dissention within one's thoughts! You are to write the history of the Moghul family, of Moghul courts, starting from the reign of my grandfather Babur, your own beloved father! And this is an edict, my great aunt, straight from the lips of the emperor."

"Alas, Your Majesty. I was only eight years old when Padishah died. Oh, what a day it was, blackness and desolation! *The First Great Moghul Emperor of Hind,* everyone said, even his enemies couldn't deny that, and we, and the rest of his subjects called him, Padishah." She sighed. "How can I write in Persian, Your Majesty, when I read and write only in Turkish?"

"You speak Persian fluently, Aunt Gulbadan. And you understand Persian more than my poetess wife, my beloved Salima." Akbar stole a glance at the glittering circle. "Salima writes couplets in Persian, and thinks that the emperor doesn't know." He whispered to his aunt confidentially. "You may learn Persian alphabets from Shaikhu Baba. You would be the greatest of all Moghul historians, aunt Gulbadan, I assure you."

"Padishah told me once that I would be a great author." Gulbadan murmured. "Besides all praise, Your Majesty, who can thwart the will of a young emperor? You are my adored nephew, and how you have grown, Your Majesty. Baba also told me several times that I would write beautiful couplets! His love for poetry inspired me to construe a few quatrains, but I could never commit them to paper. In the breath of wind, my words would lay neglected and forgotten. Like the babes whose lips were sealed by the hands of death, 'ere, they could cry back to life for breath and sustenance."

"Ah, the poetess again!" Akbar exclaimed laughingly. "Death is an illusion, dear Aunt, and the words never die! Unfortunately, they are repeated too often, by the whim of each scribe who fail to catch the essence of thoughts beyond words. They tend to weaken each expression in tongues loud and harsh. Yes, on the battlefield of translations—Turkish, Persian, Hindi, and what next! Babel of tongues!"

"Gulbadan's words, Your Majesty, would be minted in gold." Haji Begum commented merrily. "Her words could be of more value to the ones who are worthy, and of no value to the scribes, who might pass them around like copper coins. Mistaking the worth of gold in the glitter of coppery worthlessness!"

"Ah, the wit and poetry in my harem, dear Mamma!" Akbar exclaimed again. "If the emperor could only have but a few crumbs of such wit in his court? And you an architect too, sitting behind the harem walls! The beauty of baba's mausoleum speaks of your love and talent. Delhi is fortunate in having baba as its guest, and you have enshrined his tomb in a garden most delightful. That garden and mausoleum are a dreamland for poets and the philosophers. Ah, the marble domes and gilded archways, and the awesome gateways in exquisite designs. Alas, that my baba died before his time and so suddenly, leaving me no opportunity to show my love and devotion to him."

"It's not me, Your Majesty, but Mirza Ghiyas, who deserves all the compliments. The designs for the tomb and the garden were mine, I admit, but he implemented them with his genius." Hajji Begum murmured in response. "Mirza's love for the late emperor made him work with energy and devotion!"

"No love, no fruit of life!" Gulbadan Begum chimed in with a poetic reverie.

"You will enjoy more fruits of life, Your Majesty, if you journeyed less, and sent others on hunting expeditions." Hamida Banu Begum chided her son. "From Agra to Bengal, you embark on such long, long journeys. The emperors should not fight hand-to-hand with the wretched rebels, but appoint able men to quell seditions."

"The emperor is doing just that! Miryam Makani, my able advisor." Akbar teased gently. "Todar Mall is in Bengal, chastising the sedition-mongers! Bhagwan Das was in Gujrat when we fought the battle, and he himself had implored to be in the lead. For his valor and resolve alone, the victory was ours. And this very evening, the emperor is going to bestow upon him the highest of honors and rewards." He paused. "I journey in this life, Mamma, with a view that somewhere on the path of trials and error, I may stumble upon the rock of sublime *truth*. Then I would wander no more, but would cling to that rock of *truth* without further follies and journeys."

"Oh, these mystic journeys of yours, Your Majesty, they lead nowhere." Hamida Banu Begum smiled indulgently. "I wish I can order you imprisoned in your newly built palace at Fatehpur Sikri. Though I would grant you the freedom of journeys in your head if your thoughts could promise to stay obedient to my will?"

"A paradise for the emperor if he could be arrested in the palace with his wives and with all the lovely ladies of the harem!" Akbar laughed, his eyes flashing mischief. "But I do promise, dear Mamma, that I would stay in the palace of Fatehpur Sikri the longest ever. Yes, I would stay there, and would order more palaces to be built, for all my wives. Well, let me start with the ones who have blessed me with heirs to my throne." His gaze was wandering and caressing. "My sweet Hira, since you are the mother of my first-born, what kind of palace would you like in Fatehpur Sikri?"

"My own palace! Your Majesty." Hira Begum was startled to her feet with the alacrity of a young girl. "I want a large palace with marble halls. Windows, windows everywhere, all overlooking the gardens! And flowers, all the way from the palace gates to the palace walls!" She sank back to her seat, overwhelmed.

"And what would you do with all those flowers, my sweet?" Akbar asked.

"I would deck the halls with garlands, Your Majesty, and would still have plenty left to weave garlands for my gods." Hira Begum breathed trance-like.

"Do your gods have dearth of flowers now, my sweet?" Akbar asked indulgently.

"No, Your Majesty." Hira Begum beamed. "But I would like to pick my own flowers in my gardens."

"And if the emperor can count on your sweet generosity, you might share some with others." Akbar shifted his gaze to Salima. "And my love, the mother of my second son! Would you like your palace as large as Hira's?"

"A small kiosk-like palace in the Persian style, Your Majesty! With no embellishments, but two tall minarets on the façade!" Salima deigned to smile.

"A splendid edifice for some widow in mourning!" Akbar laughed without mirth. "I would plant a lovely garden next to that Persian monastery, and that garden would serve me as my lonesome abode. You would have your sanctuary if that's all you desire, my sweet." His attention was shifting to Usha. "My lovely Usha, what would you choose? A palace grand and opulent!"

"A palace studded with jewels, Your Majesty!" Was Usha Begum's sing-song exclamation! "A palace carved with flowers in mother-of-pearl! Oh, the pillars, the grilles and the balconies, all of marble and sandstone. The wide, imposing chambers, all gilt and damask and a gold chain to summon the servants!" She concluded breathlessly.

"The loveliest of all the palaces the emperor would not ever cease to visit, after returning from his journeys on land and sea, his hunting expeditions!" Akbar intoned wistfully. "My sweet, your palace would be a poet's dream, indeed. Mirza Ghiyas would be ordered to embellish it with all the precious jewels, the emperor could retrieve from his treasury, if not from the oceans of Hind."

"Your Majesty." Sultanum Begum appealed charmingly. "Now that you are in a mood to granting boons, may I request a pilgrimage to Mecca?"

"How can I deny such a sweet request, my sweet Aunt?" Akbar responded graciously. "You, who cared for me when I was a child, a helpless child!" He teased.

"You were never a helpless child, Your Majesty." Gulbadan Begum laughed. "You as a child-prince wandering alone, heedless and fearless! Chasing wild beasts in the pine-valleys of Kabul!" She paused, her eyes attaining a wistful appeal. "May I have the boon of joining Sultanum Begum in this pilgrimage?" She asked abruptly. "A pilgrimage to Mecca has been my dearest wish since a long, long time."

"To grant your dearest wish, my dear Aunt, is the emperor's dearest pleasure." Akbar responded genially. "All the ladies in my harem are free to go on this pilgrimage, if they desire." He added generously.

"Your Majesty. May I join Sultanum Begum and Gulbadan Begum on this pilgrimage?" Sarvaqad Begum sang happily.

"The emperor would be most delighted, if you accompanied them." Akbar consented happily. "Our treasury would furnish all the needs of the happy pilgrims."

"Your Majesty, may I be a pilgrim on this journey, too?" Gulnar Aghacha requested with the elation of a happy child.

"The most charming of the pilgrims!" Akbar laughed. "My grandfather would be happy in his grave if he could but see you journey thus."

"Your Majesty, may I be an escort to the ladies?" Prince Murad was all agog. "I would be the best escort, Your Majesty, to take them to—to, wherever they are going."

"My royal cavalier! How far would you go?" Akbar indulged happily.

"To the garden of Fat—eh Sikri." Prince Murad responded cheerfully.

"The sweet pilgrims would never reach Mecca, then!" Akbar laughed. "But, how would you escort them?"

"I would ride my pony, Your Majesty." Prince Murad commenced most earnestly. "And ladies would ride in gilded howdahs."

But the emperor had ceased to heed. His attention was diverted to Salima, who had just eased herself up, and was now approaching the emperor.

"Your Majesty. May I be a part of this happy pilgrimage?" Salima murmured. "I too had wished, rather dreamed of this pilgrimage since, since—" She could not continue, for the mirth in the emperor's eyes was replaced by stark anguish.

"You, my love." Akbar murmured back. "You, Salima, my lily nurtured on the pond of purest love, would wilt, would not last, from here to Surat."

"All the ladies are free to choose, you yourself said so, Your Majesty." Salima murmured again. "Yet, it seems, you will deny me my request."

"Against my will, my love, I might consent." Akbar smiled.

"Your will is my will, Your Majesty." Salima's eyes mocked the emperor.

"A jest most profane, my sweet." Akbar got his feet, summoning Jouhar. "Come, Jouhar, you have neglected the emperor thus far! Fill his cup with fresh wine."

While the wine was being poured, Salima had slipped back to the circle of the emperor's other wives. Akbar drained his cup and turned his attention to Abdur Rahim.

"Come, my son, accompany the emperor to the abode of the blossoms. The loveliest of all my gardens where beauty injures not but with its perfume of joy in living!" Akbar commanded, turning to his heels without looking back.

The deep grove of pipals and poplars with tamarind trees in the background was the abode that Akbar had chosen for his stroll, not the lovely garden in front of the palace. Abdur Rahim was strolling along with the emperor, quietly and obediently.

The first opportunity of escape and my Beloved is fleeing from the emperor, seeking refuge in Mecca. Akbar was thinking. The whirlwind in his mute contemplations was plunging him into the tides of utter chaos and indecision. He was the emperor despised, and the emperor unloved, suffering torments indescribable.

A year at the most, before she returns? I must let her go. Does the emperor have a choice? What did I say—did I grant her request? What madness escapes the lips of the emperor! Akbar's thoughts were whirling in a stupor of pain and loneliness.

Torment such as mine can reduce my heart to ashes, but it's all on fire with flames pure and eternal. Burning always, inside the liquid flames of my passions, and undying on its pyre of love. His feet were coming to a slow halt.

"Have you ever been in love, Abdur Rahim?" Was Akbar's abrupt inquiry!

"Your Majesty!" Was Abdur Rahim's startled response! "I am not sure, Your Majesty. I love Mamma, and you. Besides that, all my love and devotion, all, for you!"

"For your love and devotion to the emperor, you would not ever suffer, my son." A ripple of anguished mirth escaped Akbar's lips. "If you have not suffered, you have not loved, and if you have not laughed, you have not lived. You rarely laugh, my son! In fact, I have never heard you laugh. Do you ever laugh?" He asked tenderly.

"Only when fools jest, Your Majesty. And when children by the treasures of their innocence touch my heart!" Abdur Rahim smiled bashfully.

"Children, my son, yes, they are no fools!" Akbar ruminated aloud. "And a fool has as much wisdom as a wise man. Only, the fool reveals not his wisdom, and by doing so, his wisdom exceeds far beyond the limits of any wise man." He turned to his heels, commanding over his shoulders. "Time for you to seek wisdom in the company of the fools, my son! The emperor is ready to inspect his precious brood of elephants, before he gets ready to commune with the fools in his court." His thoughts were murmuring. *Fools, wearing the garbs of wise men! And wise men, not even wearing hair to protect the bruised intellect in their heads?*

7

Nine Jewels of The Court

The citron evening had descended swiftly, while Akbar sat enthroned in the Audience Hall of his Agra palace. Its damasked galleries were teeming with the poets, the scholars, the courtiers, the musicians and the theologians, all donned in colorful robes with plumed turbans on their heads.

In conformity with the Moghul etiquette, all present in the court were to remain standing, unless granted permission to sit beside the emperor as a special mark of his favor and inclination. There was one exception though, the musicians, who were always seated in their gallery to entertain the guests, while the guests stood talking, or waiting to be presented to the emperor. This evening, the musician's gallery was garlanded with white tuberoses to honor a new musician, Sur Das. Sur Das had joined the Moghul court quite recently, being an adept musician, and an illustrious poet of chaste, Hindi lyrics.

Tansen, of course, the most favored by the emperor, was also there in the music gallery. Amongst the group of musicians, a few more favored by the emperor were, Baz Bahadur, Lal Kalawant, and two ladies endowed with beauty and talent. They were both great musicians, Zainul, the queen of veena, and Candani, the goddess of her golden harp. Right beneath the music gallery, on the carpeted stage, were the dancing girls.

Jouhar, along with the other ewer-bearers, was busy replenishing the goblets of all the guests. The poets, the painters, the mullahs and the scholars, all were spilling their comments in a cauldron of syllogisms. Akbar had favored Aziz Koka and Bhagwan Das to be seated close to him. Gleaning much information from them, concerning wars and rebellions in Bengal. He had absorbed all details with as much stoic resignation as he could muster, his heart still troubled by the thought of Salima's request for a pilgrimage.

The full accounts of insurrections in Bengal were arrested in Akbar's thoughts. But as soon as those evil details had ceased their downpour, he had begun to recite the names of his favorite elephants in his head. This kind of recitation was one of his mental exercises, which was beneficial to his own self-restraint. While indulged in this sort of activity, he could refrain from chaining his faculties to wrath and hasty decisions.

Lone, Hawai, Sabdilia, Bulsandar, Dilshankar, Rantahman, Asman Shakoh— Akbar's thoughts were straying, trundling down the terrains of Bengal.

The arch rebels Daud and Gujar had entrenched themselves in the fort of Patna to fight the Moghuls. The emperor had proceeded toward Patna with a grand fleet of one thousand boats. The monsoon rains had wreaked havoc, and quite a few of the boats were lost in the waters. Including, the large boat, laden with cheetahs, parrots and peacocks. The loss of this boat was felt greatly by the emperor, for it was designed solely for the entertainment of his royal children. Despite the loss of the boats and the monsoon rains, Akbar had continued his journey through Ganges on his elephant. A cavalcade of five hundred elephants had followed. Only one elephant was drowned, the rest landing safely on the shore. Akbar had then sent his harem to Juanpur.

Before marching toward Patna, Akbar had found it expedient to capture the fortress of Hajipur, since this fortress was the main source of food and armament for the garrison of enemy at Patna. To win the fortress of Hajipur, the battle was fought both by land and water, and the Moghuls had gained victory without much resistance from the enemy. This victory of the Moghuls had such a frightening affect upon Daud and Gujar that they had abandoned the fort of Patna, and had fled by boat, toward Bengal.

At this point, Akbar had decided to send a large army under the leaderships of Munim Khan and Todar Mall in chase of the fugitives. They were instructed to chastise the fugitives, and to curb further rebellions in the provinces of Bengal. Akbar had then returned to Fatehpur Sikri. Enroute Juanpur, he had collected his children and ladies of the harem, gathering once again joy and peace in the company of his family.

Munim Khan had recently returned from Bengal, with disturbing news over his shoulders and wounds on his legs. Daud and Gujar Khan, as expected, were claiming Bengal as their territory, and were confronting the Moghuls. A great battle was fought at the site of Tukaroi, where Munim Khan had been injured. According to Munim Khan's recent reports, Gujar Khan was mortally wounded, and Daud was still resisting the assaults of Todar Mall. Munim Khan's injuries were quite healed by now, and he was anxious to return to the side of Todar Mall. But Akbar had not given his consent to this request of Munim Khan's as yet, much to the chagrin of the valiant general.

Such a galaxy of war-encrusted thoughts were trooping forth in Akbar's mind, as he sat conversant with Shaikh Salim, whom he had just invited to sit beside him. Aziz Koka and Bhagwan Das were also a part of this royal parlance.

Victory is ours. Bengal, and the entire kingdoms of Hind too, we would have all! Soon, soon. Akbar's thoughts were foundering inside the blue oceans of Salima's eyes. *Victory! What does it mean? Can I count my strengths and weaknesses? Weaknesses, many! The only weakness, I can think of right now, is my weakness for love. My love for one woman alone, my great, great lovetorment for Salima, Salima!*

Do I wish to conquer this weakness of mine? No, a thousand times, no! Weakness becomes a wonderful gift from God, if one can see the reflection of one's weakness in the mirror of Divine Power. Where fear of God kindles the flame of wisdom in admitting one's weakness! Weak flesh holds on to the great strength of the soul, till it loses its little measure of strength. Clinging further to the mighty spirit of life everlasting! Akbar's thoughts were reaching out to Shaikh Salim.

"Shaikhu Baba, though the laurels of victory belong to God, Who keeps me under the shadow of His mercy in times of war and peace, I am grateful that you pray for the emperor. Your prayers have blessed me with a lovely daughter and three sons. And through your prayers alone, I have achieved more success than I deserve." Akbar smiled.

"All praise belongs to God, Your Majesty. My prayers are but a litany of the ignorant, seeking guidance in blindness." Shaikh Salim responded modestly. "No victories can be gained without courage, Your Majesty. And your *spirit* conquers all."

"Great victories begin with courage, and end in prayers, my good sage." Akbar laughed suddenly. "For your devotion to the emperor, Shaikhu Baba, I have decided to build you a palace near the tomb of Muinuldin Chishti. It would be a palace of all marble and sandstone, with luxurious baths and a garden brimming with flowers. The facade of this palace would be embellished with gold and jewel-flowers."

"Life's pleasures are not for me, Your Majesty. I lead a simple life, hoping for spiritual rewards after death." Shaikh Salim protested amiably.

"Shaikhu Baba!" Akbar exclaimed heedlessly. "Shunning life's pleasures for a life hereafter, one relinquishes not only the pleasures in this life, but the fruits of spiritual life after death. For, all our actions and experiences are like the seeds, they must be sown in the fields of our consciousness. To be reaped as the harvests of *illusion,* in this world of truth and reality." The enigmatic gleam in his eyes was gathering mirth and mischief.

"Your Majesty, your wisdom is beyond the meager lot of my perception!" Shaikh Salim confessed humbly. "I only feel that love for the riches of the world breeds evil. It overwhelms one with a desire to gain more, even at the cost of pain and injustice."

"How can evil overwhelm those, who are schooled to reward evil with good?" The glints of mirth and mischief in Akbar's gaze were departing. "And you are one of those men, Shaikhu Baba, upon whom the evil loses its power to tempt. You are a sage for everyone, and for all ages! Hindus claim you as their own saint, and Muslims, as their own pir. So do Jains, Sikhs and Parsees. A universal saint, you are. My late baba, may God have peace on him, built a house of worship, where saints and scholars participated in all sorts of discussions. He named it Din Panah, which means, Asylum of the Faithful. Did you ever hear of Din Panah?"

"Yes, Your Majesty, the reports of Din Panah did reach me in Ajmer. It was a center of great literary and theology discussions. Emperor Humayun, such tragedy, his foot slipped from the—" Shaikh Salim couldn't repeat that scene of death.

"Yes." Akbar murmured low. "A tragic death indeed for the emperor, who, while still ascending the steps of learning, fell victim to the snares of wise death. I have been thinking. Yes, I too would order a house of worship to be built. I would call it Ibadat Khana, but it would be a grand arena for the poets, the scholars and the theologians. I would invite scholars and theologians from all over the world, and they would be permitted to hold discussions on any topic they chose. Religions of the world would find voice in the Ibadat Khana, accommodating all faiths in the camaraderie of wisdom, learning, and understanding. Do you think it wise, Shaikhu Baba, for a Muslim emperor to build such a house of worship? It would be in Fatehpur Sikri, of course."

"Fathehpur Sikri." Shaikh Salim murmured happily. "Yes, Your Majesty, it would be a monument of your wise and generous spirit. With the diversity of faiths in Hind, Your Majesty, people are living in some sort of spiritual desert, and Ibadat Khana would become a happy abode for those, who are seeking the garden of bliss."

"A poet-sage!" Akbar exclaimed. "*Spiritual desert,* I like that expression. I like it immensely! It gives me the feeling of space and vacuity. Vacuity and space, one can wander in these realms forever, not ever knowing that spiritual silence is all that one needs for inner bliss, not the clamor of words or thoughts." His gaze was drifting toward Munim Khan, who approached the throne without attracting any notice.

"Your Majesty." Munim Khan offered his taslim. "My wounds are healed, Your Majesty, and my legs are quite strong. May I request again the privilege of joining Todar Mall? Todar Mall is a brave general, but Daud is still evading him, and I can be of great assistance to him." He seemed to be pleading than requesting.

"This red turban doesn't suit you, Munim Khan. It is not lending your pallor the color of health and exuberance." Akbar commented evasively. "You still look ill to me, and you must be carried in a litter to Bengal, if you wish to participate in the battle. My advice is that you stay in Agra, or repair to Fatehpur Sikri for a long, long rest."

"Your Majesty, I am fit to ride a fiery steed from here to eternity!" Munim Khan protested with much zeal. "Please, Your Majesty, grant me the permission to leave. I can't wait to subjugate Bengal!" He appealed passionately.

"In that case, eternity awaits you in the jungles of Bengal, my valorous knight." Akbar laughed. "You have my permission. Any more news from the quarters of our heedless foes!" He asked with a bantering tone.

"Nothing much is new in that quarter, Your Majesty." Munim Khan responded cheerfully. "A fleeing enemy is a dull subject to pursue. Daud is fleeing toward Katak now, wishing to find refuge in Orissa."

Since the next one to seek the emperor's attention was Fath Ullah, Akbar's gaze was welcoming his friend who was dearest to his heart.

"Your Majesty." Fath Ullah offered a buoyant curtsy. "Many peasants are suffering poverty on the verge of hunger and homelessness, since much of their crops has been damaged during the past few campaigns. Especially, in Gujrat, where fields upon fields lay spoiled by wars, incult and barren! My apologies, Your Majesty, for parading such dire needs of the people, but their needs must be satisfied!"

"No trumpets sound as sweet as the voice of suffering, which can be heard and soothed by the edicts of justice." A mist of sadness was replacing the glint of mockery in Akbar's eyes. "You are the most precious of jewels in my Moghul court, Fath Ullah, didn't I tell you before. And you alone have the purity of heart to bring this painful matter to the emperor's notice. To remedy the wrong, this Farman of mine must reach out to all without delay. You are to appoint Dilawar Khan to post armed guards on either side of the fields, so that the marching armies dare not ruin the crops. But before that, issue orders that immediate compensation should be made to the farmers, whose crops have been damaged by the army or by the caprice of nature. Instant cash must be paid to the peasants in dire need. And the rest can draw compensations from the royal treasury which keeps record of all the revenue accounts."

"Yes, Your Majesty. Your Farman would be voiced and executed throughout the land of Hind, most efficiently." Fath Ullah bowed low, giving way to Abdunnabi.

"Your Majesty." Abdunnabi offered kornish exigently. "If I may intercede, Your Majesty? If your Farman goes into affect, Your Majesty, the revenues in the royal treasury would be depleted considerably." His eyes were smoldering with zeal.

"*If?*" Akbar's eyes were gathering rage. "Emperor's Farman must be obeyed, always, unless one cares not to keep his head over his shoulders! What good are revenues in the emperor's treasury, if the needs of his subjects are not satisfied?"

Abdunnabi almost stumbled back into Mukhdum-ul-Mulk, who was the next to voice his concern.

"Must you arch your brows in that unseemly manner, Mukhdum-ul-Mulk? They make your face wrinkle in more folds than the ones that are in your turban." Akbar flung a rebuke at him even before he could finish his kornish.

"Pardon me, Your Majesty." Mukhdum-ul-Mulk's eyebrows arched the more. "If you could reconsider, Your Majesty! Compensating the peasants little at a time. That way, the treasury would not suffer depletion."

"One, who gives a share of his riches, gives not enough. And the one, who gives his share from little, earns riches beyond imagination." Akbar's gaze was turning to Birbal. "Another of my fine jewels of the Moghul court, and that is you, Birbal. Do you have a couplet or two to entertain the emperor?" He asked abruptly.

"Since Faizi spills couplets like the raindrops, Your Majesty, I keep mine safe inside the thunder of my heart. One of these days, this thunder would murmur in thunderous fury, and its bolts of lightning would strike through my thoughts. Then I might be able to pen a few." Birbal laughed generously. "But right now, my concern is concerning the state and the stately beasts. Your regulations, Your Majesty, in allotting the officers royal funds to maintain a certain amount of horses and troops, are not being fully complied. Some of the officers are collecting gold, instead of maintaining the required number of horses or troops. Some of them are even purchasing the inferior quality of horses, which are not suitable for warfare."

"Royal thieves, living royally!" Akbar's thoughts were gleaning more edicts. "Such greed and corruption in our imperial ranks would not be tolerated by the emperor. In order to check this fraud, I order branding of the horses. And if the horses are not of the finest quality to be found in the possession of the Moghul officers, they themselves will be branded with shame. Stripped off their honors and possessions!"

"Your Majesty!" Aziz Koka exclaimed suddenly, some sort of protest shining in his eyes. His unuttered protest was further silenced by a fit of coughing. "Does the emperor's edict choke you, Aziz? Or, does your gall is urging you to some rude act of hasty protests!" Akbar flashed him a look brimming with rebuke.

"Pardon me, Your Majesty." Aziz Koka managed to dispel his fit of coughing. "If I may persuade the emperor, not to adopt this system of branding the horses? It is cruel—cruel to the animals." He concluded.

"Branding is harmless, my kind brother. Yet, *cruel* is the tyranny of greed in men's souls, which must be checked by the law and virtue of edicts just and noble. Yes, it must be checked, before the soul of the entire nation grows cankerous with the seeds of fraud, deception and wickedness." Akbar responded without anger. "Tyranny, in any form or manner, should not reside in men's hearts, and it must be rendered unlawful in the hearts of everyone. Especially, in the heart of a sovereign, who deems himself a guardian of this world!" His gaze was settling on Bhagwan Das. "No protests on the lips of my favorite jewel! Such jewels should be treasured in the Moghul court. For your valor in Gujrat, Bhagwan Das, and for your devotion to the emperor, the emperor has decided to bestow on you signal honors." He clapped his hands. "My dear friends and courtiers, the emperor is bestowing a great honor on Bhagwan Das for the sheer merit of his valor, and for his fidelity toward his sovereign. From henceforth, he is granted the honor of using Moghul banner and kettledrums, whenever he chooses to do so, at his palace or in public. At his own pleasure, whenever he wishes." He announced happily.

The entire court was filled with the thunder of applause from all, for Bhagwan Das was loved and respected by his peers. The music had picked its tempo too, and the dancing girls were whirling on their toes more seductively. Bhagwan Das was bereft of words and overwhelmed by the burden of gratitude.

"Now, you may introduce your guest-scholar to the emperor, my valorous friend." Akbar commanded Bhagwan Das.

"Your Majesty." Bhagwan Das murmured reverently. "First, I wish to introduce another scholar, not Banduani, but someone I met during one of my rambling pursuits for knowledge, and wish to have the privilege of presenting him to you."

"An invisible scholar!" Akbar exclaimed. "No alien face I have seen in my court, which I do not recognize." His gaze was sweeping over his guests, but before it could return to Bhagwan Das, it was arrested to Faizi, who was reciting one of his poems.

"That very light which is yielded by the world-adoring sun
Is produced from the brows of the sublime
That Akbar is allied to Aftab, Sun
Is proved by the evidence of the names."

Faizi's recitation was engulfed into a volley of applause.

"If the world's New Year be destroyed
Let the hundred-leafed rose remain."

Abdul Hai could not help but boast of his oft-repeated couplet.

"You recited that at the accession ceremony of the emperor! And since then you have not written a couplet worth a rupee." Poet Nurriddin was teasing Abdul Hai.

Akbar was amused by the flattering verse of Faizi. Also, enchanted by the assiduity of his court-poets, but his senses were absorbing more than he could glean.

"Babel of tongues! The words divesting their heritage, and donning the mantles of languages harsh and alien. Hindi, Arabic, Persian, Turkish, Sanskrit? Todar Mall was right: a new language is emanating from all alien tongues. This new mixture of languages, what did he call it, *Urdu*, why? Why, Urdu?" Man Singh was engaging Muhammad Hussain in the discussion of this new language at hand.

Akbar had bestowed the title of Zarrinqalam—golden pen on Muhammad Hussain, for his skill in creating beautiful scripts on paper and canvas. Now as he watched him embroiled in discussion with Man Singh, he was wondering if Zarrinqalam could paint his words as beautifully as his script. Akbar's gaze was wandering, and lingering more than once on Abul Fazl and Mubarak Shah.

"The essence of Hindu tradition is that in the acquisition of learning, or of wealth, a man should so toil as if he were never to grow old, or die—" Puru was expounding to Khatam with the air of wisdom and benevolence.

"My good Pundit." Akbar commented aloud, catching the attention of both the Brahman priests. "In my estimation, since the rich fear more of old age and death, they withhold themselves from labor. So, in acquiring the needs of wealth and learning, we should regard each morrow as our last, and postpone not the work of one day to the next."

"Your Majesty, pardon my boldness. May I voice my opinion?" Debi— another Brahman priest was requesting the honor to be a part of this discussion. Reading consent from the emperor's eyes, he continued avidly. "I believe the words of Hindu philosophers, as they say, that in the garnering of good works, one should have death constantly in view. And placing no reliance on life, and never relaxing one's efforts."

"We need to understand the pain in living, not the peace in death." Akbar was thinking aloud. "Ah, the virtue in living and the pursuit of knowledge! To satisfy these twin needs, one should not entertain the idea of death so that liberated from hopes and fears we could practice virtue for the sake of its own worth. But the emperor is contradicting himself! Continue your discussions with good cheers, my prudent friends, and the emperor would entertain himself with unwise thoughts. Now, my honorable friend, introduce your mystery guest." Akbar's eyes were teasing Bhagwan Das.

"The mystery lies only in his youth and talent, Your Majesty." Bhagwan Das quipped brightly. With his eyes alone, he was communing with Bahlul to fetch Nizami. "His name is Nizamuddin Ahmed, Your Majesty. Todah is his birth-place. For his studies, he went to the town of Basawar. He is a scholar and a poet in his own right."

"In his court, the emperor needs more poets than mullahs." Akbar reached out for his goblet of wine on the ivory table. "I prefer, that one should write down a quatrain of Omar Khayyam, after reading one ode of Hafiz, otherwise, the latter is like drinking wine without relish." He drained his cup quickly.

Nizamuddin Ahmed, accompanied by Bahlul and Man Singh, was being presented to the emperor. The emperor sat sipping his wine, and watching the tall, fair youth with a keen interest. He was impressed by the dark, intelligent eyes of this young man and thinking to himself: *his eyes contain depths of the oceans!*

"Your Majesty." Nizamuddin Ahmed offered a perfect taslim.

"You are welcome to our Moghul court, my young scholar." Akbar acknowledged his curtsy. "I hear you are a poet. Do you write quatrains?"

"Yes, Your Majesty." Was Nizamuddin Ahmed's laconic response!

"Such brevity of speech is commendable." Akbar laughed. "If you can construe one quatrain right now, you can join the circle of eminent poets in my court. Do you accept this challenge, my young poet?" He asked capriciously.

"Yes, Your Majesty." Nizamuddin Ahmed murmured in response.

"Though the foot of speech be long of stride
Thy curtain-stone hath shattered it
Though speech be fat and lusty
It is lean, when it reaches Thy table."

"A poet incarnate! Your speech would mend with age." Akbar commented, scooping a handful of gold coins from his coffer, and offering them to Nizamuddin Ahmed. "Your reward for the day, Nizamuddin, and now you are accepted to be the disciple of Faizi and Birbal." He dismissed him graciously. "I hope, your next guest is as intelligent as this one, Bhagwan Das?" Akbar's gaze was returned to Bhagwan Das.

"Sunni by sect, he is well versed in religion and theology, Your Majesty." Bhagwan Das commented low. "His birth-place is in Basawar too, in Rajasthan. He is a friend of the Parsee priest, Dastur, and claims to have extensive knowledge of Hindu texts. And, he is hasty! He is approaching your throne, right now, Your Majesty."

"Your Majesty." Baduani offered a swift kornish, after he was presented to the emperor by Bhagwan Das.

"You are welcome to our Moghul court, Baduani." Akbar intoned kindly. "I hear you are a scholar of great wisdom and learning. Also, well versed in the subjects of theology! In the manner of languages, how wide is your learning?" He asked testingly.

"Arabic, Persian, Turkish, are like the mother-tongues to me, Your Majesty. And I know Hindi and Sanskrit."

"You would be of great assistance to my court scholars, then." Akbar contemplated aloud. "The emperor is interested, that all the great works could be translated into Persian. Faizi is translating Lilavati, a Hindi text on arithmetic. My own son, Abdur Rahim, is translating the memoirs of my grandfather from Turkic to Persian. The task of translating Tajak—a book on astronomy is subject to the intellect of Muhammad Hussain. Ibrahim Khan is working on Atharva Veda. Maulana Sheri is assigned to translate, The Haribas, a book on the life of Lord Krishna. I am most interested in having the Mahabharata translated. Several scholars are working on this sacred text. Now, you can assist them in their endeavor to bring it to completion."

"I fear, Your Majesty, I am unfit, temporally and spiritually, for this holy task of translating Mahabharata." Was Baduani's flustered response! "But I hope, my lack of understanding on this subject may not become any cause of displeasure to the emperor."

"Whoever walks in the way of fear and hope, his temporal and spiritual affairs would prosper in my court. Neglect of them would result in misfortune." Akbar's gaze as well as his gesture was dismissing the zealous scholar.

The emperor's gaze was already summoning Mubarak Shah to his presence, so that he could present his younger son, Abul Fazl, to him. A sudden spark of kindness was alighting in the emperor's gaze, as it fell on Abul Fazl. Mubarak Shah, after a graceful kornish, was presenting his son to the emperor.

"Your Majesty." Abul Fazl murmured with all reverence. "I have no worldly treasures to offer at the feet of the emperor. But I have written a commentary on the Ayat-ul-Kursi from the Quran, for Your Majesty's perusal and recommendation." He held out a scroll to the emperor, who claimed it eagerly.

"The emperor welcomes you as the ninth jewel of my Moghul court. And the last one of the precious jewels, I hope, for my set of naurattan, nine jewels, is complete." Akbar smiled. "It is strange that in the time of our Prophet, no commentaries on the Quran were made, so that the differences of interpretation might not afterwards arise." He handed the scroll to Naqib Khan. "Your eyes are offering the purity of your heart and friendship, Abul. The emperor has never been offered such precious gifts before. And now, the gifts of your tongue would be forever welcome in my presence." He favored both Abul Fazl and Mubarak Shah to be seated beside him. "Abul, why is this paper tied with a rope of cypress leaves?" Akbar was fascinated, his look tender and amused.

"This is a small gift for you, Your Majesty. A gift, that I wrapped myself." Abul Fazl's eyes darkened with the warmth of inner joy. "A poem that I wrote just the night before, for you, Your Majesty." Without meeting the emperor's gaze, he began to recite.

"In honor of my liege, the king
With all true loyalty I bring
A cypress set in garden fair
Wherein shall trysting all repair
And full draught of wine elate
Its happy growth commemorate."

"Such exquisite flattery, molded in the leaves of wisdom, is most pleasant to the emperor's ears." Akbar beamed with sheer delight. "Flatter me more, my wise poet, with a couplet or two, if you have some more to recite."

"Your Majesty." Abul Fazl responded joyfully.

"The light that o'er seven spheres celestial plays
Wins all its radiance from imperial rays
The blind need no more a staff to take
While those that see find luminous their way."

"The emperor can't absorb so much flattery in one day." Akbar laughed. "You would be taxed with the burden of writing the history of my reign."

"A burden so pleasant, which I can carry in my eyes, Your Majesty! And a burden so light, that it will sit on my shoulders like the caress of a feather." Abul Fazl responded warmly, the candles of devotion in his eyes dark and profound.

"If the burden be both light and pleasant, then the task should be done in a few years, Abul. Not like Firdausi, who spent thirty years in writing his Book of Kings." Akbar laughed, his gaze turning to Mubarak Shah. "You have been in my court for more than a year, Mubarak Shah, and you must have noticed, that the emperor is surrounded by quite a few of the men, who are proud, stupid and selfish. They are boastful too, though they happen to be the scholars of this age, and claim wisdom as their birth-right. Although I am the master of so vast a kingdom, and all the appliances of the government are to my hand, yet since true greatness consists in doing the will of God, my mind is not at ease in this diversity of sects and creeds, and my heart is oppressed by this outward pomp of circumstance. Oh, how I had wished for the coming of some pious man, who would resolve the distractions of my heart! And now, I have found this man in your younger son, yes, my heart tells me so." He flashed a warm glance at Abul Fazl.

"Your Majesty, I feel honored that my son pleases you so." Mubarak Shah murmured gratefully.

"Both your sons, my wise friend and courtier!" Akbar murmured back warmly. "Faizi, the emerald of my naurattan, the jewel of my pride! No jewel shines as bright in my turban as Faizi does amidst the jewels of Moghul court. Abul Fazl, what jewel would suit his name the best? He would stay in my heart like a well-preserved pearl! And now, my friend, lend me your advice. With what satisfaction can I undertake the conquest of this empire, when zeal of the few stifles the voice of spiritual learning in my court?"

"Your Majesty, you are the head of the spiritual kingdom." Mubarak Shah responded quickly. "To prevent the ulemas from misusing their powers, you could easily assume the authority of a primate, their spiritual leader to govern over the issues of faith, belief or ritual." He added with much enthusiasm.

"The emperor must dwell on this." Akbar got to his feet, his gaze settling on Bahlul, while Fath Ullah was trying to catch the emperor's attention.

"Your Majesty, I hope, we here sitting near your throne, are innocent, rather guiltless of harboring any zeal." Fath Ullah caught the emperor's attention.

"No man is innocent, until proven guiltless before the judgment of his soul." Akbar laughed sadly.

"If soul be the arbiter, judging itself to be guilty, then it can also purge its guilt with prayer and penance." Bhagwan Das commented to himself.

"How can one cleanse the defilements from within?" Akbar murmured to himself, summoning Bahlul to his presence. Without addressing anyone, he repeated aloud. "How could one when one carries the seeds of pride, deceit, bigotry, wickedness and corruption in one's soul? Nurturing them to full bloom, till the harvest of evil renders one heartless and sightless." He began to dismount his throne.

Bahlul was following the emperor at a distance, and so were the favored ones who had kept him company near the throne. Abul Fazl was right behind the emperor, and could not help murmuring to himself under the spell of his ponderous reverie.

"Wisdom is the answer to all the evils in this world, even the evils from within and without. The men who claim to be wise should find no obstacles in conquering all evils, even pride, deceit, bigotry in their hearts, or corruption in their souls!" Abul Fazl was not even aware that the whole procession had stopped and the emperor too.

"The wisdom that they possess, my wise scholar, is the child of their conceit." Akbar commented amusedly, before turning on his heels. "True wisdom comes to those, who claim not to be wise." He paraded out of the audience hall, now only Bahlul following him.

"Request Salima Begum to join me in the east garden." Akbar commanded.

Even my solitude is nursing some unforgettable hope to win the love of my Beloved. Akbar murmured, his senses overwhelmed by the perfume of Rat-Ki-Rani.

Akbar and Salima were strolling side-by-side, under the shadows of the cypresses. They were both silent, both painfully aware of the silent hush all around. They had been strolling for quite a while, absorbed in their own contemplations, as if bewitched by the beauty of the night. The livid moon up there appeared to be chasing them, creating patterns of old lace through the thicket of leaves, and illuminating the jewels on the royal person of both the emperor and the Beloved. For some strange reason, his thoughts were reaching out to his grandfather. One of Babur's poems was teasing his thoughts. His pace was slackening, the words of Babur's couplet breathing on his lips.

Parting from thee were perdition
How else could I depart from this world

Akbar's feet were coming to a slow halt.

"My grandfather wrote this couplet." Akbar murmured softly.

"Is there peace in death, God
No toil for the dead
No torments of the heart
Or perdition everlasting."

Salima recited her own verse under some spell of daze.

"A poetess, my Beloved!" Akbar laughed without mirth. "You wrote that, the emperor knows. Did some evil spirits inspire you to write this verse, my love? Or does your hatred for the emperor lends you such beautiful inspiration?"

"There is no hatred in my heart for you, Your Majesty, only respect and reverence." Salima found her voice.

"And no love! How else could you think of fleeing from the emperor?" Akbar asked rather charmingly. "A pilgrimage to Mecca, continents away. How would the emperor live, without you?"

"Only a year, Your Majesty." Was Salima's flustered response!

"A year." Akbar murmured aloud. "The longest year in my life, it would be."

"Many, many years, perhaps, Your Majesty." Salima teased. "Those years, amidst the tides of your hunting trips, and of your victories, would seem like the interludes between court affairs. All those years scarcely noticed by the emperor!"

"Time would be my thief, love! Stealing away my love, and chaining me in the shackles of torments supreme." Akbar murmured to himself. "You can't even imagine the agony of such a parting, my heartless Beloved. Strange, that when I am thinking about you, I think about God. And when I am thinking about God, I think about you. Both you, and God, help alleviate my despair and hopelessness in life! You, lending me the reason to live and He the hope not to welcome death!" He caught her into his arms.

Akbar was kissing her under the stars, against the bower of roses, with the moon-lit madness of a passion wild and terrible. Suddenly, as if whipped by the very waves of agony in his soul, his kisses were truncated. He released her reluctantly.

"It's no use holding a cold, throbbing star to one's heart, my love." Akbar murmured, claiming her hand, and leading her back toward the palace. "Such star, by its remote, luminous glory, is destined to steal the warmth from a loving heart." He held her close to him, his senses welcoming pain and delirium. "When you are in Mecca, love, pray for this lone pilgrim who cannot accompany you. And come back with the warmth of love in your heart. Abandon your hatred and the glaciers of ice in your soul in the desert-shrines of lands holy and unwanting—"

The emperor was seeking the comfort of his library, where Naqib Khan would be waiting for the emperor to satisfy his hunger for books. The scent of delirium was fading in Akbar's thoughts, as he entered his vast library. Naqib Khan was talking to a young girl in tender, cajoling tones.

"Morning-glory, blooming wild in the middle of the night." Akbar commented. Turning to Naqib Khan with his usual, bantering tone, which he could assume without effort whenever he was alone with him. "Who is this beautiful child you are holding prisoner in the emperor's library?" He asked.

"She is my youngest daughter, Your Majesty. She stole into the library without my permission. Wanting to know if I could take her to Fatehpur Sikri, the next time that I go there—rather demanding! Being the youngest, she is rather spoiled." Naqib Khan flashed an accusing, yet tender look at his daughter.

"And she would go to Fatehpur Sikri, this sweet rebel!" Akbar smiled, returning his gaze to the wonder of beauty. "The emperor himself would take you there. What is your name, sweet child?" He asked, fascinated by this bloom of grace and beauty.

"Zebunisa, Your Majesty." Zebunisa curtsied. "May I go, Your Majesty?"

"If I yielded to my wishes, child, you would stay with the emperor, forever. But you must enjoy the pleasures of your youth with your friends." Akbar laughed. "You may leave."

Zebunisa fled with the speed of a bullet. The heavy silks on her small person rustling behind her in giggling protests.

"When can she be the emperor's bride?" Akbar turned to Naqib Khan, laughingly.

"She is of age, Your Majesty. Turned twelve, this year." Naqib Khan responded.

"Still a child, Naqib." Laughter faded from Akbar's lips and eyes. He began to pace. "I did issue a Farman, didn't I, regarding marriage, that the marriageable age for the girls should be sixteen, and for the boys, eighteen." His feet came to a slow halt before Naqib Khan. "What virtue is in living and loving, my friend? Is there a sane answer to this question?" He began to pace.

"To love unselfishly, and to live unwisely." Was Naqib Khan's quick response.

"A virtue turned to vice then." Akbar pondered aloud. "And when virtues turn to vices, vices attain the nobility of virtues, letting vices breathe and thrive. Alive and unconquerable they remain, then." He sought the comfort of his gilded chair, and lowered himself into its velvety depths. "Read to me the verses of Rumi, all night."

As Naqib Khan stirred to fetch the Mystical Poems of Rumi, Akbar stalled him.

"Better yet, sit with me, Naqib. Talk with the emperor. Tell me of old tales, or recite some verses which have never been recorded."

"What kind of tales would please the emperor? Of what clime, of what context, Your Majesty?" Naqib Khan seated himself at the emperor's feet.

"Start with Adam. Does anyone know how he looked like?" Akbar closed his eyes.

"He was lofty of stature, Your Majesty, I read somewhere. He was considered very handsome, had curly hair and wheaten complexion. Our true ancestor, it seems, though he is the father of all. He died in Hind, and was buried on a mountain near Ceylon. It is called Adam's Hill, and his footprints can be seen on it. Noah carried the coffin of Adam and Eve on his Ark at the time of the Deluge, and buried them in Jerusalem." Naqib Khan appeared to exhaust his store of knowledge on Adam.

"In the times of great sufferings, one clings to the past. For, future holds no better promise! Isn't that right, Naqib?" Akbar queried, his eyes still closed.

"I hope, no great sufferings have touched your heart recently, Your Majesty." Naqib Khan murmured rather apprehensively.

"No." Akbar's voice was barely audible. "Only the sufferings in love. The emperor loves too selfishly, I guess. I wish I had the wisdom of Solomon."

"You are the Solomon of this age, Your Majesty, as if Solomon himself has put his ring on your finger," Naqib Khan intoned with such devotion, that his eyes appeared to shine with the light of secrets untold. "A quarry of Solomon's stone is in Kashmir, Your Majesty, of which utensils are fashioned. When you get a chance to visit Kashmir, order a vessel made out of this stone, for me, and I would drink deep of Solomon's wisdom. Maybe, I would become half as wise as Solomon, and would plead the other half from the emperor, returning all the wisdom to the nine jewels of the court." The very look in his eyes was attesting that he was failing in his effort to amuse the emperor.

"No use, no use." Akbar murmured to himself. "To be wise and in love, to hold on to the reed of wisdom, and to live unwisely! Leave the emperor, kind friend. Read to him at dawn, he would still be here in this very seat." He commanded low.

Naqib Khan got to his feet slowly, and lumbered toward the door with quiet, reluctant steps. His loving heart was throbbing to leap out, to comfort the lonesome emperor.

The most wretched of emperors who can't find a loving abode to lay his unloving head to rest. A pang of hopeless, helpless pain was uncurling its wings in Akbar's head to fan the emperor to sleep.

8

A House of Worship

The rose garden behind the emperor's palace in Fatehpur Sikri was bursting with blooms. The silk marquees erected in the garden for the emperor's harem, were a gilded splendor while the emperor floated from one rich abode to the other, gaily and restlessly.

Kindness was a gracious host in the emperor's eyes, as he stopped to greet his mother under the shade of the gul mohur tree, its gold-scattering blooms trembling in the wind. Hamida Banu was quick to voice the gossip of the harem, but Akbar's thoughts were embarking on a distant journey of their own, alighting on his new bride, Qasima Banu, whom he had married recently after his conquest of Bengal.

Bengal was conquered, the wrangling prince, Daud, had joined the abode of the dead. Shah Tahmasp, the king of Iran, had also died this very year. Cabral, the Portuguese ambassador, whom Akbar had met at the siege of Surat, was much favored by the emperor. The emperor's keen interest in learning about the customs of Europe and the doctrines of Christianity had encouraged Cabral to introduce two Portuguese Fathers, who had come to Bengal as the missionaries. The names of these Fathers were, Peter Dias and Anthony Vaz. They were now residing in Fatehpur Sikri, and had become active participants in the religious discussions at Ibadat Khana.

Akbar's thoughts were reaching out to Aziz Koka. Aziz Koka was under arrest, and brought to Fatehpur Sikri recently, for defying the edict of branding the horses. The emperor's thoughts were suspended all of a sudden as princess Khanam claimed his immediate attention, her three royal brothers lingering by her side. She was telling the emperor something about the butterflies, but Akbar's thoughts were accosting his uncle, Sulaiman Mirza, whom he was to receive this very day.

Sulaiman Mirza had ruled Badakhshan since the reign of Akbar's grandfather, emperor Babur, but was lately ousted by his own grandson, Shahrukh Mirza. Driven away from Badakhshan, he had sought refuge in Kabul with his son-in-law, Hakim Mirza—Akbar's step-brother. Hakim Mirza had not welcomed

Sulaiman Mirza, and had urged him to seek the help of the emperor in Hind. Akbar, upon learning the plight of Sulaiman Mirza had invited him to Hind. This very afternoon, Sulaiman Mirza was to arrive in Fatehpur Sikri, and Akbar had ordered a grand reception.

"Your Majesty, what are the nine jewels of the court?" Prince Salim asked. Almost on the verge of seven springs he looked more like a youth of twelve.

"Not what, Shaikhu Baba, but who?" Akbar laughed. "The nine jewels in my court are the poets, the scholars, the musicians and the learned men of this *time* and *age*.

"Like the knights in King Arthur's court Your Majesty." Prince Murad chirped.

"Your tutor, Faizi, is filling your sweet head with legends from Europe, I presume." Akbar turned his laughing eyes to prince Murad. "Unlike the knights of Arthur, the Moghul knights fight with words, not with gleaming swords. Though they do fight wars, a few of them—the jewels of my court."

"Why jewels, Your Majesty? Have I seen them?" Prince Daniyal couldn't resist his agog. The youngest of the three princes he was turning out to be a child prodigy.

"The jewels, my jewel of a prince, you have not only seen, but have talked with!" Akbar's gaze was wistful and embracing. "Birbal is Ruby, with the fire of poetry in his heart. Abul Fazl is the precious Pearl of wisdom. Fath Ullah, with the flame of compassion in his heart, shines like the Sapphire. Faizi is Emerald, fiery, yet green like the meadows in his poetry and eloquence. Man Singh, the ever-changing Opal, with his inner strength and knowledge. Tansen, a polished Garnet, the deep, boundless gem of song and mystery. Bhagwan Das, a Carnelian most bright, with its purity of heart. Nizamuddin Ahmed is my Jade, the hunter-green of knowledge and understanding. Todar Mall is my Diamond, honed to the precision of a sword, which can cut through the hearts of our enemy with the power of its will and strength. And now, my royal jewels, the emperor must commune with the jewels of his soul." He turned abruptly.

Nine wives—nine Moghul knights, Akbar was thinking. *Ruqaiya, Suriya, Mahmooda, Salima, Hira, Nighat, Farida, Usha, Jagruti and Qasima Banu! Number ten exceeding the seal of number nine. The number of transgression some say.*

"Such costly reception for your uncle, Your Majesty. Even cheetahs are wearing the collars of gold to greet Sulaiman Mirza." Qasima Banu Begum tossed a shy comment at the emperor, as his feet came to a slow halt opposite her.

"And five thousand elephants equipped with velvet and brocade howdahs! Marching from here to Mathura in great splendor to greet the great prince?" Farida Begum joined in, agog and excitement shining in her eyes.

"Don't forget to mention the gold and silver chains on the necks and trunks of the royal elephants, dear Farida." Usha Begum was chirping most sweetly.

"Not as costly as the sum of gold, which the emperor showers on the pilgrims since Salima and the other ladies left for Mecca." Hira Begum sang happily.

"My jealous, wondrous queens!" Akbar stood there laughing most genuinely.

"The pilgrimage, and now the reception of my uncle, both are sacred events to be embellished with gold. Venerable through age, my uncle requires respect and veneration from the emperor despite the fact that he coveted Kabul vainly and unsuccessfully. Besides, he will bring the memories of Kabul with him, and of my royal grandfather. And for this reason alone, he must be treated royally. And the pilgrimage—the annual hajj! It is an age-old custom adopted by Prophet Muhammed with utmost devotion. So, the pilgrims must share the bounties of God, given to the emperor, by the mercy of God."

"Five lakhs of rupees, Your Majesty! Not to mention the sum in gold and jewels, to the hajjis." Hamida Banu Begum teased.

"One tenth of what is spent to deck the royal person of the emperor's one bride alone." Akbar softened the challenge in his mother's eyes with his tender mirth.

"Five lakhs!" Nighat Begum exclaimed!

"Money is of no value in the treasuries, my sweet, as compared to the riches in one's soul." Akbar's gaze rested on her adoringly. "For a soul gains tenfold in spiritual delights, if the heart could suffer to lose even one lakh in worldly possessions, a mere pittance from the treasuries of the rich and the God-fearing."

"From such treasuries of yours, Your Majesty, may I ask a boon?" Was Ruqaiya Begum's abrupt request!

"The emperor would lay kingdoms at your feet, sweet Ruqaiya, if you but desire." Akbar responded tenderly.

"I desire only the city of forgiveness, Your Majesty, inside the kingdoms of your heart." Ruqaiya Begum murmured poetically. "Aziz Koka is much too wretched, and feeling contrite. He is suffering the torments of remorse and loneliness. Would you, Your Majesty, consider forgiving him?"

"My noble queen." Akbar murmured back. "I have always known, you, carrying the burden of evil in men's hearts inside your great soul, which keeps brimming with kindness and compassion. Forgiveness is my policy, my dear, but to show leniency to my kin will be unjust in the eyes of my subjects, who accept punishments for their follies as the rewards of my benevolence. Though a milk of river which I cannot cross, flows between me and Aziz Koka, I must punish him to maintain justice in my empire." He espied Abdur Rahim who stood talking with prince Salim. "Abdur Rahim, go, summon the lone prisoner, Aziz Koka, from his prison of gold and damask." He commanded, returning his attention to his wife. "The emperor won't be too harsh with Aziz Koka, my sweet." His gaze was returning to prince Salim. "My prince, you are admiring the arrow, but do you know from what metal it is designed?"

"Of metal, Your Majesty!" Prince Salim exclaimed. "This is made out of wood!

"Of what wood, then?" Akbar prodded.

"Of the many-pillared banyan tree, Your Majesty." Prince Salim murmured.

"Ah, the banyan tree! The symbol of Hindu Sankh ya doctrine of vitality ever-fresh and rejuvenescent." Akbar intoned thoughtfully. "No, my wise prince, this arrow is fashioned out of the wood of the cypress tree. The slender and aspiring cypress, which all Muslims hold in awe and reverence! Cypress is the tree of mourning, many Muslims believe, but it is also the emblem of undying *hope*. This *hope* never leaves us, it has been our legacy from the southern slopes of Bolar Dagh to the sources of Nile. And from the Iranian highlands to the Pillars of Hercules and the China shore of the Pacific." Noticing his son's bewilderment, he asked. "What subjects you are studying?"

"Besides arts and sciences, Your Majesty, I have become skilled in archery and riding." Prince Salim responded precociously.

"Your sister has learned much more than that, my prudent lord." Akbar laughed. "Khanam has been reading to me from the books on astronomy, and she can write verses more sublime than your great-aunt, Gulbadan Begum, or your—" His attention was diverted by the slow approach of Aziz Koka, accompanied by Bahlul and Abdur Rahim.

"Your Majesty." Aziz Koka fell into a lengthy kornish before the emperor.

"Your disobedience to my Farman concerning the branding of horses? What made you rebel against the emperor?" Akbar's look was both harsh and searching.

"I beg a thousand pardons for this folly of mine, Your Majesty." Aziz Koka murmured with implicit misery. His eyes were lowered and his head bowed.

"Pardon for follies unpardonable." Akbar murmured back. "For this folly, my brother, you would wear chains of gold inside the cell of your ignominy."

"The wretched me, Your Majesty, crushed by misfortunes all." Aziz Koka muttered, without lifting his eyes.

"The most wretched of all, indeed! If you are crushed by misfortunes, and abandoned by God as well, my rebel brother." Akbar demurred profoundly.

"Tragedies after tragedies." Aziz Koka sighed.

"If tragedies do not destroy you, Aziz, then you may see the eyes of fortunes smiling upon you from under the heap of misfortunes." Akbar's gaze alone was intense and searching. "Begone, brother! The measure of your imprisonment would be discussed later." He dismissed him, turning his full attention to his son.

Bahlul and Abdur Rahim were quick to escort the wretched prisoner back to his gilded cell of a palace.

"Now, my noble prince, Qutbuddin Khan would be reinstated as your teacher, so that you can learn prose and poetry, and verses in praise of God. Abdur Rahim has been lax in his teaching, I presume." Akbar smiled at prince Salim.

"Abdur Rahim has taught me to read and recite a few verses from the Quran, Your Majesty. *A pillar of moral precepts*, he always says, though I don't quite know what he means by that." Prince Salim's eyes were now gathering mirth and confusion.

"Morality is the luxury of the rich, Shaikhu Baba." Akbar laughed suddenly. "The rich, with eloquent words, taint the purity of the word, *morals.* Holding such corrupted form of morality dear to their hearts, and concealing the fruits of their immorality with their lying and deceiving tongues. Oh, the conceit and hypocrisy of the—" His vehemence was truncated with a realization that his son was too young for such profundities. "You need the experience of years and time to understand these things, Shaikhu Baba. Till then, might as well enjoy the purity and innocence of your youth." His gaze was greeting Abul Fazl, who was approaching gracefully.

"Your Majesty." Abul Fazl bowed low. "Prince Sulaiman Mirza has reached the gates of Fathehpur Sikri, Your Majesty. As instructed, I bring the good tidings of his regal approach to you, Your Majesty." His smile was but a sliver of warmth and devotion.

"You are always the messenger of good tidings, my revered scholar." Akbar beamed graciously. "And is he being received royally, throughout this journey?"

"How can it be otherwise, Your Majesty!" Abul Fazl began with a low comment, his expression both subtle and fervent. "From Mathura to Fatehpur Sikri, the streets are paved with gold and jewels, it seems. He is being entertained at each step with music and refreshments, with fruits and viands, and with wines cooled in snows from the very bosom of the Himalayas. Cradled in such luxuries, the aged Prince is in a perpetual daze, watching and admiring the sea of opulence before him with speechless awe. Any farther orders concerning his reception at the palace, Your Majesty?"

"You are forgetting the gold-broidered stalls, my good friend! And the circus beasts, and cheetahs with gold collars!" Akbar opined aloud, as if for the sole delight of Abul Fazl. "My lovely wives reminded me about the cheetahs with gold collars, and I can't wait to see these proud and chivalrous beasts in their gilded cages." He continued fervently. "And as to further orders? Are the emperor's caparisoned and bedizened horses ready to take us to the heart of Fatehpur Sikri?"

"Yes, Your Majesty. All the nobles and courtiers are waiting for your august presence to commence the grand journey to greet prince Sulaiman." Abul Fazl smiled.

"Come, Shaikhu Baba." Akbar turned to prince Salim, after bestowing a fond smile on Abul Fazl. "One flash of this experience would lend you much learning than the years of tutoring. Though the object of your tutoring is in my head, this very moment! You would meet Qutubuddin Khan once again, and be installed as his student in courtly fashion. You would also see the royal cavalcade of Moghul splendor in honor of prince Sulaiman's reception. Later, you would be presented to the Prince, along with your sister and brothers at the Ibadat Khana before we commence our weekly discussions." He turned, beckoning prince Salim and Abul Fazl to follow.

"Do not walk behind the emperor, but beside him, this blessed day." Akbar commanded over his shoulders.

Akbar had also commanded Birbal to ride with him along with his young prince and favored scholar. His gaze was sweeping past this entourage toward the lilac-tinted blooms of saffron. He had imported the bulbs of these plants from Kashmir.

"Which flower is the best flower of all?" Akbar asked abruptly. "Shaikhu Baba, what is your response to the emperor's caprice?"

"Rose, Your Majesty. I like the scent of roses." Prince Salim responded.

"Abul Fazl, can you add flavor to the noncommittal response of my son?" Akbar shot this query at his friend, the challenge in his eyes bright and searching.

"Rat-Ki-Rani, Your Majesty, spilling perfume in the night, the scent of purity concealed in its silken petals." Was Abul Fazl's quick response!

"Sweet perfumes are not the best of the reasons to qualify flowers as the very best." Akbar laughed, turning his gaze to Birbal. "My wise poet, can you extract wisdom out of these perfumed flowers already named, and name yet the very best?"

"Your Majesty, I know only of one!" Birbal's eyes were spilling sunshine. "And that flower is the one, from which the whole world's clothing is made."

"You confound the reason of the emperor with such wisdom, my wise poet that the emperor's preference over the flowers flies away like the cotton-clouds." Akbar laughed again. "How the puffed silence of the cotton blooms derides the beauty of all flowers, and weaves its spools of wisdom to clothe the universe! Saffron, by the virtue of its sole beauty, had captivated my thoughts, in naming it the best of the flowers."

Just outside the palace gates, the lovely gardens still in view, the royal procession was halted for a few minutes to receive Qutubuddin Khan as the mentor of prince Salim. After the ceremony, several caskets full of pearls were emptied in abundance of showers over the head of prince Salim as he rode back toward the palace, attended by courtiers.

Now, Abul Fazl was the only one riding beside the emperor. The time was swift in its flight, and the royal procession was already nearing the road leading toward the gates of Fathehpur Sikri. Akbar's gaze was reaching over to the Jami Masjid, its white minarets splashed with gold, and gleaming under the sun like an artist's dream.

A handiwork of man and God, Akbar's gaze was reaching up to the gateway named Buland Darwaza. His thoughts were reciting the gold inscription on its façade which he himself had had inscribed.

Jesus son of Mary, on whom be peace, said: This world is a bridge, pass over it, but built no house upon it. Who hopes for an hour, hopes for eternity. The world is an hour. Spend it in prayer, for the rest is unseen.

Suddenly, the light and warmth in sunshine was shut off from Akbar's sight. His joy in life was carving its way into the black hole of silence, where the flames of pain were the only light kindling the gulf of separation from his Beloved.

Wisdom I embrace, the noble queen in my soul. And the glorious knowledge escapes me inside the mire of my love boundless.

"What is a thought, Abul? So illusive that one cannot hold on to it, but for a moment?" Was Akbar's another abrupt inquiry.

"Thought is a seed of the spirit, Your Majesty. It is the flower of the soul and fruit of the body." Abul Fazl responded poetically. "It may seem illusive, but it is lodged in one's body and spirit, creating and recreating its cycle of birth and death."

"Ah, each thought a spirit! A soul and body of the mind!" Akbar exclaimed. "So is mind, the seed, the kernel, and the fruit, ploughing the sun-baked field of knowledge to reap wisdom and understanding. God is my witness, how I keep foundering amidst the diversity of creeds in this land of Hind, in search of one absolute truth. Tell me, my wise Muse, why is one branded with heresy in worshipping one's God against the ones worshipping their God or gods in this land of diverse faiths?"

"Because people make gods of men, Your Majesty. While the same man-made gods fly to God for mercy and understanding!" Abul Fazl responded cheerfully.

"Then one must not be communing truthfully with one's God, or not heeding the commandments of the One Whom one worships." Akbar pondered aloud. "How the emperor keeps warring with gods in the heavens, while the wars on earth can't afford him a moment of sane contemplation! Bengal is conquered now! A brief interval of peace, I suppose. Daud, though deceitful and conspiring, was a brave soldier, I must admit."

"Brave and despotic, Your Majesty." Abul Fazl murmured reminiscently. "Much like his Bengali ancestors, Daud was class conscious and caste conscious, ruling with the rod of zeal. Suppressing all, the privileged and the underprivileged to gain power at the expense of his greed and riches! Bengalis, even under the sovereign rule of King Sulaiman were greedy and avaricious. Most of those former kings were assassinated by their servants, whom they had shackled in chains of inferiority. With Daud dead, now Bengalis would be ruled with justice by the Moghuls. People are already singing on the streets of Bengal, *From Daud's hand passed Sulaiman's land.*"

"Death, inevitable as it is, leaves behind regret and sorrow for the living. As if pouring out its sadness of life ill-spent or well-spent onto the living, who are also encumbered with the sadness of their own. I hope, the dead take along with them some sort of peace. Peace which is missing in this life!" Akbar reminisced profoundly. "Munim Khan, I regret his unfortunate death. In my thoughts, he still remains as my devoted vizier. Though lacking good judgment, at times, he served me well."

"He served his fate well, too, Your Majesty, and succumbed to the dictates of his unkind will." Abul Fazl commented. "Had he heeded your advice, Your Majesty! Tending his wounds at home, not flying off to the battlefield of Tandah, he might have saved his life, by not tempting the fates which show no mercy."

"Fates can't be averted, even with prayers and penance, the sages of the East tell us." Akbar began as if reciting songs of the minstrels. "And I hope, fates are kind to Baduani in Gogandah. Remember, Abul, when I was sending Man Singh to Gogandah, how Baduani had pleaded to join this expedition. I can't help recalling his words: *I wish to dye my black beard and mustachios in blood of the enemy through loyalty to Your Majesty.* What skill in flattery, but I had consented just to test his mettle on the battlefield. How the bigoted ulemas of my empire withstand the rigors of wars, I have yet to discover? I would rather that Baduani was here, fighting with his pen, working on my book, Muntakhabut Tawarikh, than conquering kingdoms for me."

"He squirms under the burden of this task, Your Majesty, and says, that in obedience to your command in writing this book, he has been sorely afflicted. This book, he says, and these are his exact words, *a constant sorrow to his faith.* No wonder, he wanted to flee the dictates of his pen, Your Majesty! Last reports from Gogandah are quite favorable and interesting. All the imperial forces under the commands of Man Singh, Asaf Khan and Baduani, have gathered at the pass of Haldighat. And Baduani is often heard reciting the line of Maulana Sheri, *A Hindu strikes, but the sword is Islam's.*"

"A whole empire of stupidity reigns in Baduani's head." Akbar exclaimed with a sudden burst of mirth. "And as to his sorrow and obedience to my command in writing this book, he will remain an unhappy wretch for a long, long time to come. Happy are the ones who rejoice in sorrow! And against the poverty of their riches and fortunes, they possess all the treasures of the worlds past and the worlds to come. I should have sent him to Gujrat to fight the wrath of God—in famine and epidemic, than to carry the wrath of the emperor against the Aravalis in Gogandah. My intuition, rather the voice of my psyche, is telling me, that the battle at Haldighat has already been won. And that our troops would be returning to Fatehpur Sikri, soon! Perhaps, this very evening! Before we gather at Ibadat Khana, we would be holding laurels of victory over our heads. Have ample provisions been made for the victims of famine and epidemic in Gujrat?"

"Yes, Your Majesty." Abul Fazl responded promptly. "Food supplies are being sent in abundance, along with the large supply of medicines. Thousands of Moghul soldiers are already there, clearing the city from the ravages of wars."

"Order the construction of food houses, Abul, where hot meals could be served to all deserving victims. No one should go hungry in this land of plenty." Akbar commanded, spurring his horse.

"Yes, Your Majesty." Was Abul Fazl's obedient response!

"I want to set a record office, Abul, to take the census of the whole empire." Akbar's tone was soft and contemplative. "The officials appointed for this task would identify each inhabitant by status and occupation, from village to village, from the northern and central borders to the south and east. To insure the property of the people as a whole, all would be employed in trade or occupation, whatever their skills suggest. No one who is able to work would be permitted to stay home. And this would be the motto of the ones selected for this giant task of census under the command of able officers." He reined his horse under the grove of elms and poplars.

Seated astride their Arabian steeds, both the emperor and the scholar were watching the procession of the elephants. The trumpets were sounding their welcoming songs, and announcing the approach of Sulaiman Mirza.

"And what are people saying behind the emperor's back? Concerning his efforts to create a semblance of peace and unity with all creeds, faiths and beliefs?" Akbar was challenging Abul Fazl in a friendly combat of words.

"*The emperor has turned heathen*, they whisper." Abul Fazl laughed.

"Those insufferable bigots!" Akbar exclaimed merrily. "If I am the heathen, they are the devils incarnate."

"Wait, till the padres from Goa join us, Your Majesty. Then those insufferable fools would invent charges of heresy to soil the very name of Islam." Abul Fazl quipped.

"Those foul heretics themselves would roast in the fires of their zeal and calumnious lies. For the emperor's true faith in Islam remains pure and unblemished." A glint of mischief in Akbar's gaze was lending his bronzed features a boyish look. "When padres visit us, Abul, we could kindle the zeal of our ulemas by adopting foreign customs to our clime and taste. And all my scholars would become pilgrims, fleeing to the holy land for sanity and refuge. Oh, the holy land, that reminds me, Abul, that I wish to make generous contributions for hajj. Remind me when I get back to my palace. I would order twelve thousand robes to be bestowed on the pilgrims for this year's pilgrimage to Mecca. From the royal treasury, six lakh in rupees and caskets of gold and jewels are to be reserved for the expenses of the pilgrims." His gaze was welcoming the procession. "That's Bulsandar, my favorite elephant, chosen signally for Sulaiman Mirza."

Sulaiman Mirza was being helped by the royal guards from his gilded howdah. He was approaching closer to the emperor. His hands were poised in an act of kornish. But they were snatched by the emperor in one gracious welcome, and he was locked into the heartwarming embrace of his nephew.

"Leave all ceremony aside, dear uncle, and feel welcome in Hind." Akbar stood facing him. "Was your journey pleasant and comfortable, dear uncle?"

"How could it have been otherwise, Your Majesty, when you have paved the streets of Hind with gold and jewels to welcome an old, foolish exile!" Sulaiman Mirza breathed happily. Love and devotion brimming in his eyes in a flood of sunshine!

"Made to look foolish by the guiles of my half-brother and of your son-in-law, I presume." Akbar murmured kindly. "But the light of love in your eyes speaks volumes of wisdom, dear uncle. Would you like to continue your journey to my palace in your howdah, or would you prefer to ride a handsome steed?"

"I am not that old as to decline the offer of a handsome steed, Your Majesty. I would feel honored to ride beside the emperor." Sulaiman Mirza sang beamishly.

"The honor is all mine dear uncle, entirely mine." Akbar smiled, commanding his guards to fetch the best of the Arabian steeds.

A white horse decked with gold and velvet trappings was brought before the prince with all due ceremony. And Sulaiman Mirza was quick to leap on its bright saddle with the alacrity of a youth. His gold turban stitched with carnelians was accentuating the coppery glow in his eyes, as he claimed his place beside the emperor.

"Were you fed and entertained royally on your journey from Agra to here, my young uncle?" Akbar could not help but tease his old uncle.

"Much too sumptuously, Your Majesty, with wines rare and viands delectable. The entertainments, well, they were delicious too, as appetizing as dream-realities." Sulaiman Mirza quipped. "I fear though, Your Majesty that I have disturbed the order of your luncheon and dinner by arriving at such an inappropriate hour." He apologized!

"The emperor eats but once a day, with no appointed hour for this one and only meal." Akbar commented, commanding both his uncle and Abul Fazl to ride beside him on their journey back to the palace. "Most of the people live for breakfast, lunch and dinner, and the rest few of us are still learning what we are living for?"

The late evening with its coppery haze was greeting dark shadows, as Akbar sat presiding over the theological discussions in his Ibadat Khana. As predicted by the emperor, Man Singh and Baduani had returned from Gogandah, wearing the laurels of victory over their shoulders. Princess Khanam, prince Salim, prince Murad and prince Daniyal were brought before Sulaiman Mirza with all due courtesy, and introduced to their grand-uncle with much pomp and ceremony. Then they were escorted back to the palace with gifts and blessings from Sulaiman Mirza. Princess Khanam had received a Badakhshani doll. Akbar was much impressed by this gift to his daughter than by the gifts of gold and jade daggers for his three sons.

Under a canopy of gold, Akbar was seated on an estrade lined with velvets and brocades. He was wearing purple robes and a large amethyst in his silk turban. Sulaiman Mirza was seated next to the emperor, so were the nine jewels of the Moghul court. From where the emperor sat, he could see the four halls of Ibadat Khana, his senses absorbing arguments from theological discussions.

The emperor had learned about the details of victory at Haldighat during his one meal of the day, which he had shared with Man Singh and Abul Fazl. Now as he sat with his set of naurattan, he had summoned Baduani to his presence.

"Your Majesty, may I offer you a gift, which came into my possession, right out of the field of victory?" Baduani implored, his eyes shining with pride.

"Ah, the gift from my spiritual scholar who holds victories sacred in his head, if not the mounds of spiritual truths!" Akbar laughed. "Yet, the emperor is tempted to receive your gift, Baduani. How unfortunate, our love for temporal things renders us sightless, so that we can't view the spiritual truths which lie hidden inside the mantle of our shame. But the emperor digresses. What is your gift, my happy scholar?"

"An elephant from the booty of war, Your Majesty. I myself captured it."
Baduani announced proudly.

"An elephant!" Akbar's interest was kindled. "Where did you capture it?"

"The imperial mahout captured it." Man Singh whispered under his breath.

"Actually, I saved the life of this elephant from a quagmire near the city of
Amber, Your Majesty." Baduani corrected himself after noticing Man Singh's
inaudible whispering. "Your imperial mahout captured this elephant at the battle
of Haldighat, when Rana's mahout was injured by an arrow. But he had entrusted this elephant to me, so that I could present it to you, Your Majesty. I had
taken good care of it throughout my journey, till I was away ten miles from Amber, when it fell into a quagmire. In my desperation, I sought the help of the villagers. They sent a few strong men who dug channels around the elephant, and
drained buckets full of water, and the elephant got out unharmed. You can't
imagine my sense of joy and relief, Your Majesty, when I saw this miracle of an
escape from that deep quagmire. Ram Prasad named this elephant after his
name, Your Majesty, the same elephant you wanted for yourself, but the Rana
always managed not to part with it. Now this elephant is my gift to you, Your
Majesty."

"That elephant has the wisdom of a sage!" Akbar exclaimed happily. "I
name that elephant Pir Prasad." He took a handful of gold coins from his coffer
and offered them to Baduani. "For your pains and valor—and more!" He turned
to Birbal. "Bestow two nakhudi shawls on my valorous knight, Birbal." His attention was returned to Baduani. "These shawls are from our royal factory,
Baduani. Maybe, the emperor's own hands have tied a few knots on these fine
gifts." Akbar laughed.

"Thank You, Your Majesty, thank You." Baduani bowed thrice, bereft of
speech.

"Tell His Majesty of your valorous deeds, Baduani, before others corrupt
your acts of valor with their malicious tongues." Man Singh teased.

"Oh, the deeds of a fakir, Your Majesty, your humble servant." Baduani's
tongue was suddenly snapped to speech. "I was fighting in the advance when I
asked Asaf Khan, what sign is there whereby we may discern between friendly
and hostile Rajputs. He said: Don't ask. *Shoot your arrow. Come what may,
Islam will be benefited, whichever side is killed.* So I shot arrows after arrows,
and not a single one missed the enemy. The heart is a true witness, I said, repeating to myself that the proof of a true lover is in his sleeve, as the Persian adage
goes. Why I repeated that, Your Majesty, I don't know, but I knew the victory
was ours."

"Victory." Akbar murmured. "Yet the vanquished escaped. I want Ram
Prasad to be captured alive, so that I can conquer deceit in his mind and subjugate it to my will."

"In despair he fled, Your Majesty, and this despair would be the death of his
soul, so that he could be brought before you alive." Was Baduani's histrionic
comment.

"Confusion—not despair, is the death of the soul." Akbar claimed his wine goblet, his gaze still fixed to Baduani.

"Despair and confusion are Ram Prasad's birthright, Your Majesty. He deems himself invulnerable though, believing his life to be everlasting, and denying the presence of death in the very face of misfortunes." Baduani murmured under the spell of zeal.

"Acceptance of life everlasting is more terrifying than the denial of death!" Was Akbar's Sufic response! "Anyone who escapes death in war or peace, gains *hope* as victory in this short journey of life. You have returned victorious, my scholar-general, and the emperor is glad to welcome you back."

"There appeared a victory from God, Your Majesty, that's what everyone said in Gogandah." Baduani began exigently before he could be dismissed. "I prayed to God to have mercy on all believing men and women, to help us all who helped the religion of Prophet Muhammad, and to abandon all who abandoned the religion of our Prophet."

"Great mystery that such prayers are granted audience, for which God be praised." Akbar murmured to himself. "Enough of wars and victories, my friend! Now your great task begins right here, in Fatehpur Sikri. You are to translate Mahabharata."

"An unhappy task, Your Majesty! To touch the forbidden—" This protest died on Baduani's lips, as he noticed the daggers of dismissal in the emperor's eyes. "But if such be my fate, Your Majesty, I submit to your royal wishes." He retraced his steps.

"You can probably guess, dear uncle, how the emperor has to contend with all the bigots in his court." Akbar whispered to Sulaiman Mirza.

"Your grandfather, Your Majesty, had to contend with the bigots all his life, but he remained steadfast in kindness and compassion." Sulaiman Mirza smiled. "Pure thoughts are the most difficult to live with, your grandfather used to tell me. Though I never understood what he meant by that, and never dared ask."

"Pure thoughts can turn to wicked lies, if mixed with zeal. Probably, that's what he meant, if I may discern the thoughts of my grandfather." Akbar murmured. "How can one banish zeal from the tongue of learning, which expounds and confounds?"

"Zeal can only be expelled with the rod of vengeance, Your Majesty." Sulaiman Mirza began with the garnered zeal of his own. "For kings and emperors are the vicergents of God, and are sanctioned to condemn bigotry, before it explodes into the living hell of perdition."

"Vengeance is God's alone, my wise uncle, and there is much wisdom in the old scriptures." Akbar's gaze was sad and troubled. "Revenge is a quality not consonant with my disposition, I always tell my viziers and courtiers." His gaze strayed toward Man Singh. "Remember, Man Singh, how I forgave Daud amidst his several bouts of rebellions. And even during his last act of rebellion, I wanted not war, but his obedience. Yes, his obedience, so that he could have the chance to come, and to lay his head at my feet in total submission to my sovereignty. His head did offer submission though, but unfortunately, after it was cut off from his shoulders." He was becoming aware of loud arguments in the lower halls. "How do you judge the ulemas in our court, Man Singh?"

"They are rich in their faith, Your Majesty, but poor in understanding the faith of others, especially, if the others are born in poverty." Man Singh demurred aloud.

"Ah, my wise soldier and scholar!" Akbar breathed kindly, his gaze warm and profound. "Rich is he in faith, who deems not poor lowly, but worthy of esteem and respect. For, poor suffer only the poverty of the riches, living in the richness of their own, sufferings for a better life to come. They despise not wealth, but stealth! And many rich have gained their riches through the labor of deceit and flattery, not through the sweat of their brows. They have cultivated brambles in the path of honest men, and have gathered fruits of honesty from the poor, as their noble rewards. Knowing, yet knowing not that these are the bitter, bitter fruits of corruption, which have the power to poison their souls, if not actually stab their hearts with the splinters of guilt and anguish. But the emperor digresses, my *Farzand*." He paused. Becoming aware that he had called him, Farzand, meaning, imperial son, even before he had bestowed this title on him. "Yes, my Farzand. I bestow this title of Farzand upon you for your valor in Gogandah. A true valor which has become rarity in this world of greed and malevolence!"

"Thank you, Your Majesty. I am greatly honored." Man Singh bowed his head.

"Man Singh, didn't you say to Rana Prasad, *If I do not humble your pride, my name is not Man Singh*?" Akbar reminisced aloud. "And just for my uncle's amusement, tell Sulaiman Mirza, how Rana Prasad responded to your challenge?"

"Your Majesty." Man Singh protested happily. "He told me, prince Sulaiman, that when I return to humble his pride, I should bring with me my phupha, meaning uncle, the emperor himself."

Sulaiman Mirza was caught into a fit of uncontrollable mirth. But his mirth was drowned amidst the hum of noise from the lower halls.

"No one should follow you in prayer, Nabi. You are undutiful to your father, and you suffer from hemorrhoids—" Mulla Abdullah was saying.

"You are a fool and a heretic." Abdunnabi was waving his fist before Abdullah.

"That bastard, that hellish dog—" Baduani was shouting in the farthest end of the south hall. "Sufism is vain and void of all sophy and Shiism is a vile sect—"

"Man does not live by breath alone, by him in whom is the power of breath—" Debi was quoting from the Upanishads.

"He truly knows Brahman who knows him beyond knowledge. He, who thinks that he knows, knows not. The ignorant think that Brahman is known, but the wise know him to be beyond knowledge—" Puru too was spilling pearls of wisdom from the Upanishads.

"You shall not take the name of the Lord your God in vain—" Anthony Vaz was quoting from the Bible.

"Faizi, write down the names of all these ill-bred wretches, who are rude and vociferous. So that I may begin the process of expelling them from my Ibadat Khana!" Akbar commanded.

"Your Majesty." Faizi leaped to his feet and bowed his head. "If I did that, Your Majesty, all would be proclaimed guilty. And no man in these halls would remain with us, all retiring to the abode of unlearning in their luxurious homes."

"Guilty! All! Yes!" Akbar swept his gaze from hall to hall. "Silence, you all!" He thundered. "This is not a den of bigotry, but a house of worship."

Suddenly, all arguments were truncated. Akbar's anger was abated as quickly as it had flared. His eyes were challenging all to test their arguments.

"Discipline, not disorder, is the law in this house of worship. You may begin when you feel certain that you can maintain courtesy and propriety in your arguments, without zeal and without rancor." Akbar's eyes were bright with a subtle challenge.

"Our God is Allah, Your Majesty." Mukhdum-ul-Mulk broke the silence, zeal still shining in his eyes. "We worship Him alone. How can we revere and worship other gods when we believe in one God alone? Now, are we to worship Buddha, Krishna, and Jesus—though we believe Jesus to be the apostle of God?"

"Each person according to his condition gives the Supreme Being a name, but in reality, to name the unknowable is vain." Akbar responded with Sufic restraint. "A reverence to worship the Creator comes from faith divine, but to respect the created apostles of God in all creeds, faiths and religions, is wisdom sublime. This wisdom is bestowed on very few of us, who strive to understand that God speaks in all tongues to all people, teaching all love and peace, not hatred and dissention."

"Vile speech does not become the servants of God, Your Majesty." Dastur Mahyarji commented. "Especially, when they are the servants of a god-fearing master?"

"No man is a servant to one another, my good priest, if he can make his heart the master of his rage and ignorance." Akbar looked at the Parsee priest kindly. "The ones who use vile speech degrade their souls. Their souls are corrupted, especially, the souls of the zealous. And they become deaf to the voice in their souls, which hungers for spiritual silence, not for empty words cast into the vessel of contention."

"All slanderers of Islam ought to be punished, Your Majesty! They revile our Prophet, may peace be upon him." Baduani ventured forth, his eyes burning.

"The emperor couldn't help but catch your slanderous remarks about Sufism and Shiism just a few minutes ago, my mentor of faith." Akbar smiled. "But as a master of free speech, I condone such baseless comments. As for your satisfaction, concerning the slandering! The prophets themselves suffered in silence, when persecuted, and they blessed those who reviled them. Yet to me, it seems, this particular evening that all the unblessed heathens have gathered here in my

Ibadat Khana, reviled by their gods, and persecuting all who believe." He paused, his eyes shining with Sufic light. "Prophets, yes, in persecution, they were not forsaken by God though. Cast down by men, yes, but not destroyed, and always remembered by God." He contemplated aloud.

"For the kingdom of God is not in word, but in power, Your Majesty." Peter Dias sang under some spell of inspiration.

"The Kingdom of God is *word* and *power*." Akbar flashed him a searching look. "Through God's word all faithful live, and through His Power all believers shudder."

"Then by the power of God, Your Majesty, that rich, insolent Brahman who abused the Prophet, should be justly punished, as I requested before." Abdunnabi couldn't contain his bitterness which he hoarded in his heart against the Hindus.

"And has God informed you, Nabi, about the manner of His just punishments?" Akbar challenged him with a piercing gaze, which rendered him speechless.

"That Brahman should be paraded on the back of a donkey, and fined heavily." Baduani vented his zeal, while the emperor's attention was still fixed to Abdunnabi.

"No, he deserves death." Abdunnabi breathed hoarsely.

"And who is to act as a judge over this harsh punishment?" Akbar asked.

"Death is always the just punishment in Nabi's realm of justice, Your Majesty." Fath Ullah began reluctantly. "He wishes death for Khan Sarwani whom he suspects, and that is just a slight suspicion, Your Majesty, that he used words of blasphemy against the Prophet. And he wants to sentence Mir Habsh to death, just because he is a Shia."

"Though this Brahman, without suspicion, is a real offender, Your Majesty, and he must die under the law of Islam. Allah commands us to punish those who blaspheme." Baduani interceded quickly in favor of Abdunnabi.

"By your unruly contentions, you all make God the author of confusion." Akbar pronounced with a dint of impatience. "God teaches mercy in different tongues, to all faiths, to all beliefs. The authority to kill should be his who can give life, and he who performs this duty at the command of right judgment, does so with reference to God. God, who is All Merciful! Human life is too sacred to be forfeited without the greatest of care and attention. Extreme caution must be exercised before putting anyone to death, and destroying what is an edifice of God." His gaze was fixed to Baduani. "And God, my great theologian, does not prescribe an unjust death under the banner of Islam. You claim your descent from Abu Hanifa, and according to the Hanifa school, the cursing of the Prophet by the unbelievers, who have submitted to Islamic law, does not absolve Muslims from their duty to protect the infidels, as you deem all those whose God is not Allah. Tell me, Baduani, if you profess to know the Hanifi principle, which states: *if there be ninety-nine traditions prescribing the death sentence for an offense, but one stating that the accused be set free,* which one the learned theologians should prefer?"

It was Baduani's turn to be speechless now. Like Abdunnabi, he could summon no arguments to refute the wisdom of the emperor. Akbar turned his attention to Sulaiman Mirza, who was absorbing all discussions with the intensity of an old seer.

"Tell me, my wise uncle, what should the emperor do with all the wrangling scholars and theologians in his court?" Akbar laughed suddenly.

"Make them perform their five daily prayers, in one sitting, right here in this Ibadat Khana, Your Majesty. Then, they would have no time to question the faiths of the others." Sulaiman Mirza's quick response was followed by his somber mirth.

"And send the Brahmans and the Buddhists to their temples and monasteries, and the priests to their gilded churches." Akbar flashed his uncle a quizzical look. "All these men professing faith, yet wavering in their belief, their prayers would dissolve like waves into the sea. Though the sea-waves turn and toss always, trying to reach the profound depths in some divine struggle between calm and chaos. Besides, the object of outward worship which these men call a new divine institute is for the awakening of the slumberers. Otherwise, the praise of God comes from the heart, not from the body."

Akbar's gaze was lured toward Saiyid Ali who was sketching the scene of discussions in this Ibadat Khana. Abdus Samad and Daswanth beside him were adding finishing touches to the silk paintings.

"A painter comes close to God by the sheer inspiration of his art." Akbar commented. "For a painter in sketching that life, and in devising its limbs, one after the other, must come to feel that he cannot bestow individuality upon his work, and is thus forced to think of God, the giver of life, and will thus increase in knowledge."

"Yet, many argue, Your Majesty, that the Quran forbids depicting any living being." Sulaiman Mirza murmured low.

"The shameless hucksters of faith, that's what these bigots are, distorting the meaning of each holy word in the Quran!" Akbar began with a great animation. "There is no such injunction in the Quran, you know that, dear uncle, don't you?" He asked.

"I have read the whole Quran over a hundred times, Your Majesty, and I couldn't find any. Mullahs are skilled in this art of misinterpretation, as long as the Holy Quran is in their hands to be interpreted." Sulaiman Mirza murmured again.

"Talking of mullahs, dear uncle, let me expose you to the flavors of matrimonial discussions concerning mutah marriages." Akbar smiled. "The emperor has several wives, as you have seen. But some of my ulemas argue that my marriages beyond the four prescribed, are illegal marriages. I don't agree with them, of course, and by invoking their discussions, I aim to succeed." His gaze was landing on Abdunnabi. "Come forward, Nabi, and tell the ulemas what you told the emperor. That one might have nine or even eighteen wives, and that all these wedlocks are considered to be legal."

"Your Majesty." Abdunnabi lumbered forward, stammering some apologies. "I—I was wrong Your Majesty. I support the view of the other Sunni ulemas that Muslim law permits only four wives at a time, and the others are considered illegal."

"Which one is more dangerous? Zeal, or conceit, I have yet to decide!" Akbar laughed. "But one of those would be your downfall, Nabi." He turned his gaze to Baduani. "Let us hear your opinion about the mutah marriages?"

"Mutah is a marriage for an agreed period, Your Majesty, for which the wife receives consideration." Baduani began with the patience of a suffered saint. "But in your case, Your Majesty, that's not the case. Your marriages are a life-long commitment, so considered illegal, I am afraid."

"So, by such standards as our little minds could devise, you jurists of the Islamic law, are ready to pronounce the marriages of Prophet Muhammed illegal." The play of mockery in Akbar's eyes was gathering the light of derision.

"God have mercy on me, Your Majesty. I would never be caught guilty of propounding such heresy!" Was Abdunnabi's flustered response!

"How does Shia doctrine judge the emperor's marriages?" Akbar, condoning Baduani's confusion, turned his attention to Fath Gilani from Gilan.

"Pardon me, Your Majesty, but in the eyes of the orthodox Shias, your marriages stand illegal." Fath Gilani professed proudly.

"In the eyes of one man." Akbar murmured to himself, questioning in turn, Mulla Muhammed of Yezd. "How do the Shias of Yezd dwell upon this matter, Muhammed? Do they think that the emperor is living in sin?"

"God forbid, Your Majesty." Mulla Muhammed protested. "But they do believe that only four wives are permitted to both Shias and Sunnis."

"Sharif of Amul, state your opinion." Akbar commanded the last Shia in this trio. "I am settled in my convictions, Your Majesty. My opinion, too, coincides with the rest of the ulemas. I have as much faith in my convictions as in the heavens above." Sharif attempted to garnish his response with poetry, but failed.

"Heavens descend to earth, when our mortal sight affords us the privilege of such bliss!" Akbar opined aloud. "How can one find heavens in the sky, when to earthly pleasures one walks blind?" He smiled, his gaze resting on Husain Arab. "Come forward, Husain. Your very eyes speak reason and wisdom. A rarity in the jungle of confusion and ignorance! Since you belong to the Maliki sect whose doctrine both Shias and Sunnis respect, you may speak without constraint. Speak like a judge, and I myself would esteem your judgment. Let us end this dispute over mutah marriages with the seal of your wisdom." He rested his head against the velvety back of his chair.

"Your Majesty." Husain Arab bowed ceremoniously. "This contention over the mutah marriages has not dug deep into the pillars of knowledge. According to the common belief, even for the Shafis and the Hanafis, mutah is a legal marriage. Since most of your marriages, Your Majesty, are alliance marriages. Falling under the jurisdiction of mutah marriages, they are all legal under the law of Sharia."

"Wisdom is the arbiter, to cut all the tongues of contention!" Akbar exclaimed happily. "For your wisdom and for your knowledge, you would be showered with gold." He offered him gold coins from his coffer. "Rich jagirs would be bestowed upon you."

"Thank you, Your Majesty." Husain Arab beamed, balancing one gold muhr on the palm of his hand. "This is round like the silver rupee, Your Majesty, but has no inscription on it." He seemed fascinated by this piece of glittering gold on his palm.

"The emperor wishes that Allah-u-Akbar to be inscribed on all the gold muhrs and on all his royal seals." Akbar announced.

Allah-u-Akbar, the loud applause from all was filling the Ibadat Khana. But Hajji Ibrahim was scampering toward the throne with discontent written all over his face.

"Your Majesty, it is not wise to have the coins inscribed with such inscriptions." Was Hajji Ibrahim's feverish appeal.

"On what grounds does your wisdom stand so tall and rude?" Akbar asked.

"This inscription is ambiguous, Your Majesty." Haji Ibrahim murmured.

"In what way, my wise rebel?" Akbar queried intensely.

"Pardon me, Your Majesty, but the phrase Allah-u-Akbar, as you know, means, God is Great. But if you have it inscribed on the coins and the royal seals, it can also be interpreted as, Akbar is God. That means, you, Your Majesty." Hajji Ibrahim murmured.

"How could this pure intention of mine be misunderstood so atrociously?" Akbar exclaimed. "How can the emperor who feels weak and helpless before the throne of God, claim to assume divinity?" His eyes were catching the fire of anger and disbelief.

Haji Ibrahim was retracing his steps in a flurry of apologies. The emperor's eyes were settling on Abdus Samad.

"Abdus Samad, you would take charge over the mint factories in Fatehpur Sikri. Without delay, issue orders, that the gold muhrs and the royal seals are to be minted with the inscription, Allah-u-Akbar." Akbar's gaze was showering commands. "And any man, who dares distort the meaning of Allah-u-Akbar, would be trampled under the feet of my new elephant, Pir Prasad." He dismissed Abdus Samad with a wave of his arm.

"Your most obedient servant, Your Majesty." Abdus Samad murmured.

"Now, all you nobles and ulemas! You may resume your recriminating discussions, but without raising your fists before the faces of your peers. The emperor needs to confer with the nine jewels of his court without the din of loud arguments." Akbar turned his attention to his uncle, rather than conferring with his set of naurattan.

"There exists a bond between the Creator and the created, which cannot be expressed in words. Do you agree with the emperor on this point, dear uncle, or would you like to instruct him with the wisdom of your own?" Akbar asked, smiling sadly.

"And a bond between man and man, Your Majesty! If one is to live in harmony with the creatures of the Creator." Sulaiman Mirza smiled back.

"It is my duty, dear uncle, to be in good understanding with all men." Akbar murmured. "Yes, with all men. If they walk in the ways of God's will, interference with them would be reprehensible. And if otherwise, they are under the malady of ignorance, and deserve my compassion. But enough of my own thoughts and quest for knowledge! Now you will taste the wisdom of the nine jewels of my court, whom you have already met. Abul Fazl, I have named him pearl, his wisdom radiates the glow of Sufic light." He turned to Abul Fazl. "Tell my uncle, Abul, some tales of wisdom and antiquity. The tales, which have so often delighted the emperor in his quest for truth!"

"In truth, Your Majesty. You are the one, from whose wisdom I benefit the most." Abul Fazl responded, turning his attention to Sulaiman Mirza. "He is the emperor whom, on account of his wisdom, we call zufunun, prince Sulaiman, meaning the possessor of the sciences, and our guide on the path to religion. Although the kings and the emperors are the shadow of God on earth, emperor Akbar is the emanation of God's light. How can we call him a shadow, then?" He concluded most passionately.

"To be cradled in royal wisdom, in the company of a wise emperor, is a privilege most coveted, from which I have stayed banished all my life, Abul Fazl. With the exception when I was in the company of the emperor's grandfather, whom people still remember as the, First Great Moghul Emperor of Hind." Sulaiman Mirza intoned softly.

"Inside the kingdom of flatteries, there is no wisdom." Akbar laughed, his gaze mocking both Abul Fazl and Sulaiman Mirza. "All men are the shadow of God who deem falsehood improper. And I, a just monarch, pronounce falsehood as unpardonable. Ah, the emperor himself is resorting to self flattery." He paused momentarily. "Your flatteries are infectious, Abul. Delight us with your wisdom, or with a couplet or two."

"A quatrain, Your Majesty. I wrote just this morning." Abul Fazl began reciting.

"The dullard's eye to sterling merit dim
True ring of minted gold tells naught to him
Worth must from noble souls unbidden blaze
And from the moon her light, from Jupiter his rays."

"Divine, divine! Divine inspiration and poetry sublime!" Akbar sang happily. "You are striving to outshine your poet-brother." He was turning to his uncle once again. "His brother Faizi is emerald amongst the nine jewels of my court. He is fiery, yet smooth like green meadows in his poetry and eloquence. Faizi, are you going to delight my uncle with some exquisite verses of you own?"

"With all the discussions in theology, Your Majesty, my thoughts are sedition-bound." Faizi quipped. "I coin epigrams in my head, and then write verses." His eyes were reaching out to Sulaiman Mirza. "Prince Sulaiman, I only hope that you don't find my epigrams unwise and provocative. When all the ulemas in this court raise their fists, striking the very air dumb with their fervent cries, I can't help saying to myself. Come, let us turn toward the pulpit of light, and let us lay the foundation of a new Kabah with stones from Mount Sinai. Often, I have restrained myself from crying out loud. The wall of the Kabah is broken, and the basis of the qiblah is gone, let us build a faultless fortress on a new foundation." He concluded passionately.

"These epigrams ring true with the poetry of wisdom and of quiet contemplation, Faizi, and I feel fortunate in sharing your inspiring thoughts." Sulaiman Mirza commented with earnest delight.

"Birbal is another great poet in the set of my naurattan, dear uncle, who keeps his poetry inside the rivers of his thoughts alone." Akbar expounded wistfully. "He is my ruby, with the fire of poetry in his heart. With what arrows of wit, Birbal, you are going to entertain us this evening?" He asked.

"I am going to don a robe of poverty, Your Majesty, and become a mendicant." Birbal responded in all earnestness.

"How strange, Birbal! Why do you wish to live like a beggar?" Akbar asked.

"Because your royal menu of sinful dishes, day after day, from the imperial kitchens, Your Majesty, is making me bilious and bellicose." Quipped Birbal.

"Fast for a year then, Birbal! And then, you would be fit to glide through an eye of the needle." Akbar laughed, prompting mirth from the cluster of his nine jewels.

"Your Majesty, if I could stay as slim as Birbal, I would not decline any of the sumptuous dishes brought before me, and would devour all." Sulaiman Mirza commented amidst a volley of laughter from the others.

"My being slim is all due to my Sufic tendencies which I savor and practice, prince Sulaiman. They help me maintain balance in life." Birbal retorted mirthfully.

"What Sufic doctrines you have learned so far, Birbal?" Sulaiman Mirza asked.

"I know them all, prince Sulaiman." Birbal began with the eloquence of a scholar. "Sufism is not only a doctrine, but my temple and sanctuary. It blesses me with the knowledge of great mysteries. The words whispering to me like the unsung mantras. One mantra that I have learned by heart is that, all individuals of this world, however infinite their number and close their succession, behold only the one and the same truly-existent Being, present in all and identical in all."

"God is my beloved, and my soul striving to know the lover." Akbar eyes were accosting Fath Ullah. "My dear friend, you have been sitting here all evening, communing with the silence in death, it seems, remote and unmoved. Are we going to benefit from your inner wisdom tonight, a few words to delight us? Fath Ullah is my sapphire, dear uncle, and his heart is kindled with the flame of compassion."

"By invoking the name of death, Your Majesty, you have judged my thoughts right." Fath Ullah smiled. "My thoughts have been trooping down the valley of death in some mysterious surge. I was thinking Your Majesty, that from the death of a seed a plant is born, and from the death of a flower we receive the gift of fruit! Such beauty and power in death, that it creates life? It itself dying, giving birth to a new awakening. Stealing the fruit of resurrection from life and granting it the miracle of breath, in the everlasting cycle of birth and death. The mating of light and darkness, creating shadows, recreating truth, as illusive as the eternal embrace of day and night in the bosom of centuries. Time begotten out of the womb of timelessness, and the unbegotten hours searching for the union of time with God in the vacuity of silence and unreality—" He seemed lost inside the vacuums of his contemplations.

"What darkness, what desolation! But wisdom supreme in the valleys of death!" Akbar murmured to himself. "I must pick another jewel, who can offer us solace and laughter, in life." His gaze fell on Todar Mall. "My diamond, honed to the perfection of a sharp sword. A sword which can cut through multitudes with the indestructible power of its will and strength! You are my invincible general, Todar Mall, fighting death with the sword of life, where valor alone survives. You know more about life than any one of us who have fought but a few battles. Battlegrounds are schools for warring men, teaching them the worth of life, which barters not honor in exchange for riches. To what degree of wisdom you hold this life dear?"

"Thank you, Your Majesty. But my thoughts, lately, that is, have been about death." Todar Mall breathed reluctantly. "After the wars in Gujrat and Bengal, I have been thinking that death doesn't annihilate us, but life! Life has a terrible power of its own, devouring our body and soul piece by piece, till death appears as a blessing to comfort and to cement those pieces in some formless mass of understanding."

"Dark imponderables in the link of life with death, against the mountains of silence!" Akbar intoned thoughtfully. "In this sea of profundities, we are neglecting our honored guest, and that is you, my dear uncle." He smiled, his gaze shifting to Man Singh. "Man Singh, my opal of inner strength and knowledge. Do your thoughts also wander into the valleys of death, when you are fighting?"

"No, Your Majesty." Man Singh flashed his majestic smile. "I barely notice death on the battlefield, strange as it may seem. I see only victory and life. When I witness the submission of our foes, this is what I say to myself. In surrender, they are born anew, for they understand the destiny of the vanquished."

"And yet they surrender not at the commands of their wills." Akbar's eyes were lit up with a profound smile. "Self-surrender is victory, if they only knew, and self-immolation, the death of courage." His eyes were shooting inquiries at Bhagwan Das. "Bhagwan Das, my bright carnelian, share *your* warring thoughts with us?"

"No warring thoughts, Your Majesty." Bhagwan Das smiled, trying to shut off the surge of voices from the adjacent halls. "I suffer the need for love."

"For such a need, you would be rich in learning. For this need alone, lends both courage and action to attain the object of one's love. As you stand on the battlefield like a mountain of strength, your sparkling wit will never fail. The emperor must turn to his precious jade for understanding." Akbar's gaze was arresting Nizamuddin Ahmed. "Nizami, what are your thoughts on the love for God?" He asked abruptly.

"To attain such love, Your Majesty, one must practice the speech of ecstasy." Was Nizamuddin Ahmed's prompt response!

"Are you learning the art of such a speech, then?" Akbar shot another question.

"With the help of Sufic writings, I am trying to learn more than I can contain." Nizamuddin Ahmed replied enigmatically.

"And what are these writings teaching you, Nizami?" Akbar asked.

"That human life is often compared to a journey, Your Majesty, in which the various stages mark progressive steps in the knowledge of God, and the last is immersion in *all*, the soul of the universe." Nizamuddin Ahmed intoned softly.

"What mysterious impulses of the mind draw us toward the mysteries of the unknown?" Akbar's gaze was greeting Tansen. "Ah, my polished garnet, the beautiful gem of song and mystery! Tansen, would you sing for the emperor, and delight our honored guest with the divine music in your throat?"

"I am obedient to your wishes, Your Majesty, if that's what you command." Tansen's voice rose above the din of arguments. "But the hour seems unpropitious."

"Yes." Akbar could touch the tides of arguments with his eyes. "Their profane cries are tearing the night into the splinters of unholy discussions." He turned to Abul Fazl. "Can you make sense of their arguments, Abul?"

"Yes, Your Majesty, they are arguing about the circumcision age for the boys." Abul Fazl, with his keen sense of hearing, offered nonchalantly.

"It is such a remarkable thing that men should insist on the ceremony of circumcision, who are otherwise excused from the burdens of all other religious obligations." Akbar clapped his hands, announcing dismissal for this evening.

The sea of ulemas and scholars was draining out of Ibadat Khana, while Akbar linked his arm in his uncle's, proceeding down the throne.

"Our solitary discussions, concerning diverse creeds, are just about to commence between you and me, dear uncle." Akbar murmured.

"The hour is late, Your Majesty." Sulaiman Mirza protested. "I am old, and I need my sleep with as much ardor as a bridegroom, his bride."

"Life is the greatest gift of God, dear uncle. It were better that it should be spent in wakefulness." Akbar laughed. His heart was yearning for the nearness of Salima.

Such little lifetimes—deeply yearning, always!

9

Nauroz Celebrations

The coliseum, where Akbar's throne was set, was a silk city of entertainment and celebration. The emperor was celebrating his twin victories and the Persian New Year, which he had introduced in conformity with the solar calendar as opposed to the lunar calendar. The entire city of Fathehpur Sikri was one great pageant, displaying silk hangings and jeweled ornaments over the facades of the imperial buildings.

Akbar, this particular moment, was watching dancing camels in the center of the arena. These camels seemed drunk, their long necks and legs moving in graceful rhythm with the music. In the background, elephants too were dancing to the wild tunes of the tablas, their snouts the wands of magic and snake-dance. At the south side of the arena, just below the raised courtyard, a group of yogis were dancing and singing. Akbar seemed to be watching, but his thoughts were restless.

The emperor was expecting the arrival of Salima and of the other ladies on their journey back from Mecca, this very day of festivity and entertainment. The ladies had left Ajmer two days hence, after visiting the shrine of Muinaldin Chishti, one courier had informed the emperor this afternoon. Since then he had been waiting and thinking.

These New Year's celebrations! No, the emperor is celebrating the birth of his daughter? Yet, to be absolutely honest, these festivities are in honor for the homecoming of my queen. The queen of my heart—oh, my soul, my life, my beloved, my Salima.

The emperor was thinking about Salima, but his thoughts were entering the bower of his new brides of political alliances. He had married Sangita in the town of Buswara, while on his way to Fathehpur Sikri, after his hunting expedition to quell unrest in Gujrat. His second wife of political alliance was Bibi Shad, whom he had married immediately after his return to Fathehpur Sikri. The number of his wives was now grown to one dozen. Bibi Shad had blessed the emperor with a daughter, whom he had named, Aram Banu. Her second daughter was born recently whom Akbar had named, Shukrunnisa. He was happy to be the father of three sons and three daughters.

Akbar's thoughts were looking into the eyes of the war-strewn years, beholding prince Salim and prince Murad, both of whom had actively participated in wars against rebels. The chief rebels were Masum Khan of Bihar, and Baba Khan of Bengal. Jointly, they had laid siege over the fort of Tanda, succeeding in luring the Moghul governor, Muzzafar, out of his fortification, under the false pretext of a peace-treaty, and murdering him on the spot. Then they had read khutba in the name of Hakim Mirza, setting up a rival government and distributing titles and territories.

Akbar, after learning about the deceit and cruelty of these murderers, had sent large forces under the command of Todar Mall to chastise these rebels. At the same time, Aziz Koka was pardoned of his offense concerning the branding of the horses, and was sent to assist Todar Mall. Both the traitors were defeated, retiring to the vile abode of their viler deeds till earth could grant them impunity from flight and captivity. Muzaffar Khan, the ex-king of Gujrat, had re-established himself in the capital city of Ahmadabad, boasting of an independent government. Abdur Rahim was commanded to quell this rebellion, and the inveterate rebel overwhelmed by the might of the Moghuls, had fled without shame. After Abdur Rahim's victorious return to Fatehpur Sikri, Akbar had bestowed upon him the title of Khan Khanan—the prince of the princes.

The major rebellion, which had caused the emperor more heartache than concern, was by Hakim Mirza from Kabul, who had decided to invade Punjab. To chastise his step-brother, Akbar himself had marched from Fathehpur Sikri with a cavalry of fifty thousand, and five hundred elephants. Prince Salim, almost thirteen year old and prince Murad, twelve, had accompanied the emperor on this hunting expedition. Hakim Mirza entrenched in his camp at Lahore had contracted a hasty retreat, even before the arrival of the emperor and his troops. Akbar had learned about this in Sirhind, but he had kept marching, leaving prince Salim in Peshawar, and sending prince Murad ahead, in chase of the ambitious rebel—the fleeing Hakim Mirza.

Man Singh had accompanied prince Murad on this first campaign of his early youth. The imperialists, under the command of prince Murad and Man Singh, were just seven miles away from Kabul, when Hakim Mirza had changed his tactics. He had launched an attack against the Prince and the General, thinking, that the young prince could be easily captured. But prince Murad had proved to be a mighty foe, emerging forth victorious, and Hakim Mirza had become a fugitive, once again. He had taken refuge with the hated Uzbeks. Akbar was so happy at his son's victory, that upon reaching Kabul, he had pardoned Hakim Mirza, inviting him to return to Kabul, and to resume his kingship. He himself, along with his son, had returned to Hind, ordering on the way the construction of a fort at Attock at the site of river Indus.

Akbar's gaze was wandering over to the three Jesuits, whom he had invited from Goa to learn about the Christian doctrines. These three Jesuits were, Father Rudolf Aquaviva, an Italian and the son of a duke; Father Montserrat, a Spaniard; and Father Francois Henriques, an Iranian of Ormuz, and a convert from Islam. The emperor had welcomed them graciously, and they in return had presented emperor with the volumes of Royal Bible in four languages, including the gift of the portraits of the Savior of the World and of the Virgin Mary.

Akbar had assumed the authority of *Mujtahid* after finding his ulemas unworthy as arbiters over religious matters. The edict, concerning the title of Mujtahid, was designed by the emperor himself, in precise terms, and with quotations from the Quran.

Obey God, and obey the Prophet, and those who have authority amongst you. We declare that the king of Islam, Amir of the faithful, shadow of God in the world, Abul Fath Jalaluddin Muhammad Akbar Padshal-i-ghazi, whose kingdom God perpetuate, is a most just, a most wise, and most God-fearing king. Should, therefore, in future, a religious question come up, regarding which the opinions of the Mujtahids are at variance, and His Majesty, in his penetrating understanding and clear wisdom, be inclined to adopt, for the benefit of nation and as a political expedient, any of the conflicting opinions which exist on that point, and issue a decree to that affect, we do hereby agree that such a decree shall be binding on us and on the whole nation.

Further we declare that, should His Majesty think fit to issue a new order, we and the nation shall likewise be bound by it, provided always that such an order be not only in accordance with some verse of the Quran, but also of real benefit for the nation and further, that any opposition on the part of the subjects to such an order as passed by His Majesty, shall involve damnation in the world to come, and loss of religion and property in this life.

Akbar's thoughts were recalling also the words of the khutba which he had read at Jami Masjid, the Friday following his role as a Mujtahid.

The Lord has given me the empire
And a wise heart and a strong arm
He has guided me in righteousness and justice
And has removed from my thoughts everything but justice
His praise surpasses man's understanding
Great is His power, Allahu Akbar.

Abdunnabi and Mukhdum-ul-Mulk were banished—sent to exile in Mecca as the unhappy pilgrims, for their irrepressible zeal and indiscipline. Abdunnabi was even charged of murdering a Brahman, but he had denied this charge quite adroitly. Recently, both had returned from their exile in good health and good spirits. Mukhdum-ul-Mulk had retired to the abode of the dead, for he had died a natural death at his home in Ahmadabad. But Abdunnabi had returned to the scholarly pursuits at Ibadat Khana.

Padres have a foul tongue! They are as bigoted as any over-zealous mullah, and as savage as any pious heathen caught in a net of his absurdities. Akbar's thoughts were leaping back four seasons in a stride.

The theological discussions at Ibadat Khana, then, had taken a strange turn, concerning a precept of holiness ascribed to the languages. Pundits were ascribing holiness to Sanskrit language. Priests were claiming Latin to be the holiest of the holy. Mullahs were asserting that each child born into this world was blessed with the knowledge of Arabic. Akbar had challenged them all by proposing an experiment to be conducted in a secluded house in Fathehpur Sikri, named gang mahal. Twenty newborn infants were sent to gang mahal under the care of dumb nurses, to be reared in seclusion for a number of years. The challenge was that after a prescribed period of time, whatever language those infants could speak, would be considered a holy language.

Four years had flown past unheeded, since the emperor had left those innocent babes into the care of the nurses at gang mahal. Akbar's thoughts were proclaiming all of a sudden that the time is ripe to refute the claims of all contenders, whose bigotry had become the cause of such an experiment. The pain of separation from his beloved which he had cherished for six, long years, was surfacing upon the waves of his silent thoughts.

Akbar's very gaze was smoldering with the light of this pain-hush within his psyche. To escape this ocean of pain, his thoughts were journeying toward gang mahal. He was about to command such a trip, when his attention was caught by a curious object on one silver tray. Asad Beg was the one carrying this tray. This object had a gourd-like base of enamel, which was encrusted with jewels. From the base of this gourd was jutting out a silver pipe, wrapped in lengths of purple silks. A long stem with patterns of gold and silver was embedded in the middle of the gourd with more folds of silks. At the tip of this stem was hoisted a jeweled bowl, half the size of its bloated base.

"Your Majesty." Asad Beg set the tray at the emperor's feet, offering kornish. "I have brought you a gift, Your Majesty."

"By the virtue of its refined contours and of its bejeweled charm, it seems, you have robbed this gift from some wealthy Raja." Akbar smiled, forcing his pain back.

"No thief would be as bold as to present his evidence of theft to the emperor, Your Majesty." Asad Beg joined the emperor in his mirth. "I designed it myself."

"The emperor is at a loss to name this beauty! Is this some object of pleasure, or of decoration?" Akbar asked, noticing a golden burner on the tray.

"This is a hookah, Your Majesty, the likes of which can't be found in Hind." Was Asad Beg's quick response!

"Have never seen one, not even heard of this name before!" Akbar murmured.

"You may call it a pipe of tobacco, Your Majesty." Asad Beg expounded hurriedly. "One can find a crude version of this in the villages, Your Majesty. The villagers design their own hookahs, with a clay base and a clay top. They use a pipe of jute or flax, woven tight or layered. The base is filled with water, and the tobacco leaves are lighted on the top. The villagers smoke hookahs, after work in the fields."

"Show the emperor how it is done?" Akbar asked with a great enthusiasm.

Asad Beg began the process of lighting the hookah. A few courtiers were gathering around him under some spell of suspicion. Amongst these men were the emperor's physicians, who were more intent on watching Asad Beg than the hookah.

"This superb artwork on the stem! Who is the author of this color and design?" Akbar asked, watching Asad Beg light the gold burner with a flint.

"Some divine disciple, blessed with the art of God's handiwork, Your Majesty! I have no way of knowing, who?" Asad Beg responded inspirationally. "This is the finest I could procure from Achin, the finest."

"What is that oval-shaped morsel you are stuffing into the mouth of the pipe?" Akbar asked with the curiosity of a child.

"This is the mouthpiece, Your Majesty, of Yemen carnelian, very rare and much sought after by the artisans of the world." Asad Beg responded proudly.

"And what kind of tobacco is this? The whole leaf is burning like a map put to torch!" Akbar's childlike curiosity was intense and fluttering.

"I got this tobacco from Bijapur, Your Majesty. You have to light but one leaf, and the whole stack would smolder for a long time, lending rich flavor when smoked." Asad Beg stuffed more tobacco leaves into the jeweled bowl.

A few more courtiers were attracted toward this active display of hookah-lighting, foremost among them, Nawab Khan. He had one hookah in his possession, and indulged in smoking at home, quite frequently. His knowledge concerning different varieties of tobacco was extensive, and now he could not help boasting with a swift animation.

"Your Majesty, this tobacco is imported from Medina, I am sure." Nawab Khan commented. "I know few physicians who personally bring this variety of tobacco from Mecca and Medina, and use it for medicinal purposes."

"Remarkable." Akbar applauded avidly.

"Would you like to try smoking this hookah, Your Majesty?" Asad Beg held out the silver pipe toward the emperor, delight shining in his eyes like quicksilver.

"My senses are longing for this pleasure." Akbar claimed the pipe, and put the mouthpiece to his lips. He sat puffing, and blowing luxuriantly.

The hookah was making gurgling sounds at each puff, and the emperor was pleasantly surprised, enjoying this luxury with the spirit of an adventurer. The royal physicians were craning their necks for a better view.

"The smoke is filtered through water before it reaches the mouthpiece, Your Majesty, so the flavor is lighter than—" Asad Beg was expounding, but the emperor had ceased to heed. He was luxuriating in this new discovery of smoking hookah.

"Tobacco is not good for your health, Your Majesty." Hakim Mirri—the senior physician murmured with great consternation. "I have not studied much about tobacco, but as little as I know about it, it may have peculiar qualities which can be harmful."

"Much study has been done on the tobacco leaf, and there is no harm attached to its use." Hakim Ali—the junior physician began with a carefree nod of his head. "Tobacco has been used for centuries in all parts of the world, its roots being originally imported from China. European doctors have written much in its praise."

"In fact I know for a fact, that tobacco is of no medicinal value. And if no harm is attached to it, no hymns of praise are sung in eulogizing its qualities either. There is no medicine, about which the European doctors have written nothing." Hakim Mirri spoke more in alarm for the emperor's health, than in opposition to the younger physician. "How can we assume that it's safe, if we are not sure about its qualities? It is not fit that His Majesty should try this foreign leaf."

"Europeans are not so foolish as not to know about it." Asad Beg mocked Hakim Mirri . "There are wise men amongst them who seldom err or commit mistakes. How can you, before you have tried a thing and have found out all its qualities, pass a judgment upon it that can be depended upon by the physicians, the kings, the great men and the nobles? Things must be judged of according to their good or bad qualities, and the decision must be made according to the facts of the case."

"We don't want to follow the Europeans, and adopt a custom which is not sanctioned by our wise men without trial." Hakim Mirri retorted.

"Don't you find it strange, that every custom in the world was new at one time or the other?" Asad Beg responded intensely. "From the days of Adam till now, all customs has gradually been invented. When a new thing is introduced amongst people and becomes well known in the world, everyone adopts it. Wise men and physicians should determine according to the good or bad qualities of a thing, the good may not appear at once! Thus the China root, known to us of ancient times, has been newly discovered, and is useful in many diseases."

"Great minds with greater reason can overcome all obstacles, on a road to greatest understanding." Akbar interceded, his gaze offering compliments to Asad Beg. "Truly, we must not reject a thing which has been adopted by the wise men of other nations, merely because we cannot find it in our books, or how shall we prosper?" His attention was caught by the recital of Faizi above the din of arguments from theologians.

"Whenever discourse deals with the knowledge of God
Our thought's praise becomes dispraise
Behold rashness, how it boils over with daring
Can a drop embrace the ocean
Think not that it is even a single letter of the Book
For the letter is muslin, and the Book moonlight
How long will thou be an embroider of speech
Stay thy foot here, with the acknowledgment of humility."

Faizi's verse was challenging theologians, their arguments getting louder.

"God Vishnu is the most famous of the false gods of Hind." Father Montserrat was blowing his rage to the face of Debi. Since Debi—the Brahman priest was smiling back with compassion, Father Monserrat's anger was falling on Abdunnabi. "Hind is the land of the Christians, not of the Hindus or Muslims. Gwalior was ruled by the Christians three hundred years from hence—and

Delhi, first of all, had been made a capital by the Christian kings. And Afghanistan, had at one time, been a Christian country! How dare you vilify the Christian doctrine, Nabi? Your own Prophet is a wicked impostor, the impious villain and a rascally babbler—"

Akbar was smiling no more, his look intense and profound. His thoughts were taking an inward journey, yet no anger was alighting in his thoughtful gaze.

"Where does time go, Birbal?" Akbar's abrupt inquiry fell on Birbal.

"Into the womb of the unborn, Your Majesty." Was Birbal's quick response!

"Where does evil go?" Another inquiry was shot forth from Akbar's lips.

"Nowhere, Your Majesty. It stays in its volcano of eternal damnation." Birbal smiled most profoundly.

"And where does good lead to?" Akbar smiled back.

"It leads one by the hand toward the luminous abode of the *self*, Your Majesty." Birbal's very look was breathing wisdom, the smile in his eyes dark and profound.

"What can be done with these heathens?" Akbar was shifting his gaze to Abul Fazl. "All these heathen-scholars, Abul, who claim to be the true believers of their own, very own true beliefs! Hurling each other into the pits of perdition, and clawing one another with the fists of their zeal and intolerance?"

"If the whip of reason doesn't lend them sense, Your Majesty, then bridle their tongues with the reins of *power*, in which Your Majesty's wisdom may invent one divine truth to judge the tides of their zeal and contention." Abul Fazl proposed most genially.

"Silence is sacred, when ignorance speaks a million lies to blacken the face of truth, my friend." Akbar's thoughtful look was gathering flashes of inspiration. "But then how can truth be ascertained, torn apart and then glued back to mend the follies of ignorant minds, if there were no arguments to test its validity. It is no unusual thing for one engaged in a disputation to hold his views to be true and those of his adversary to be false. Yet, respect and prudence must be sought in all manner of discussion. What divine truth can the emperor invent, my prudent friend?" He asked suddenly.

"You have erected several altars in your soul, Your Majesty, if I am not mistaken. Each altar revealing the face of one truth most pure! If I am not too presumptuous, Your Majesty, you can weave all these truths in one whole garland of *truth* by the light of your wisdom, and present it to the world infested with wars, holy and unholy, where men keep warring with ignorance, not ever confronting the shields of wisdom."

"Ah, truth and wisdom, always running parallel, neither diverging, nor colliding! Seeking, always seeking something unattainable, the *mind* of cosmic reality." Akbar commented. "Your flattery has a sting of truth in it, my friend. Yes, I have many altars in my heart and soul, but none as holy as the one which worships *love* alone. Yet, I have pondered much on the diversity of creeds and religions. There is truth in every religion, and in each religion a handful of good, pious and honest men can be found. Islam alone does not hold monopoly over truth and virtue. We ought therefore to bring them all into one, but in such a fashion that there should be both *one* and *all* with the great advantage of not losing what is good in any one religion, while gaining whatever is better in another. If all truths could be manifested in one, I would call that truth, *Din-i-Ilahi;* meaning, God's religion, universal truth, noble wisdom. The Throne of God, where tolerance toward all faiths is received with blessings for all."

"The law of Mahomet is a tissue of errors and lies!" Father Monserrat's voice was rising above the din of equally heretic calumnies by the ulemas.

"Summon this son of Jesus to the emperor's presence, and let me question his erring tongue." Akbar commanded Abul Fazl.

Father Montserrat was still boiling with rage, while being led by Abul Fazl; Father Rudolf following.

"Oh, the hideous and heinous name of Mahomet, I can't bear it—" Father Rudolf could be heard murmuring while Father Montserrat stood bowing before the emperor.

"My good Father, I deemed you kind and gentle." Akbar began most patiently. "You are mentor to my son, prince Murad! Is this the way the padres of my court conduct themselves when exposed to arguments, which seem beyond the knowledge of their understanding?" His chest was constricting with a sudden assault of pain.

"These mullahs try the patience of the very saints, Your Majesty. Not that I claim myself to be of a saintly disposition." Father Montserrat breathed humbly. "The great sorrow and suffering in my soul is renewed, whenever I repeat the truth: *Jesus, the Son of God.* For one ulema cries out *God forbid*, and another covers his ears with his hands and a third mocks, while another blasphemes."

"And yet, I heard you, blaspheme the Prophet, Padre." Akbar murmured softly. "Is tolerance not the virtue of the learned in such theological disputes, Father? To keep the fire of learning kindled, does the emperor have to suffer stupidity, bigotry and intolerance of the learned?" He was trying to dispel the pangs of pain.

"Tolerance, Your Majesty, when they attack my true belief in Christianity with the swords of Islam—and Hindu gods shooting their arrows at the very heart of Christendom." Father Montserrat murmured low.

"True belief, good Padre, is in the heart of every believer, no matter what his faith." Akbar's pain was in abeyance. "If you believed in the gods of the others, you would believe in your own God, most truly."

"A true Christian does not believe in the gods of others, Your Majesty." Was Father Monserrat's discomfited response! "Christianity is the only true religion, and Bible the only holy book revealing truth of the Lord."

"Have you studied other religions, Father, besides Christianity? Brahmanism, Buddhism, Zoroastrianism, just to name a few?" Akbar asked testily.

"Only Islam and Judaism, Your Majesty." Father Montserrat muttered piously.

"Then you can't compare, learned Father, you can't compare." Akbar repeated, as if in despair of his own need to know all. "Judaism, Christianity and Islam, breed and constitute the People of the Book, who hold their own individual beliefs sacred. Believing in one God, yet disputing over the mere names, Yahweh, Jesus, Allah, and also remaining ignorant of the other diverse creeds which expound the belief in one God alone, though naming this *one entity* in different names. Knowing one's religion and not wishing to learn the other's, is like a man being ignorant of his spiritual thirsts. Seeking only one drop of water in the vast ocean of holy knowledge! Standing aloof by the very waters which quench the thirsts of the fortunate few, yet withdraw their favors from many whose thirsts are satisfied but with little!"

"I know enough about other creeds, Your Majesty, to say that Christianity alone offers salvation, and that all sins are forgiven to those who accept Jesus Christ as their Lord." Father Montserrat intoned persistently.

"You mean, Father, that my sins will be forgiven if I accept Jesus Christ as my Lord?" Akbar caught and held the glint of zeal in Father's eyes into his own gaze.

"Yes, Your Majesty. Absolutely." Father Monserrat's eyes were lit up with zeal.

"What about some pious Hindu, who has not accepted Jesus Christ as his Lord, but has known no sin all his life?" Akbar began intensely. "And who has offered his love, goodness and kindness to the world? Is he not blessed to earn his salvation by practicing only the virtue of compassion, through prayer and devotion to his gods?"

"But he has sinned in not accepting the word of God through Jesus Christ, Your Majesty." Father Montserrat protested hastily.

"So he remains sinful, though piety is his shield and armor?" Akbar asked.

"Salvation is not promised to the ones, who do not accept Jesus Christ as their Lord and Savior, Your Majesty." Was Father Monserrat's tremulous response!

"Does a Muslim get one half the share of Salvation, since he believes Jesus Christ to be the apostle of God?" Akbar laughed suddenly.

"Salvation is in believing Jesus Christ to be the Son of God, Your Majesty." Father Montserrat murmured under the spell of some nameless misery and constraint.

"Metaphorically, you mean, good Father." Akbar murmured back profoundly.

"No, Your Majesty. Truly, and absolutely believing Jesus Christ to be the Son of God!" Was Father Monserrat's quick response!

"How can the *son of man*, as written in the Bible, become a Son of God? Jesus Christ never claimed divinity himself. *Get thee hence, Satan, for it is written, thou shalt worship the Lord thy God, and him only shalt thou serve.* That's what he said when he was tempted by Satan. Now, good Father, tell me, did Jesus Christ ever claim to be the Son of God at any time in his own words as recorded in the Bible?"

"He called God his Father, Your Majesty." Father Montserrat murmured.

"Father, Abba! Metaphorically, God is the father of us all." Akbar countered.

"But Jesus Christ was born holy, of Virgin Birth." Father Montserrat protested.

"Metaphorically, good Father, metaphorically." Akbar repeated genially.

"All Muslims believe in the Virgin Birth, Your Majesty, and the whole nation of Islam would be scandalized, if the word got around that one Muslim emperor does not believe in Virgin Birth." Father Monserrat's rage and vehemence were returning.

"The emperor does believe in Virgin Birth." Akbar's gaze was gathering mirth and sadness. "Yes, I do believe in Virgin Birth, absolutely and irrevocably. But in a context much different than the merely professed belief in holy mysteries! I believe with the lamp of reason in one hand, and with the candle of understanding with the other. The eyes of ancient wisdom beheld Virgin Birth as the purity of the spirit. In that age and time, virtue and holiness were of the soul, not of the flesh. Many gods and kings are believed to be the issues of virgin births in the history of mankind. Starting with the Sumerians who wrote the story Creation, depicting heaven as the garden, furnished with the serpent and the scene of the Fall, the Expulsion and the Expiation. Alexander the Great believed himself to be the issue of Virgin Birth. Egyptian goddess, Isis, is depicted as Virgin Mother with her son Horus, as Madonna and the child. Her husband, Osiris, is the Savior God, who died and was resurrected. Dionysus, the Roman god, was killed in a cave by the Titans, and resurrected as a Savior God."

"God forbid, God forbid, God save us all from believing in these heathen gods, Your Majesty." Father Montserrat was covering his ears. "Christianity is unique with the essence of godhead, relating to the divine nature of Jesus Christ—the God, the Son, the Holy Ghost. No other religion in the world has this concept of Trinity, Your Majesty, this divine blessing in Baptism and Salvation." He concluded incoherently.

"Much in the manner of my ulemas, you couldn't help covering your ears, Father! Thinking *pagan*, evil, and branding their sacred beliefs as heathen lies." Akbar mocked. "Irreverent pagans and unblessed heathens indeed! And as to the concept of Trinity, Padre, Hinduism has such a concept, in different terms, with different names. Hindu Trinity names Brahma as the Creator, Vishnu as the Preserver, against whom you were blaspheming in terms of the *most famous of the false gods of Hind,* and Shiva as the Destroyer. You didn't know, Father that the concept of Trinity exists in other religions?"

"But no other religion claims the Son of God as their sole Savior, Your Majesty." Father Montserrat murmured in great misery.

"For the salvation of their souls, it is much better that they don't ascribe divinity to Jesus Christ, the apostle." Akbar's voice was low and ponderous. "By becoming the Son of God, Christ becomes mortal. By becoming mortal, he is fated to die. Death is not the attribute of God, neither is birth! God is the unborn, the unbegotten, and the uncreated. The Creator, the Supreme, the Immortal, the

Absolute Divine. By being Absolute, He has no opposite. By being Divine, He challenges the oneness of the Absolute. If Absolute accepts the Divine, then oneness are both Divine and Absolute. Absolute suppressing the Divine! The Divine killing the Absolute, both challenging the Essence of Oneness! Essence divides and disintegrates. Absolute becomes Divine, and Divine, the Absolute. Both attaining the sin of mortality, both retaining the attributes of godly within the ungodly—both sundering apart. Godly, tainted with the virtue of evil and goodness. And ungodly scarred with the vice of sin and perdition."

All men were silent as portraits caught on the canvas of life. Even the beasts in the arena were suspended under some sort of hush, it seemed.

"Since men cannot be both divine and mortal, God ceases to live inside the boundaries of their souls. Since man is not divine, he lives in eternal quest to find God, who appears to have abandoned man. Actually God has not abandoned man, but has severed the link of mortality with the divine. Waiting for mortality to reject its false sense of Absoluteness, so that the Divine could enter man's own Divinity! If Christ is both mortal and divine, both Man and God, both Son and Father, then the essence of Son, Man, God, and Father attains divinity beyond mortality, which is the pulse of time in its everlasting cycle of birth and death. And renewal of life with all its pain and suffering, with all its rapture and Union! Absolute dies. Divinity lives. Time digs the grave of Oneness. Nature opens the womb of Essence. Miracle of life becomes the orgy of death. Death becomes the harlot of life." Akbar's gaze was sailing beyond the confines of nature and time. "Sublime lives in the *nobility* of evil and good, of beauty and ugliness, of justice and injustice, of kindness and wickedness, of mercy and cruelty, of sin and virtue, of prayer and blasphemy! Sacred and profane! In the holiness of the holy of the holies, where *light* embraces *darkness*, with as much sanctity as the virgin bed of lilies bathing its white purity in the mud of this sacred earth. Ah, the Ganges pure and muddied, the river holy and sacred! Purging the sins of the suffered and the suffering!" His gaze was arrested to Duster Maharaja. "Duster, since you are a priest, a great scholar and a devout Parsee, you are well versed with the holy texts on Hinduism. Can you expound to us in the tongue of the great Upanishads, why Man and God, man-made god, or men-made gods cannot live in harmony with each other?"

"Great Upanishads, Your Majesty, is a source of enlightenment to all, who embrace its teaching as a path to learning, not as a dweller in the street of knowledge." Duster Maharaja responded with a swift bow of his head. "I feel fortunate in recalling this holy wisdom from the Upanishads, which fits aptly to your inquiry. *The distinction between God and man is that God controls ignorance, man is controlled by it.*"

"Ah, the truth and mystery of wisdom!" Akbar exclaimed, favoring Duster Maharaja with a warm smile. "For this profound mating of thoughts with wisdom, the emperor bestows upon you a fertile pargana of two hundred acres." He returned his gaze to Father Montserrat. "Ponder upon this adage, good Father: *in the shadow of present, the past lingers like a snail, but the veil of future reveals nothing.*"

Father Montserrat was stricken mute, so Akbar's gaze was shifting to Todar Mall.

"What sadness dares visit the emperor in this festive bazaar of wisdom and theology, Todar Mall?" Akbar chanted happily. "I have been thinking for quite a while, that you stand unrivaled in the knowledge and experience of our civil administration. I have decided to grant you the post of Prime Minister to the emperor."

"Your Majesty." Todar Mall bowed thrice, mute and overwhelmed.

"Such poverty of gratitude." Akbar teased. "Yet, the emperor needs no overt show of gratitude from you, my brave general, for you have earned the reputation of an incorruptible man. By granting you the sword of power over all, you would be burdened with duties most suitable to you. You are instructed, first of all, in honor of your enviable post, to build two houses in the precincts of Fathehpur Sikri. These houses should be designed to serve meals to the poor and the saintly. Both Hindus and Muslims, who deserve alms, can come to either one of the houses, but I have decided to assign separate names to these alms-houses. One will be called Dharmpura, for dharma amongst the Hindus for their charity. And the other will be named Khairpura, from khair for charity amongst the Muslims."

"Yes, Your Majesty." Todar Mall bowed again.

"*Yes, Your Majesty.*" Akbar repeated to himself. "Todar Mall, I have never seen you bereft of words, before! Sadness still sits in your eyes like the Scythian night. What heavy burden weighs on your mind, which has crushed your joy in acquiring power and might over the cruelty and injustice of all men?" He asked kindly.

"I am overwhelmed with joy and gratitude, Your Majesty." Todar Mall was able to express the rhythm of his joy. "My sadness is just a part of the evil news which I carry like a burden of lead. But now, my heart is brimming with such joy, that it forbids me to talk of evil and sadness."

"Yet, the emperor commands it." Akbar's gaze was gathering turbulent waves.

"Jala, Your Majesty, your favorite Chief Trade Commissioner, has committed a heinous crime." Todar Mall complied promptly. "He has violently debauched a Brahman girl, and her parents are grief-stricken beyond despair, unfit to seek justice—" He could not speak further. The emperor had leaped to his feet with a sudden alacrity.

"Justice, in my Moghul court, considers all men equal. The favorite of the emperor will fall as ignominiously as any poor man on the street, who dares commit evil in the eyes of man and God." Akbar thundered aloud. "By the emperor's orders, Jala, this evil wretch of a parasite, is to be scourged, and then strangled without mercy." The emperor was descending his throne pressed by his anger and sorrow. The viziers, the priests, the ulemas, and a brood of theologians were following the emperor.

"Many good Muslims are falling under the bastinadoes by the Hindus, merely, on the accusations of evil crimes." Abdunnabi was heard murmuring.

Akbar was in an act of walking away, when he stalled himself before the bigoted ulema with the fury of a lion.

"Good Muslims, you say, you vile liar! Your corrupt tongue can cut through the purity of a diamond. The emperor is not ignorant of your guilt, which is sitting proudly on your shoulders. You evaded the charge of murdering a Brahman, but now you stand convicted. That Brahman of Mathura! Now all the evidence is against you and you cannot escape the gallows." The flash of anger in Akbar's eyes was gathering a storm. "Send this ignorant viper into his own hell of tortures. The prison of the damned, where he would be strangled by the silence of the four walls alone." He thundered over his shoulders at no one in particular, and marched past the stunned spectators.

Fath Ullah, who was right behind the emperor, seized Abdunnabi by the collar, and handed him over to the Imperial guards. The emperor was scampering past the arena, where a water-buffalo fight was evoking much cheer from the wild spectators. In the background, Tansen had begun to sing a ghazal. Akbar's feet were coming to a slow halt, his anger dissipating, and he was becoming aware of Shah Mansur approaching at the head of a procession, followed by a caparisoned elephant.

Shah Mansur was nicknamed Longtailed Star, for in his scholarly pursuits, he was prone to neglect the court custom, and let the end of his carelessly folded turban hang down behind his back. He had assumed this guise after the appearance of a comet in Year 1577, this comet boding misfortunes and worldly disasters. The prophecies of the pious were fulfilled a year later after the appearance of this comet, for Shah Tahmasp of Persia had died, and Persia was plunged into the throes of civil wars and anarchy. Shah Mansur, even today, amidst this arena of grand festivities, was careless in his dressing, the long end of his red turban loose and unkempt.

"The elephants are welcome in the arena, Shah Mansur, but not on this path leading toward the emperor's palaces, not today." Akbar admonished.

"Your Majesty, this elephant is welcome even in the heavens!" Shah Mansur exclaimed histrionically. "This elephant, Your Majesty, is carrying a sacred object on its back." His eyes were commanding the two men behind him to step forward. "Mir Abu and Itamid Khan, Your Majesty, have brought this stone all the way from Mecca. This stone is no ordinary stone, it bears the impression of the foot of the Prophet."

"We are blessed to have this sacred object amidst us, then. And we must pay homage to it, in the memory of our Prophet." Akbar's gaze was assessing the sanctity of this stone. "We would carry it on our shoulders on the streets of Fathehpur Sikri. I myself would carry it a few paces to let the citizens of Hind behold its sanctity with devotion and reverence." He returned his gaze to Shah Mansur. "But first, Longtailed Star, tell the emperor, when are the royal ladies expected to arrive in Fathehpur Sikri, the only pilgrims from Mecca the emperor has been anxiously waiting for?"

"The grand cavalcade of your royal ladies would be arriving here this evening, Your Majesty, if not this very afternoon." Shah Mansur elicited a smile.

"And if they don't, Shah Mansur, your turban would be thrown into the very deeps of Ganges, by the emperor's express orders." Akbar laughed, turning to face the brood of his viziers and theologians. "We would carry this stone toward gang mahal, where we would test our experiment. The emperor would be the first one to carry this stone, but don't let him carry it for too long, or he would melt under the burden of its holiness. Abul Fazl would carry it next, then Fath Ullah. Faizi, Nizamuddin Ahmed and Bhagwan Das would take turns after that." He espied prince Salim amongst them. "Come, Shaikhu Baba. You have proven your valor, already. The proof of your devotion to your bride, Man Bai, is beyond compare. Now prove your devotion to the emperor as the son of a Muslim sovereign by carrying this stone over your shoulders."

And I will be a living proof of love and devotion to my second bride, Sahiba Jamali, also. Prince Salim's thoughts chuckled in silence as he followed his father.

Accompanied by the sound of the imperial band, this stone was paraded before the citizens over a float of royal shoulders. Akbar was the first one to carry it, his chosen courtiers were the next, and then this honor had fallen on to nobles and the ulemas. Right now, his gaze was chasing prince Salim, who could not be denied the privilege of carrying this stone, time after time. Laughter was alighting in Akbar's eyes, his voice rising above the din of music, and drawing Bhagwan Das's attention toward his son.

"Look, Bhagwan Das, how tall and princely my son has grown!" Akbar exclaimed. "Your lovely daughter, Man Bai, is a lucky bride, indeed. But find more beautiful brides for him. He must learn to share his love with others as a lesson to prove his love and duty toward his countrymen. Happy alliances!"

"Many comely wives I have in mind, Your Majesty, if the ulemas don't raise objections." Bhagwan Das joined the emperor in his mirth.

"If they do, they would be roasted in hellfire! Their bodies would be consumed in hoary flames, instead of their sacred texts." Akbar laughed. "Surely, you have not forgotten about the discussions between our mullahs and the padres?"

"No one can forget such discussions, Your Majesty." Bhagwan Das rejoined mirthfully. "The scene stays vivid in my head, each man claiming the sanctity for the holy book of his own religion, and denying others the claim of such holiness. And when they could not be pacified through arguments, how Your Majesty proposed that both Bible and Quran could be set on a pyre of burning wood! And, that if either, or both the holy books could withstand this test, and were not reduced to ashes, their sanctity could be ascertained. If they were to accept the challenge, they would have been left with ashes, and no holy arguments." He concluded beamishly.

"Only with the rod of reason, one can destroy ignorance, Bhagwan Das." Akbar was feeling dull pangs in his stomach again. "But if reason fails, one should hold on to the hem of patience, compassion and tolerance."

"Ibadat Khana is the seat of learning, Your Majesty, as we all know, but these men of learning have learnt no discipline. They are always there, to command war with words in quest of peace, yet never practice the virtue of peace with their actions." Bhagwan Das intoned thoughtfully.

"Only God commands, Bhagwan Das, only God commands." Akbar repeated to himself. "God commands, men only scream in hopelessness to comfort their plight of despair. Only, if ignorance could heed the voice of wisdom! Bonds of ignorance fetter us all, as we think that we have arrested truth within the confines of our small minds. The veils of ignorance are many, and each veil resists the brutal touch of truth. Ignorance itself shudders in fear that its blind faith in matters sublime might crumble by this brutal touch of truth—fire-wisdom. Many fools have tasted this fire-wisdom, though, knowing not that its flames are to be cherished, not to be devoured. Many such men I have come across, whose minds are bloated with greed, searching for the key to immortality, and heeding not the cries of their souls which yearn to be free."

"Immortality sleeps in the pine-valleys of Kashmir, Your Majesty." Abul Fazl commented softly, stealing a look at Bhagwan Das, and seeking the emperor's attention.

"What a subtle way to remind the emperor about the issue of Kashmir, my prudent friend." Akbar flashed him a searching look. "Kashmir is the immortal foe of the Moghuls, and the emperor must confront this beautiful foe face-to-face, one of these days. With Ali Shah dead, and Yusuf Shah being reinstated as the emperor's vassal, the chance of rebellion is not likely to fall on us. Not very soon, I should think. Besides, his son, Yaqub, is still in our imperial army. The emperor treats his son with affection, but he can be held as a ransom to instill loyalty, if thoughts of rebellion breed in Yusuf Shah's head. Is Haider Shah plotting rebellion?" He asked abruptly.

"Haider Shah, Your Majesty, since being the eldest son of Yusuf Shah, thinks himself the sovereign of Kashmir." Abul Fazl responded smoothly. "Though, Your Majesty sent him back with a kind letter to his father, he is filling his father's ears with lies that Your Majesty wishes to usurp Yusuf Shah's rule with some other favorite Moghul noble from Hind." He concluded rather ominously.

"Rebellion is on its way then, and our next hunting trip would be to Kashmir." One prophecy of a thought escaped Akbar's awareness. "Right now, our journey is only up to the fortress of gang mahal, so let us employ this time in thinking about reforms for the good of our empire. The emperor wishes to hear proposals from all. Shaikhu Baba, since you are the heir to my throne, you are commanded to voice a proposal to whet the appetites of the others. Think of something which can add luster to our glorious reign."

"I propose, Your Majesty that the child marriages should be abolished, and that no one should be permitted to marry before the age of twelve." Prince Salim intoned with the precocity of a noble youth.

"Splendid as it sounds, Shaikhu Baba, it has already been taken care of. The marriageable age I proposed was eighteen for boys and sixteen for girls. But you are thirteen and already married?" Akbar laughed, his eyes gathering waves of mischief.

"I propose, Your Majesty that the preservation of the fish, the birds and the reptiles should be taken into consideration. They are being killed indiscriminately." Abdur Rahim proposed quickly.

"A humane proposal most sublime!" Akbar favored him with a brilliant smile. "We would issue an edict, in which it would be dictated that constraint must be preserved while hawking, hunting, or fishing."

"Your Majesty, I propose that alms should be distributed everyday at the royal palace, and that the imperial staff should be asked to furnish a list of the poor and the needy, week-by-week." Todar Mall was swift to voice his proposal.

"A gracious proposal which would take precedence over the rest mentioned before!" Akbar announced, flashing him a warm smile.

"My proposal, Your Majesty, is that a daily newspaper of important happenings should be written and copied by the royal scribes." Yusuf Khan offered his proposal.

"A literary proposal, most prized by the emperor." Akbar responded with the heightening of interest. "A newspaper laying bare the corruptions of all and clothing great events into the raiments of joy and pride!"

"Since all the proposals are being graciously accepted by the emperor, I feel bold to voice mine. I propose that several groups of able and impartial officers be appointed at different posts, who could report the cases of the oppressed and of the suitors for justice. They should also send to our court an account of the unavoidable calamities in their respective jurisdictions." Birbal broke his silence with this lengthy proposal.

"An angelic proposal from the lips of an angel." Akbar flashed him a smile. "The emperor would be ruled by the poets most wisely." He murmured under his breath.

"I propose that the rest houses should be constructed along the roads throughout the empire, for the benefit of the travelers." Qasim Khan proposed cheerfully.

"A healthy proposal which the emperor accepts most warmly!" Was Akbar's prompt response!

"I propose that able and experienced men should be dispatched to bring to court the men in want and distress." Bhaikh Jamal joined the current of the proposals.

"The emperor accepts this one most gratefully, and with the spirit of peace and goodwill to all." Akbar's gaze was warm and encouraging.

"I propose that arrangements should be made in lowering the prices of the articles of consumption." Faizi emerged from his poetic reverie into this material world.

"Feed the poor with compassion, and the rich with kindness! This motto of yours could fetch a higher price, if it was not fed to the peasants with fixed prices wrapped inside the morsels of ethics and morality." Akbar teased him mirthfully.

"I propose, Your Majesty that public hospitals should be built in every city." Was Hakim Ali's hasty proposal.

"Health, wealth and prosperity! The emperor cannot help but agree." Akbar laughed again.

"Your Majesty, I propose that the soldiers, who are not on an active duty, should enlist the names and professions of the householders, assessing their income and expenditure. And that they should report to the state of the ones who avoid working, for they expose their families to the indignity of poverty and beggary." Abul Fazl appealed.

"A dear, dear proposal from the dearest of my friends." Akbar's warm gaze was lingering on Abul Fazl. "Two bright lamps, hoarding many mysteries, are forever kindled in your eyes, Abul. I stumble not into the dark alleys of doubt and ignorance, when you choose to lend me the staff of your genius." He was becoming aware of the precincts of gang mahal. "Our journey on foot has been swifter than riding. Let this stone from Kaaba continue its own journey, while we repair to gang mahal."

The fervor and the jubilation of the procession were at their peak, as the men marched on, singing and making merry on the streets of Fathehpur Sikri. The emperor's royal entourage was entering the stone-hewn path toward gang mahal. The gang mahal with its lofty pinnacles and smothered with bridal ivy, seemed to be a formidable abode awaiting the arrival of the emperor. Baduani was the last one to enter, but the first one, finding himself in one large chamber with silk hangings and Persian carpets. His eyes were searching the dumb nurses and the mute children.

Akbar had accosted the nurses slowly, and was now standing there, cajoling the children into the act of speech. But no sound was issuing forth from the lips of those innocent babes. Suddenly, Akbar had begun to laugh, his laughter sad and mirthless.

"Now, they would be taught the language of the birds! The language divine, of the seers?" Akbar exclaimed, his gaze flashing some mad challenge.

The theologians, who had wrangled over the holiness of a language, were stricken dumb like the babes and the nurses. Akbar's laughter was truncated as quickly as it had begun, and he intoned sadly.

"The ear is the sentinel of voice. When the speaker becomes deaf, he loses the need of speech." Akbar's mirth was completely vanished.

"Silence is the speech of the angels." Abul Fazl's lips were lowering a couplet.

"He who knows speech knows
What kind of speech this is."

"A divine couplet, concealing the wisdom of the Divine." Akbar complimented.

"Faith is sacred. Language only the means to express one's Faith." Baduani peered from behind with a kindling of zeal. "No rivers of knowledge are more sacred than the revelations of wisdom in the Quran."

"The source of mighty rivers, from mountain-tops to the very deeps is in the knowledge of a cosmic reality, which expresses that these mighty rivers derive bliss and refuge from their humbling experience of expanding and shrinking into shallow puddles, not from pride and wisdom in their bottomless depths." Akbar commented.

"I wish to return to Goa, Your Majesty." Was Father Monserrat's abrupt plea.

"Your wish is granted, good Father." Akbar responded absently. He was hugging one child with the intensity of a loving father. "You would be my messenger to the Philip II of Spain, entrusted with a letter to invite more padres to our court."

"I too wish to return to Goa, Your Majesty." Father Aquaviva chanted from behind, as if to confirm the feelings of unrest in Monserrat's soul.

"Your wish will be granted just the same, kind Father." Akbar looked over his shoulders. "The emperor would bestow upon you both the gifts of gold and jewels."

"Your generous gifts we must decline, Your Majesty, in conformity with our vows of poverty. But may I implore a great favor from the bounty of your great compassion!" Father Aquaviva pleaded with a quavering voice. "May I be allowed to take with me the Russian, Christian slaves, who are residing in your palace?"

"We don't have slaves, but disciples, good Father." Akbar responded firmly. "Besides, that Russian man with a Polish wife and two children, they are under the care of my queen mother. The emperor himself has to request his mother, if she wishes to part with them. But what haste, what urgency! Why this sudden chant of returning to Goa?"

"My faith, Your Majesty—my soul is burdened. I can't live in a land with many gods—" Father Montserrat murmured incoherently.

"Ah, gods!" Akbar laughed suddenly. "God is one and should be worshipped in every possible way. God is one, and is everywhere, and in everything, including man. The God of the Jews, of the Muslims, of the Christians, of the Jains, of the Sikhs, of the Parsees, One and One alone! Hindus believe in one God in the Trinity of their gods, or inside the pantheon of their gods and goddesses. To praise God with every name, in every tongue, in every heart is love, not discord. I too, a Muslim emperor, pray to my Merciful God, loving Him in every creed. Holding Him in reverence, and not ever fearing him, even if I utter the name of Vishnu as the Preserver, or love to sing the hymn of the Upanishads to Brahma, its wisdom you must hear, Father.

Of all religions thou art the source
The light of thy knowledge shining
There is neither day nor night
Nor being nor non-being
Thou alone art."

He recited passionately. "I fear not my God, even if I pray in the manner of the Christians, for Allah is always with me, the Merciful, the Gracious, and the Magnificent. God, my good Father, ought to be adored with every kind of adoration, with love, and without the burden of fear, or guilt." He turned away, heading straight for the door. "And now a game of polo might stir our thoughts from mute idiocy to dull compassion."

The furtive shadows of the dusk were swallowed by darkness in the night, and the game of polo was still at its peak. This polo-ground was not far from the palace of Fathehpur Sikri, so the emperor was indulging in this pleasure to his heart's content. The moon was waxing high, and a myriad of stars were lowering their beacons of light over the velvety carpet of grass. The polo balls made out of palas wood were glowing like the globes of jade. The polo sticks with the knobs of gold and silver were a glorious heap by the fence. The polo players were doing justice to this heap of polo sticks, claiming quickly the new ones, when their old ones were broken or damaged.

Akbar was propelling the ball forward from under the feet of his horse with an unerring skill. This ball had veered toward the right, but Abul Fazl was quick to snatch it from the pouncing aim of the opponent, and had sent it flying toward Faizi. Faizi was swift in claiming this ball from his left side, and had rolled it craftily beyond the victory lines. Amidst the jubilant shouts of his team, Akbar was ready to announce another polo match, when a night rider intruded upon the players with the speed of a hurricane.

"Your Majesty." The night rider bowed his head, without alighting from his fiery steed. "The royal ladies from Mecca have finally arrived." He breathed happily.

The emperor was flying toward the palace unescorted. He was forcing back the pangs of pain in his stomach, fearing, lest they taint the joy of union with his Beloved.

The drums were sounding their beats to announce the arrival of the emperor at the palace, but his heart was thundering louder than the drum-beats as he mounted the steps of his palace. Through the flung-open portals, he had floated past the curtsying servants into the parlor, all damasked and garlanded. Sultanum Begum had abandoned herself on the velvety couch, and Gulzar Begum was reclining beside her with utmost ease. Gulnar Aghacha and Sarvaqad Begum were standing by the marble hearth, and whispering to each other, oblivious of the others. Most of the ladies were laughing as the emperor had stormed into the parlor, but now they were curtsying and greeting the emperor with giddy pleasure. The sober amongst them was the emperor's aunt, Gulbadan Begum.

Akbar was hugging and kissing all with joyful impatience, but his eyes were searching, rather thirsting for one glimpse of Salima. He was on the verge of inquiring about her, when the beloved herself had sailed into the parlor, arrayed in purest of silks, with no jewels to vie with her chaste beauty.

Like a flash of lightning, Akbar was beside her. He had folded her into his arms, and was kissing her hair and eyes, and murmuring endearments.

"The emperor's heart is breaking with joy, my love. Can joy kill one with its pain and bliss—" Akbar's lips, grazing her cheek were contorted from some inward torment of the body, not of the soul.

The emperor was slumping down to his feet, his eyes blazing with pain, and a sudden pallor sweeping over his features like the mask of death.

Salima was standing there mute and stunned. Her glazed look was fixed to the emperor at her feet, and terror was shining in her eyes like the moonlit glaciers.

10

Death of a Poet

Akbar was donned in a blue, woolen robe, broidered in gold. He was pacing to and fro in his garden at Fathehpur Sikri, while dictating a letter to Naqib Khan. A galaxy of wars had been fought and won since the recovery from his brief illness. A severe case of dyspepsia was the prognosis of the royal physicians. They had decided to treat the emperor with a Greek method, which was the most potent, healing slowly, but effectively. This method was named, Unani, in which natural herbs with the concoction of oils were used, to heal small lesions in the stomach. The emperor was not to touch solid food for three days, then subsisting on rice and vegetables, cooked in mild sauces! After one month and six days, the emperor was fully recovered.

This time of convalescence had proved to be a supreme bliss for the emperor, for he had kept Salima by his side at all hours of the day and night. In such utter bliss, Akbar had begun to believe that Salima did love him. Alas, this sense of bliss was not to last long, as Akbar had discovered soon at the eve of his full recovery. He was left with the sense of loneliness, realizing too soon that Salima's devotion toward him during his convalescence was more the outcome of her piety than of love.

Yet, she has grown tender and affectionate. Akbar would often drift into moments of quiet contemplations. *My Beloved suffers too! Yes, suffered and suffering, both the lack of her love, and the abundance of mine own? Yes, my turbulent and undying love, which only moves her to pity and remorse? And to a sense of tenderness, as if she is fated to love one terrible child, once happily neglected? If we rejoice not when the pain leaves, how can we weep when joy takes flight?*

Din-i-Ilahi had become Akbar's beautiful white *rose* of noble wisdom! Embodying one God, one truth, manifested in all religions, in all hearts, in everything! This truth expounding, that all religions speak to one another in the tongues of their own belief. The emperor—the author of Din-i-Ilahi, was under constant siege by the arguments of the padres, the pundits and the mullahs alike.

But his wisdom could drive such bigots and zealots miles away, attracting *noble unity* in thought and action.

Father Montserrat had left for Goa, carrying the emperor's letter for Philip II of Spain. In this letter, the emperor had shown keen interest in Christianity, inviting more priests to his Moghul court. A year later, Father Aquaviva was the next to leave for Goa. He was permitted to take along with him the Russian, Christian family, but he himself was faced with a tragic end during the course of his journey. Keeping in mind that the Jesuits were not well liked by the general public, Akbar had provided guards for the safe journey of Father Montserrat to his country. And now, Akbar had wished to do the same for Father Aquaviva, but he had declined the emperor's offer of the guards.

It is our glory to die for the faith which we preach. Father Aquaviva had said. He had embarked on his journey without the guards.

Father Aquaviva had withstood the hardships of a journey, but he could not withstand the arrows of hatred, and was murdered near Goa at Cuncolim close to Salsette.

Akbar's thoughts were leaving the chamber of death and seeking the colonnades of joy and sunshine. He had bestowed upon Birbal the title of Kavirai— the poet laureate of Hindi during a poetry contest at Lahore. Also bestowing upon him the perghana of Nagarkot in the district of Kangra. Prince Salim's wife, Man Bai, had blessed the royal prince with a daughter, whom Akbar had named Sultanunnisa. A year later, she had blessed the prince with a son, whom Akbar had named Khusrau. Both these grandchildren had become the center of emperor's attention. Prince Salim's marriage with Sahiba Jamali was also solemnized with much pomp and grandeur.

The haze of joy in Babur's thoughts was soiled by the dust of intrigues and rebellions. At Daman, the Portuguese had oppressed the pilgrims on their way to Mecca, and were duly chastised by the Moghuls. Nine of the Portuguese pilots were captured and executed. Then Mulla Yazdi had risen against the emperor, issuing a fatwa and proclaiming: *the emperor has strayed from the religion of Islam, and has in his dominions made encroachments on the grant-in-lands belonging to us and to God.*

The fires of rebellions were kindled in the cities of Kari, Nadot, Bihar, Patan, Gujrat, Bengal, Baroda and Ahmadabad, finally quenched through alliance or warfare. The imperialists under the command of Todar Mall had succeeded in Bihar, and Aziz Koka had quelled the insurrections in Bengal. Nizamuddin Ahmed had been victorious in Ahmadabad, while Abdur Rahim had succeeded in reconquering the cities of Nadot and Gujrat. Amidst these conquests, Itamid Khan and Shihabuddin were entrenched in Patan by the bold rebels, and Nizamuddin was being besieged in the city of Kari, and Baroda had fallen into the hands of Muzafar khan. After learning about these details, Akbar himself had decided to go hunting, and had gained victory after victory in all quarters. Muzafar khan was no match for the emperor, and noticing the advance of the imperialists, had fled to Gondal near the city of Junagarh.

Hakim Mirza, through his overindulgence in wine, had died suddenly. Leaving Kabul prey to anarchy and confusion, down to the very borders of Afghanistan! Badakhshan was captured by Abdullah of TransOxiana. He had also annexed Balkh, Bokhara, Tashkent and the whole of Turkistan into his empire.

Akbar had sent Man Singh to Kabul, at the head of a large army to secure peace amongst those warring kingdoms. The emperor himself had followed Man Singh soon after, with fresh reinforcements at his command. He had marched by the way of Delhi, Sonpat and Panipat. No sooner had the emperor reached Thaneshwar, when he was informed that Man Singh had reached Peshawar, and that the Afghans had submitted to him without much resistance. Shah Beg, the leader of the Afghans, at the sight of the imperialists marching forward, had taken flight out of sheer terror.

The emperor had continued his march via Punjab, and had learned about the unrest in Kashmir on his way to Kalanar. The ruler of Kashmir, Yusuf Shah, was charged of plotting intrigue and rebellion. Besides, Yusuf Shah's son, Yaqub, had fled from the emperor's camp to Srinagar, without permission. Reaching Kalanar, Akbar had sent orders to Yusuf Shah to appear before the emperor without delay. Resuming his march onward, Akbar had barely reached the precincts of Rawalpindi, when Man Singh had joined him. Man Singh had left Kabul under the governorship of his son, Jagat Singh, and had fetched the sons of late Hakim Mirza to be presented to the emperor. Hakim Mirza's sons, fourteen year old Afrasiab, and fifteen year old Khaiquabad, were presented before the emperor with all due courtesy, and they were received by the emperor most kindly. Man Singh was made the governor of Kabul. Akbar himself had repaired to the resort of Hasan Abdal, to wash off the soot of wars fought and of wars impending, with the intention of indulging in great qamargah hunt.

While still in Hasan Abdal, the emperor was informed of the fresh rebellions in Swat, Bajuar, Kashmir and Baluchistan. By now, Akbar was accustomed to the deluge of such rebellions, so he had calmly dispatched a powerful army to Kashmir under the command of Bhagwan Das. He had sent two more contingents of army to Swat and Bajuar under the command of Zain Koka. Zain Koka was ordered to chastise the Yusufzais, specifically, for they were plotting to block the road to Kabul. Another heavy contingent was sent to Baluchistan under the command of Quli Khan. The emperor himself had decided to march back to Lahore to take control of the affairs in Punjab.

Inexhaustible in his journeys and warring tactics, barely had Akbar reached Benares, when he had received reports from Kabul that Man Singh was facing another band of fanatical foes. These mighty rebels were known as the Raushaniyas, followers of Pir Raushan. They were plundering all caravans near the Khaiber Pass, thus making the road unsafe between Hind and Afghanistan. Akbar had great faith in Man Singh's might and valor, and he had continued his journey toward Lahore, without any thought of turning back. As soon as the emperor had reached Lahore, a swift messenger from Man Singh had brought the news that the Raushaniyas were ignominiously defeated.

Akbar had journeyed from Lahore to Fathehpur Sikri with much haste, gaining obedience on the way from the rebels and the intriguers alike. Even before he had entered his palace, he was faced with the alarming news that the Yusufzais at Swat and Bajuar were proving to be the foes most formidable. Zain Koka had sent a messenger, requesting urgently more troops and fresh enforcements. Soon, a powerful army was appointed by the emperor, but the decision as to who was to head that army was subjected to debates and controversies. Since Birbal and Abul Fazl had gained high posts without any military credits, they were foremost to be recommended by the generals. Both Birbal and Abul Fazl had no objections to this cause, but the decision of choosing one general had fallen to the discretion of the emperor. The lots were drawn and Birbal was chosen to lead the imperialists.

Birbal had marched forth at the head of a formidable army with joy and pride. But woeful was the day, when the news of his death had reached the emperor. The Afghans were staying in ambush at the Balandri Pass to repel the reinforcements of the Moghuls. Misinformed as the Moghul forces were as to the guerrilla tactics of the rebels, they had approached closer to the Balandri Pass without expecting any attack or obstruction. Caught unawares, the imperialists were trapped under the Balandri Pass. Eight thousand Moghuls were slain by the Yusufzais, foremost among them, Birbal at the head of his army. Zain Koka was too late to reach the scene of this woe and slaughter.

Akbar was inconsolable at the death of his poet-friend. He had shut himself up in his chamber for two whole days and nights, refusing all entreaties of food or drink, and admitting no audience. Though lamenting the loss of all his soldiers, he was suffering greatest of agonies for the death of his friend, Birbal.

Alas, they could not bring Birbal's body out of that defile, that it might have been committed to the flames. Akbar had lamented for days.

Not until Birbal's son, Lala had pleaded with Akbar that he had emerged out of his chamber. Lala had succeeded in making the emperor partake of food, and Akbar had elicited a spark of buoyancy, more so to comfort Lala than to console himself.

Birbal is now free of all earthly fetters. And as the rays of the sun were sufficient for him, there was no necessity that he should be cleansed by fire.

Shah Abbas of Iran, after saving Persia from strife, which had followed after the death of Shah Tahmasp, was now threatened by Abdullah Khan of TransOxiana. Abdullah Khan had already captured Herat and Badakhshan, and was coveting more territories. Abdullah Khan, being a Sunni himself and despising Shias in all of Persia, had proposed to Akbar to join his forces with him to invade the country of Iran. Akbar had declined this proposal most strongly.

The emperor deplores the fact that a Sultan of Turkey is taking advantage of Iran's feebleness and is sending expeditions to conquer the land of the Muslims, just because it is the country of the Shias, and not of the Sunnis! Though the Safavids profess Shiism, they deserve respect because of their connection with the Prophet's family. The emperor is bound to the Iranis with the ties of old and values their friendship.

Further exchange of embassies amongst Akbar and Abdullah Khan had resulted in an agreement to stabilize the boundaries between their respective empires by accepting Hindu Kush Mountain as the dividing feature. It was explicitly clear to both the parties that Akbar would not disturb Abdullah Khan's possession of Badakhshan, and that Abdullah Khan would not covet Kabul and its close territories.

This very day as Akbar paced to and fro, dictating another letter to Abdullah Khan, he was being reminded of Birbal's death by a surge of sadness in his thoughts.

If I was with Birbal at the Balandri Pass, I might have saved his life.

And why did the emperor feel more grief at the loss of his poet-friend than of his brother's? Akbar's thoughts were recalling his comments to Fatehullah Shirazi—a scholar and scientist from Persia who had recently joined his court.

Hakim Mirza is a memorial of the late emperor Humayun. Though he has acted ungratefully, I can be no other than forbearing. A child brought to condign punishment might be easily replaced, but a brother once lost can never be regained. The names of the old and the new theologians were trickling in Akbar's mind, as he kept pacing, his gaze now and then resting on the cluster of roses bordering the yonder terraces.

Zoroastrian priest, Dastur Mahyarji. Parsee priest, Dastur Ardeshir. Commandant, Pedro Tavares. Henriquez, a Persian convert from Islam, now a priest. Jain scholars, Buddhi Sagar; Khartar Gachha; Hirvijaya Suri.

If I had not entered the service of this adorer of multiplicity, and chooser of unity, I would not have become a traveler on the road to divine knowledge. Akbar was recalling the words of Fatehullah Shirazi, which this scholar had uttered at his first meeting with the emperor, addressing the emperor as the *Adorer of Multiplicity.* His feet were coming to a slow halt before Naqib Khan.

"Read to the emperor what you have written so far, Naqib." Akbar commanded.

"Your Majesty." Naqib Khan obeyed promptly. *"I have kept before my eyes the truth that all this autocracy and world-rule, all this sword-bearing and clime-conquering, are for the purpose of shepherding and for doing the work of watch and word, not for the amassing of treasure of gold and silver, or for decorating the throne and diadem, or for letting one's feet halt in the mud of transitory pleasure, or for sinking the head into the collar of unstable desires. Hence there has ever been naught but goodness and goodwill toward friend and foe, kinsman and stranger. There hath been a constant stirring toward the soothment of mortals, whether high or low and for graciousness to men of the age, whether near or afar. In accordance with the principle: Do good as God doth good to thee. I have been devoting my energies toward promulgating the laws of kindness, the laying of the foundations of justice, the spreading of the lights of benevolence and the irrigating of the gardens and men's hopes and peace."*

"Not another word to add." Akbar smiled to himself. "Strange epistle, but it needs no embellishing, except my royal seal. Get it ready to be dispatched immediately, Naqib. As for now, leave the emperor to his solitude." He dismissed him.

Akbar was immersed in the absolute luxury of his solitude after Naqib Khan was gone. His feet, on the will of their own, were leading him toward the marble terraces, overlooking the fountains. A flock of pigeons were pecking at the remains of their breakfast around the fountains, served earlier by the royal servants, it was obvious.

Akbar began to whistle as was his wont, to see the pigeons dance and somersault. He himself had trained these pigeons for such grand performances, and they were obedient to his will, when their wills matched the emperor's. One pair of the emperor's favorite pigeons had begun to heed the emperor's summons. This couple was stretching their wings for a grand performance. Catching the rhythm of the royal whistle, they began to dance, somersaulting in the air, and then landing at the emperor's feet.

More pigeons were joining this couple, and now they were an orderly group, landing at the emperor's feet in unison at the rhythmic end of each whistling. So absorbed was the emperor in his act of whistling, and of watching the dancing pigeons, that he didn't even notice the slow approach Abul Fazl.

"Still grieving the loss of your wise poet, Your Majesty?" Abul Fazl curtsied, his eyes begging a million pardons for this rude intrusion.

"The emperor's grief has taken wings, and is gone, my friend." Akbar smiled. "I was just hoping that time could come back to me somersaulting. And that if I could hold it into my palm for one brief moment, I would speak with Birbal."

"Is it true then, Your Majesty, that your need for the company of Birbal is more urgent than your need for spiritual understanding in the realms of life and death?" Abul Fazl thought aloud.

"My good friend, my quest for spiritual understanding is a disease, not a need." Akbar stood studying the palms of his hands. "Rather, a paralysis of the mind and the soul! I am afflicted with both, something cankerous festering inside my flesh, while the body as a whole lumbers onward to the path of ruin and decay, of pain and surcease."

"If such a disease can emanate the light of truth, Your Majesty, as it has from your ocean of wisdom and judgment, then I would love to be afflicted by it." Abul Fazl challenged with the precocity of his wisdom.

"Truth is blind, my sage friend! It is crushed by its weight of light, rendering all sightless, who dare look upon its face." Akbar knotted his fingers together in the shape of a castle. "Is truth, love?" He asked whimsically.

"Both are one, Your Majesty. Naked and absolute as the sun with all its warmth and radiance!" Abul Fazl responded poetically.

"Then I have not found it! My quest has been a mirage of absurdities." Akbar laughed suddenly.

"Truth is your talisman, Your Majesty. You may not see it, but you possess it, absolutely." Abul Fazl laughed in return. "Truth is your companion, in wisdom, in compassion, and in your virtue of tolerance toward all religions."

"That is not truth, Abul, but the influence of Sufism on me. Sufism, which is called the *creed of love*!" Akbar's eyes were shining like the shafts of sunlight.

"Then, we should talk more about Sufism at the Ibadat Khana, Your Majesty." Was Abul Fazl's abrupt plea. "Muslims are quick to accuse the emperor! Some say that you have become a Hindu and some that you have become a Christian?"

"Let the men say what they want, Abul." Akbar retorted mirthfully. "Judgment falls from God into the hearts of men who are close to Him. And God knows, I am as true to Islam as I could be to Hinduism if I was born a Hindu, or remaining true to Christianity if I were the son of a Christian. And if I were born in a Jewish family, I would continue to love Yahweh with all my heart. Yet, Buddhism is the seat of my worship these days, if the emperor may confess. Seeking enlightenment, under the mercy of God, as Allah is my witness."

"Yet, discretion is necessary in these times of war and zeal, Your Majesty." Abul Fazl murmured apprehensively. "God, may He grant our Muslim brothers the sight to see truth as seen by the wisdom of our emperor."

"Don't invoke the name of the Lord, in vain, Abul." Akbar teased. "The emperor has not seen truth, he is still searching. Besides, insight, not sight, beholds the truth. The sight has only two eyes, while insight, a myriad. Though, it looks more into the heart of lies than into the soul of truth!"

"As your devoted friend, Your Majesty, I live in constant fear, concerned about the safety of your life." Abul Fazl began assiduously. "The zeal of the Muslims is fanned by other sects in Hinduism, who deems you the avatar of their gods. Brahmans hail you as a saint, as the incarnation of Brahma!"

"Don't fear for my life, Abul. I plan to live as long as the very last of avatars in the pantheon of holy gods of the Hindus." Akbar snapped rather cheerfully. "These people, my friend, who hail me as a saint now, would persecute me later, as a heretic. After my death, I hope. And as for our Muslim brothers, their zeal matches their sense of bigotry. Such times, when virtue, justice and goodness are branded as the very acts of heresy! Before their judgment, the emperor is an infidel, I know too well!"

"May Your Majesty's sense of tolerance heal the cankers of bigotry, injustice and ignorance inside the hearts of our Muslim brethren!" Abul Fazl exclaimed prayerfully.

"Tolerance! Especially, the emperor's sense of tolerance, in the hands of the bigots, is a smoldering flame. A flame, which, after my death, would leap forth like a wild fire! Annihilating all, but the rich and the malefic, the emperor can predict. My only hope is, that prince Salim would enforce the edicts of tolerance as his legacy, to rule and to be ruled, wisely." Akbar demurred aloud.

"Prince Salim is a noble youth, Your Majesty." Abul Fazl commented in response. "But please, Your Majesty, may I request that you shun the subject of your death. My heart sinks, when you talk about your death, I do confess. May the wicked of tongue and of heart, I pray, roast inside the fires of their conceit."

"Wicked, you say, my suffered friend." Akbar began with a subtle humor. "My dear Abul, wicked are never scorched by the fires of their conceit, for it only warms their hearts. Its warmth alone blackens the simmering cauldrons in their souls with the soot of self-righteousness." He paused. "It's almost noon, Abul. Do you know the special significance of this time, this particular day?"

"With the sun shining so radiantly, Your Majesty, how can I forget?" Abul Fazl smiled. "The Sun is entering Aries approximately nineteenth degree in a sharp angle, and today is the thirtieth of March. I have come prepared, Your Majesty." His hand reached down to his pocket, procuring a stone named, *Surajkrant*, along with one white strip of cotton. "Last year, exactly on this same spot, we committed the Surajkrant to the rays of the Sun, building a celestial fire, which was preserved in the fire-pot called the *agingir*. See! Your Majesty, I remember every detail. That fire has lasted us a whole year, and this will too, if I succeed in kindling it." He held the strip of cotton close to the stone.

"I have confidence in you, Abul that you would succeed in kindling this celestial fire. The Sun is gracious and benevolent this brilliant noon-day." Akbar watched him thoughtfully. "You kindle this fire, Abul, and the emperor would go and seek the company of his brides." He kept watching. "The cooks and the torch-bearers would be pleased to see the renewal of this celestial fire. And I hope they spend the whole year in great prosperity, getting much use out of this fire, and preserving it wisely." He was looking at the fire-pot, which Abul Fazl had procured from the pouch at his waist. "Don't forget to bring twelve candles in silver and gold each to the pavilion at sunset. We would recite poetry and sing the melodies of peace." He turned abruptly.

"Please, wait, Your Majesty, wait a moment longer." Abul Fazl exclaimed! In a flash the strip of cotton was lit to a living flame. He was quick to dip this flaming strip into oil inside the fire-pot. The celestial fire was preserved.

"Since you are the guardian of the sacred flame inside the harem, Abul, come, show it to the royal ladies, yourself." Akbar laughed, turning to his heels.

The emperor was feeling much joy in the company of his royal ladies in this new palace at Fathepur Sikri. Prince Salim, with his wives Man Bai and Sahiba Jamali, was drinking and laughing. His daughter Sultanunnisa by Man Bai, only two year old, was entertaining the emperor with her little attempts in song and dancing. Not giving any chance to her younger brother, Khusrau, to claim the emperor's attention. Sahiba Jamali was heavy with child, hoping to bless prince Salim with a royal son.

Abdur Rahim and Aziz Koka were seated by the emperor, welcomed most graciously by the Queen Mother, Hamida Banu Begum herself. Akbar's Hindu wives, Hira, Usha, Jagruti and Sangita were lingering near the alcove where the fire-pot with its celestial fire burned vividly. Suriya and Ruqaiya had also joined the Hindu wives where they stood admiring the sacred flame. Nighat and Mahmooda were seated on the gilded divan. Farida and Bibi Shad were cradled in amiable conversation with the Queen Mother. Salima was listening most attentively to the emperor's aunt, Gulbadan Begum.

"Your Majesty, what means this celestial flame?" Hamida Banu Begum commented. "It should be left in the royal kitchens, where the cooks can benefit from it. It should not have been brought inside the harem walls to be watched as some divine object of worship and curiosity. Most of us, as instructed by the holy Quran, do not favor this celestial flame as an object of veneration. Are we to worship fire and light now?"

"Sweet Mamma, how your thoughts are swayed by the gossip in our court?" Akbar laughed. "It is the emperor's religious duty to offer divine praise, and to worship fire and light, since his Hindu wives love and cherish this practice. But be assured, dear Mamma, only the ignorant consider this practice as forgetfulness of the Almighty, and call it fire worship. The deep-sighted know better, and the emperor with his wisdom, not only knows, but feels the presence of Allah in every ritual and essence of things."

"You must guard yourself against calumny, Your Majesty, and practice restraint in what you say. And in what you do, no matter how noble your thoughts or how deep your wisdom!" Hamida Banu Begum warned. "People are bent on making a god out of you. Jains, Hindus, Brahmins, all think that you are the avatar of their personal gods!"

"This is the second time today that I have been honored with the privilege of being avatar of the holy gods, Miryam Makani. One of these blessed days, I might even start feeling and acting like a god." Akbar laughed. "How can I appear as an avatar to Jains, Hindus, or Brahmins, when I, a mere mortal, profess to all, that in a spiritual sense, I feel I am an unholy worm intoxicated by the power of God. And that I am thirsting for the oceans of knowledge, while holding Islam as my talisman. Yet, I keep wandering astray into the jungles of truth, my hungers and thirsts unslaked, my thoughts impenitent and inconsolable. Tell me, dear Mamma, what kind of an avatar the emperor appears to be before the eyes of the ignorant men?"

"I don't know, Your Majesty, I don't know, my son." Hamida Banu Begum smiled. "I only know that you are surrounded by enemies, right here in your Moghul court, and abroad. Base accusations against you reach me every hour of the day. In the eyes of the mullahs, you are not only an infidel, but have become a Christian!"

"And do you believe in such lies, dear Mamma?" Akbar challenged.

"No, Your Majesty." Hamida Banu Begum murmured. "Though I should be the one accusing my son, for you favored Father Montserrat against your mother in permitting him to take away the Russian slave, his Polish wife and their two children."

"There is no concept of slavery in Islam, Mamma, as you know, and Islam teaches equality for all men, regardless of their race, creed, or religion." Akbar responded. "You should be glad that I relieved you from the burden of sin, and cast it to the winds."

"The only sin I know myself to be burdened with, Your Majesty, is the sin of loving my son more than God. And suffering in eternal fear for his safety!" Hamida Banu Begum sighed, her gaze warm and adoring.

"Ah, Miryam Makani, this subtle irony!" Akbar exclaimed poetically. "Our sins we conceal inside our hearts. And our sufferings we carry over our shoulders, for all to see and empathize." He stole a glance at Salima who was talking with Gulbadan.

After this poetic comment of the emperor, a chorus of complaints was erupting forth from the lips of the ladies, as if rehearsed in advance to chide the emperor.

"How we suffer and suffer, Your Majesty." Gulbadan Begum was the first one to voice her complaint. "A Muslim emperor inviting Christian priests to his court—"

"And how Father Aquaviva was installed right here in the emperor's palace, and prince Murad instructed to take lessons from him—" Salima was the next to validate Gulbadan Begum's fears.

"And the portraits of the Virgin Mary and of the Jesus Christ held in reverence—" Hira Begum could not resist her protest.

"And Bibles displayed along with the Quran in our imperial library—" Nighat Begum opined aloud.

"And prince Daniyal adopting the customs of—"

"Ah, crusade against Christianity by the divine lips of the ladies!" Akbar declared. "A wise and virtuous man has only two choices in this world. An eternal torment in life, or eternal damnation in death! But he rejects both, inventing a third one? Which leads him toward the path of righteousness in this desert, called the world of diversity, if not the world of adversity and of adverse choices." He flashed a quick glance at prince Salim. "Do you understand the truth of this mystical epigram from the very cores of the emperor's psyche, Shaikhu Baba?" He asked abruptly.

"Moderately so, Your Majesty, in relative to Din-i-Ilahi." Prince Salim murmured cautiously. "But in my estimation, truth, which is the core of righteousness, is arbitrary."

"Truth is neither arbitrary, nor judgmental, my presumptuous Prince." Akbar chided firmly. "Truth shines through the virtues of its own deeds performed by the men of understanding, whose knowledge of the Divine is not restricted, but open to a multitude of ways. All *ways* carving one single path—the path of righteousness, which is not absolute, but relative to the terms of age and time." His gaze was alighting on Abdur Rahim. "What are your thoughts concerning the truth divine or unholy, my son?"

"Truth resides in one's heart, Your Majesty. Its divinity or un-holiness resting on one's thoughts profound or undisciplined." Abdur Rahim responded smoothly.

"The emperor must disagree with you too, my son." Akbar intoned sadly. "Truth speaks through the divine wisdom of speech. It refutes not the truths of others, but accepts them as its own legacy. Treating all truths like the siblings of one cosmic truth, not like the infants slaughtered amidst the warfare of ignorance. Ah, one cosmic truth, kindred to all beliefs!" His gaze was reaching out to his daughters. "One of these days, my loves, we would go on a picnic in our royal safina. And my dear princesses would study stars under the moonlit nights."

"These moods and whims of yours, Your Majesty! You need rest, not excursions." Hamida Banu Begum sought the emperor's attention.

"And the fears and protests of my lovely wives!" Akbar's gaze was lured toward the dancers before he approached his mother. "My wives, who must cultivate the need for poetry and music, besides being entertained with song and dancing. I have been thinking, Mamma, that for the harmony of families in general, all families should share one meal and expenses, and practice the art of love and understanding! Then all members of the family would stay happy, without anyone intruding upon the moods and the whims of each other." He smiled, turning toward Salima.

"No love, no fruit of life." Gulbadan Begum commented aloud.

"The emperor needs a shower of warmth and sunshine, dear Salima. Would you be kind enough to honor him with your presence?" Akbar held out his hands, and assisted Salima to her feet.

"Watch out, Your Majesty, the Sun might lower its banner of lies on your very head." Hamida Banu Begum could not help voicing her concern. "Accusations against you are being floated and exchanged, that the emperor worships the Sun."

"I neither worship Sun, nor any other celestial deities, Mamma, but beauty inside the temples of my heart, where all my wives have equal share of my love!" Akbar declared laughingly, holding Salima prisoner and dragging her along out of the chamber.

The small garden with its bower of roses was welcoming the emperor and his beloved. Salima was recollecting, rather than talking about the incidents of her journey from Mecca back to Agra. How the royal ladies were delayed at Aden after the shipwreck? How Bayezid had espied one royal boat in search of a ship? How the Portuguese had caused delay at the port of Surat? Many more recollections were erupting forth, but amidst the string of her thoughts, she was lingering behind and asking abruptly.

"Do you really worship the Sun, Your Majesty?"

"How imperfect is our vision, my love, which deems the shining orbs in the galaxies, including the stars and the moons, as holy and inconceivable? While living on this earth, we are in constant fear of desecrating holiness inside the shrines of our hearts." Was Akbar's low response!

"Are you still in mourning over the death of Birbal, Your Majesty?" Another lone inquiry was chased out of Salima's thoughts.

"Yes, my jewel. I am still grieving that great loss and the loss of love in your heart—for the emperor."

"That's not true, Your Majesty." Salima murmured wretchedly.

"The emperor was happily deceived in believing that you loved him. That was when I was ill." Akbar murmured to himself. "Did you truly love me then?"

"Yes, I did, Your Majesty, truly." Salima could only choke her bitterness under the mantle of white lies.

"Yes, like a rich heiress, bestowing crumbs of affection on her poor slave." Akbar challenged tenderly.

"You can be a slave to none, Your Majesty, but to your own mighty will. And poverty can never dare approach you, fearing, lest you breathe on it the curse-of-the-riches." Salima summoned the aid of her caustic wit.

"Ah, my nemesis!" Akbar laughed wistfully. "You did love me during my illness I would like to believe, even if it was a deception. More likely, an illusion! And now, do you love me, now?"

"I do, Your Majesty. How can I prove?" Salima murmured.

"By melting sweetly into my arms, my love, you can prove your love. Not by enduring my kisses in sweet revulsion, till you can be free to absolve your body from the taint of passionate sweetness." Akbar hummed softly.

The late afternoon had arrived swiftly, and Akbar's companion now was Faizi, as he sauntered toward Ibadat Khana. The tall pipal trees on both sides with their thick, interlocking canopies were offering comfort and quietude, lending soporific warmth to the poet and the emperor. The Ibadat Khana with its domed roofs, turrets and balconies, was looming not far, awaiting the arrival of the royal host in majestic silence.

"You look so lonesome, Faizi! Why?" Akbar asked abruptly.

"The companion of my loneliness is my comprehensive genius
The scratching of my pen is harmony for my ear
If I were to bring forth what is in my mind
I wonder whether the spirit of age could bear it."

Faizi's thoughts broke forth into an impromptu quatrain.

"No jewels are worth one single breath of your poetry, my divine poet." Akbar complimented. "I hope, you excel beyond words and beyond your genius."

"Hope leads me to the door of oblivion, Your Majesty. I consider hope my enemy, than a friend." Faizi commented under some spell of poetic profundity.

"Oblivion, not enlightenment, leads one to the abode of truth, my poet-genius." Akbar responded thoughtfully. "But the emperor does agree with you. Hope is the life-long foe of us mortals, who let it live at the risk of their misery, despair and hopelessness. Such an agony of the mind and soul! Sublime, sublime! A torment everlasting!" He laughed suddenly. "Such anarchy in fire and light, in thoughts, in thoughts!"

"Fire lends warmth to thoughts, Your Majesty. And they kindle into the radiant revelations of their own." Faizi commented in response.

"Yes, fire burns and scorches, also. But it does give light, of revelation, I mean." The poet-mystic in Akbar expounded cheerfully. "This light, then, is quickly consumed by cinders, which soon turn to ashes. The ashes without warmth, so light and so humble! Knowing the essence of light in their cold humility, not in the scalding ripple of the flames already dead in their pride! Anarchy in thoughts, indeed! I have forgotten my dream, not the dream of law and stability in my empire, but a real dream which I dreamt a longtime hence—" He paused as if recalling that strange dream. "Yes, that dream! I saw a woman's body emerging out of the coils of a snake in three pieces. The lower part danced as the sensuous emblem of lust. The middle one expanded like the furnace of pain and torment. And the upper one was all purity."

"Maybe, Your Majesty had gone to bed angry that night." Faizi commented. "I have noticed that when I go to bed professing to myself, that I hate so and so, though actually not hating in a true sense of the word! I spend a restless night flanked by turbulent dreams." He murmured softly, as if divining the emperor's thoughts.

"Anger is difficult to swallow, and hate more difficult to digest, when both plunge headlong into the profounder deeps of one's noble soul. Disrupting its calm and filling it with chaos." Akbar opined aloud. "Oh, the fogs of bigotry, will they ever fade? Well, we have settled on the twelve provinces, so far. Agra, Delhi, Oudh, Ajmer, Malwa, Multan, Bihar, Kabul, Bengal, Lahore, Ahmadabad, Allahbad. And the revenues from them are bountiful. Lahore alone can boast of one thousand workshops, which specialize in making shawls. I want the taxes on such merchandise abolished, so that the trade of foreign goods could prosper. Also, the harbor taxes and the river tolls must be reduced, so that the merchants could feel welcome in Hind, and can travel freely. Well, look." He was becoming aware of the horses and the elephants right in front of the Ibadat Khana. "The Arab and Persian horses with the saddles of silver! And the emperor loves the housings of velvet and brocade on these elephants. Is there something of happy import, about which the emperor has not been informed?" His feet were coming to a sudden halt.

"The gifts to the emperor!" Was Faizi's quick response!

"The emperor can tell." Akbar breathed delight. "What embassies?"

"The embassies from Iran and Turan, Your Majesty. And from Queen Elizabeth 1 from England." Faizi informed happily.

The highest gallery in the Ibadat Khana was all carpeted and damasked. At the foot of the Akbar's velvet throne were heaps of gifts from ambassadors of rich countries. The caskets of gold and silver, brimming to the top with heaps of pearls, rubies and garnets! The silver vases and vessels of gold and silver! And the chains wrought in gold, just to name a few of the precious gifts. The emperor seemed not aware of these gifts, his thoughts accosting mysteries of the mysterious.

Were the gods of the pagans not merciful and truthful? Is the God of the Jews, of the Muslims, of the Christians not One? Was Yahweh born out of nothingness? Was Jesus the god of the Underworld? Did Prophet Muhammed ascend to heaven? Did Nothingness become the God of the People of the Book? Splintering their Faiths into three warring tribes! This mighty God, sending commandments! Commanding all, always commanding. Befuddling all, and thundering parables upon all. Sundering all apart, and cutting them into three bleeding lumps of deformity. All bandaged with the divine ropes of wrath, chastisement and vengeance most terrible and irrevocable. Were the deities of the Greeks, the Romans, the Egyptians, and of the Sumerians, not born before Yahweh? Out of Nothingness, into the empty skulls of the aborigines! Was Truth ever revealed? Truth, isn't it a lie? The biggest lie, a man could ever invent. Do lies need to be revealed? Nay, they cannot be concealed, even if the lying tongues were plucked out of the mouths of the wretched liars! So, where does the truth stand? Inside the mire of countless lies, chaste and unrevealed—this truth! Ah, God's curse! Holy wisdom! Divine jest! Akbar's thoughts were awakening to absorb all arguments.

"Hinduism is the only seat of worship, which permits men to fashion their own gods and goddesses in the images of man-god and mother-goddess." Debi, a learned Brahman was commenting, rather than arguing with the poet Nurruddin.

"O, Mankind! we created
you from a single pair
of male and a female,
and made you into
nations and tribes, that
you may know one another
verily, the most honorable
of you in the Sight of Allah,
is that believer who is best in
religion and best in good deeds.
Verily!
Allah is All-knowing,
All-Aware."

Fatehullah Shirazi was reciting from the Quran.

"Sun is the source of wisdom and understanding, if we only but look upon its countenance with devotion and worship." Dastur Mahyarji, the Zoroastrian priest was expounding to the Jain scholars.

"Fire and light are the souls of cosmic wisdom—" Dustur Ardeshir, a Parsee priest was voicing his wisdom amidst the din and clamor of other voices.

"Poverty and chastity should be the dharma of all living. And the practice of ahisma which is non-injury, alone leads one to the portals of truth—" Hirvijaya Suri, a Jain Pontiff was trying his best to be heard amidst the tides of epigrams.

"Christ is the Son of God. He suffered pain and calumny, and died for our sins" Cabral, a Portuguese merchant was loud in voicing his creed.

"Without pain and suffering, there would be no music in poetry, no color in art." Akbar turned to Faizi. "Sin, evil, violence and wickedness, if they were absent, life would be dull and uninteresting. What would you add to such mundane thoughts of the emperor, my royal poet?"

"Something very subtle to match your wisdom, Your Majesty." Faizi smiled. "If your thoughts are inspired by the turn of these arguments around here, then I may find myself fortunate in eliciting a suitable response. If Christ had died a natural death or even his ascension to the heaven as we Muslims believe, not on the Cross with suffering as his talisman, he would not have been exalted by the Christians as the Son of God."

"Christ is our prophet, not our Lord, if that's the only contention between the Muslims and the Christians!" Akbar's eyes were kindling the stars of amusement. "And yet, if the prophets had not suffered, there would be no holy wars, but unholy peace."

"Unholy peace! Your Majesty. You have just touched a painful wound in my heart." Faizi intoned wistfully. "Alas, peace is gone from me. I am in love again. Denial and suffering have become my lot, the only means to feel closer to the soul of my beloved. How violent is my heart these days, Your Majesty, you can't imagine? Seeking evil and taking vengeance on my poor soul, which practices denial and suffering."

"Evil indeed is violence and vengeance inside one's heart, but not denial and suffering!" Akbar commented. "Denial and suffering bring one close to perfection! The only kind of *perfection*, a mortal soul could embrace. But a poet in love is vulnerable." His attention was diverted to the chain of loud arguments.

"And what is this new religion, Din-i-Ilahi? Pray, tell me." Julian Pereira, the Portuguese priest was assiduous in his arguments with Baduani.

"How do I know?" Was Baduani's caustic exclamation. "Ask the emperor. He is not sitting on some throne in the seventh heavens, but on an earthly throne! Where all the lowly or exalted have access to His Majesty's audience!"

"Yes, I will. I shall, indeed!" Julian Pereira was already wading his way through the sea of scholars, toward the emperor.

"Of God, people have said that He had a son;

of a Prophet they have said that he was a sorcerer.

Neither God, nor the prophet has escaped the slander of men, much less I." Akbar sat hugging his impromptu couplet.

"What sort of religion is this Din-i-Ilahi, Your Majesty, if I may be as bold as to ask?" Julian Pereira stood there flushed.

"Din-i-Ilahi is not a religion, my good priest, but a prayer to let each man revere one's own God, and to find manifestation of truth in one's soul." Akbar began thoughtfully. "Yes, not a religion, but a hymnal, set to music by the law and virtue of one's wisdom. A ghazal, telling all! Not to flaunt one's belief to the face of the other. Not to condemn any man into the jungles of perdition! Not to vilify the gods of the others, which are but one *essence* under different names? Yes, a prayer, a hymnal, and a sublime note inside the very heart of nature. Singing that rituals and prayers are only the means to flatter one's ignorance! And the ignorant would remain blind to truth, even if it came face-to-face to challenge one's faith." He concluded poetically.

"Your Majesty." Julian Pereira murmured in awe. "Yet, people say. I have heard, Din-i-Ilahi is a religion."

"To know one's God through the path of righteousness is a religion, indeed." Akbar expounded. "*Din* means, religion. *Ilahi* means, God's, Allah's. In essence, *God's Mercy* accepts all *Faiths* in one universal Faith—in God. Inculcating the sense of tolerance toward all religions! Tolerance itself should be the religion, which all men should adopt as their duty toward piety and goodwill. Yet, my besotted priest, have you seen any religious scriptures concerning Din-

i-Ilahi? Have you heard any prayer which belongs to Din-i-Ilahi? For each religion has one simple prayer, at least! Have you seen a temple, a mosque, or a
synagogue, where the adherents of Din-i-Ilahi prostrate themselves before some
unknown deity?" He asked kindly.

"No, Your Majesty." Julian Pereira murmured.

"What heathen lies, the emperor has to endure, for his sense of tolerance
toward all religions!" Akbar turned to Abul Fazl while watching Baduani approach the throne.

"Your Majesty, I feel it heart-rending to hear accusations against you from
the tongues of common people. Who, in fact, are incited by the men of wealth!"
Baduani bowed hastily. "Especially when those base, wretched canards affirm
that Your Majesty worships the sun, not God." His own eyes were accusing the
emperor.

"And who are the authors of such base, wretched canards, my wise scholar?" Akbar laughed. "How can the common people possessed only with the
desire of gain, look with respect upon the sordid men of wealth! From ignorance
those fail in reverence to this fountain of light, and reproach him who prays to it.
If their understanding were not at fault, how could they forget this sura in the
Quran? *By the Sun and its rising brightness; by the moon when she followeth
him; by the day when it showeth its splendor; by the night when it coverth him
with darkness; by the heaven and him who built it; by the earth and him who
spread it forth.* How is he who hath purified the same, happy, but he who hath
corrupted the same is miserable." He turned his gaze to Abul Fazl. "My friend,
tell this scholar of Islam, what the holy book of Quran says concerning the sun.
Though, I revere life and nature in its entirety, Him alone I worship."

"Your Majesty, my pleasure to refresh Baduani's memory. Though, I am
sure, he reads his Quran daily." Abul Fazl looked at Baduani. "A couple of suras
come to my mind, Baduani, which can be interpreted in seven different ways.
But they still retain the essence of worshipping only one God. *Surely your God
is one. Lord of the heavens and the earth and all that is between them and the
Lord of the sun's risings.* You surely can recall this one, Baduani, for I have
heard you recite it so often. *They say, our Lord, hasten to us our portion of the
punishment before the Day of Reckoning. Bear patiently what they say, and remember Our servant David, man of strong hands, surely he was always turning
to God. We subjected to him the mountains. They celebrated God's praises with
him at nightfall and sunrise.* I would welcome your interpretations to these suras, Baduani, when you could spare some time from your pious contemplations."

"Since the emperor is under this holy inquisition, he wishes to shed more
light on this subject." Akbar's gaze shifted from Abul Fazl to Baduani. "Al-Nur,
is one of the ninety-nine names of God in the Hadith. Al-Ghazali, its author,
calls Al-Nur the Light of Allah, which is manifest to all in its flow of mercy and
kindness. *Existence is a light streaming to all things from the light of His essence, for He is the light of the heavens and the earth*, Al-Ghazali expounds.
*And as there is not an atom of the light of the sun which does not by itself lead
one to the existence of the sun which illuminates it, so there is not a single atom*

from the existents of the heavens and the earth and what lies between them
which does not lead one by the very possibility of its existence to the necessary
existence who brings them into being. This holy inquisition may find rest in this
verse by some poet, whose name the emperor can't recall.

The glass is fine and the wine is pure
So alike are they that the facts are confused
As if there were wine and no glass
Or a glass and no wine."

He was trying to catch the words of prayer from Fatehullah Shirazi in the
lower gallery.

"O God, I am your servant, and the son of Your servant, and the son of
Your bondmaids, my forelock is in Your hand, Your judgment concerning me is
done. I implore You by every name which is Yours, by which You have named
Yourself, or which You revealed in Your book, or which You taught to anyone
from Your creation, or which You appropriated to Yourself in Your knowledge
of hidden things, that You might make the Quran a renewal of my heart, a light
from my inmost thoughts, a way through my affliction, and the unraveling of my
distress—" Fatehullah Shirazi was reciting this prayer from the Hadith by Al-
Ghazali.

"The beginning of wisdom is the fear of God, as Prophet Muhammed said."
Faizi was concluding his comments in response to Akbar's quest for truth.

"Yes." Akbar sat quoting Al-Ghazali. *"And wisdom guides us to the happi-*
ness of the world to come in a manner free from rebuke or harshness, fanaticism
or disputation. The best way of being benevolent open to man, lies in attracting
others to accept the truth by one's own good qualities, pleasing comportment,
and exemplary actions. For, they are more effective and more benign, than elo-
quent exhortation."

"Part of the attractiveness of a man of Islam is to leave alone that which
does not concern him, here is one more of Prophet Muhammad's sayings." Abul
Fazl opined aloud. Thinking, that the emperor was immersed in his sad rumina-
tions!

"The doctrines of Islam are most grossly misinterpreted, as you are well
aware, Abul." Akbar began slowly and thoughtfully. "This evening, my thoughts
seem to cling to the cloak of Al-Ghazali. I can't help, but ponder upon what he
wrote. *What is most evident is perceived by the senses, and the most evident of*
these is what is perceived by the sense of sight, and the most evident of the
things perceived by the sense of sight is the light of the sun shining on bodies, by
which everything becomes manifest, not itself be manifest." He turned his gaze
to Baduani. "Show me your translations of the Mahabharata, Baduani. How far
you have proceeded?" He asked abruptly.

"Your Majesty, they are with Naqib Khan." Baduani's voice quivered with
some inward emotion, which he could not restrain. "I will fetch, eighteen chapters are done."

"You have mistranslated a few chapters, I hear." Akbar shot this challenge
at him, thoughtfully and menacingly.

"That is not true, Your Majesty. How could you believe in such accusations?" Baduani could only murmur in explicit misery.

"For, everything Muslim is good, and everything non-Muslim evil, in your pious judgment." Akbar's gaze was intense and searching.

"There is no truth in this either, Your Majesty. How can—" Baduani appeared to crumble before the light of anger and accusation in the emperor's eyes.

"May God Almighty protect those who are engaged in this work! Is not that what you said in the presence of the other scholars? Deny that, Baduani, if you will?" Akbar challenged intensely.

"Yes, Your Majesty, but the work—" Baduani's protest died on his lips.

"But, that your zeal is bigger than your ego." Akbar interrupted. *"These useless absurdities are enough to confound the eighteen worlds!* Are these not your own words? And you were impudent enough to confess to the other scholars, while translating this holy text. Are you going to deny your own words?"

"But the languages, Your Majesty. Sanskrit is so very difficult to—" Baduani was confounded by the flashing of rage in the emperor's eyes.

"We should all learn only one language, my friend. And that language is the language of perception. Then, we can all live in conformity with each other." Akbar's anger was hushed, but flaring.

"Your Majesty." Abul Fazl interceded. "I attest to Baduani's integrity, concerning the translations, Your Majesty. Though, he is bold of speech, and stands accused for uttering those words, which he himself doesn't deny. If I may be bold to speak in his favor, Your Majesty? He looks contrite, and seeks your pardon."

"I had thought, Abul, that Baduani was an unworldly man of the Sufi tendencies." Akbar's flashing eyes now rested on Abul Fazl. "But, now, I have discovered, that he is such a bigoted lawyer that no sword can sever the jugular vein of his bigotry." He returned his gaze to Baduani. "Begone, Baduani, Begone. And wear the mantle of propriety, if not of wisdom, when you speak. For the words shot through lips are most dangerous, than the bullets piercing one's heart." Akbar clapped his hands as a signal for courtly sessions. "The emperor is ready to receive the embassies."

"Here, in the Ibadat Khana, Your Majesty?" Faizi commented.

"Yes, the great ceremonies can wait, till the emperor visits Kashmir." Akbar commented back. "The fatigue and the weariness of my hunting expeditions bid me to practice economy in time. Besides, I have grown quite greedy of time amidst the galaxies of my spiritual needs and spiritual quests." He murmured low.

The first embassy presented before the emperor was from the ambassador from Thatta. Raja Basu appearing in person to pledge allegiance to the emperor! He was presented by Muhammad Hussain of Kashmir, upon which the emperor had bestowed the title of Zarrinqalam.

"Ah, my Zarrinqalam! The proud son of Kashmir. You would be the emperor's guide, when I visit Kashmir." Akbar turned his attention to Raja Basu.

"Your Majesty, your most devoted subject." Raja Basu bowed low. "This casket of jewels is my humble gift, with a pledge of obedience to your will."

"The jewel of your friendship is much more precious to the emperor, than all the worldly treasures, my friend. Yet, you and your gifts bring immense delight to the emperor." Akbar invited Basu to be seated near the throne.

The next embassy was from the rebel and the dethroned ruler of Kashmir, Yusuf Shah. He was presented by Shahrukh Mirza.

"I thought Bhagwan Das was assigned the privilege to conduct Yusuf Shah to our presence?" Akbar's kind gaze was probing Shahrukh Mirza.

"Bhagwan Das is indisposed, Your Majesty. Since he has been recalled from Kashmir, he has been suffering some fits of insanity. He attempted suicide." Shahrukh Mirza breathed this crumb of information, quite reluctantly.

"Death and insanity have become the plague of these constant wars. And the emperor is being robbed of his treasures, of his jewel-friends." One anguished comment broke forth on Akbar's lips. "First, I lost my Ruby, my Birbal. And now, my carnelian, Bhagwan Das is fading from my sight. Send my royal physicians to him, at once, Shahrukh, without any delay." He commanded.

"Your Majesty, your royal physicians, Fath Gilani and Hakim Ali, are already by his side day and night." Shahrukh Mirza confessed.

Akbar's gaze was slowly turning to Yusuf Shah.

"Your Majesty. Your humble servant in the chains of obedience and contrition!" Yusuf Shah breathed low.

"Cast away these links of contrition, Yusuf, and wear only the chains of obedience." Akbar commanded. "What were your reasons for rebellion?"

Yusuf Shah stood there mute. Wearing only a mantle of shame and silence!

"Yet, your contrition is enough to grant you the boon of clemency." Akbar softened his tones. "The emperor would send you back to Kashmir as a ruler, on one condition, that you would wear the chains of obedience even in your sleep." He dismissed him with a wave of his arm.

The third embassy was from the queen of England, Queen Elizabeth 1. She had sent three merchants, along with a letter addressed to the emperor. These three merchants, Ralph Fitch, John Newbery and William Leeds, were presented to the emperor by Nizamuddin Ahmed.

"Your Majesty, I have a letter from our queen, Queen Elizabeth 1, which says." John Newbery unfolded the document, and continued. *"The most invincible and the most mighty prince, Jalaluddin Akbar, the king of Cambaya—"*

"Cut short the formalities, good merchant, and state the intent of your generous Queen." Akbar commanded. "Besides, I am not the king of Cambay, but the emperor of Hind. And the emperor wishes to know, why your Queen has sent you across the ocean with greetings kind and flattering?"

"Your Majesty, we are the English merchants, as you are informed." John Newbery obeyed quickly. "And our Queen wishes to open trade between Hind and England. We have the fine European cloth and the woolens. And excellent quality of furniture. Our Queen wishes us to trade these for spices, silks and the jewels from here."

"We welcome you, and convey our thanks to your Queen for her gracious offer." Akbar smiled. "The emperor will trade knowledge with caskets-full of jewels from Hind. What manner of life abounds in England? Does your Queen encourage the cultivation of the arts, the sciences, and of the literary pursuits in culture and religion?"

"There are much song and poetry in nature, there, Your Majesty. And we do have the poets and the theaters." John Newbery complied disinterestedly.

"Your Queen, is she a devout Christian?" Akbar prodded Ralph Finch.

"Yes, Your Majesty. She is a Protestant." Ralph Finch responded laconically.

"Isn't that the off-shoot of Catholicism? What's the difference?" Akbar demurred aloud. His gaze still fixed to Ralph Finch.

"Very little, Your Majesty, very little." Ralph Finch murmured rather bashfully. Being not a religious man himself, and totally ignorant of the Christian doctrines, he couldn't think of the differences between Protestants and the Catholics. "Protestants believe in a humble living, Your Majesty." He added doubtfully.

"And your priests, what do they teach?" Akbar persisted amusedly.

"They, Your Majesty, most of them have taken a vow of poverty. They too preach and practice humble living." Was Ralph Fitch's flustered response!

"Ah, the poverty and humble living!" Akbar laughed. "How can men preach of a humble living, when their gods live in such glory in temples, churches, mosques and the synagogues? If poverty be a mark of blessing, then why all these humble shrines are appareled in the wealths most coveted, which claim their hearths as the holy of the holies?" His eyes were turning to William Leeds. "One prudent response from you, and the emperor would be delighted to host you in his favor. Do you have an abundance of philosophers and the theologians in your country?"

"Too many, Your Majesty." William Leeds began with a great enthusiasm. "I have heard of quite a few of the philosophers. But Francis Bacon is the most popular of them all." He added with a pride akin to the love for learning.

"Francis Bacon." Akbar murmured. "This name sounds like the name of a priest, not of a philosopher. Leeds, and your name, I like the sound of it. Do you believe in Salvation, Leeds?" He asked abruptly.

"These days, the name Salvation, plunges my heart into deep sorrow, Your Majesty." William Leeds commenced in all earnestness. "In sorrow, because the Protestants and the Catholics are bent on killing each other on the charges of heresy!"

"The Salvation is not sorrow, but gladness of the spirit, my friend, as I have judged it after talking with the padres from Goa." Akbar commented kindly. "Do you have mosques in your country?"

"No, Your Majesty, we don't have many Muslims in our country." William Leeds responded discreetly.

"And we don't have many Christians in Hind, but we have churches." Akbar smiled.

"Do you mean, Your Majesty that you being a Muslim emperor, permit Christians to build churches in your country!" Was William Leeds baffled response.

"My great vizier here, Abul Fazl, will satisfy your curiosity, Leeds." Akbar turned to Abul Fazl, laughter brimming in his eyes.

"It is the emperor's Farman, William Leeds that he wishes all in his dominions to follow what faith they please." Abul Fazl began with a kindness matching the emperor's. "And his Farman is that no man should be interfered with, on account of his religion. And that anyone has the option to accept any faith they choose. If anyone chooses to build a church, or synagogue, or a temple, or the tower of silence—Parsee temple, no one has the authority to hinder him."

"Besides being a merchant, Leeds, what are your interests? Do you have any special skills?" Akbar asked.

"I might as well be a jeweler by trade, Your Majesty." Was William Leeds dreamy response! "I adopted this trade as a hobby. I am quite skilled in this trade now, and I can very well pass as the best jeweler in my town."

"And the best would excel to excellence in the service of the emperor." Akbar announced happily. "You are to fashion jewelry for my queens. And for my daughters, they are to be married soon. And for the wives of my sons, of course!" He dismissed all the three Englishmen with a kind gesture, becoming aware of Aziz Koka.

"Your Majesty, I bring good tidings. The news of great import for the peace in Hind." Aziz Koka curtsied. "Qasim Khan has quelled the rebellions in Kashmir. And Yaqub, the chief instigator, has fled to the hills of Kurakh. And Arab Bahadur, who was retreating after his ignominious defeat in Audh, fell into a pit and died. And the rebellions in Swat, Kabul and Bajuar are completely crushed, also. And now, we can sing the songs of victories, Your Majesty." He concluded hastily.

"With Tansen as our singer, we don't need any musicians to adorn the laurels of victories with tunes strange and wordless." Akbar clapped his hands, summoning Tansen to his presence! "But peace must be retained, and we should be vigilant of all intrigue and wickedness." He motioned both Tansen and Aziz Koka to take their seats near his throne. "The emperor has decided to move his court to Lahore, for reasons which demand urgency, not grandeur. Our further plans for peace and conquest can be attained expediently, if we took our residence in Punjab with Lahore as its capital. The north-western regions of our empire need constant attention. The affairs of Kashmir, as well as of Kabul and Badakhshan can be speedily dealt with, as Lahore being the heart of the Punjab. Yet, peace reigns for now, and the emperor longs to visit Kashmir."

"Your Majesty, we should not move our court from Fathehpur Sikri, if I may be so bold as to suggest." Baduani began humbly, but with great consternation. "A world of treasures would be lost to us in art and architecture. Our palaces would be abandoned. Ibadat Khana would mourn the loss of its occupants." He protested under some spell of earnest concern. "We should fight all the wars from here, if need be! For Fathehpur Sikri abounds in treasures, which have become a delight to us all!"

"We should fight the wars of greed and avarice, of hatred and enmity, of zeal and ignorance, of intolerance and malevolence, inside our hearts." Akbar responded calmly. "And if we come out as victors from those wars, we will discover that all the treasures of the world are within us. Then, we will be worthy to reject all the treasures of many worlds! For, such treasures enrich not those, who remain disobedient to the true nature of their noble wills." He got to his feet. "Come Tansen, and Abul and Faizi. Accompany the emperor to his palace. He needs the company of the poets, the singers and the scholars. The theologians may continue their discussions till the dawn of reason." He descended his throne, Faizi, Tansen and Abul Fazl following him.

"A great feast awaits the emperor at the palace. I was informed earlier that Prince Salim has some happy news to share with the emperor, along with a grand entertainment." Tansen sought the emperor's attention.

"One crumb of knowledge from God's table is sweeter than all the delicious viands dressed and garnished by human ingenuity." Akbar commented without looking back. "Happy news, I know! Prince Murad is engaged to be married."

Oblivious to the pale dusk ringed with crimson streaks, the emperor was approaching closer to the palace gates. At last, the beauty in sunset had arrested his attention. Much in rapport with the wounded throbs, wringing his heart into convulsion of longings fresh and inviolate!

11

Beautiful Kashmir

Akbar was seated on his makeshift throne of sandalwood within the heart of his capital, the city of Lahore. Three beautiful summers had already sailed past on a winged flight, since Akbar had made this city of gardens into one of his prosperous capitals. This particular day, the emperor was seated amongst his viziers and grandees, as if celebrating a high festival. But actually, it was a tragic event marking the end of Tansen's life.

Tansen had died suddenly, and Akbar concealing his grief inside his heart had ordered his court musicians and the musicians from all over the city to join in this funeral rite for the greatest of the singers in Hind. They were to carry Tansen's body to the graveyard with song and music, as if evoking the sweetest of tunes for a wedding march.

Tansen would prefer songs than tears. And this is the way he would love to go to his resting place, with music still sailing in the wind. Akbar had told Abul Fazl.

The people from all over the city were milling around the garlanded bier of Tansen in sober ranks, while the emperor sat watching from his throne. The notes from the lutes and the flutes, accompanied by veena and sitar were cutting through the air, and reaching aloft to the highest of the heavens. This very morning, everything around Akbar was the mist-illusions. Life, death, victories, even quests from within and without!

Illusions, illusions all! Even Salima's love and hate!

Peace had been restored in most of the cities in the vast empire of Akbar. Swat, Kabul, Gujrat, Bengal, Bajuar, Kashmir, Punjab, Baluchistan, all were savoring a breath of respite from wars and rebellions. To Akbar's judicious planning in times of war or peace, he was well aware of unrest in Deccan. And of Abdullah Khan's despotic rule over the North West Frontier Provinces. But the emperor is wearied of wars! *Akbar's thoughts were teasing the buds of joys.*

Princess Shukrunnisa was married to Shahrukh Mirza and Princess Khanam to the son of Hindal. Prince Salim was blessed with a son from Sahiba Jamali, whom Akbar had named Pervez. Much before the birth of Pervez, prince

Salim had contracted another marriage with Jagat Gosaini, the daughter of Mota Raja. Less than a year ago, Akbar had bestowed upon Faizi, the title of Poet Laureate.

Akbar's thoughts this bright morning, as he sat mourning, were entering the chamber of Salima in the palace of Lahore, and then flying off to Bhimbhar, where all his other wives had gone on an excursion. In the absence of the emperor's other wives, Salima had become so loving that Akbar was bewildered than gratified.

Two weeks. Exactly two weeks! So, my Beloved is jealous! Jealous of the other wives! How stupid any lover could be? And in this case, an emperor, who can't search the soul of his Beloved? But these illusions!

Akbar had decided to visit Kashmir. Prince Murad was to be wedded in Kashmir. Prince Salim was sent to Bhimbhar to fetch the emperor's wives to Lahore. The emperor was to leave this very day, after the funeral rites. The garlanded bier was being hoisted on men's shoulders and floating away amidst the chorus of song and music. An anguished cry of pain was constricting Akbar's heart. But his thoughts were enveloping all in the mists of illusions! He was becoming aware of Faizi and Abul Fazl.

"What mystery in silence, Abul? What repose, what sadness?" Akbar opined aloud. "Melt this sadness into the wine of wisdom, and cheer the emperor."

"Alas, Your Majesty, I have vowed to practice silence from now on." Abul Fazl suppressed a sigh. "For my wisdom is impoverished to such a grain of salt, that it can kindle no tears of pain or joy in the eyes of any man. Especially, when that man is the man of reason with a sense of pride and buoyancy!" He failed in his attempt to smile.

"Why so, Abul? Do you grieve thus?" Akbar prodded.

"I grieve only for my sorrowful tongue, Your Majesty." Abul Fazl began gravely. "Whenever I open my mouth, my wives find my speech shallow, and jarring to their ears. They get irritated so! They even say that to my face."

"All men get to be irritating at a certain age, Abul." Was Akbar's low response! "And the husbands, much more irritating that all the living species in any color or form. Yes, much more irritating, for the wives have to live with them. I have studied the souls of my wives, my friend, and have reached to a sad conclusion. Most of the wives pity their husbands, than love! Not that we are some strange, pitiful animals, but our lusts, desires and ambitions make us despicable in their eyes. They, who want the proof of love, not the love itself!" His gaze was following the bier, dipped in the gold of marigolds. "Ah, there goes the annihilation of a *melody*." He murmured.

"God's ways are mysterious, and His thoughts not to be revealed to us mortals." Abul Fazl murmured to himself, thoughtlessly.

"God doesn't have to think, my wise friend. He knows." Akbar murmured back.

"God." Abul Fazl demurred prayerfully. "May He grant the sight of *reason* to all, Your Majesty, who ascribe the power of magic and miracles to your noble deeds!"

"*My Jonathan*! Isn't that what the blasphemers say? That you are the emperor's Jonathan." Akbar intoned with a sudden brightness. "Though, I prefer the sound of Jonathan than of Abul. Now, the emperor wishes that he could claim and hold even one crumb of Divinity! So that he could raise Tansen out of his grave, just like Lazarus who was granted life after death by Christ!" He laughed mirthlessly.

"Your divine attributes, Your Majesty, I can prove them so. They tempt me to deification. But I love and revere you as one disciple his patron-saint. Loving the noble emperor, even his few faults, yet knowing no weaknesses!" Abul Fazl declared.

"Ah, my weaknesses too, and my compassion lacerated with doubts." Akbar intoned. "As for the disciples, my wise scholar! To make a disciple is to instruct one in the service of God, not to make one a personal attendant. Don't I tolerate scathing absurdities from all the bigots in my court and in my empire? The men, who deem themselves as wise, learned Muslims. Don't they revile each other with the tongues of fire? Slashing each other's throats with hideous lies! And becoming the very Jews and Egyptians for the hatred of each other! And yet, for the sake of truth, I let them dig the grave of lies. And yet, for the vile odium in their hearts and on their tongues, I would like to fill their mouths with coals, if not with offal." He added without bitterness. "What did Baduani say when Birbal died, do you remember?"

"Alas, Your Majesty, his tongue exaggerates more than his mind or heart." Abul Fazl responded evasively. His eyes pleading pardon for Baduani.

"Refresh the emperor's memory about what Baduani said after Birbal's death, my poet, since my scholar refuses to obey the emperor." Akbar turned quickly to Faizi.

"Your Majesty." Faizi muttered. "*That Birbal entered the pack of the dogs of hell.*"

"For this outrage alone, the emperor should have cast him alive into some dungeon of a hell-fire on this earth." Akbar reflected aloud. "But jails and dungeons are non-existent in our empire. Ah, yes, he still has a chance to be dethroned from his heap of *pardons*, and to be imprisoned inside the fort of Gwalior. That stinking fort where the royal rebels rot in filth and chains!" He smiled.

"Your kind *pardons* are his only refuge, Your Majesty, keeping him away from the sanctuary of Gwalior Fort." Abul Fazl was watching Baduani and other courtiers approaching the throne. "Right now, he is hugging Ramayana. His book of cherished translations for which he needs rewards, than punishments! I have watched him holding the works of his translations to his breast possessively, since morning, and repeating to himself. *I have labored on this for years—for four years.*"

"I hope his Persian is as poetic as Hindi of the Tulsidas." Akbar commented.

"Your Majesty, I hope I have done justice to the great work of Tulsidas. And that Ramayana breathes the true words of its great author." Baduani intoned humbly. "And now I present this complete translation to you, Your Majesty, for your approval.

"If your zeal were less than your intelligence, my proud scholar, you could touch stars in the heavens." Akbar claimed the book with reverence. "Your wisdom, I fear, matches equally with your zeal! The only reason, you stay in the emperor's favor. You would be rewarded bounteously after I return from Kashmir. This pearl of your labor would be illumined, of course, and added to the imperial library. Naqib Khan would do justice in reciting these holy texts to the emperor during his journey to Kashmir."

"Your Majesty, may I ask a boon?" Baduani shot a plea, encouraged by the emperor's warm gaze. "May I appeal, that grants for the hajj pilgrimage be restored?"

"Only when the holy men at Mecca cease to be malefic and avaricious, my wise scholar!" Akbar's look was thoughtful. "Meanwhile, you continue writing great works, besides these great translations. The emperor wishes that the history of the world be written, covering one thousand years after the death of the Prophet. Abul Fazl, Naqib Khan, Fatehullah Shirazi and Nizamuddin Ahmed would assist you in this endeavor."

"Your Majesty, this history of the world." Nizamuddin Ahmed sought the emperor's attention. "Would that be illumined like the other books? Like Daman, Damnah, Khalilah, Ayar Danish and the story of Humza?"

"What kind of illumination would you prefer on this history of one thousand years? The emperor has already chosen a title for it, Tarikh-i-Alfi." Akbar asked.

"If the ulemas don't object, Your Majesty! The title page might be illustrated and illumined with the picture of Prophet Muhammed riding on his horse, the Buraq, and ascending to the heavens." Nizamuddin Ahmed responded ecstatically.

"If the emperor lives that long to hold such a book in his hands, he would demolish objections of all the ulemas with the Grace of God's Mercy!" Akbar ruminated aloud. "So far, the emperor has found no injunction in the Quran forbidding the depiction of images. You have turned out to be quite a theologian, Nizamuddin. I didn't know you had such tendencies?" He murmured, as if to himself.

"I hope, Your Majesty that Tarikh-i-Alfi with such a depiction of holy art on its title page, is not to be sold in the bazaars like the poems of Urfi and Hussain Sanai." Fatehullah Shirazi was the next to seek the emperor's attention. "People are buying their books at great costs, and running the scribes ragged with further demands."

"If this book of history unwrit yet, gains such popularity, my dear friend, you would be the first one turning all the denizens of Hind into scribes! And suggesting that the whole empire of Hind should live on words alone?" Akbar's heart missed a beat, as if he could see some sort of doom lurking over the head of his friend.

"Your Majesty, since the books-yet-to-be are gaining popularity in the eyes of all present! I wish to present to the emperor my Persian translation of the Chagatai memoirs of Babur." Abdur Rahim stepped forward, holding out a large book.

"Ah, Babur. My beloved grandfather!" Akbar claimed the book with a bright smile. "I would cherish this book above all. Several copies of this book would be ordered. One for you to keep and the rest to be distributed amongst the scholars!"

"Your Majesty, prince Abdur Rahim should be under your royal surveillance at all times. People say, he has deviated from orthodoxy to such an extent, that he has become like one of those Shias who practice taqiyyah—fear, caution, proclaiming themselves Sunnis." Fatehullah Shirazi commented to reclaim emperor's attention!

"Orthodoxy, the vice of this age better be left into the hands of the bigots, my dear friend." Akbar's gaze was alighting on Jouher. "Ah, my wine-bearer, without a flagon of wine, and with a bottle of ink within his reach! What are you writing, Jouher?"

"Your Majesty's sayings, Your Majesty. Since I am relieved of my duties for the time being, Your Majesty, not to serve wine here—" Was Jouher's flustered response! His eyes were gathering mists of fear and apprehension!

"And next, you would be writing your own memoirs, the emperor predicts." Akbar laughed, sadly and indulgently.

"Great revenues from the books for the empire of Hind, if Jouher ever completes his memoirs, Your Majesty!" Bhagwan Das could not help tossing one jest to the winds.

"Ah, the revenues from spices, opium and indigo, Bhagwan Das! May you remain in good health and good spirits, so that you could collect such revenues for the patronage of art and literature." Akbar's heart was lurching as if Bhagwan Das was also the part of this same tragedy which stood lurking over the head of Fatehullah Shirazi? "Since, the emperor would be in Kashmir, pray, do not tempt fate by attempting to take your life. Life is a great gift of God, spend it wisely. Shunning melancholia and most of all collecting revenues since you are entrusted with this task!" He smiled. "What goods fetch the most revenues, my friend? Refresh the emperor's memory, as well as your own, if you can boast the knowledge of such a trade?"

"My melancholia is drained out of my mind and soul, Your Majesty, by your kindness and benevolence." Bhagwan Das smiled in return. "And as to the revenues, Your Majesty has named the most coveted of all the goods. The spices, especially, the black pepper is in great demand in the whole of Western Europe. Since it is used as a preservative for meat! Another important good is cotton. Our cotton textiles are the best, and fetch mighty gains from all the countries far and alien."

"The treasures of Persia and Tartary, Your Majesty." Todar Mall broke his silence. "Our imports enrich our empire, as well as our exports. The velvets, the brocades and the carpets! And precious stones and the metals of all kind! Though wars have loomed over my head all my life, I have enjoyed riches and great pleasures all my life. Now that I have grown old, I care neither for jewels, nor for riches."

"You are making the emperor look older than he really is, Todar Mall! Though, the passion of youth still courses in his veins like the rivulets of fire." Akbar was feeling the sense of doom as if Todar Mall too was wearing some nameless shroud of tragedy. "Though age accentuates our sadness, it enriches our hearts with joys deeper than the oceans. Knowledge surfacing on the ocean of experience in calm, tender waves! Wisdom and learning are the gifts of *age*, which a man of learning dares not exchange for the fickle pleasures of youth. You are the master of affairs in Punjab, Todar Mall, while the emperor is away. And you better summon your youth as your guide, if age robs you of such strength." He turned his attention to Faizi. "Poetry is the language of the seers, Faizi. Delight us with a couplet or two. The emperor feels bereft of wisdom."

"Your Majesty, Tansen has taken away all my couplets with him." Was Faizi's thoughtless response!

"What! All thousands and thousands of them! Not even leaving one behind?" Akbar laughed. More so, to encourage the poet than to conceal his grief!

"I cannot show ungratefulness to Love
Has he not overwhelmed me—sadness and sadness?"

A sad couplet broke forth on Faizi's lips, before he could crush its wild surge.

"A sadness most divine!" Akbar applauded, turning quickly toward Abul Fazl. "We must find a cure for this sadness. And what balm more potent, than the balm of learning and knowledge? The emperor wishes you to write, Abul, with the pen of sincerity, an account of the victories and of the other events during our reign."

"A great honor and pleasure, Your Majesty." Abul Fazl bowed his head. His own thoughts breaking forth into an impromptu quatrain.

"My pen its point-deep in my heart's blood dyes
To write such prose as far all verse out vies
For prose in its degree doth verse excel
As unbored pearls the rarest price compel."

"Oh divinity, most sublime! That is your poetic genius, Abul." Akbar got to his feet. "The emperor must repair to his palace, and then we journey to Kashmir."

A caparisoned horse was brought to the emperor for his ride toward the palace. But before the emperor could mount this graceful steed, Abul Fazl edged closer.

"Your Majesty. Could you postpone your journey to Kashmir, till the royal ladies reach Lahore? They might be here, early tomorrow. Then, we can commence our journey without delay." Abul Fazl pleaded, rather than requested.

"Grief bids me to hasten, to get away from life—death. I can feel my very soul floating! Moving closer to another death, to another life? In some new place, in continents far and wide! With new desires and alien affections—" Akbar stroked the mane of his horse sadly and tenderly.

"I just fear, Your Majesty that Prince Salim, in his preference to drink, might neglect to—" Abul Fazl's concern was silenced by downpour of mirth from Akbar's lips.

"I know, Abul, my sons drink." Akbar's mirth was dwindling. "But I console myself with the thought, that though my sons have the vice of drinking to excess, their virtue is no less, in remaining sober. I have failed in a way." He spurred his horse.

Akbar was pacing inside his bedroom in his palace at Lahore. A gold candelabra was shedding its warmth on Salima, where she sat quietly on the velvety divan, her hands resting in her lap, pale and listless. She appeared to be praying, but her thoughts and prayers were not touching the emperor's grief.

Actually, the emperor was not grieving, this very moment. His thoughts were longing for the journey to Kashmir while thinking about Salima his very own beloved. *She has no love in her heart, but pity for the emperor!* He was thinking. *Keeping her soul chaste and her body tainted with the religion of hatred!* His thoughts were touching the hem of grief. *Tansen, and Birbal, two of my beloved friends, gone. This canker of grief! Yet the pain in love—for my beloved I would suffer, always?* Akbar's thoughts were losing their rhythm. For some strange reason, he wanted to cry.

"Would you like to see the emperor cry, my love?" Akbar pondered aloud.

"I would rather that your eyes were filled with joys, Your Majesty, not with tears." Was Salima's startled response, out of the very silence in her thoughts!

"Only, you, my dear, only you have the power to fill them with the light of joy. No one else, no one else can." Akbar's feet came to a slow halt before her. "And, my heart too." He murmured.

"Had I known, Your Majesty. Could I believe—" The tears of pity, shame and regret were shining in Salima's eyes.

"Love." Akbar folded her into his arms, absolving the canker of pity out of her eyes with his kisses wild and hungry!

This hunger and violence in love was swallowed by time, as far as Akbar could recall this early dusk in the evening. He was watching the juggler tricks of his elephants on the field of Degrama where his encampment was settled on the way to Kashmir. Abul Fazl was holding out the silken, knotted ropes before these elephants. And they were untying each knot with much patience and obedience. Fatehullah Shirazi across from Abul Fazl was scattering wisps of straw before the pragmatic elephants. And these elephants were gathering straw into small bundles in their curled up snouts, and presenting these bundles to their master.

The emperor was delighted, of course, and watching these acts of juggling by the elephants with much interest. But since his entire day's journey from Lahore to Degrama, his anger had been flaring on account, that prince Salim had still not escorted the ladies from Bhimbhar. Salima had tried to defend the Prince, but Akbar had vented his anger on her by violating her altar of solitude by making love to her in the middle of the day!

Such violence of passion, he didn't know he possessed! Such beastly hunger and thirst in his body and soul? Akbar was becoming aware of the gold coin in his hand. The gold coin which he had snatched out of his jade coffer before abandoning his damasked abode! There was an inscription on it, which his thoughts were fondling!

Uprightness is the means of pleasing God
I never saw anyone lost in the straight road.

He tossed this coin over the loose straws, where his *Lone* elephant was gathering them into an uneven bundle. Chasing away the straws in one gust of his breath, the elephant had balanced the gold coin on his snout, holding it out to the emperor within his arm's reach. Akbar retrieved the coin, laughing.

"Even the beasts obey the emperor." Fatehullah Shirazi commented mirthfully.

"And the emperor's own son sits on the throne of disobedience." Akbar retorted.

"Prince Salim has not disobeyed you, Your Majesty." Fatehullah Shirazi began thoughtfully. "There can be several reasons for his delay, and he will come prepared to offer them to you. With utmost obedience, I am sure." He smiled. "Fortunes smile on us, while we wait here! Five thousand stone-cutters, and the mine experts and the diggers, whom Your Majesty have sent ahead to smooth the roads, might be halfway to Kashmir. Working their way through laboriously, and making the roads swifter for us to travel. God's ways are mysterious and His mercy bountiful."

"We cling to something mysterious above us, though the *mystery* is within us, which we are incapable of exploring." Akbar murmured to himself.

"In my quests and explorations, within the chronicles of history, Your Majesty, I have discovered that Kashmir is destined to fall under your sway, foretold by a Brahman nine hundred years from hence." Abul Fazl flung this comment to the winds, it seemed.

"Some ghost story, Abul, which you have recently studied with all the skill of a mystery writer, I am sure! Your history is trying to woo the facts to come to their rescue. Yaqub is still rebelling out there somewhere. And his father, Yusuf Shah is journeying with us. Pardoned, and permitted to rule Kashmir under our suzerainty. So far, the history is edging close to truth?" Akbar smiled sadly. "Yaqub is quite vile and devious, Abul, trying to cause unrest and anarchy, and Kashmir is far from safe."

"Abul Fath, your devoted vizier, Your Majesty, is also journeying with us, as you know. To capture Yaqub and to bring him to Your Majesty in chains of submission." Abul Fazl almost kneeled to the ground to retrieve the gold coin at the emperor's feet.

"Ah, you remind me of my childhood, Abul, while kneeling thus!" Akbar exclaimed suddenly. "When I was a child, my father made me a present of his cap. I put the cap on, and kneeled, but finding the cap too large, laid my hand on it in fear of losing. My father liked this childish act of mine so much, that he incorporated it into the royal curtsy—the kornish. Strange, that this curtsy is still practiced in our court. And passing strange, that this thought is coming to my head while you are talking about Abul Fath! And while I am thinking about his brother Human, whom I have sent on the Turanian embassy, and—" His thoughts were truncated, as he became aware of the sound of the hoof-beats.

The dusk itself appeared to be slashed with powdery dust from under the hoofs of the horses. Prince Salim was riding ahead of the cavalcade toward the emperor, where the emperor stood thoughtful amongst the company of his friends and elephants.

"Your Majesty, my deepest apologies in coming late! But all unimaginable delays have crossed my path in my haste to reach you." Prince Salim curtsied.

"The emperor wishes to postpone these stories of delay for reprimanding you later, Shaikhu Baba." Akbar intoned firmly. "How far behind are the ladies? While the chosen escort stands before me with apologies, and no sign of the carriages in view?"

"Your Majesty." Was prince Salim's flustered response! "I. Your Majesty—the roads are very difficult due to rains. Not fit for the Begums to travel. I have left them at Naushahra—" His words were drowned by the thundering of rage in Akbar's voice.

"Left them at Naushahra! You presumptuous Prince!" Akbar's eyes were flashing. "You have dared disobey the emperor, while I strictly commanded you to bring the ladies here. And you stand here before me with a pack of lies as your only defense! Your brother is getting married in Kashmir, were you not informed? And, is he going to get married without the presence of his mothers and aunts? Oh, begone before the emperor's rage whips you to a lump of wounded obedience." He waved him away.

Prince Salim attempted to speak, but words failed him. He fled toward the silken city of tents, as if fleeing the very thunder in his mind and heart.

"Fetch my horse, Abul. The emperor himself would escort his wives. They must be present at prince Murad's wedding." Akbar commanded.

"Your Majesty." Fatehullah Shirazi interceded quickly. "I, myself would bring the Begums post haste. No need to expose yourself to unnecessary fatigue."

"Yes, Your Majesty." Abul Fazl voiced his appeal. "We would both ride back. And in less than a day's journey, we would return, along with the begums.

"The briars of disobedience!" Akbar murmured to himself. His rage dying!

The emperor turned to his heels, tracing the steps of his disobedient son, but his steps were goading him toward the silken tent of Salima. So overwhelmed with rage was he at the behavior of his son, that he did not utter a word as he entered his royal tent. Salima noticing torment in her husband's eyes decided to stay silent. Akbar began to pace, his rage dwindling, as if by the very silence of his beloved.

"I have failed. Absolutely, and wretchedly failed in disciplining my sons, Salima." Akbar voiced his thoughts, still pacing.

"You have not failed, Your Majesty." Salima murmured softly.

"I have exposed them to all sorts of knowledge in ethics and religion. In arts and sciences, and they have learnt nothing, nothing! No love for knowledge is kindled in their hearts, but indulgence in the pleasure of the senses. My sons, all my sons! What have they learnt? No restraint, but excesses in drinking." Akbar thought aloud.

"They adore and respect you, Your Majesty." Salima began cautiously. "They are in awe of your power, strength, and wisdom. Perhaps, they fear you?"

"Fear!" Akbar exclaimed suddenly. "So, the emperor incites fear, not love!" His eyes were flashing a subtle challenge. "Do you fear the emperor, my love?"

"No, Your Majesty." Salima murmured feebly.

"Yes, hatred knows no fear, my pearl." Akbar poured himself wine.

"You accuse me unjustly, Your Majesty." Salima protested. "Hatred dies, as well as love." She breathed low.

"Not my love, sweet flower." Akbar murmured back, not turning to face her. "My love for you will live, even after my death. Wandering restlessly to entice you to the galaxies and continents, wherever my dark abode would be! Maybe, love is the only *truth* worth seeking? And I have neglected it in my search for absurdities, in wisdom, knowledge and learning. The intellect of the fools!"

"What dark thoughts have taken hold of you, Your Majesty? The look of grieving and suffering when you came in!" Salima looked bewildered. "I hope, no tragic news is the cause of such quiet mourning?"

"Only the tragedy of disobedience, my love!" Akbar turned to face her. "My precious fool of a son, Shaikhu Baba, has returned without the Begums! And with an odious excuse, that the roads are not fit for the royal ladies to venture such a journey."

"You misjudge him harshly, Your Majesty." Salima interceded on his behalf, quickly. "Disobedience is not his intent, I am sure. He is young and inexperienced."

"Young and heedless! That is what, my Shaikhu baba has turned to be." Akbar reflected aloud. "And my intent is to explore the realms of love prayerfully."

Time again was engaged in quicksilver flight, this time revealing the beauty of Kashmir. The grand wooden palace in Kashmir was decked with silken hangings and perfumed flowers to enhance the festivities of prince Murad's wedding. Prince Murad was wedded to the daughter of Aziz Koka with all grand ceremonies befitting the son of a Moghul emperor. Akbar had blessed the wedded couple, and then had sought refuge in his large chamber upstairs. He was overwhelmed with fatigue, and so were the ladies of his harem, leaving the newlyweds to their entertainment, and joining the emperor.

Akbar, though enjoying the company of his wives and of the other harem ladies, was feeling some strange discomfort in the pit of his stomach. His thoughts were ascribing this pain to the half cooked, Kashmiri rice and the Himalayan trout. After a few spasms of pain, one serpent of a doubt had entered his head, that perhaps he was poisoned. This serpent of a doubt was hissing the name of prince Salim, and accosting his son with its sibilant tongue, and accusing him as the possible suspect.

Prince Salim, since his reprimand from the emperor on the site of Degrama, had shut himself up in his cloister of solitude. Amidst the flurry of sightseeing in Kashmir and preparations for Prince Murad's wedding, the emperor had neglected to comfort the prince. Yet, he could not help noticing his son's taciturn presence, or rather his absence!

"How romantic! His Majesty's choice fell on the poets, when it was time to shower gold on the bride's head. And the same favored poets too! Faizi and Mir Sharif, who had showered gold on the poor and the devotees when we entered Kashmir!" Ruqaiya Begum was responding to one of Suriya Begum's comments.

"Kashmir is heaven on earth, and romance blooms in its lovely saffron." Suriya Begum was laughing in return.

"Well, this whole country is regarded holy by the Hindu sages. Forty-five shrines are dedicated to Mahadeva, sixty-four to Vishnu, three to Brahma, and twenty-two to Durga." Hira Begum was telling Mahmooda Begum.

"Not to mention the hideous serpent-shrines. And oh, that frightful monastery on the hill of Koh-i-Sulaiman, smelling of damp wood!" Mahmooda Begum was laughing.

"Oh, the clear, bubbling springs. My favorite one is Kokar Nag." Nighat Begum was bursting with joy at the memories of those recent excursions.

"I like the one, where they make the offerings of goat and sheep. It irrigates the five villages, they say." Farida Begum was reminiscing aloud.

"Matan hill is the place where I would like to have a palace of my own, with that large temple in the background. Not a wooden palace, but a palace of marble and red sandstone. Did you see that small pool near the temple? They say, it is the well of Babylon. And in Wulnar, that lofty mountain with its salt spring, I spotted a Kashmiri stag there. When the water of that spring recedes, an image of Mahadeva in sandalwood appears." Usha Begum was dreaming aloud.

"With your wild imagination, you should live in the village of Aish, Usha. There, they say, Baba Zainuddin found his abode and was lost to the world. When he came near the hill in Aish, it held no water. But when he took his abode there, a spring began to flow. He stayed there in his cell for twelve years, and closed its mouth with a large stone. Never did he come out again, and no one ever found any trace of him either." Jagruti Begum was shattering the dreams of Usha with her flare for anecdotes.

"I will never go near that spring in Dakhamur, where the water builds up and becomes turbid with straw and rubbish floating on top. Who can believe that, that is the Solomon's stone close to it, out of which the villagers fashion utensils?" Sangita Begum was revealing her fears, than concealing her distaste for such a place.

The emperor's gaze was wandering toward the princesses, where they sat playing cards. Amongst them, there was an alien face, whose name the emperor could not recall. Actually, it was a familiar and comely face. A face, which he had seen before, Akbar was thinking, but his gaze was seeking the attention of Salima.

My disenchanted beloved. Not even showing much joy at the wedding of her own son, and mine, our handsome prince, Murad. Akbar was thinking.

"We should all visit those woods again in that village of Matalnamah. All those herons with their colorful plumes, what a charming sight it was?" Bibi Shad Begum was painting that memory in words.

"Who would not like to sit near that spring called Nilah Nag in Nagam, and read poetry under the stars!" Qasima Banu Begum was poetically effusive.

"Oh, all those vile springs with their omens and incantations." Gulbadan Begum was chiding the poetess bride of the emperor. "Don't you feel revolted by all the odious myths attached to those springs? Were you there, when some peasants were talking about the auguries and divinations? They divide the nut into four equal parts, and throw it into the spring of Nilah Nag. If an odd number floats on the top, the augury is favorable. If otherwise, the reverse is true. They also practice divinations by throwing the parts of the same nut into a bowl of milk. If the odd number sinks, it's a good omen, if not, it is unpropitious. And strangest of all the myths! They claim that a book named Nilmat arose from the depths of Nilah Nag, containing the history of the temples in Kashmir. And yet another strange one, that a lofty city is buried under its waters. And that one Brahman descended into its depths, and returned after three days, bringing back some rarities of this city. Then, he narrated his experiences."

"It seems, my dear Aunt, you are not impressed by the beauty of Kashmir." Akbar could not help but smile. "The beauty of Kashmir, its heavenly mysteries wrought in garlands of art and architecture." He added softly, smiling to himself.

"These mysteries, Your Majesty, gather lies in layers upon layers of thick moss." Gulbadan Begum smiled. "And who is to believe in them, but the rishis and the hermits, in the caves of the Himalayas. Blowing their conches and practicing austerities!"

"To miss the sense of beauty is to deviate from the path of truth, my dear Aunt." Akbar's look was thoughtful and indulgent. "And austerities have their noble rewards, for the ones who yearn for truth with a passionate fortitude. Truth is known to be slaughtered by brutal lies, but in the end, its mysterious renewal slays all lies."

"And you are blamed for deviating from God's truth, Your Majesty. Rather, for rejecting it in your quest for discovering something else, some truth absolute!" Hamida Banu Begum's silent reproof in her eyes was transformed into words.

"Recollection of God's truth is my aim in searching one absolute truth, Miryam Makani." Was Akbar's Sufic response! "And yet, the blame rests in your eyes, dear Mamma. You are accusing your son, believing in vile canards. Can you tell why the emperor deserves such reproof, rather than love and kindness from his mother?"

"My blame, Your Majesty, is only for your leniency toward all the heretics, who revile Islam and prosper inside the mire of their heresy." Hamida Banu Begum breathed hastily. "It is no canard, Your Majesty that the Portuguese tied a copy of Quran around the neck of a dog, and paraded it on the streets of Ormuz. And even after this sacrilege, they roam free on the streets of Hind. Unpunished and gloating. You should punish those heretics, Your Majesty. And order, that a Bible be suspended from the neck of a donkey, and paraded on the streets of Agra." She looked shocked by her words.

"It behooves not the emperor to requite ill with ill, dear Mamma. For the contempt of any religion is the contempt of God." Akbar responded with implicit regret. "Islam has withstood the heresies of the ages, and its mighty foundations would not ever crumble. Leave alone be shaken by the impious acts of man or beast." He got to his feet. "Muslims often tend to forget, that Bible is one of their holy books."

"Sinful acts, and blasphemies such as these should not be condoned, Your Majesty." Gulbadan Begum was quick to voice her disapproval.

"This kind of sin is the folly of the ignorant, dear Aunt." Akbar flashed her a smile! "Yes, a folly of the ignorant, not the highest blasphemy against any religion. Though it seems that way! If the wise too wear the veil of ignorance, and must be numbered amongst the fools!" He was approaching the circle of the younger princesses.

"And who is this rare bloom, blessing the festive occasion of prince Murad's wedding with her lovely presence?" Akbar muttered aloud.

"Zebunisa, Your Majesty." Was Zebunisa's flustered response!

"I have not seen you before! Yet, I have, whose daughter?" Akbar's gaze was intense and searching.

"I am Naqib Khan's daughter, Your Majesty, your—" Zebunisa could not continue against a volley of mirth on the emperor's lips.

"Ah, that bird of beauty and innocence! Now a fragrant blossom!" Akbar's mirth was kindling ardent stars in his eyes. "Now the emperor remembers." He turned away.

She shall be my bride. For the eternal hatred in Salima's heart, the emperor must be justified. Akbar's thoughts were courting anguish, as he approached Salima.

"And my lovely queen sitting here joyless at the wedding of her son!" Akbar's eyes searched his Beloved's. "You should be dancing, my love, and stringing garlands of joys into the wedding songs." He teased rather tenderly.

"Garlands of festivities have exhausted me, Your Majesty." Salima elicited a cold smile. "Though, the dance of joy in my heart remains unseen. Even by the soul-searching gaze of the emperor." She murmured low.

"The soul-searching gaze of the emperor sees only—" Akbar paused, feeling a sudden flaring of pain in his stomach. "Well, my love, the emperor would find much joy under the warmth of sunshine. And inside the heart of this valley in Kashmir." He smiled, abandoning the company of his beloved and stepping out into the garden.

Akbar stood breathing cool air on the wooden terrace with a sense of bliss and reverie. The Alpine lake down yonder was a blue mirror of magic and mystery. He was dismounting the wooden steps, while espying one lone figure down yonder, becoming aware that this young person in the distance was his son. Prince Salim was pacing to and fro under some spell of anguish and despair.

Suddenly, the knot of pain in the pit of Akbar's stomach was tightening. His pain was surfacing, and so were his doubts—that strange link to pain? Akbar stood there at a distance, motionless. Prince Salim was oblivious to his surroundings.

"Come hither, Shaikhu Baba. What despair drives you to loneliness and seclusion?" Akbar's voice splintered the mask of serenity in this valley.

"Your Majesty." Prince Salim rushed toward the emperor, pale and speechless.

"You have been avoiding the emperor, Shaikhuji." Akbar's voice was softened. "You seem alienated from the emperor, as if plotting some revenge?"

"No, Your Majesty." Prince Salim protested. "I, I have been worried concerning Yaqub. He is still hiding in some deep valleys of Kashmir. You yourself, Your Majesty, instructed me to watch over his moves." He concluded incoherently.

"If you can unveil Himalayas from the clouds of presage, my son, then the heavens would be yours! Along with the valleys of Kashmir, this paradise on earth!" Akbar laughed suddenly. "What fears, Shaikhu Baba, when the paradise itself kisses your feet in the valleys of Kashmir?" His gaze was intense and probing.

"A fear for you, Your Majesty. Now that you have gained full possession of Kashmir, it might be lost if the rebels wander around unchecked." Prince Salim responded with a diplomatic flourish.

"No fears assault the emperor's mind, Shaikhu Baba." Akbar's gaze was piercing. "I have come to a conclusion, that the fear to lose what we have gained is much more dangerous than the desire to achieve what always seems illusive and fleeting."

But, Your Majesty." Prince Salim began under some spell of confusion. "You have attained peace in the empire of Hind, and in Kashmir. And to lose all!"

"The semblance of peace, that is, not even that! If peace it is! It floats on the stormy waters of intrigue and plotting, Shaikhu Baba." Akbar smiled. "Yet, my efforts for peace would ripen in time like the blooms of saffron! Gold and ruddy inside the mists of timelessness itself!" He could see Abul Fazl sailing toward them.

"May I be excused, Your Majesty?" Prince Salim appealed.

"No, Shaikhuji, stay. You might learn some wisdom from the lips of this sage, philosopher and historian. He is all three in one." Akbar murmured.

"Your Majesty, if I am not imposing on this royal parlance, may I request your audience?" Abul Fazl bowed before the emperor. Greeting the prince in turn!

"Your presence is welcome, Abul. And you may delight my son with the wondrous story of that cave, called Amar Nat." Akbar's eyes were gathering sunshine.

"With great delight, Your Majesty." Abul Fazl's gaze was returning to prince Salim. "Prince Salim, this cave Amar Nat belongs to a small town. Daechhinparah is the name of this town, which lies cradled against a large mountain bordering the mountainous land, the Great Tibet. This cave has a spring of its own on the slope of a hillock. The people of Kashmir ascribe great sanctity to this cave. They say when the new moon rises from her throne of rays, a bubble, as if it were of ice is formed on the cave, which daily increases. But when the moon wanes, the bubble disappears. And these people believe that this bubble is the image of Mahadeva who comes here to fulfill the desires of the supplicants. Below the mouth of this cave is a rill called Amraoti. Its clay is white as snow. And people smear themselves with it for spiritual cleansing."

"And now, Abul, recite that poem. That divine inspiration of yours, which I made you carve on the wall of that holy temple, in the very heart of Kashmir."

"Kashmir is my inspiration, Your Majesty. And that poem is my prayer. I would never tire of reciting it." Abul Fazl commenced with a great fervor.

"O, God in every temple I see people that seek Thee
And in every language I hear spoken, praise Thee
Polytheism and Islam feel after Thee
Each religion says, Thou art one, without equal
If it be a mosque, people murmur the holy prayers
And if it be a Christian church, people ring the bell from love to Thee
Sometimes I frequent the Christian cloister, Hindu temple
And sometime the mosque
But it is Thou when I search from temple to temple
The elect have no dealing with kufr and orthodoxy
For neither of them stand behind the curtain of Thy Islam
Heresy to the heretic, and religion to the orthodox
But the dust of rose petal belongs to the heart of the perfume seller."

Akbar, standing there rapt, had the misfortune of looking at his son, and detecting the daggers of hatred in there directed at Abul Fazl. For the first time in his entire life Akbar was puzzled than outraged as to why his son should hate this man of learning! A bold rider was coming into view no other than Faizi himself. He alighted from his horse with the speed of lightning, and stumbled forth.

"Your Majesty. Fatehullah Shirazi, died, suddenly. I was with him, he—" Faizi could not continue. He was becoming aware of the emperor's pallor.

The emperor could not speak. His grief for the death of his friend stifling the assault of pain in his stomach!

"Oh, that man of wisdom and learning." Abul Fazl lamented. "If the books of antiquity had been lost, Fatehullah would have laid a new foundation of knowledge."

"His feats of strength no Rustam could emulate." Faizi murmured to himself.

"My friend, my friend. This world is bereft of wisdom without him." Akbar's voice was barely audible. "Fatehullah, my dearest of friends, dead! Had he fallen into the hands of Franks, not into the volcano of death, I would have given all my wealth as a ransom for him, and would have gained by the bargain."

Amidst the throes of his mental and physical agony, a strange revelation was dawning upon Akbar. His thoughts were shooting blame at his son, that prince Salim might have poisoned his food at the feasting. The Pain was becoming intolerable.

"Oh, my son. Did you poison the emperor?" Akbar's gaze was fixed to his son.

"Baba Shaikhuji since all this
Sultanate will devolve on thee, why
Hast thou made this attack on me
I would have given it to thee
If thou hast asked me."

Akbar collapsed into the arms of Faizi and Abul Fazl.

The valley of Kashmir with its serpent of doubt was left leagues behind. Now the hills of Khistwar enveloped in violet mists, were just one gossamer background against the silk city of tents. The emperor had encamped here on his homeward journey toward Lahore. He had been the victim of colic pains when he had fainted that evening, and had recovered quickly. Though he could not forget the death of his dearest of friends, but he had no recollection of the accusations which had breathed upon his lips against his son in that moment of despair. Upon learning the import of his accusations from Abul Fazl, the emperor had felt astonished. He had summoned prince Salim to his presence, and had favored him with all sorts of gifts and kindnesses. Prince Salim's fears thus allayed, he had begun to serve the emperor with all obedience and humbleness.

Another of Akbar's dear friends Abul Fath had died during this journey from Kashmir, via Srinagar. Abul Fath had died of a brief illness at Damtur, on the frontier of Kashmir. During his lifetime, Abul Fath had built a tomb for himself to be buried at Hasan Abdal. So Akbar, honoring his wish, had sent his friend's body to its destined abode under the command of Khwaja Shumsuddin. Abul Fath was buried on the site of Takht-i-Sulaiman near Srinagar, in the very heart of Hasan Abdal.

The royal entourage was still in Khistwar, when the emperor was informed about the hideout of the inveterate rebel, Yaqub. Actually, after arriving at Khistwar, Akbar had decided to encamp for a longer period of time in Khistwar, planning improvements. He had ordered that the irrigation channels in the valleys of Kashmir should be thoroughly cleaned, and then maintained properly under the care of the tribal chiefs at all times, in all seasons. Gardeners were instructed to plant large orchards of apples, peaches and apricots. Poplars and plane trees were to be planted at the slopes of the hills from the valleys of Srinagar to the plains of Rawalpindi. He had selected the lofty rock of Hari Prabat for his wooden palace.

Right now, the emperor was examining the accouterments of artillery and gunnery near his royal encampment. His feet were coming to an abrupt halt before the solid array of polished guns, and he stood reconnoitering. His gaze was fixed to his favorite gun named *gajna*, which he himself had designed, much lighter than the ones which his master-gunner had devised and crafted. He was now examining his big invention called *mitrailleuse*. Mitrailleuse was similar to cannon, where seventeen guns were chained together, and all those could be fired simultaneously with one single ball of fire.

"In cold climates such as Kabul and Kashmir, guns should be made thicker than ordinary, so that cold and dryness may not crack them. Don't you think so, Abul, that only the heavy guns should be used in Kashmir where the clime and the landscape render the lighter ones unfit?" Akbar voiced his thoughts aloud.

"In that paradise, Your Majesty, no guns should be employed, only swift arrows from the bows of the archers." Abul Fazl responded with a poetic élan.

"Ah, my poet-philosopher! You are drunk with the beauty of Kashmir." Akbar laughed, his gaze espying his son down the slope practicing archery. "Isn't Prince Salim the best of archers in the whole of Hind?"

"The best in the world, Your Majesty, as far as I know!" Abul Fazl agreed with a pleasant smile. "If the Prince employed all his skills, his arrows could pierce through the very heart of Yaqub. Though, that rebel rests concealed in some thick forests inside the very heart of these pine-valleys." He stood guarding, for some strange reason, the secret of Yaqub already being in custody of the Imperialists.

"No more deaths, Abul. I am wearied of deaths." Akbar's gaze was profound. "Death has followed me to the valleys of Kashmir, and I wish to appease its hunger with the morsels of clemency." His gaze was sailing above the tall cedars.

"Death is an illusion, Your Majesty, and so is life! This illusion burdening our senses with dregs of grief and sadness!" Abul Fazl began thoughtfully. "Only the perception of joy and beauty in its attire of unreality rewards our senses with the breath of life. This life, as real as reality could be perceived in the sense of unreality. Amidst this dance of reality and illusion, it is better that we catch only the tunes of laughter and renewal, not of tears and surcease."

"Ah, my poet-philosopher again!" Akbar exclaimed. "Fatehullah's great life itself had been his greatest of rewards. Nobler it was, and noble it would remain! And nobler yet, it would breathe forever within the sanctuary of death. Awakening to the rhythm of time in timelessness!" He smiled. "You are the only one, Abul, who can dispel the emperor's sadness, with your presence, and with your wisdom! And right now, if you wish to succeed, delight the emperor with a couplet or two. This divine valley is all inspiration, in your eyes, I can see?"

"If my couplets can dispel your sadness, Your Majesty, I will pluck the very stars from the heavens, and make them sing your praises." Abul Fazl declared.

"No praise, Abul, only the stars of light and wisdom." Akbar laughed. "If one can humble oneself to the level of dust, one can reach the sky in a chariot of stars in one's soul—inside the vast heavens in one's mind! Not lured by the little stars in the heavens, but by the shining galaxies within one's abyss." He concluded fervently.

"Then, in dust I will stand, Your Majesty, and smear my lips with dust. And with this dust on my lips, I will rise above the stars against the shadow of my humble verse." Abul Fazl's eyes were gathering stars of inspiration.

"For ever, and so long as there are stars in the firmament
For ever, and so long as there are bodies with souls
May there be no revolution of the spheres without thy pleasure
No movement of the heavenly bodies except according to thy will."

"Such divine flattery shall drag you down to perdition, Abul." A genuine peal of laughter escaped Akbar's lips. "My fears and sadness' are gone. And now I pray under the canopy of these mists which conceal the stars, that Todar Mall be restored to complete health. What kind of missive did Todar Mall send? I forget. I only remember about his illness. And what response did I send?" He asked happily.

"Todar Mall, Your Majesty, had written, that due to his old age and feebleness of body, he requests Your Majesty's permission to retire. And to spend his remaining days on the bank of Ganga at Hardwar! Thus, spending his last days *in remembering God*, his request stated explicitly." Abul Fazl responded intensely. "Your royal response accorded him the necessary permission to resign and retire."

"Old! We are all getting old, Abul." Akbar exclaimed. "Though, I don't feel old. I have grown a little plump, that's all. And a little colic too! No visible wrinkles. A sprinkling of gray in my hair and mustache! I still have the strength of a teenager. And virility too, with all the passions of youth! Dispatch another missive, Abul. And command Todar Mall that he can't resign. The emperor forbids it. Add further, that the emperor declares, that no worship of God is equal to the service of mankind. And that it would be better for him to give up his idea of retirement, and to spend his last breath in serving man. This way, he is sure to make a glorious provision for his final journey. My prayers are with him for a long and healthy life."

"Yes, Your Majesty." Abul Fazl bowed his head in acknowledgment.

"And send him gifts, which I received from the rulers of Little Tibet and Great Tibet." Akbar murmured. "These allies of affliction! They wouldn't have sent me such gifts and such flattering embassies, if I was not here in Kashmir. They fear the emperor!" He smiled. "And Yaqub, in his so-called hiding, how did he treat my messengers?"

"With great honor, Your Majesty." Abul Fazl murmured back. "He said: *Now let only the slipper of His Majesty be sent to me, and I will place it on my head, and then venture to approach and prostrate myself at the sacred threshold.*"

"And this sacred threshold is getting wearied of wait." Akbar's hand flew to his breast with a gesture of impatience.

"No more wait, Your Majesty. Yaqub is already in the custody of the imperialists. Waiting for your permission to prostrate himself at Your Majesty's feet!" Abul Fazl confessed with glowing pride.

"And you kept the emperor ignorant, all this time!" Akbar began to laugh without restraint. His feet carrying him toward the harem of his silk city!

Months, rather seasons had flitted past in a flurry of fortunes and tragedies, since the emperor's journey from Kashmir to Lahore. Todar Mall had died in Lahore, serving mankind and performing the duties of his governorship as the emperor had commanded.

Akbar was seated under one ornamental arch in the solitary chamber of his palace at Lahore. He had aged, all of a sudden. His features were pale and haggard. He was dressed in white silks with no embellishments, except the ropes of pearls around his turban. He seemed oblivious to the presence of Abul Fazl.

After three days of mourning in his own chamber of solitary self-confinement, Akbar had summoned Abul Fazl to his presence. Inconsolable as he was, he had listened to his friend's solicitations, murmuring that Hind's great statesman was lost to mankind.

"You should not mourn Todar Mall thus, Your Majesty." Abul Fazl commented. "He was a pillar of strength, in times of sorrows and tragedies. There are no words to compliment the richness of his integrity and experience in the affairs of Hind. He would like to be remembered as the bloom of joy, unfolding year after year in the purity of its inner strength—in his works. His noble actions would never die."

"And what did Baduani say the day after he died?" Akbar declared suddenly.

"You don't wish that odious verse to be repeated, Your Majesty." One quick protest escaped Abul Fazl's lips.

"Yes, my friend, I do. I want you to recite it." Akbar murmured. "The emperor wishes to exchange his pain with rage. His rage supreme against all the bigots in Hind!"

"Todar Mall is he, whose tyranny had oppressed the world
When he went to hell, people became merry
I asked the date of his going, from the old man of intellect
Cheerfully replied that wise, old man, he is gone to hell."
Abul Fazl complied obediently.

"We have to clean the gutters of his zeal, Abul, with a severe reprimand, and just punishment. So that he can find wisdom in the silence of his inner purity, if he possesses such a treasure." Akbar murmured again.

"That sinner deserves pity, than reprimand, Your Majesty. His zeal is nothing, but ignorance. He truly and sincerely believes that the word of God comes to him in his poetry, and in his everlasting search for truth in the realms of the-

ology. Most of the time, he is not even aware of his folly in speech or manner."
Abul Fazl murmured soothingly.

"That pious heathen!" Akbar exclaimed without rage. "Word of God never
comes to men, whose hearts burn in hatred and malice for their fellowmen.
What do you think, Abul, should his tongue be sucked out of his foul mouth?
Or, should his throat be singed with the hot pincers, if he is not to be sent to the
tower of silence?"

"His penance and the rituals of piety, may yet earn him the rewards of mercy from the emperor, Your Majesty." Abul Fazl intoned discreetly.

"Ah, my noble counselor. You are too wise to heed emperor's threats." Akbar ruminated aloud. "Penance and rituals, and even the prayers, are for the ones
who doubt the mercy of God. And who live in perpetual fear for the sins in their
minds and hearts. When one has absolved one's soul from all the impurities, one
reaches closer to God without the outward rituals of prayer and penance."

The look of serenity in the emperor's eyes had left Abul Fazl bereft of all
speech.

"This iced water tastes sweeter than wine, Abul. Had we not discovered
saltpeter, we would not have had the luxury of this cool nectar." Akbar cupped
the jeweled goblet in both his hands. "Strange discovery! We pour water over
saltpeter, boil it, and let it stand till the saltpeter is crystallized again? Who
would have—" His thoughts were truncated, as Nizamuddin Ahmed came flying
through the bronzed portals.

"Your Majesty. Pardon me, but I am the messenger of grievous news." Nizamuddin Ahmed bowed low. "Bhagwan Das died this afternoon."

"How did he die?" Akbar asked, holding on to the mock string of his serenity.

"Your Majesty." Nizamuddin Ahmed murmured apologetically. "He
seemed to have caught cold after the funeral of Todar Mall. Your royal physicians claim, that the sudden cause of his death are strangury and excessive vom-
iting."

"Instruct Prince Salim to repair to the house of Amber with my personal
condolences. Also, furnish Man Singh with a robe and a swift horse. And with
trays of jewels for the bereaved family at Amber. He is to accompany Prince
Salim. Naqib Khan would pen the letter of condolence." Akbar got to his feet,
slowly and thoughtfully.

"Yes, Your Majesty." Nizamuddin Ahmed retreated hastily.

"The emperor has returned to the valley of death." Was Akbar's low lament! He drifted close to Abul Fazl, who was startled to his feet. "Leave the
emperor to his luxury of solitude, my friend." He commanded. And as Abul Fazl
seemed glued to one spot, he smiled kindly. "The emperor is not going to die of
grief, Abul. So many deaths in such a brief period have finally cured me of my
griefs and despairs. I don't consider myself as the victim, anymore. I have become like a lone observer, watching the dance of death as a conqueror would! A
conqueror who would not accept defeat until tragedies pierce his heart with the
sword of destiny! Now, leave me, my kind friend."

The emperor had begun to pace the length of the Persian carpet woven in gold and crimson rosettes. Abul Fazl had left reluctantly, weighed down by his grief and sorrow. Akbar's pace was dwindling, his feet coming to an abrupt halt. He was standing motionless by one large tapestry, sightless and unthinking. The voice in his psyche was like dry lightning from one smoldering command.

To enjoy the sanctuary of the present, one must not mourn over the grave of the past. Or, to puncture the chaste womb of future with fears, doubts, anxieties—Akbar was seeking the sanctuary of his beloved in this vast palace.

12

The Tavern of Theology

The red sandstone palace at Lahore was bustling with excitement amidst the preparations for Nauroz festivities. The royal servants in white robes and crimson turbans were decking the palace from marble steps to the tapering domes on the rooftops with candles and colorful lamps, to be lighted from dusk till dawn.

Akbar, standing at the large window of his damasked chamber, was admiring the glory of his sprawling gardens. His sight was absorbing the bounty in color and sunshine, but his thoughts were sailing back to the adjacent bathroom where Salima was taking a bath scented with oils and perfumes.

Luxuriating there in her pool of solitude! Probably, scrubbing off the emperor's kisses from her body, and absolving her soul from the passion-violence of love.

Actually, the emperor was luxuriating in the sense of his newly discovered peace. This twice-born peace, both times, the product of his longed-for union with his Beloved.

If love could offer me such peace, then why should I war with hatreds and quests for truth in the whirlwind of sovereignty? Akbar was feeling pain in his leg.

During one of his hunts, he had fallen from his horse, and had received a slight injury to his left leg. That leg had become susceptible to pain, especially, when he was compelled to march endlessly on long, hunting expeditions.

Right after his return from Kashmir, the emperor had sent diplomatic embassies to Little Tibet—Balistan and the Great Tibet—Ladakh. Two years later, the ruler of Little Tibet had sent his daughter as a bride for prince Salim. Prince Salim was blessed with another son by Jagat Gosaini known as Jodh Bai by the ladies of the harem, and the emperor had named him Khurram. The emperor had marched to Baluchistan to subdue the rebellions there, before Shah Abbas of Persia could claim that kingdom as his own. The Baluchi chiefs had submitted to the emperor without resistance and the emperor had restored their kingdoms to them under the laws of his suzerainty. At the same time, Orissa was annexed to the Moghul Empire. And the rebellions in Sindh were quelled. The emperor had returned to Lahore, then, and had sent Faizi to Deccan as an ambassador, since prince Murad and Abdur Rahim were unsuccessful in gaining any positive results from the warring factions in that contingent. Prince Murad was recalled, and assigned the post of governorship in Malwa. Soon, Kandahar was besieged by the warring troops from Iran. And Abdur Rahim, who had also been recalled from Deccan, was sent via Baluchistan to route the Iranis, and to conquer Kandahar.

At Lahore, Akbar was able to recommence his practice of religious discussions, after the arrival of the second mission of Jesuit priests from Goa. A Greek sub deacon, Leon Grimmon, was the first one to present himself before the emperor. A year later, Father Duarte Leitao, Christoval de Vega, and a lay brother by the name of Estevao Ribeiro, had paid their respects to the emperor. Two more Jain Scholars, Bhanu Chandra and Jina Suri, had also joined this theological group. While Akbar was busy planting the seeds of tolerance, he was cheered by good news that Abdur Rahim had conquered Kandahar, and had completed the conquest of Umarkot, the birth-place of the emperor.

The victory of Umarkot had such a pleasant affect upon Akbar that he had decided to celebrate this victory by visiting Kashmir, once again. Meanwhile, the Jesuit priests, unable to proselytize the emperor of Hind, had decided to return to Goa. The emperor had entrusted them with a letter to their king, requesting the company of more priests, in his longing to gain knowledge and understanding of the Christian Faith.

Before his journey to Kashmir, Akbar had married Zebunisa.

Once in Kashmir, Shamsuddin Chak had offered the hand of his daughter in marriage to the emperor. The wedding ceremonies were performed on the same day as the festival of Diwali, and Umbrine had become the emperor's youngest of brides. On this very same day, the daughters of Husain Chak and Mubarak Khan were accepted to be the brides for prince Salim in strengthening alliances with the Kashmiri lords.

Before leaving Kashmir, Akbar had visited jogis and qalandars in their humble abodes. One holy qalandar, Shaikhul Khairabadi, had declined the emperor's gift of land, but had consented to visit the emperor.

Amidst the preparations for his journey back to Lahore, Akbar had deputed Abul Fazl to fetch a recluse by the name of Wahid Sufi. Abul Fazl had returned without Wahid Sufi, for the mystic had declined to visit the emperor. Akbar was more impressed than displeased and had decided to visit the mystic himself.

Lahore, with its gardens and palaces, was a den of omens and conflicts, as soon as the emperor had set foot in this capital of Hind. He was faced with the daggers of bigotry once again, proclaiming an edict of complete tolerance toward all faiths in the whole empire of Hind. Aziz Koka, who had been sent to Deccan for conciliatory measures, was recalled back to join the emperor in Lahore. Aziz Koka, instead of returning to Lahore, had decided to flee to Mecca. Another embassy was dispatched to Deccan, with poet Faizi as the most eminent of the ambassadors. Faizi had succeeded in gaining the submission of one of the Deccani leaders, Raja Ali Khan. And in proof of his submission, had sent his daughter as a bride for prince Salim. Burhanul Mulk, and the other rulers of Deccan had refused to submit to Akbar. Akbar, after exhausting all conciliatory efforts, had then resolved to invade Deccan by force. Prince Murad was ordered by the emperor to prepare his army for a mighty attack.

While prince Murad was still gathering forces for his campaign to Deccan, Aziz Koka had returned to Lahore after being fleeced by the avaricious men at the holy shrines in Mecca. Much tormented by his act of disobedience, Aziz Koka had laid his head at the emperor's feet in utter remorse, pleading forgiveness. Akbar had pardoned him and had reinstated him to his former position of Khan Khanan, ordering him to join prince Murad.

Meanwhile, Mubarak Shah, the father of Faizi and Abul Fazl had died suddenly. Three years later Mubarak Shah's wife had died and she was buried beside her husband at Agra in Baghi-Bihist built by Babur during his brief reign in Hind.

The third Jesuit mission from Goa had arrived, Father Jerome Xavier and two other Portuguese priests, Father Emmanuel Pinheiro and Brother Benedict de Goes. At the same time, a third Jain mission had arrived in Lahore at the head of Vijaya Sen. He was accompanied by his disciple, Nandi Vijaya, including a group of one hundred monks.

The news from north-western frontier of the empire had brought much joy to the emperor for the victory over Kandahar. When its rebellious leader, Muzaffar Hussain, was brought before the emperor, he was pardoned and received by the emperor graciously. Prince Murad, on his way to Deccan, had learned that the chief rebel, Burhanul Mulk, had died suddenly. And that the war of succession had broken out in that region like a wildfire. Chand Bibi was appointed as a regent for Burhanul Mulk's grandson, Bahadur Nizam, to defend the fort of Deccan.

Nizamuddin Ahmed, Akbar's best-loved poet had died suddenly, leaving behind the fruits of his labor, Tabakat-i-Akbari. A year later, Faizi too had died suddenly.

The emperor was still standing by the window, witnessing all those memories. He was turning slowly, his fingers pressing his temples. Reflected before his gaze, this moment, were the shining mists of beauty and wonder. Salima, Beloved, Reality!

Salima had returned to the room much too quietly, caught under the spell of her wonder and enchantment. Akbar was charmed, rather dazed. *Embodied in the cold, chaste marble of her hatred and tenderness*, his thoughts were chuckling.

"Your Majesty, you have been neglecting the pain in your leg for too long." Salima breathed apprehensively. "How long has it been? Almost six years, since you fell from your horse. The royal physicians are here to serve you, Your Majesty. Listen to their pleas, if not to mine." Her eyes were gathering clouds of presage.

"From concern in your voice, my love, it seems that you love the emperor." Akbar folded her into his arms, kissing her softly on the lips. "Come, love, sit with the emperor, and let me worship you like a suppliant at the altar of a devi."

"What about the other devis in the harem, Your Majesty! All waiting for your love and devotion?" Salima quipped.

"Ah, my love, you are my one and only devi." Akbar resumed happily. "If only, I could prove my love? The naked hatred in your eyes, I can see and absorb. Yet, my own eyes! Well, somehow, they fail to reveal the ocean of love in my soul, for you, for you.

"Alas, Your Majesty. I do see the oceans of love in your eyes, the waves in there drifting to yonder shores in many a tumultuous loves." Salima mocked!

"You delude your very sight, my love, when you deem these waves drifting and wandering." Akbar began thoughtfully. "Yet, if those waves which you see, cannot abide in the grace of their ocean, then how would that ocean dare call itself an ocean? If there were no waves, the passions vast and terrible would perish in their parched lands!"

"Women's passions, of love and hate, are different than the passions of men, Your Majesty." Salima began enigmatically. "Men's passions are clouded by the rags of their ambitions. Those passions shuddering without tears behind the doors of their needs, desires and possessions! The passions of women, they remain strong and rooted, like fixed stars on the face of a remote galaxy. Women cultivate their passions of love or hatred with a single-minded tenacity, while men, in multiplicity of their passions, cannot separate them from the countless gateways of their ambitions and aspirations. What women can share or withhold, in terms of passions, with the simple purity or corruption inside their hearts, men cannot afford to part with? Fearing, that they would lose a part of their *self, being, or multiple-being—*" She lost her chain of thoughts.

"Men, my lovely poetess, are no different than the women. Being is *one* in all sexes." Akbar began softly. "Being is *one and all in one*. The only thing we can barely afford to give away from our *being* is vanity! And the rest, we cannot suffer to lose. Love and hatred! Anger and compassion! Greed and malevolence! And yes, ambition and stupidity! And valor and wisdom, of course! Not to mention, our joys and sadness', and our weaknesses too. And our agonies and torments! And our bliss and rapture, all these we must keep. Or, the pain in living can become so unendurable, that we will ransom life for the peace in death."

"The pain in your leg, Your Majesty, was my most urgent concern, which you have succeeded in avoiding so mystically." Salima smiled.

"The pain in my heart demands immediate attention, my love. And be assured, there is no pain in any other part of my body." Akbar laughed. "The much scribbled book in your soul, I can read. The only book, which I am capable of reading! Yet, some words in there, smudged and rewritten, confound my sense of perception."

"Tell me, what you have read so far, Your Majesty?" Salima challenged.

"A medley of names, fears, doubts, apprehensions." Akbar responded smoothly. "The dancing text in your soul itself is wondering, why the emperor, especially, after issuing this edict, that no one is allowed to have more than one wife, acquired two more brides? And why does he claim to love you alone, when he shares his love with a harem-full of wives?" His look was tender and searching.

"The emperor has the right to wed as many times as he wishes, Your Majesty." Salima murmured.

"The emperor has no right to wed, my love, and no right in claiming the purity of love for *one*. Though his love, in its purest form—for *one* refuses to die!" Akbar got to his feet, filling his cup with wine from gold flagon on the table. "To seek more than one wife is to work one's undoing. Had I been wiser, I would have married no one, but you, my true love. Especially, I would not have taken any woman from my kingdom into my seraglio, for my subjects are to me in the place of children."

"And the right to open a wine shop for medicinal purposes." Salima was not heeding, but voicing her fears.

"Wine shop, that was—" Akbar turned, catching sparks of fear in her eyes. "Can you read the emperor's soul? What do you see in my eyes, love?"

"Texts alien and undecipherable, Your Majesty." Salima complied hastily. "Hindi, Latin and Sanskrit. Not a word in Urdu, Persian or Turkish. And a horde of faces in the drifting fogs. Jains and Jesuits, padres and priests, pundits and mullahs! All those discussions, Your Majesty! What are you searching for?"

"Those discussions lead to the rungs of truth, my love, or of *love,* the highest abode in the realms of knowledge." Akbar took a few steps, and then stood still. "Even if I could drink the holy Ganga dry, my thirst for knowledge would not ever be slaked. What is this fear, which is stealing light from you eyes, love? It has no link with the wine shop, has it? That wine shop, which was opened in Fatehpur Sikri, years ago! You are worried about our prince Murad in Deccan, perhaps. About his safety, his life! I can't read your thoughts, love? Not, always."

"His life is much safe on the battleground, Your Majesty, than on the field of oblivion. His state of inebriation, whenever leisure dictates his moods and he drinks and drinks!" Salima's inmost fears were trembling on her lips.

"So, wine is the link to your fears!" Akbar contemplated aloud. "Has the Prince written to you about his lapses of oblivion and drunkenness, lately? Drinking, his only vice, which he shields from the emperor, much to the chagrin of his impenitent heart?"

"No, Your Majesty." Was Salima's quick response! "He boasts, quite truly, of his valor, and of his duty and obedience to your will. The most recent letter which I received from him a couple of weeks ago is quite enchanting. He says, that Chand Bibi who is guarding the fort at Ahmadnagar, is a mighty match to his valor. She is the queen over all in shooting, horse-riding and sword-fighting, as well as in statecraft. Our Prince is so impressed by her valor and beauty, that he calls her, Chand Sultan. Though, he remains adamant in foiling all her defensive strategies."

"And you have so deliciously averted the emperor's attention from the valleys of love and hate in your bosom!" Akbar exclaimed. "Though, I have ceased to hope for your love, my love. But even in the ocean of your hatred, I find a blessed home."

"No such ocean of hatred rages inside my heart, Your Majesty!" Salima protested. "But if I fail to convince you, in heaven we might meet in perfect love."

"I am in heaven, right now, my love. Whenever I am near you, that's heaven for me!" Akbar kneeled, kissing her hands. "I would rather lose all the joys in heaven and endure all the fires in hell if that is the only choice I have to stay close to you forever!"

"And next time I see you, Your Majesty, you would be wedded to another princess, in the name of love or alliance." Salima Begum laughed bitterly.

"Next time, if I have the urge to wed or the need for an alliance, I would espouse the bride of meditation." Akbar got to his feet. "And now, I must find repose in the arms of theological discussions. And next time, if you happen to reach out and touch the fogs of Latin and Sanskrit in the emperor's head, summon him to your presence. He would dissolve those alphabets with the wand of his love." He laughed, turning to leave.

"You are forgetting the promise to your wives, Your Majesty. You are to visit them in the chamber of Hira Begum, before you leave for your theological discussions." Salima Begum reminded softly. "They are waiting, and they would be disappointed if you didn't keep your promise."

"My time is happily consumed with you, my love. They would not even miss the emperor, save alone wait for him." He stood contemplating.

"Yes, they will, Your Majesty." Salima Begum teased. "Especially, Umbrine and Zebunisa!"

"Why only two out of all my heedless brides?" Akbar headed toward the door.

"Because, they are the newly-weds." Salima murmured to herself.

"More than three years since I wedded them! Three brief eons, and you still refer to them as the newly-weds, my love." Akbar disappeared into the damasked hallway.

The large gallery overlooking the courtyard of the palace was teeming with theologians. This gallery, as well as the domes and the balconies of this palace were decked with candles and colorful lamps in commemoration of the Nauroz festival. The estrade upon which the emperor sat was cushioned with gold and maroon velvets, and heaped with satiny pillows. Abul Fazl was seated next to the emperor, recounting the worth of all the gifts which were being presented. *And of many, many more, which could not be brought into this gallery.* The gifts which could not be displayed in this gallery were the horses and the mares and the camels housed in green and crimson velvets. The chariots of silver and gold! The elephants furnished with gilded howdahs.

"Do you find comfort, rather solace, in theological discussions, Abul?" Akbar's gaze was both profound and piercing.

"Yes, Your Majesty, my only solace and comfort, against the lamps of tragedies since these past few years!" Was Abul Fazl's quick response!

"How long would you lament the death of your noble brother, Abul?" Akbar's tones were soft and soothing. "Learn from the emperor's heart. Sorrows can be easily banished, once that one learns to relinquish the claim to affections, attachments! Whether they belong to the dearest of kin or to the dearest of friends!"

"I have ceased to lament, Your Majesty. The pain in my heart is stilled." Abul Fazl lied quite smoothly. "And when I do long for Faizi's company, I read his poems. And feel his presence, closer to me than ever." He confessed.

"Then recite one of his poems, Abul. The one, which he wrote in your praise? And we would command Faizi to stay with us, this evening." Akbar requested.

"I am unworthy of that praise, Your Majesty. His great love for me is the only reason, which his poetic genius expressed itself in that poem." Abul Fazl demurred.

"The emperor feels every inch worthy of Faizi's praise, for he made him the subject of his noble eloquence. And by reciting his couplets, I would summon him to my presence." Akbar began thoughtfully. "And if you wish to share his company, you must recite that praise-worthy poem of your brother's love. Otherwise, he would stay with me alone, shunning the company of his brother." He challenged, reciting.

"O king, give me at night the lamp of hope, bestow upon my taper the everlasting ray

Of the light which illuminates the eye of Thy heart, give me an atom, by the light of the sun

If you wish to see the path of guidance as I have done

You will never see it without having seen the king

Thy old-fashioned prostration is of no advantage to thee

See Akbar, and you see God

Such aggrandizement, Abul, from the very pen of your brother! Don't you think that the ulemas would find it blasphemous? Yet, in their ignorance, they would miss the spiritual beauty of this quatrain, if they interpreted it literally. God can be manifested in all of us, from one lowly beggar to the highest king, if only one dares look? And now, Abul, don't you think you can accept your brother's praise with gratitude? And thank the Almighty God that his genius would live forever. Faizi is with me, now! And you can see him too, if you have the heart to recite the mantra of his sublime poetry."

"My verse may share both great and little worth

Its theme sublime—I lowlier than the earth

A father's virtues shall it far proclaim

And vaunt the glory of a brother's fame

He, touchstone of all wisdom, who inspires

My strain with sweetness that a world admires

If through a riper age, I pass him by

In merit, centuries between us lie
What though the branching savin taller grows
What gardener mates its beauty with the rose."

Abul Fazl appeared to cherish the very words on his lips with his eyes closed.

"Serene be the night and pleasant the moonshine
 That I may talk with thee on every subject"

Akbar recited his own couplet.

"You have taken me back to Deccan, Your Majesty. And Faizi is with us. Such an unforgettable night! With all the poetry of joy and beauty—" Abul Fazl was following the emperor's gaze, where Baduani stood alone. "And such a selfish brute I have been, Your Majesty! Wallowing in my misery and self-pity! Not even knowing, that the emperor has countless worries and burdens, which can be shared with friends."

"Living in oblivion and neglecting your duty toward the emperor is a sure cause for reprisal." Akbar returned his gaze to Abul Fazl. "Yet, emperor's worries are not as much as half the weight of his conscience, which keeps the just and noble spirits in check. I can't help but notice that Baduani has become taciturn, of late. Can you enlighten me as to why he has burdened himself with the task of avoiding the emperor?"

"He is afraid of you, Your Majesty, since he stands accused of accusing you unjustly of heresy. Proclaiming, that under your sovereign rule, the mosques stand empty and are transformed into stables, granaries and storehouses! His imaginations run quite wild, when he is drunk with zeal. He is under the impression, these days, that he has depleted all the resources of your great clemency." Abul Fazl intoned cautiously. "His fears are heightened since his couplet against you has made all the tongues rattling."

"How could the emperor forget? I have not thought about that couplet since—" He laughed suddenly. "What was it? Yes!

The ulemas avoid the schools as they avoid taverns in the fasting month of Ramadan

The Quran wanders as a pledge to the pawn-brokers.

What fear has he when his zeal and ignorance have ceased to annoy the emperor? His base canards and vile accusations are but reeds in the wind. He has received no reprimand from me! What indeed is his fear?"

"He fears his zeal, Your Majesty. For, he lacks the strength to discipline his mind." Abul Fazl began reluctantly. "By the law and virtue of his nature which breeds more vice than virtue, he cannot help but exploit his well of wisdom and learning. Now, he has drawn a fresh list of charges against you, Your Majesty. Rather, a list of heresies, which a very few of us have read." He whispered regretfully.

"And you have imbibed the contents of that list, I am sure." Akbar's gaze was kind and searching. "And what are those blooming absurdities, this time?" He asked.

"Your Majesty!" Abul Fazl's reluctance was but one silent plea. "That the emperor has forbidden fasting and the call to prayers. That the Muslim festivals are banned! That the emperor has plundered the mosques! That capital punishment is inflicted on those who slaughter the cows!"

"The holy cows!" Akbar exclaimed! "Just because the emperor has granted permission to the pious Hindu, Vitthalashwar, the freedom to let his cows graze wherever they are? And just because he has granted freedom to the pundits of Goverdhan temple grazing of their cows in the neighboring villages of Savi! The emperor is being charged, what, of capital punishment? Oh, such odious lies. The emperor's policy of tolerance toward all religions doesn't make him less of a Muslim, does it? But it does attract swarms of hideous lies from the lips of the zealots. The brotherhood of Islam, they dare call themselves Muslims, with malefic lies breathing through their very teeth. And how many in my court would fan these absurdities, Abul?"

"Only a few, Your Majesty." Abul Fazl was tracing the emperor's gaze again. "Only a handful, whose zeal is as blind as their learning and whose sightless ignorance guides them to the path of a false reckoning."

"Only one, Abul, the emperor predicts. Baduani himself the author of great lies!" Akbar returned his gaze to his friend. "He would believe to the end, that his God and my God are different. And that my God is in absolute power to persecute the Muslims with His Grace of Mercy, Justice and Compassion. Only Baduani's learning, of which he possesses but a few grains, save him from my anger. I have the urge to feed him alive to the holy cows, this very instant. Well, he might learn the virtue of piety and discretion in their warm bellies. He had a great share in translating Mahabharata from Sanskrit to Persian. And for that alone, he deserves to live! Not in the stomachs of the holy cows, but inside the unholy lumps of his flesh. Though, other works of equal holiness were translated by others with much greater intellect than his. Atharva-veda; Bhagawat Geeta; the Ramayan; the Harvarsh Purana; Panch Tantra; Katha Sarit; Sagar; Nala-Damayanti, and a lot more divine works of sublime merit. Refresh the emperor's memory, Abul, of more translations?"

"There is one, Khirad Afza, Your Majesty." Abul Fazl began quickly. "Tazuke-Babari, which is translated from Turki. Quran, Majma-ul-Buldan, and Samart-ul-Filsaga, all these from Arabic to Persian. And Bible from Greek to Persian, and many, many more books on law, history, religion and philosophy. The names elude me, right this moment. Yes, a Lexicon of Persian language is being compiled by Dustur Ardeshir. You invited him from Persia, Your Majesty, if you recall."

"Yes." Akbar's gaze was lured toward prince Salim and Father Xavier, joined by Baduani. "What is that book Father Xavier is cradling to his breast so possessively?"

"No other than the book about the life of Jesus Christ, Your Majesty. The book which he himself translated from Portuguese into Persian!" Abul Fazl smiled to himself. "The same one, Your Majesty, which was read to you. And it had made such a great impression on you, that you had conferred upon it the title, The Mirror of Purity."

"And have I seen that portrait before, which my princely son is holding for all to see? It is evoking such mute veneration from my Prince?" Akbar asked.

"Yes, Your Majesty, you have seen it. You yourself ordered that exquisite frame, which houses the portrait of Mary Magdalene. Nothing like it exists in the whole of Hind." Abul Fazl smiled. "The beauty of the frame compliments the portrait, prince Salim showed it to you last week, Your Majesty. The painter copied it from an Italian picture by the explicit orders of prince Salim." He added.

"You seem more enchanted by the exquisite frame, Abul, than by the divine portrait itself." Akbar commented amusedly. "Yet, what interest does Baduani have in this portrait, my sage friend? He might be stricken blind by watching this wonder of sanctity, someone should warn him. For, to him, this is the handiwork of the devil."

"The devil in him, Your Majesty, is gloating inwardly. He is gleaning all sorts of hidden meanings from the Biblical mysteries, in order to challenge or malign the Christian beliefs as I have been informed!" Abul Fazl blurted out amusedly.

"So, the zealous fool is studying the Bible, these days! I have my own sources, Abul, if you choose not to inform the emperor about the whimsical pursuits of my ulemas. Due to your love and devotion for the emperor, I believe?" Akbar laughed. "And what lies he has concocted out of the deepest truths in mysteries sublime?"

"Your Majesty!" Abul Fazl protested low. "He intends to refute Christ's claim to celibacy. His studies reveal, he says, that Mary Magdalene is the bride of the Christ."

"And if he dares utter such blasphemy without some divine evidence as his only refuge, he would be crucified alive by the very tongues of the Fathers, here in my court." Akbar thought aloud. "Yet, marriage in no sin for the Man of God, or god-man, as he is represented to us, the spiritual guide of us all. Divine prophets know they are sinless, for they see divinity in all of us, more so in the hearts of the women, who are known to us from the annals of history as the mother-brides, sister-brides, and brides of the gods. If we all decided to stay celibate, there would be no one left to praise God. With the exception of violence in nature! And what other muskets of vile discovery is he holding captive in his wild imagination?" He asked probingly.

"A cannonade of discoveries, rather assertions! All lacking proof, Your Majesty." Abul Fazl commenced doubtfully. "He is naming the Biblical James, Joses, Jude and Simon, as the brothers of Jesus Christ, the sons of Virgin Mary."

"Instead of learning wisdom from Holy Scriptures, men of weak intellect are bound to fall into the folly of base disputes." Akbar's thoughts were disrupted by the volley of arguments amongst a young man and two Fathers. "Isn't he that Armenian Christian? What is his name? Yes, Peres, who married a Hindu girl! And Father Aquaviva was there to interpret the sermon for the bride.

How long has it been since he wedded that Hindu girl, a decade at least?" He returned his gaze to Abul Fazl.

"Almost thirteen years, Your Majesty." Was Abul Fazl's thoughtful response!

"And what fire is erupting forth flames of anger from the lips of the Fathers, do you know? Has the Armenian offended the holy Fathers?" Akbar asked quickly.

"Peres lost his wife a few months ago, Your Majesty." Was Abul Fazl's prompt response! "And now, he wishes to marry the niece of his deceased wife. The Fathers forbid it on the grounds, that it is an abominable sin. The church doesn't sanction such a marriage, to any kin of the acquired wife, even if she is dead. Peres have threatened the Fathers with his intention of becoming a Muslim, and marrying the niece of his late wife, if the Fathers insist upon prohibiting such a match. I was hoping, Your Majesty that the Fathers won't bring this dispute before you, not this evening, at least. But their spirit of martyrdom has over-ruled their judgment for postponing this dispute, I guess."

"Summon these sons of Christ to my presence, Abul." Akbar commanded.

Father Xavier, Father Pignero, and Peres were brought before the emperor without delay. Peres had merely bowed his head, standing there stunned.

"What is this heathen uproar, holy Fathers? Why must you rage and rant? The cinders of your intellect turning to ashes on your very lips!" Akbar demanded.

"Your Majesty. This apostate here is digressing from the Christian Faith." Father Xavier was trying his best to digest his anger. "He is abandoning his True Faith! Simply, because he has fallen victim to the vile charms of his late wife's niece, and wishes to marry her. And that is the highest of sins in the eyes of our church. Perdition is allotted to those, who desire such an incestuous union. Our aim is to save him from this act of sin and damnation. Eve beguiled Adam, and—" His vehemence was silenced by one impatient gesture of the emperor.

"The devil charmed the serpent, and the serpent beguiled Eve. And Eve captivated the heart of Adam. The root of evil from man to man! The serpent is the emblem of *wisdom*, and Eve, the mother of *virtue*. Both becoming the victims of evil from beginning to end! And Man, not accepting the blame for his weakness. And the woman, yes, enduring the burden of evil, while cradling truth inside the purity of her heart. And that is the truth, Holy Father, so ingeniously misconstrued." Was Akbar's Sufic reproof! "The issue here is not of sin and damnation, Father, but of love and marriage. What harm is there if a man wishes to marry the lady of his choice, under the jurisdiction of Muslim law?"

"The harm, Your Majesty, is that he is abandoning the road to paradise for the road to hell." Father Xavier intoned tremulously. "And anyone who abandons his Faith for the lust of a woman is surely to be damned, finding no mercy from man or God."

"Hell and damnation are in the souls of the ones, whose hearts burn in the everlasting fires of ignorance. These fires scorching the very fibres of virtue, reason, tolerance, and feeding the flames of unreason with rage and malevolence! Or rather, with hatred and insolence." Akbar commented without rage. "Divine mercy attaches itself to every form of creed, and supreme exertions must be made to bring oneself to the ever vernal flower-garden of peace with all. The eternal God is bounteous to all souls and conditions of men. Under the edict of tolerance in our empire, Peres is free to choose any religion he wishes, without the interference of holy men with the tongues of unholy fire."

"Your Majesty, we have come here to defend our faith, or die, if you sanction such a marriage. Christianity prides itself in martyrdom, and we would die as martyrs, bearing crosses in our arms." Father Pignero could not control his zeal.

"Cross, a symbol of torture! How can one venerate something, which reminds one of pain and suffering!" Akbar shifted his gaze from Father Pignero to Father Xavier. "The word, martyrdom is as much distorted in meaning as the word, jihad. Both meaning: to conquer evil in one's heart. To fight the passions of rage, hatred and avarice! To kill pride and prejudice! To appease the passions of envy and jealousy! To assuage the hungers of gluttony and rapacity!"

"Pardon us, Your Majesty." Father Xavier implored suddenly. "We came here— if you grant us the permission, to talk about the Christian doctrines. Our fervent desire is to converse with you on this subject." He appealed humbly.

"Peres, retire to that chamber yonder, and brood over the *lord of love*." Akbar commanded, after bestowing a kind smile on Father Xavier. "The emperor will summon you much before these discussions come to a congenial repast. You would find the emperor a kind witness to your second wedding, also."

"Your most humble servant, Your Majesty." Peres fled without another word.

"Wasn't it Voltaire, Your Majesty, who wrote? *And if you must be damned, at least be damned for pleasant sins.*" Abul Fazl sought the emperor's attention.

Akbar laughed, inhaling the scent of a couplet recited by prince Salim.

*"Always, everywhere, with everyone, and in every circumstance
Keep the eye of thy heart secretly fixed on the beloved."*

"Come hither, Shaikhu Baba, and show that beloved portrait of yours to the emperor again." Akbar commanded, reciting his couplet, his gaze shifting to Jouhar.

*"In the era of the fault forgiving king
The Qazi drained flagons, the Mufti quaffed cups.*

Come, saki, fill the cups of all men, till sense and sensibility start flowing in their thoughts, and from their very tongues." He claimed the portrait held out by prince Salim.

Mary Magdalene was seated with her hands clasped, and a silvery halo was suspended over her head. The book in her lap was forgotten. The alabaster jar at her feet neglected. She was wearing a gown of green, a red cloak tossed over her shoulders carelessly. The emperor was so rapt in studying the face of Mary Magdalene, that he could barely hear Father Xavier, who had begun to speak suddenly.

"Your Majesty, you should see the picture of Madonna and the Savior, painted on the east side of Prince Salim's bedroom window!" Father Xavier murmured. "Your Majesty, we are still waiting for your gracious consent to build a church at Lahore."

"The emperor not only grants you the permission to build a church at Lahore, but all its expenses will be paid from our royal treasury too." Akbar intoned kindly. "Yet, what need you have for churches, when you can openly preach in the whole of Hind. And you have converted many *heathen*, as you call them, to the true faith of Christianity. Didn't you recently convert a ninety year old Jew to Christianity? Isn't he condemned to hell by abandoning his true faith?" He asked.

Father Xavier stood there nonplused.

"Your Majesty. God, in His mercy, has shed the light of the heavens on that Jew. He is converted to Christianity, and is finally baptized." Father Pignero appeared to sing to himself. "We of pure Faith, Your Majesty, believe that God in His justice forgives not those who disobey our Lord, Jesus Christ."

"To question the justice of God, and to know not His mercy, is like falling into an abyss without tasting the bliss of wisdom and understanding. It's like burying a treasure-chest of divine knowledge in one's bosom into some neglected tomb, where the altar of truth could never be erected. This neglected tomb could be reached within the altars of one's soul, if one were to journey in an everlasting quest for truth, nothing but the truth. Where is Brother Benedict de Goes, the master of proselytizing?" Akbar asked.

"He, Your Majesty." Father Xavier began since Father Pignero couldn't speak. "He, Brother Benedict is praying for us, I guess. We came here—well, to protest against the heresy of Peres, donning the mantles of martyrdom? Besides, Brother Benedict was engaged in the baptismal rites of the children before we left." He added thoughtlessly.

"Ah, the children!" Akbar exclaimed. "Don't they die as soon as you baptize them? I have heard such reports like these. Are those reports true, holy Father?"

"True only amongst the most recent cases, Your Majesty. Mainly, because those children were sickly, even before they were brought to us." Father Xavier admitted reluctantly. "But they die in peace, Your Majesty, and they would dwell in heaven."

"Yes! Heaven is always the abode of the dead, who are forbidden to taste the joys of heaven on this earth, this living hell and paradise of ours!" Akbar demurred aloud.

"Pardon me, Your Majesty." Baduani broke his cup of silence. "Islam is profounder than the truth itself. And it seems to me, our discussions around here are leading us more and more toward Sufism. Sufism is not what Islam is, it unspools but a few parables through the tongues the Sufis, or the mystics."

"All religions, Baduani, they are God's religions, created by Him, and shared by us all." Akbar responded patiently. "And Sufism is as much a part of Islam, as one's body to its soul. Sufism, to me, is the child of all religions. Pure and innocent and without guile! Untainted by the scars of disputes, and embracing all faiths, which reach out in love to comfort its vulnerability. Was Prophet Muhammed not a mystic? Didn't our holy Prophet seek solitude in the silence of Mount Hira, and prayed in utter seclusion? It was there, that he fell into a mystical ecstasy, and the holy Quran was revealed to him." He smiled. "Though professing Sufism as the one divine attributes of Islam, I do not claim myself as a prophet. The divine virtues of prophethood are not acquired, but bestowed upon a few holy men by the grace of God. I am neither holy, nor wise, and God is not about to bless me with the soma of truth. But I do seek truth in knowledge, and do possess a few grains of wisdom. Though, this humble wisdom of mine is tortured by the sand-dunes of ignorance from all the planets on earth, whose inhabitants come to my court, preaching the edicts of intolerance. And not learning the *art of truth* in the universal language of love, peace and compassion."

Now it was Baduani's turn to be cast into the ocean of bewilderment.

"It is our humble request, Your Majesty, to discuss with you the Gospels." Father Pignero looked contrite. "Especially, the miracles of our Lord! No other religion in the world has any miracles compared with the glory of the miracles in Christianity."

"You have my permission, Father Pignero, to discuss the glorious miracles, and to preach, if you will." Akbar smiled. "Though, in my estimation, only vulgar believe in miracles, the wise man accepts nothing without adequate proof. Yet, all religions abound with the wealth of miracles, even Islam. Prophet Muhammed rode on his horse named, Buraq, and ascended to the heaven. Once, the angel Gabriel, cut open the chest of Prophet Muhammed, and purged his heart of all mortal impurities, sealing it back and leaving no scar. See, Holy Father, if one must believe in the scriptures, when God's angels cut and heal, they leave no scars on the flesh."

"The miracle of Virgin Birth, Your Majesty! Even Muslims believe in that." Father Xavier interceded quickly. "No other religion has blessed mankind with the Son of God through the miracle of Virgin Birth."

"Many sons were born of Virgin Mothers, holy Father. And worshipped like the gods in many religions, beginning from ancient to the so-called civilized ones." Akbar responded thoughtfully. "It is believed that Buddha descended from heaven into his mother's womb in the shape of a milk-white elephant. All the pagan gods are the issues of virgin births, too. Dionysus was conceived of a goddess, whom Zeus visited as a snake. The Virgin goddess bore the ever-dying, ever-living god of bread and wine, the Dionysus himself. He was nurtured in a cave, torn to pieces by the Titans, and then resurrected as a Savior God. I have the painting of the Egyptian goddess, Isis. Her husband Osiris is worshipped as a Savior God, who had died and was resurrected. She herself, with her son Horus is depicted as, Madonna and the Child."

Both the Fathers were standing there spellbound, disbelief shining in their eyes.

"The Christian Son of God was crucified. But Christ, the Messiah, as believed by the Muslims, was ascended to the heavens by the mercy of the same

God Whom we worship as Allah." Baduani's murmurous tones didn't escape the emperor's notice.

"Christ would have never been crucified, if he was to preach in Hind." Akbar, though responding to Baduani's murmurous comments, was turning his attention to the Jesuits. "Yes, if granted the opportunity of telling the Hindus that he is the Son of God, the Christ would have gathered disciples in hordes. The Hindus would have fallen at his feet, calling him Bhagwan, and worshipping him as one of their own gods."

"Christ, our Lord, is the Son and the Vassal of God, the true God of Christianity." Father Pignero murmured to himself.

"And the Vessel of God Himself!" Was Father Xavier's feeble comment! "A Vessel filled to the brim with the spirit of truth. And whoever drank out of this Vessel became drunk with desire to seek, as well as to protect the Tree of Knowledge, which grows and blooms in Bible with the scent of divine truth."

"The roots of this Tree of Knowledge, holy Father, can be traced in all the holy books. In holy Geeta and in holy Quran! In holy Torah, and in all the holy books, which were ever written to guide all men to the path of righteousness?"

"The Godhead in Christianity is unique, Your Majesty." Father Pignero began with all haste. "No other religion has the concept of Trinity."

"Hinduism has the concept of Trinity, good Father." Akbar intoned merrily. "Brahma as the Creator, Vishnu as the Preserver, and Shiva as the Destroyer! I thing I have said this before over and over again."

"But Hindus pray to many gods, Your Majesty." Father Xavier protested. "They have many idols, and many, many more gods and goddesses."

"Tell the holy Fathers, Chandra Siri." Akbar flashed a kind smile at the Jain scholar. "Yes, enlighten them as to how the Hindus pray to one God through many, since you have studied Hinduism more extensively than any Pundit. Where do the idols stand in the cosmic reality of oneness?"

"Hinduism is as complex as any other religion of the world, Your Majesty, but I will try my best. Fortunately, two verses from Holy Geeta are coming to my mind, which may suffice to explain the concept of oneness in Hinduism." Chandra Siri commenced happily. "Lord Krishna is another of the Hindu gods whom all Hindus invoke as, our Father, but they worship only one and that is Brahma. Holy Geeta says: *When one sees the whole variety-of-beings, as resting in the One, and spreading forth from That One alone, one then becomes Brahman.* And again, the wisdom of Holy Geeta: *I am the Goal, the Supporter, the Lord, the Witness, the Abode, the Shelter, the Friend, the Origin, the Dissolution, the Foundation, the Treasure-house and the seed imperishable.* Hindus pray, but to one God. And as to the idols, they are the divine seats of our divine concentration. For our mortal imperfections do not permit us to perceive or to attach our thoughts to *one* with a single-pointed devotedness. They are not much different than the intermediaries to reach one's God. Much like kneeling before the Cross, or praying before the portrait of Jesus Christ! Or venerating the purity of Madonna and the Child. Or even sitting in supplication at the feet of the image of the Buddha!"

"But some of the idols, carved so shamelessly, in obscene depictions!" Father Pignero muttered, before he could check his zeal.

"Obviously, Father Pignero, you have not read about the phallic pillars of the Solomon Temple. And Solomon is as much a prophet of the Christians as of the Muslims. Though, both these sects wallow in their rituals of piety and self-righteousness. Condoning, rather concealing the so-called shameful facts, and erecting tombs of lies, where the truths lay buried still." Akbar shot him a look of reproof.

"The Lover and the Beloved are in reality one
Idle talkers speak of the Brahman as distinct from his idol."
Abul Fazl could not help but recite.

"Poetry has no place in the realm of theology, Abul Fazl." Father Xavier opined aloud. "At the throne of God, the words Lover and the Beloved are not to be uttered."

"God, Lover and Beloved are the same in Sufic language, revered padre." Abul Fazl commented. "One Sufi poet Al-Hallaj wrote.

"I am He whom I love, and whom I love is I
We are two spirits dwelling in one body
If thou seest me, thou seest Him
If thou seest Him, thou seest us both
Truly! If one loves God with the devotion of a Lover to his Beloved, one attains union with God with the help of love, not Reason."

"And Al-Hallaj was executed at Baghdad in Year 922 for such heresy." Baduani muttered derisively. "Impious men have changed the divine laws of God, and now the blasphemers roam free on the face of this earth."

"To change the course of such laws is not human but divine by Whose will all suffer or rejoice according to their capacity in surrendering to His will." Abul Fazl responded calmly. "Even nature suffers blight, yet obeys the laws of its Nature."

"If great nature in its entirety doesn't deviate from its laws, then how us lowly mortals can deviate from the laws of our natures?" Akbar turned to Abul Fazl.

"This subtle epigram is embedded inside a million incarnations, Your Majesty, like a great puzzle. Ever-complete and ever-changing, as Bhanu Chandra says." Abul Fazl's gaze was pleading with Jain sage. "He is the scholar of many such puzzles. And if I may recommend him for Your Majesty's pleasure and edification."

"Enlighten us about the essence of the Divine, Bhanu Chandra. And about the laws of nature, its change, creation and destruction!" Akbar welcomed the sage. "Your silence puzzles me more, than your wisdom, my eminent sage."

"Your Majesty, silence is wisdom. Yet, I possess only its first half, and the other half escapes me." Bhanu Chandra responded. "My puny perception of the Divine doesn't permit me to elucidate, but I do try to seek knowledge for the sake of my own peace. So far in my quest, I have discovered this much, that the laws of the Divine are changeless in the cycle of creation and destruction.

Change in creation means chaos and blight. From uncreated, no change occurs but stability. So, from nothingness into being, is the stable law of nature. Remaining changeless in its cycles of birth and death!"

"Much profounder than truths, are the fruits of your quests, my sage-philosopher." Akbar's gaze was shifting to Baduani. "Baduani, the discussions such as these have led you to believe, that the emperor has renounced Islam? Do you have more arrows of heresy left to shoot at the emperor?"

"Many times, Your Majesty, I have been accused unjustly. Though, my heart is forever devoted to you." Baduani protested vehemently. "I have never as much as thought, that you have renounced your faith. All these charges of heresy against you are merely fabricated lies concocted by malicious tongues. Inside the mirror of your heart are altars pure and noble, Your Majesty. Reflected in there, you see sensible men in all religions. You have found true knowledge in every religion, preferring not one over the other, yet remaining true to Islam. A true Muslim sovereign, indeed, Your Majesty! With justice and equality, as his banners of Islam. The highest virtues in Islam, justice and equality!"

"Equality!" Father Pignero exclaimed. "Equality, when fakirs roam hungry on the streets and the kings sit high on their thrones! Poor wallow in the mud, and the rich are weighed in gold!" He bit his tongue, horror shining in his eyes at his audacity.

"Equality, good Father, doesn't mean sharing one's wealth with the idlers, or abasing one's dearly won status in life before the sight of the rude simpletons." Akbar began calmly. "Or, giving away one's jewels of wisdom to the unintelligent herd of fools! Or, enduring the edicts of stupidity! But equality in thought and reason! In respect and discipline! In tolerance toward all, whether one has attained the throne of kingship, or whether one has mired oneself into the pit of degradation. Lowly or high, both demand respect in respect to their attained or unattained station in life."

"How can truth of the Gospels be proclaimed when thoughts stray from religion to—" A cry of despair escaped Father Xavier's lips. "Where do these discussions lead to, Your Majesty?" He cried with utmost dejection.

"To the soul of noble reasoning." Akbar appeared to console the Father. "For the soul shines forth best in stirring talk. Our minds are forever tyrannized by the bullets of inquiries, and the truth half-slain in this debacle pleads mercy against the shield of lies."

"Lies one can easily understand, Your Majesty. But the concept of equality! How can one know? How does one attain—equality?" Father Xavier lamented.

"Only in death, one achieves equality, holy Father." Akbar was listening to the edicts of his psyche. "Only in death! All are buried in the mud, no marble tombs or glorious monuments can lift the fortunate dead from the blankets of dust. Knowing not the fool from the wise! Rich from the poor! Or a sinner from the righteous one! Evil, along with the good, dies! As well as the passions noble or wicked, only to renew the link of time with nature, in the scale of creation and destruction."

"Islam grants equality to the living, Your Majesty." Baduani began pontifically. "When one prays to one God, bending one's head in the same direction, there is no distinction left, but the sense of brotherhood. A Muslim, by the sheer act of reciting Kalima understands the concept of equality. Further, purifying his body and soul in the sacred rite of circumcision, which is another aspect of equality, leading one to the door of peace, justice and understanding. We Muslims believe in one God alone, and this is the religion of the pure and the wise."

"Pure and wise are born in every religion, if they practice not zeal and intolerance." Akbar smiled to himself. "Religion does not consist in repeating the Kalima, or circumcising oneself, or bending one's head outwardly in prayer. The first step for any religionist is to conquer his carnal desires and passions. Such as lust, anger and greed, and then cultivate the purity of thought." He added rather sadly.

"The message of Jesus through the Gospels makes one realize the worth of this religion, Your Majesty. And by learning the doctrines of Christianity, one finds oneself face-to-face with truth." Father Xavier appeared ready to deliver a sermon.

"The message of Jesus, wise Father, it seems, was corrupted by his apostles, just like the message of Prophet Muhammed by the false disciples of Islam. Foremost amongst them, the ignorant mullahs and the learned ulemas, burdened by the weight of their false prides." Akbar was feeling the familiar pulse of presage.

"The throne of God is in the heavens, and wisdom belongs to Him alone. And to reach that throne, even the emperor needs the light of truth through His Grace, in the name of Jesus Christ." Father Xavier murmured to himself.

"Royalty is a light emanating from God, and a ray from the sun, learned padre." Abul Fazl commenced since Akbar didn't speak. "Some call this light a divine light and some, a sublime halo. It is communicated by God to kings without the intermediate assistance of anyone, and the men in the presence of it, bend their forehead of praise toward the ground of submission. Many excellent qualities flow from the possession of this light! His Majesty is blessed with this light of truth, and thousands find rest in his love and wisdom. With such wisdom, the emperor understands the spirit of the age, and shapes his plans accordingly. In his thoughts, as well as in his actions and commands! He considers God as the real doer of all."

"Such flatteries, Abul, can even tempt a saint to follow the path to perdition." Akbar laughed suddenly.

"No kingdoms on earth, Your Majesty, are equal to the kingdom of heaven, which you will discover in the Gospels. Wars and conquests divert your attention from seeking the kernel of truth, which your noble soul yearns for." Father Xavier intoned assiduously.

"By the law of nature, Father, I am commanded to conquer and secure peace. And in the warring arguments, reach closer to the truth which all gospels hold sacred, in all faiths." Akbar responded mirthfully.

"And yet, Your Majesty, the men who refuse the boon of Salvation, lead the life of sin. Suffering great misfortunes, and not knowing the bliss of pure Faith." Was Father Xavier's urgent and despondent plea!

"Sinner and sufferer both, I live the life of a saint." Akbar was watching the slow approach of Aziz Koka. "My valorous knight, welcome to the court of war and theology. What woeful news you bring, that the emperor's heart flutters so rudely?"

"Happy news, Your Majesty. Only glad tidings and the laurels of victories!" Aziz Koka announced joyfully. "The conquest of Sindh is now complete. Muzaffar Hussain has submitted without resistance. Qara Beg is to bring him to Lahore for his formal submission to the emperor. The strong fort of Sibi is also conquered. And this entire land upto Kandahar, Kutch and Mekran is in the possession of the imperialists."

"Ah, from the coast of Mekran to the borders of Kandahar! And that celebrated fort in Baluchistan." Akbar's joy was boundless. "This fort of Sibi lies north-east of Quetta, isn't it? And where is prince Murad? Has he taken Ahmadnagar by storm?"

"The Prince is waiting outside, Your Majesty, anxious to seek your audience." Aziz Koka responded evasively. "He wanted me to deliver the good news, first."

"Is he the messenger of bad news, then?" Akbar interrupted quickly. "Summon the sad knight to my presence, at once." He commanded impatiently.

Prince Murad didn't need to be summoned. He was seen approaching.

"What sad news you bring the emperor, my charming prince?" Akbar asked.

"Only the happy news, Your Majesty, if you judge me kindly?" Prince Murad smiled winsomely. "I have signed a treaty with Chand Bibi. In this treaty, Berar is ceded to the Moghul Empire, but Bahadur Nizam, Chand Bibi's nephew will retain Ahmadnagar as a fief from the emperor."

"And my valorous son is bewitched by the beauty of Chand Bibi, is that true?" Akbar's heart was still shooting the arrows of presage.

"Charmed by her valor, Your Majesty, not bewitched by her beauty! Though she is beautiful!" Prince Murad confessed.

"And how do you rate her valor superior than her beauty? In relation to her valor which charmed you and to her beauty which failed to bewitch you?" Akbar asked.

"No comparison, Your Majesty. Her beauty humbles one to silence, and her valor moves one to awe and disbelief." Prince Murad responded. "Only, I saw her valor first, in the darkness of the night! That night, when a part of the fort was blown up by our soldiers! She rushed out barefoot, with a naked sword poised before her, exhorting her soldiers to repair the wall. And it was done before daybreak." He was quiet suddenly.

"For your chivalry alone, my Prince, you are promoted to the rank of eight thousand." Akbar announced. "Now, you stand accused with a sense of elevation, as well as with the sense of humiliation." He teased.

"Your most devoted son, Your Majesty." Prince Murad curtsied.

"Prince Murad is endowed with the sense of spirituality, Your Majesty. For, he is most keen in learning the Gospels." Father Xavier could not help boast about his student.

"If we can buy spirituality in little vials of perfume, Father, everyone would be cured of all the worldly prides and prejudices. With Faith as a panacea for Salvation!" Akbar turned toward Abul Fazl. "You have sealed your lips, my noble scholar. Let the rivers of your spirituality flow in smooth rivulets. And delight us with couplets."

"Your Majesty." Abul Fazl was startled out of his reveries.

"Of me a hundred fictions rumored fly
And the world stares if I a word reply."

"Divine inspiration flows forth from your very lips, Abul. Especially, when I feel the most famished for song and poetry." Akbar complimented happily. "Arrest your inspiration a little longer, and coin a few more couplets the worth of gold.

"The dullard's eye to sterling merit dim
True ring of minted gold tells naught to him
Worth must from noble souls unhidden blaze
As from the moon her light, from Jupiter her rays."

Abul Fazl's very thoughts were spilling this quatrain.

"Divine, divine, my noble friend." Akbar complimented. "If we were born blind, how would we praise the sparkling eyes of the moon and the Jupiter? Would the sightless then, bow to the darkness above, or to the light beyond, inside their dark souls! Learning the art of devotion inside the very abyss in their psyche!" He espied Vijaya Sen making his way toward the throne in all haste.

"Your Majesty, my master, Vijaya Suri, is seriously ill." Vijaya Sen breathed apologetically. "Please grant me the permission to leave for Gujrat. I may be able to lend him a little comfort in—" He could not continue, overwhelmed by grief.

Akbar was about to respond, when commotion broke forth in the balcony.

The fire, the palace is on fire.

In a flash, the emperor was on his feet, possessed by his need to get to the balcony from where he could see his palace burning and smoldering. All occupants of the palace were rescued. Akbar's thoughts were heaving a sigh of relief.

"God, have mercy on us. In the name of Jesus Christ, forgive us, Lord." Father Xavier's voice was making the sign of Cross over his breast. "God, and his only Son, Jesus Christ, he came to save the world. And whoever refuses to believe in him, cannot escape the everlasting torment. Lord, do not punish the emperor for his disbelief. Have mercy on him, our Lord, I pray in the name of Jesus Christ."

"Oh, these fogs of bigotry, will they ever fade!" Akbar turned his back on the crumbling ruins of his palace. "This fire burns but material wealths. And the fire, which burns in the emperor's heart in quest of a truth, will remain kindled forever." He made his way slowly into the hall of emptiness.

13

Beautiful Anarkali

The emperor was standing on a hill named Korhi, watching his garrisons. Beside him was standing his favorite grandson, Khusrau, the eldest of prince Salim's three sons. Both the prince and the emperor seemed to be a part of this hill, at the foot of which were sprawled the royal encampments in colorful silks. This city of Deccan had become the emperor's abode, since he had laid siege on the fort of Asirgarh. The rebellion of Bahadur Shah had incited the emperor on this hunting expedition.

The sense of doom was in Akbar's heart and psyche, though victories upon victories were heaped at his feet, wherever he had journeyed on campaigns long and arduous. Alas, those victories were tainted with the breath of fates, summoning *death, tragedy and misfortune* on the battleground of joys and sorrows.

Right after fire at the palace in Lahore which had reduced all its opulent wealths to cinders, Akbar had decided to visit Kashmir. The journey from Agra to Kashmir was delayed by an unfortunate accident. While hunting outside the city of Agra, the emperor was attacked by a wild deer, his testicles badly lacerated. His sufferings were exacerbated by the rumors proclaiming the emperor dead, if not laying prostrate on his death-bed. Upon his recovery, the emperor was informed about the excesses in drinking of all his sons, which were becoming more of a disease than pleasure.

The preparations for the journey to Kashmir were drawing to an end, when Akbar was faced with a dilemma he had not ever encountered before. Prince Salim had fallen in love with a dancing girl by the name of Sharifunnisa. This girl was the favorite of the Akbar's harem, and he himself had bestowed upon her the title of Anarkali as a reward for her great talent in singing and dancing. Anarkali was banished beyond the walls of the harem, commanded, not ever to sing or dance. Prince Salim was ordered to be sent on a campaign in the very heart of Allahabad, but he had shut himself up in his room with his wine-cup as his only companion. Anarkali was offered gifts in gold and jewels, if she could convince the prince that she did not love him, but she had rejected all offers.

Anarkali was sentenced to death by the orders of the emperor, yet her life was spared by the wisdom of Abul Fazl. Abul Fazl had proposed a solution in which the life of the girl could be spared, and the honor of the prince to be restored. Anarkali was to wed the prince for just one day, if she was willing to depart from his life forever. Abul Fazl had succeeded in winning Anarkali's consent to go along with this plan in exchange for all the wealth she desired. Anarkali was to be wedded to the prince, and was to make him drunk with wine mixed with opium. By dawn, she was to slip out of her bridal chamber, and meet her escorts, who would convey her to a secret place of luxury, where she would live like a queen to the end of her life. Prince Salim was not aware of this ruse of a wedding, stunned with grief upon finding his bride dead in the morning.

Inside the heartland of Kashmir

Once in Kashmir, Akbar was immersed deep in fighting the battle of famine of which he was duly informed, while prince Salim was left on his own to nurse his pain and loneliness. One evening, as prince Salim was exploring the rugged trails of Rajuri he was informed that the emperor was encamping nearby to inspect the construction of the sarais. Neglecting, rather forgetting his manners that he was not to appear before the emperor uninvited, prince Salim had stumbled forth into the tent to greet the emperor. The emperor was busy consulting with his viziers, and noticing his son sail into the tent, he was highly incensed, dismissing prince Salim immediately. Soon, Abul Fazl was sent after him to convey further the emperor's displeasure for his son's lack of etiquette.

The prince and the emperor were estranged once again, but this rift was soothed by Abul Fazl's temperate persuasions. The emperor had noticed his son's hatred toward Abul Fazl, and had been concerned. But Abul Fazl had soothed the emperor's fears.

I am much closer to you, Your Majesty, not with the ties of blood, but with the bond of wisdom and friendship, and the prince feels alienated.

More estrangements!

One of prince Salim's men was killed while Fath Gilani was guarding the Bhimbhar Pass, and could not allow any visitor to enter Kashmir without the permission of the emperor. The emperor was duly informed about this tragedy, and he had sent Fath Gilani in person to commune with the prince, stating that he was leaving this matter into his son's hands to punish or to pardon the man responsible for his friend's death. Prince Salim was pacified by the emperor's kindness in permitting him to choose his course of action, and had sent Fath Gilani back without inflicting any punishment on him.

A few months after this tragic incident, the emperor had ventured forth on a boating trip near Wulnar Lake. Late in the evening on his way back to his resort in Lain Lanka, Akbar had espied prince Salim in a state of half inebriation and half exhilaration. Incensed once again, the emperor had ordered his guards to escort the prince back to his palace. The same evening, the emperor's royal attendant, Khwaja Bhul, was dispatched to the prince to convey the emperor's reprimands, verbally.

Khwaja Bhul, inflated by the sense of his pride and importance had delivered the emperor's message to prince Salim in a manner both rude and presumptuous. Outraged in return, prince Salim had sent a missive to the emperor, professing his rage against this lowly messenger, yet confirming his devotion to the emperor.

The emperor had inquired about the behavior of his messenger, and was informed that Khwaja Bhul, indeed, had been insolent, distorting the emperor's message, and behaving discourteously. Weighed down by the burdens of royal duties, and now confronted with this outrage of discourtesy, he had ordered Khwaja Bhul's tongue to be cut off. Thus ended the rift between the prince and the emperor?

And the journey back to Lahore!

The discord and calamity were to follow the emperor to the very gates of Lahore, where more calamitous news were in store for him. Prince Murad's son, Rustam, had suddenly died, and prince Murad was in grievous state of mind and health.

At Agra, preparations for the Deccan campaign were moving swiftly, when the news of prince Murad's sudden death had scattered all those plans to the winds. Salima was inconsolable, drawing closer to the emperor with the ties of grief, and becoming a part of himself as she had never been before. The emperor had aged suddenly, both mentally and physically. His quest for truth was still his bewildering companion, where each life could lend breath to the chilling deeps in death! There was God somewhere?

After forty days of mourning and funeral rites, Akbar had instructed prince Salim to take charge of the rebellion in Ahmadnagar, but since the Prince had appeared disinclined, prince Daniyal was chosen to lead this campaign.

Two months later, the emperor himself was on his way toward Asirgarh. No sooner had the emperor reached Burhanpur, that prince Daniyal had come galloping his way, wearing the banners of victory in his very eyes.

The victorious Daniyal! The exultant Daniyal! The valorous prince!

Prince Daniyal had approached closer to the precincts of Ahmadnagar when he was confronted with news awful and strange. Bahadur Nizam had learned from his spies that the Moghuls were marching toward Ahmadnagar to sign another peace-treaty with Chand Bibi. Blinded by zeal that his aunt would befriend the Moghuls, Bahadur Nizam had ordered his slaves and his eunuch Hamid to murder Chand Bibi.

Thus ended the life of a brave queen!

Prince Daniyal had been shocked after learning about the death of this brave queen, but this shock alone had lent him the courage to avenge the murder of the queen. At dawn, when the blue stone fortress was stormed, there was no Chand Sultan to fight the Imperialists. The breech was made with the precision of a craftsman, and fifteen hundred of the enemy's garrison was put to sword. All the members of the ruling house, including Bahadur Nizam, were taken prisoners. The Imperialists had also gained the booty of silks, the jewels and the embossed arms and armaments. A gold crown, twenty-five elephants, and an extensive library with valuable books!

Now, prince Daniyal was with the emperor in Asirgarh. Honing his skills in constructing the earthworks! A succession of thoughts were trooping down the alleys in the emperor's head, his gaze was searching prince Daniyal, but espying Abul Fazl and Father Xavier, instead. He turned with the intention of trekking down this hill, but his steps were arrested by the light of adoration in prince Khusrau's eyes.

"You love your grandfather! Don't you, Khusrau?" Akbar laughed. Holding out his arms to him, and helping him scale the uneven path down to the rugged slopes below.

"You are my idol, Your Majesty, and I worship you." Prince Khusrau chanted happily. "My baba called me *heathen* for saying, that I worship you."

"Ah, my heedless prince! And that is your father, my beloved Khusrau. And that heedless prince of a father is the heir to my throne." Akbar ruminated aloud. "Since I have encouraged you to accompany me on all the campaigns, your father is shunning my company. My own son! Even disobeying the emperor? Unwilling to head any campaigns, and neglecting his royal duties, where they are needed the most."

"My baba is jealous, Your Majesty, I think." Prince Khusrau murmured. "I heard him say to my mamma. *Why do I have the privilege of talking to you, Your Majesty, whenever I want to, while he has to get permission whenever he wishes to see you?*"

"Ah, you have touched the chord of truth, my profound scholar!" Akbar exclaimed. "You are too young to know the viper of jealousy in each man's heart. Or, inside the heart of each woman! How is you mamma? Is she jealous, I mean, of the other brides in the harem? Man Bai, yes, she is the emperor's favorite too, of all Shaikhu Baba's wives. She has not been feeling well, and I wonder, if the cause of her ill health or ill-humor is, jealousy?" He appeared to ponder aloud.

"No, Your Majesty, mamma is not jealous, I can tell." Prince Khusrau murmured low, as if thinking to himself. "She is unhappy, I guess."

"Ah, you ought to learn about the difference between jealousy and unhappiness, my young scholar. Rather, the similarity between the two!" Akbar indulged merrily. "Why is she unhappy, if she is not jealous?"

"She loves baba too much, and thinks I don't like my baba, Your Majesty. And that—that I rebel. I mean, go against his wishes." Prince Khusrau murmured.

"And do you—rebel, my prince?" Akbar asked. "Now, your grandfather is not here to spoil you, is he? He may grant you many privileges, but obedience to your father is your first duty. Why does your mamma think that you don't like your baba?"

"Because, I like to stay with you, Your Majesty, and talk with you!" Prince Khusrau's responded reluctantly.

"And you don't like to talk with your father, is that it?" Akbar prodded gently.

"No, Your Majesty. He doesn't like me." Prince Khusrau confessed without bitterness. "He likes Perwiz and Khurram and stays—well, I don't know.

"And spends his time in revelry and drunkenness! Royal secrets, my innocent child! The emperor knows all." Akbar drew him closer and hugged him.

Both the emperor and the grandson had landed at the foot of the hill, laughing. The merry companionship of the emperor and prince Khusrau was intercepted by prince Daniyal. He had sent prince Khusrau flying to some military errand, and himself had become the emperor's companion. At the approach of prince Daniyal and the emperor, Abul Fazl and Father Xavier were offering their curtsies and greetings.

"It is always a delight to see Prince Daniyal with you, Your Majesty. This brings to my mind, the picture of a disciple with his patron saint." Father Xavier remarked warmly. "He is my favorite student, Your Majesty. And if he can walk in the footsteps of Jesus, he will have the kingdom of joys to claim, and to restore to others."

"In your ignorance, Father, you have alluded to something wondrous." Akbar teased. "Jesus walking in the footsteps of his Father! And this disciple here will walk in the footsteps of his own father? In essence, you have sketched the portrait of the disciple—the son. Patron-saint, the Father! Thus, the emperor, the God!"

"I wouldn't utter such heresy, Your Majesty." Father Xavier was appalled.

"A great compliment to the emperor, Father Xavier." Akbar began to laugh.

"Imagine, Your Majesty, prince Daniyal gained victory without the provision of the Portuguese weapons, which Your Majesty had requested." Abul Fazl commented.

"Yes, Father! What did you say, when I requested you to procure suitable guns and ammunition from the Portuguese port of Chaul?" Akbar asked. "Remember, what you said? *Compliance with such a request would violate the Christian law!"*

"And that is the truth, Your Majesty." Father Xavier murmured hopelessly.

"And behind that pious truth, Holy Father lurks the fact that the Portuguese have made an alliance with Bahadur Shah." Akbar's mirth and mischief were fading.

"Permit me, Your Majesty, to rescue Father Xavier from this embarrassing inquisition." Prince Daniyal interceded amiably. "I would take him into my confidence, and would learn more about this recent alliance, Your Majesty." He appealed.

"With all my heart, my valorous prince!" Akbar declared a bit soberly. "You are well suited to converse with this holy mentor, while the emperor digresses."

"Your Majesty. True Belief has nothing to do with war and weaponry." Father Xavier implored. "I came here to preach the *truth*, the teachings of our Lord, Jesus Christ, not to fight the wars. It has been almost five years, and I have achieved nothing."

"Were you in Hind one century and a half earlier, Father, and were you given the opportunity to proclaim: Jesus—the Son of God. You would have been impaled alive, if not flayed to death without mercy! And yet, now, you can say those words openly. You baptize and proselytize freely. You are granted the permission of building churches in Hind, and that alone is a privilege not to be granted to the Jesuits in the other Muslim countries. Then, how can you say that you have not achieved anything? And as for the truth! Such a lesson ought to be learnt and explored through teaching, not preaching. And True Belief, Father, is that if you believed in the gods of others, you will believe in your God, most truly." He waved dismissal.

"God Almighty has already promised us the boon of victories over those insurgent lords, Your Majesty. And without the need for the Portuguese arms, I can feel that." Abul Fazl attempted to cheer the emperor.

"My heart is already kneeling in gratitude to Allah, for such anticipated boons, my friend." Was Akbar's merry response! "And what makes you presume, my prophetic scholar, that we will claim victories over our insurgent foes? No, no need to comment on that. I feel the same way, yet the siege of Sapan and Maligarh is trying my patience. Bahadur Shah has claimed Asirgarh, and has proclaimed himself the king of Khandesh. He is unwilling to submit, unless we take this fort of Asirgarh by force. And how long the preparations for such a siege will last? The emperor is getting wearied of wars."

"The forts of Sapan and Maligarh are soon to fall into the hands of the Imperialists, Your Majesty." Abul Fazl began with a renewed surge of divinations. "The Moghul spies have supplied Qara Beg with the information about a secret path leading toward the fort of Mali. I thought, prince Daniyal informed you. We were there. Prince Daniyal himself devised all the plans for a decisive attack. With his nonpareil skill in warfare, prince Daniyal was quick to mark all the right spots for mine digging, before assigning the post of leadership to Qara Beg. Victory will be ours, I am most certain. As for Asirgarh, Bahadur Shah is already disheartened by the fall of Ahmadnagar. Besides, there is an epidemic in the fort of Asirgarh, I hear. Many people are dying every day!"

"An epidemic!" Akbar ruminated aloud. "Since man and beast have made their abode together in that damp sepulcher of a fort, epidemic should not come as a surprise to them. How many men, women, and children are squeezed in there, besides fifteen thousand artisans, laborers and shop keepers, not to mention his household, and soldiers? Sadness, sadness all! War might spare their lives, but epidemic won't."

"He has a large supply of drugs and aromatic herbs, I hear, Your Majesty. To cure his men, if not drug them with opium, our spies told us. He has great quantities of opium stored inside the fort, much greater than the supply of food provisions, I hear."

"I am growing old, Abul. And I see death and doom everywhere!" Akbar's look was wistful. "Lend me the light of your wisdom, my friend. And light the lamp of your understanding, so that I may behold my weaknesses as well as my strengths."

"Akbar, the emperor, illumines Hind's night
And is as a lamp in the court of the House of Timur."
One impromptu couplet broke forth on Abul Fazl's lips.

"A divine couplet, Abul." Akbar laughed. "Your friendship alone elevates me to the heights undeserved."

"Behold the recompense of noble toil
That guards the Caesar's halls from time's despoil."
Abul Fazl's response was another impromptu couplet, his eyes shining with inspiration.

"Your genius, Abul, if not your flattering couplets, is worth many kingdoms on this earth and in heaven." Akbar declared happily. "And yet, these couplets may reveal my toils? But they do conceal my whims and my weaknesses. And yet again, you must compile all your verses in a book. It would fetch gold in praises and riches."

"My thoughts do modestly my works decry
While Gebirs, Muslims hawking run, 'who will buy'."
Abul Fazl's font of inspiration was spilling forth couplets upon couplets.

"The emperor himself may have to write the history of your genius, my poet-scholar, if you decline. And you will write the history of wars under my turbulent reign." Akbar's eyes were kindling the stars of mysticism. "Any more couplets, my friend, to arrest emperor's joy in pearls of time?"

"I can sing your praises all life long, Your Majesty, if you will let me." Abul Fazl chanted against the surge of his kindled inspiration.

"You have my permission, Abul, since I can see the ocean of inspiration in your eyes, bubbling forth to swallow the cries of wars."

"With joyful omens blest, my strain
Shall celebrate his glorious reign
His praises shall my pen proclaim
And here enshrine his royal name."
Abul Fazl sang happily. Some anguished cry inside him was shooting a warning.

"What maddening thoughts, Abul? Why do I feel this way? I have a feeling that I am going to lose you. This joy would be sprinkled with grief." Akbar seemed to voice Abul Fazl's mute anguish. "But go on, my divine poet. I see couplets dancing in your very eyes. Spill them, Abul, I wish to be drowned in their shower of sweetness, than seek the puddles of grief and sorrow, which lurk in the future."

"May joy alone await you in future, Your Majesty!" Abul Fazl murmured.

"Then, let your couplets rain flowers, Abul. This moment with you, in the raiments of poetry, is joy eternal and joy boundless." Akbar intoned poetically.

"The princely heart that virtue dowers
For him gems bloom instead of flowers
And hill and dale his kingdom round
Shall with their monarch's praise resound."
Abul Fazl recited warmly.

"What black magic makes you sing such praises, Abul?" Akbar exclaimed teasingly. "I feel drunk with your poetry and praise, and yet the thought of winning wars is not leaving me. It is shooting arrows inside the very battlefield of my joy. To deflect that thought, I must seek the realms of wisdom and learning. How much you have accomplished in writing the Akbarnamah?" He asked abruptly.

"Volumes upon volumes, Your Majesty." Was Abul Fazl's quick response!

"And have you thought of some quaint verse to embellish those volumes?" Akbar asked. His heart had begun to throb with a sudden presage.

"I have already written it, Your Majesty." Abul Fazl responded quickly.

"Recite it then, Abul. I want to capture the essence of your poetry, before I capture the fort of Asirgarh in its entirety."

"I bear from wisdom's inmost store
The royal house this treasured lore
And pray its justice and its grace
May ne'er my memory efface
And let this loyal offering be
Accepted of its Majesty
May God His favor grant benign
And His acceptance deign with thine
And raise its dignity on high
With thy name's gracious currency
That it from thee may win renown
And link my fortunes with the throne."

Abul Fazl recited, as if melting under the strain of his words.

"If I lost you, Abul, I would surely die." Akbar murmured.

"My worthless life is of no account, Your Majesty. But yours would be the greatest loss to the very soil of Hind, if you—" Abul Fazl could not imagine, even in his thoughts, the death of this divine emperor. "So, please, Your Majesty, do not think of dying, but of keeping me in mind as the souvenir of time."

"My most precious souvenirs, if—" Akbar could see Qara Beg riding closer.

"Splendid news, Your Majesty." Qara Beg alighted from his horse, curtsying. "The forts of Sapan and Maligarh are captured." He announced happily.

"Man and God be praised for these victories, my friend." Was Akbar's jubilant response! "Both man and God is praiseworthy. But the great man, who has earned the praise for valor this day, is you, Qara Beg. And our great God is the one and only, Whom we call, Allah. To Whose will, we surrender with absolute humility, regardless of our defeats or victories." He paused, absorbing the warmth of sunshine in Qara Beg's eyes. "And how did you accomplish such a great feat, my great commander?"

"With the beating of the drums alone, Your Majesty. The garrisons of the enemy were quivering with fright by the mere sound of the royal drums, it seemed." Qara Beg was glad for the opportunity to flaunt his maneuvers. "From the top of the Sapan hills, we were able to send three batches of troops at the very gates of the fortress. The night was dark and rainy. After the second batch was sent, their garrison had retreated to the main fortress. With the third batch in view, their soldiers had lost heart to confront the Imperialists. The fort was captured with a very little resistance on the part of the enemy."

"Great strategies, I have heard. The emperor is blessed with great commanders as his devoted subjects." Akbar complimented profusely. "Now, you would command the siege of Asirgarh. Is Bahadur Shah aware of our sweeping victories?"

"Yes, Your Majesty." Qara Beg's enthusiasm was rising and culminating. "Bahadur Shah has no choice but to surrender, Your Majesty. I hear he is trying to gather enough courage, so that he can pay homage to the emperor in person. With Sapan and Maligarh capitulated, Your Majesty, he has no chance but to surrender."

"Yes, the unfortunate wretch! He is hemmed in on all sides. Between the north-west and the north lie Sapan and Maligarh, he should be well aware of our gateway to his fortress. And south-east can afford him no flight, for our batteries and trenches await him like one heavy ax into the hands of an executioner." Akbar's gaze was turning to Abul Fazl. "Would it be wise, Abul, to accept his submission, and to pardon the wretch?"

"Confinement in the fort of Gwalior would be a gentle abode for this inveterate rebel, Your Majesty." Abul Fazl laughed without joy. "Wisdom seeks peace, not war!"

"This joy of recent victories has intoxicated your judgment, my prophetic counselor." Akbar's gaze was now returning to Qara Beg. "Qara Beg, Summon prince Daniyal, and let us—" His thoughts were disrupted by the sound of hoof-beats.

Bahadur Shah was approaching closer, attended by a few of his retinue. Before he could ride past the silk tents, his advance was intercepted by prince Daniyal.

The fall of Sapan and Maligarh! These news must have flown to Asirgarh with the swiftness of fire. And to escape its flames, Bahadur Shah has ventured forth to offer his submission. Besides, Malai, the fort of Sapan, and Antar Malai, the fort of Maligarh are connected to Asirgarh with secret pathways buried inside the very tombs of the hills, and these hills themselves whisper secrets to their masters of their gains or losses.

Prince Daniyal was thinking. Now, both the prince and the humble suppliant of a king were scurrying toward the emperor. The air was charged with a sudden hush. Abul Fazl's eyes were speaking volumes, and Qara Beg's lips were forming soundless words, but Akbar's gaze was brimming with warmth and kindness.

"Your Majesty, I offer my total submission, and entreat your mercy and kindness." Bahadur Shah implored. "My garrison would surrender to you without resistance. Just one request, Your Majesty, if your kindness could spare the lives of all the occupants, and if I may rule Khandesh under your suzerainty?"

"Life and honor, we all should hold worthy, even beyond the confines of greed and wealth." Akbar intoned kindly. "The lives of all your family, friends and soldiers would be spared. You are also granted the permission to rule Khandesh, but under the strict vigilance of the Imperialists. The emperor would watch you too, and you would always submit to his sovereign authority, not rebel against it. Is your garrison in agreement with your proposal, Bahadur Shah? Considering their unruly spirits and scheming minds, are they not plotting deceit and insurrection?"

"Your kindness compels me to be honest, Your Majesty. "My commander, Yaqut Khan opposes me in my decision to surrender this fort to you, but his son, Muqarib Khan is my strongest ally, Your Majesty." Bahadur Shah responded. "Muqarib Khan supports me in my decision. He also requests that if an agreement can be signed by the emperor, granting the safety of all lives, he will convince his father in surrendering this fort."

"Qara Beg, summon Naqib Khan, and get this agreement in readiness for the emperor to sign. We would enter the fort peacefully." Akbar commanded.

The lamps of the torch-bearers were splintering the bosom of the night, and drawing the hills together with their shafts of light. The shadows themselves appeared to be groaning, as Akbar unlocked the gates of this mighty fortress of Asirgarh. He was fascinated by the large key fashioned out of pure gold, which was presented to him by Bahadur Shah himself. The narrow passages were lit by candles and oil lamps. At the end of each passage were vast, airless chambers, the size of granaries.

The emperor was exploring the maze of this fortress with agog and caution. One large room with tall ceiling was hosting tons of ammunition. *In every bastion, there are cauldrons of oil, which are stored for the purpose of boiling, and to be poured over the heads of the assailants*, the emperor's thoughts were his sleepless guides. One entire room was filled with sacks of opium, where the chests of medicines and aromatic roots were stored. Large vessels brimming with grain! Mounds upon mounds of rice, lentils and dried fruit! And gold flagons, bloated with the aroma of sweet-scented wines.

Caskets of precious gems and heaps of gold coins!

Gardens and courtyards!

The emperor and his companions were wending their way through the wide, serpentine paths into the very heart of the city, called Takhti. Looming before their sight, were the palaces of the lords and the mighty minarets. Abul Fazl and Bahadur Shah was keeping pace with the emperor, rather lagging behind a little, immersed in their quiet contemplations. The emperor was becoming aware of the shadows over the balconies. Suddenly, one loud voice was cutting through the night-air like a naked sword.

The royal guards were at once alert and attentive. The torch-bearers were standing there with their lamps poised before them in some ritual of ceremonial silence. Yaqub Khan was recognized by the imperialists by his scraggly demeanor and blistering tongue. He was reviling his son for surrendering this fort of Asirgarh to the Moghuls.

"Just like a galley salve—" Yaqut Khan could be heard amidst his tirade of invectives. Suddenly, Muqarib Khan was seen stabbing himself with his own sword.

"Bahadur Shah, fly to the side of this wretched youth, and tend his wound. He may bleed to death, if he is already not dead." Akbar's very gaze was shooting commands. "And the emperor's message to this cruel father is that the lives of all his men would be spared. Also, his family and his wealths would be restored to him, as soon as he recovers from his maddening fits of rage and despair." He retraced his steps.

A few men of strong physique had appeared on the parapet, and were seen cradling Muqarib Khan into their arms. Yaqut Khan was seen bending over his son and crying for help, all were lost somewhere in the palace inside the death-valley of silence. Bahadur Shah was racing toward the palace like a man pressed by fate. The torch-bearers were now following the emperor, Abul Fazl his sole companion by his side.

"Your wise and valorous son, Abul! Yes, Abdur Rahman, appoint him as the governor of Deccan, and we will march back to Agra. Agra might offer us respite from the wars? For a few years, at least." Akbar was seeking the refuge of his encampment. "Though, the emperor longs for eternal peace." He murmured to himself.

Some sort of peace in the semblance of cloistered joys, had befriended the emperor on his month long journey from Deccan toward Agra. Agra was still oceans apart, but peace was in view toward the garden of Kiraoli. This garden was designed by Salima Begum against the majestic sight of her private palace. Akbar's horse was now racing down the unpaved path, edged by magnolia trees on both sides. This garden was boasting a lovely kiosk and a grand palace in the distance.

My Beloved's retreat. Her cherished abode, which she chose in favor of Agra or Lahore to receive the victorious emperor." Akbar was thinking.

The quaint chamber with gilded arches was housing the queen of the emperor's heart, Salima. The dancing girls in shimmering chiffons were nimble on their feet to the rhythm of tempura. He was quick to wave away all the dancers and musicians.

"I haven't seen you for centuries, my love! Come, sit with the emperor, and let him feast on your beauty." Akbar claimed her hand, kissing it passionately. "Is it love, my love, which has summoned me to this paradise on earth? Or some sweet intrigue simmering in your sweet head, has granted me this boon?" He asked happily.

"Nothing is hidden from you, Your Majesty, as I have learned. Alas, but too late." Salima smiled. "Yet, I wanted you to rest here, Your Majesty, before you went to Agra. The atmosphere at Agra is rather dismal, for the time being, that is. Gulbadan Begum is poor in health, and Miryam Makani is not quite well, either."

"So, the emperor is to rest here, without the boon of love." Akbar squeezed her closer and closed his eyes.

"You know, Your Majesty, you have been loved always. And you have known it, always." Salima murmured a protest.

"Let me look into your eyes, love, again and again and forever." Akbar's eyes were shot open. "Yes, love born out of pity! Though, I do feel fortunate in receiving even one crumb of love from the ocean of your pity. I don't see any rills of hatred in there, no, not any more. Yet sadness, sadness all!" He continued profoundly. "Are you not glad to see the emperor alive and in good health?"

"I am, Your Majesty, I am. And may God grant you a long, long life for the peace and glory of Hind." Salima murmured quickly.

"A curse, my dear! Long life, that is." Akbar laughed. "I have already lived a long, long life. Somehow, all parents hope and think that their children would outlive them. I am already old, but my heart will stay young, forever. Yet, I am growing old, and my heart is wearied of wars." He kissed her on the lips.

"Talking of wars, Your Majesty. You should let prince Salim carry half the burden of your royal duties and campaigns." Salima Begum appealed softly.

"Ah, prince Salim. Is he not the author of mental and physical agonies for both my aunt and my revered mamma?" Akbar commented without bitterness. "My prince is vain and disobedient. He is flattered by his vanity, and is charged with plots to gain speedy access to my throne. The throne of his desires! You know that, don't you?"

"You misjudge him, Your Majesty." Salima protested quickly. "Prince Salim is devoted to you. He loves you, Your Majesty. He has no intention of usurping your throne. He seeks pardon for any offenses, unintentional or seemingly vile. He is in sheer misery, thinking to himself that he might have offended you, though knowing not how. He is requesting audience with you, so that he can plead forgiveness. *For any misunderstanding, which have become the cause of your displeasure,* he says."

"Prince Salim loves no one, my dear, but himself. First, foremost and last, his own dear self. He loves his comfort, and loves the pleasures of the table. Perhaps, his wives too?" Akbar commented soothingly. "Though, I hear, his wife Man Bai is going through the spells of her dark moods and ill humor. Is he neglecting her? Last time, I saw my prince, he was very drunk? Has he espoused wine as his favorite of brides?"

"No, Your Majesty." Salima began with a sudden passion. "Prince Salim is devoted to Man Bai. And she in turn, is devoted to him. She has this wild notion in her head that prince Khusrau is disobedient to both her, and his father. We can't understand her fears. She thinks, prince Khusrau hates his father. Her fear is that, he might harm his father in some way. She can't drive this insane thought out of her head."

"The emperor is fortunate in having you as his only beloved, my love." Akbar smiled. "For you stay constant in your moods. Even amidst the sea of violence in love or hatred. Moderation and discretion, the best of your virtues, my sweet! And no mountain of fear can ever rule over your sense of right or wrong." Akbar smiled. "And now, since prince Salim's own mother, Hira is not here to plead her son's cause! Tell me, my love, have all the ladies of the harem chosen you to intercede for prince Salim?"

"Yes, Your Majesty." Salima confessed.

"And do you know, my sweet, that prince Salim marched to Agra with a large body of troops, to fight for throne in the emperor's absence? And in such haste he was, that he neglected to visit Miryam Makani, who had requested him to visit her before going to Agra. He had crossed Jamna, without even giving a thought to his grandmother's request. Perhaps, fearing, that she would advise him contrary to his wishes? Thus, neglecting his duty and offending my great mamma."

"Prince Salim misunderstood the message, Your Majesty. He thought that Miryam Makani wished to see him at Agra, not in her palace near Jamna." Salima was trying to win favor for prince Salim. "And as to the troops, Your Majesty. He always journeys at the head of many soldiers. In case, the necessity of a combat confronts him, all of a sudden."

"And thousands of them, just to see the emperor." Akbar laughed. "No, my dear, the pomp of a vicergal household is far more to his taste, than the privations and fatigues of wars. Didn't he abandon the campaign of Mewar and chose the life of dissipation?"

"And yet, he seeks pardon, Your Majesty. He desires your love and forgiveness." Salima murmured hopelessly.

"My prince, our prince, my love, desires only two things, and they have nothing to do with love and forgiveness. His first desire is to stay in Allahabad, and his second, his ambition to gain independent sovereignty."

"But he is wasting away in misery and wretchedness, Your Majesty, pleading audience. Won't you grant him that, if you love me?" Salima Begum pleaded.

"I love no one, my sweet, but you. That's the whole truth I have been seeking all these years, and didn't even know that it is within me. I am willing to lay down kingdoms at your feet, if you but ask." Akbar's tones were sad and tender. "And if you asked pardon for the most hated man in Hind, he would be forgiven. Then, why can't I forgive my own son, whom I do love. Yes, I will forgive him. He is forgiven, absolutely and completely forgiven." He held her close, circling his arms around her waist. "Remember, my sweet, you are my only love. My only truth, always has been, and will always be, in life or even after death." He kept holding her tenderly and reverently.

"Won't you have some refreshments, Your Majesty? How I have neglected your needs. Those fresh melons and the choicest of fruits I ordered from—" Salima murmured incoherently.

"My need, Love, is the need for your love alone. Your true love, once in a lifetime, perhaps! I hunger for the fruits of love on your lips."

Agra once again

The court at Agra, despite its peace and splendor, was in constant deluge from the foreign embassies for trade or alliances. The notable amongst them was a trade mission from the Queen of England, Elizabeth 1. The Queen had sent

Mildenhall at the head of other Englishmen to seek permission from the emperor for the free access of English ships to the Moghul ports. As the emperor had granted them permission, the Portuguese fathers were weaving all sorts of lies, and branding Mildenhall and his men with the epithet, *savage pirates*. The savage pirates, who had taken hold of the ports in Hind!

Besides these canards floating around unchecked, the emperor was pressed for time by the burden of his royal duties. He had been unable to grant prince Salim a private audience, as promised by him on his return to Agra. Prince Salim had sent his troops back to Allahabad, and was now patiently waiting for the emperor's summons.

The court at Agra, with its damasked walls and silken canopies, was still in session, but the emperor was getting wearied of the unbroken chain of the embassies. His thoughts were flying back to prince Salim. He was dismissing all with a wave of his arm, commanding Man Singh to summon prince Salim to his presence. Only Abul Fazl and Naqib Khan were to stay with the emperor, the rest were dismissed. Father Xavier, uninvited, was lingering behind.

"Father, the emperor is wearied. Why do you linger on the peril of invoking my anger?" Akbar made another signal of dismissal with a flourish of his arm.

"I have no such intention, Your Majesty." Father Xavier bowed humbly. "Burdened by the weight of my troubles, I can't move fast. May I plead a boon before I leave, Your Majesty?" He asked.

"Yes, wise Father." Akbar smiled kindly. "If this boon doesn't rob me of my three hours of sleep, which the empire of Hind grants me, but grudgingly?"

"Your Majesty! Since Mildenhall and his men have gained the greatest of boons, in securing a trade company to their name, here in Hind, for trade and—" Father Xavier's speech was truncated by the emperor's quick command.

"No more accusations, Father!" Akbar commanded. "Only request a boon, and then leave this court."

"Your Majesty. Would you kindly commit your Farman to writing! So that we are protected from opposition, while we build St. Peter's cathedral close to Shri Krishna?" Father Xavier implored quickly.

"So, you have already chosen the Datt Paliwal Park for your holy cathedral." Akbar smiled, recalling his Farman of this afternoon in granting him the permission to build a church. He turned to Naqib Khan. "Let your golden pen record my Farman, Naqib. Or the emperor would neither have time for sleep, nor for his daily meal." He began to dictate. "It has been represented to us that Reverend Fathers are desirous of erecting in this city a house for worship. We accordingly grant this our imperial Farman, and implicit obedience to which is necessary, and order that all officers concerned must under no circumstances interfere in the erection of the said house of worship, or molest the Reverend Fathers. This order must be respected by all."

"Thank you, Your Majesty, thank you." Father Xavier murmured chokingly.

The emperor's gaze was following Father Xavier. He had forgotten about his order to the cooks for his one meal of the day, but they were already trooping along with the steaming dishes. The emperor was eating ravenously, but Abul Fazl was eating abstemiously. His thoughts were feeding more on the subject of prince Salim's private audience, than on the taste for these rare delicacies heaped before him.

"I should be leaving, Your Majesty, before prince Salim arrives." Abul Fazl murmured low. "The prince wishes to speak with you alone, Your Majesty."

"No, my friend, stay." Akbar commanded. "Since fatigue and weariness are the emperor's companions, he will feel at ease in the company of his devoted friend. Besides, it is not easy for the emperor to converse with his estranged son."

"My company has a chilling affect on the prince, Your Majesty. Prince Salim hates me." An involuntary confession broke forth on the lips of Abul Fazl.

"Hate you!" Akbar exclaimed suddenly. "He is not a callow youth anymore, Abul. And he must learn to restrain his loves and hatreds. And your presence alone, might discipline his whims and weaknesses." He began to eat quietly.

The emperor was still eating, when prince Salim was announced.

"Welcome, Shaikhu Baba." Akbar intoned kindly. "Come, sit with the emperor. May wisdom guide your speech and intention!" His gaze was fond and thoughtful.

"By the font of your great wisdom, I seek to be guided, Your Majesty." Prince Salim responded with a gallant bow of his head. "Greatness in your manners, Your Majesty, and kingship in your lineage make me wonder, if the Solomon himself has put his ring on your finger." He complimented with ready wit.

"Your flattery alone can win you many kingdoms, Shaikhu Baba. Once Naqib Khan also flattered me with the, *ring of Solomon.*" Akbar laughed. "Come, join me in this pure cuisine of the vegetable delights."

"Pardon me, Your Majesty, for declining this sumptuous invitation. But my palate craves meat, when hunger strikes me with its own pangs for nourishment." Prince Salim joined the emperor in his mirth.

"Blood contains the principle of life, my glutton of a prince." Akbar commented lightly. "To avoid eating meat, thereof, is to honor life. And it is not right that man should make his stomach the grave of animals. I hope, you have been made aware, Shaikhu Baba, that your undisciplined acts of caprice and defiance caused not only great pain to the emperor, but have affected my aunt and mamma in the deepest sense of grief and agony. Your grandmothers, just the same, they are ailing"

"Pardon me, Your Majesty. I am too-well aware of the rumors, which did float unchecked from Agra to Deccan." Prince Salim began humbly. "Ignorance is my only defense, Your Majesty. I didn't think that my coming to Agra would cause rift and unrest in your royal household. I have been visiting the ladies religiously, now that they are lodged in this palace. I craved your audience, Your Majesty, so that you could guide me in ruling the little kingdom of Allahabad. Small men with great faiths in the diversity of their creeds are clouding my judgment. I desire justice for everyone. Yet justice itself proves to be injustice to others, as I have come to view it."

"Men, who fear God, know what justice is! And injustice is not done to any, if one but holds the scepter of kindness and compassion at all times." Akbar commented. "The emperor can guide you but little, Shaikhu Baba. Experience alone would teach you volumes upon volumes of discipline and discretion. When prince Murad was appointed the governor of Malwa, I had sent one little advice to him. This same advice might grant you some insight into the affairs of others. I had written to him: let not the difference of religion interfere with your good policy, and be not violent in inflicting retribution. Adorn the confidential council with men who know their work. If apologies be made, accept them. You need a trusted friend like Abul Fazl by your side, Shaikhu Baba."

"I am not so fortunate, Your Majesty, as to gain the trust of such a friend, like Abul Fazl." Prince Salim murmured. "May I be as bold as to ask, Your Majesty, why you have forbidden all to prevent or to interfere with the building of the temples?"

"And what makes you ask such a question, my prince? When you already know the emperor's policy of complete tolerance toward all religions?" Akbar sipped his wine.

"I have been conversing with the ulemas, Your Majesty, since I came to Agra." Prince Salim commenced soberly. "Their comments have fed my brain to such motley of thoughts, that I feel tortured by my thoughts, at times. Do you know, Your Majesty, that they call these holy temples, the haunts of idolatry! I was just wondering, if they are justified in their thoughts that only mosques should be constructed in Agra?"

"These ulemas, Shaikhu Baba, though zealous and ignorant, accept the emperor as their mighty monarch, the shadow of God upon earth." Akbar began ruminatively. "I have seen, Shaikhu Baba, that God bestows the blessings of His gracious providence upon all His creatures without distinction. Ill should I discharge the duties of my exalted station, were I to withhold my compassion and indulgence from any of those entrusted to my charge. With all of human race, with all God's creatures, I am at peace. Why then should I permit myself under any consideration, to be the cause of aggression or molestation to anyone? Temples, as well as the churches and mosques, are the houses of worship. And they can be built anywhere on God's earth, without the sanction of any man. Even, if that man happens to be a Muslim sovereign, ruling over the lands of Godless or God-fearing people." He concluded, shifting his attention to Abul Fazl.

"Your Majesty. If ulemas had the power to rule over this world, three-fourths of its population would be slaughtered like animals. Just because the men of other faiths would not consent to profess the faith of Islam! Heathens all, this entire horde of men as perceived by the bigots and the zealots!" Abul Fazl commented thoughtlessly.

"Gather the priests and the pundits together, Your Majesty, and there will be the holy crusades on the very streets of Agra." Prince Salim sought the emperor's attention. "Hindus, Muslims and Christians, cutting each other's throats in the name of God, or in the name of gods and goddesses. I aspire for your wisdom, not power, Your Majesty."

"Wisdom comes to those who surrender their wills to the will of God, Shaikhu Baba." Akbar intoned endearingly. "The Almighty God alone in his eternal goodness and changeless mercy and in spite of so many obstacles and such a world of work and occupation has inclined my heart ever to seek after Him. He has entrusted to me the sovereignty over many powerful princes, and I strive to guide and rule them, that all my subjects may dwell in happiness and contentment. Offer your praises to the Lord God, Allah, Shaikhu Baba, and discharge your duties under the protection of His divine will and mercy. And that should be the aim of all your aspirations. Too much theology in one day is making me opiate. Or, maybe the food is? Tell me, Shaikhu Baba, how is Man Bai? Have you been offending her in some unseemly fashion? I hear she is ill again? All the royal ladies should be treated with great respect and affection. You were instructed in this art of love and marriage, have you forgotten that?" He demanded.

"No, Your Majesty." Prince Salim protested passionately. "I am devoted to her, and she is devoted to me. Her only unhappiness she thinks is prince Khusrau—"

"I know all that, Shaikhu Baba." Akbar made an impatient gesture. "Prince Khurram is as dear to me as prince Khusrau, and prince Perwiz, and I indulge them all with equal love and tenderness. Do you think that the emperor favors prince Khusrau over you, Shaikhu Baba?"

"No, Your Majesty." Prince Salim murmured wretchedly.

"Since you look penitent, Shaikhu Baba—" Akbar paused, his look thoughtful. "I have decided to entrust you with the kingdoms of Bengal and Orissa. Rule over them justly and wisely. And stay worthy of respect from all, like the heir-prince to my throne. Write to prince Daniyal, he is drinking too much, I hear. One day, you would rule Hind."

"Your Majesty!" Prince Salim protested. "May you live long, and I would stay obedient to your wishes all my life."

"Now, leave us, Shaikhu Baba." Akbar announced. "I have promised to visit Miryam Makani and Gulbadan Begum, and I better not keep them waiting."

"Your most devoted subject, Your Majesty." Prince Salim bowed low, and then retraced his steps without uttering another word.

"There is an island of gloom and doom in my head, Abul. And the strangest thing is that I can see it." Akbar eased himself out of his seat, without looking at his friend.

"No such gloom and doom reign in Agra, Your Majesty. Only peace and prosperity! You have the power to dissolve this island of gloom in your head, even with one reed of your practiced will." Abul Fazl got to his feet slowly.

"No, my friend, this island is very real and solid. And yet, I can face any gloom or doom on that island, if you can stay by my side." Akbar averted his gaze.

The emperor was drifting away, his soul intoxicated with the spirit of God.

God is inconceivable, unknowable, unapproachable. He is the God of the East and the West. Of the North and the South! Of the heavens and the earth. Of the sea and the mountain! Eternal and everlasting. Of ages past, and of the ages to come! Manifesting Himself in the Present, in the heart of all men, and inside the soul of cosmic Wisdom. He is the God of the Sumerians, the Babylonians, Mesopotamians, and of the Greeks and the Romans. The God of the Jews, the Christians, and of the Muslims! In essence, the God of all Creeds, Faiths, Beliefs and Religions. God is an entity. And its Throne of such colossal heights, that no mind wise or spiritual could ever encompass even one grain of its boundless wealth. How can one profess to know Truth, when Truth, by the virtue of its divine essence is veiled in mystic knowledge of the Mysteries, ever since the creation of man and beast? How can one perceive the Sacred, when the purity of a mind, heart and the soul is tainted with the darkness in Understanding? How can one fathom the Sacrosanct, when by the law and virtue of Nature, sanctity belongs only to the Mysterious One. That Mysterious One is the God of all nations. Speaking to each living, breathing creature, to the measure of their own Understanding! God, creating gods inside the hearts of men, and men recreating God in the image of their ancestors. Praising God in different tongues, with different rituals, with names as countless as songs in the wind! To know God is to know that He knows all, and man, nothing. And through His will, all sustenance comes to all. Mercy is His alone. And against His wrath, misfortunes breed. Evil escapes not His judgment, and goodness goes not unrewarded. Sages, in their quests to approach the Throne of God, have journeyed far, and so have ascetics as well as the shamans. The very first godless men on this earth, to the all present heretics still living, have taken such a journey. The Jains, Sikhs, Hindus, Jews, Christians, Muslims, all have felt His presence. All receiving riches from His bounties, according to their own measure of faith and perseverance! The emperor was standing under the shade of one gul mohur tree, forlorn and entranced.

14

Death of the Emperor

The emperor was donned in saffron silks. Strolling alone like a spirit weighed down by grief and despair. The mighty stoic of an emperor, in one year of agony and loneliness since the death of Abul Fazl, had been transformed to an emperor of bereavement. This death stained with the brand of *murder*, had plunged the emperor's spirit into the profoundest of agonies. And the murderer was prince Salim. This particular evening the ladies of the harem were to intercede on behalf of the prince.

Suddenly, the emperor's heart was thundering with all its renewal of grief and suffering. His thoughts were returning to the dark alleys of the past for answers. After being appointed as the governor of Bengal and Orissa, prince Salim had left Agra. But soon after, he had abandoned the post of his governorship, and had returned to Allahabad, assuming the title of kingship. The emperor had conveyed his reproof through a letter, to which, prince Salim had responded that those were merely rumors, requesting an audience with the emperor. Akbar had countered his son's request with a reprimand that the prince should practice obedience before he could be permitted to see the emperor. Meanwhile, prince Daniyal, in Deccan, was given to such bouts of drunkenness that the emperor had decided to send Abul Fazl to discipline his wayward prince. Another request from prince Salim, pleading audience too was denied, for the emperor had received the reports of his drunkenness.

During that time, Man Singh was promoted to the rank of seven thousand horse and personal. Aziz Koka's daughter was married to prince Khusrau. Prince Khusrau had become the most favored of Akbar's grandsons. While the victim of his own drunkenness and hallucination, prince Salim had begun to think that his son was chosen as an heir to the throne by the emperor. He had begun to hate all who were favored by the emperor, especially Abul Fazl.

After receiving the news of Abul Fazl's imminent arrival in Agra, prince Salim had jolted himself out of his drunkenness, entrusting Bir Singh Deo—the Raja of Bundehah Rajput with the task of murdering Abul Fazl. Attended only by a few of his devoted guards, Abul Fazl had just proceeded on the small road joining the villages of Antri and Sarai Barki, when he was attacked by five hundred soldiers, headed by Bir Singh Deo. Abul Fazl's devoted guards, Gadai Khan and his sons were killed. Abul Fazl was stabbed in the back by a spear wielded by Bir Singh Deo.

No one had the courage to break such tragic news to the emperor. But the messenger, who was appointed to announce Abul Fazl's arrival, had wrapped a blue handkerchief around his waist, in accordance with the old custom of the Timuirids. The emperor had noticed that blue handkerchief, even before the messenger had approached closer to the throne. And the emperor had lamented aloud.

The empire of Hind has lost its pearl of wisdom. The emperor had fainted.

Prince Salim was forbidden to see the emperor, and was incarcerated inside his palace at Allahabad. A large body of Moghul soldiers was dispatched to hunt down Bir Singh Deo, but all their endeavors had remained unsuccessful.

More memories were surfacing in Akbar's thoughts, as he kept strolling.

The night before this fateful tragedy, Abul Fazl was warned by a seer, that his life was in peril. To this warning, Abul Fazl's only response was one profound statement.

The fear of death is vain, for its period cannot be deferred.

Watching the band of murderers with naked swords, Gadai Khan had pleaded with Abul Fazl to flee, before they could get any closer. But Abul Fazl had declared:

My gracious sovereign has raised me from the rank of a student to the lofty position of a vizier and general. On this day, if I act contrary to His Majesty's opinion of me, by what name shall I be called amongst men, and how shall I have a clear countenance amongst my rivals? Were Abul Fazl's last words!

These words were piercing Akbar's heart, his thoughts lamenting.

*What is grief? Grief—is! Yes, the pain soaring toward culmination. When pain reaches at its sense of grief inconsolable! When everything inside one's little heart is literally tearing and screaming. Each little part weeping and bleeding! Each little wound cutting the very pain into splinters of agony. Each splinter shedding tears, each tear gasping for breath! Unwilling to dissolve into the ocean of torment! Each shred of pain suspended loose! Spent and exhausted. Mending and healing. Gathering its tortured shreds, and weaving them into the tapestry of anguished knots. The heart feeling nothing but sadness! Kneading the pain in living into one blister of shock. The body and soul churning and lamenting! Sliced and glued. Unhealing inside the scars of time! The pain wedding grief and both seeking the terrible, terrible knowledge of the mystery and the—*Akbar was becoming aware of Aziz Koka approaching slowly.

"So, the ladies are waiting the emperor's verdict." Akbar commented.

"Your guess is accurate as always, Your Majesty." Aziz Koka curtsied. "And they are armed with a battery of pleas." He unfolded one gold-sprinkled paper. "One anonymous poet from the Bundela court sent this poem in memory of our deceased friend, Abul Fazl. May I read it to you, Your Majesty?"

"Yes." Was Akbar's laconic consent.

"How can I run away
A warrior must die where he is molested
You say, run away
The enemy is thundering on all sides
If I am killed running away
What shall people say of me
Both in running and fighting death is certain
I shall run away, if I can
But I have the fetters of honor in my feet
And the burden of the emperor's love on my head."
Aziz Koka recited softly.

"The emperor himself has composed one couplet to heal his fatal wounds, my brother. Though, these wounds, unfestering they remain." Akbar lamented.

"My Shaikh in his zeal, hastened to meet me
He wished to kiss my feet, and gave up his life."

He walked away. "Abul Fazl lives in his deeds and works. His books are my precious companions. How diligently he worked! A genius most unfortunate!"

"He was a perfectionist, Your Majesty." Aziz Koka followed behind. "He labored through his manuscripts like a slave. Revising them five times, at least."

"And would have revised yet another time, if he was alive? Could never be content with what he originally wrote." Akbar kept strolling toward the palace. "Mubarak family, geniuses all! Faizi, how long has it been? How many books of poetry did he leave behind, I forget?"

"Faizi, the pride of Hind, Your Majesty. He left forty-six hundred bound volumes of poetry." Aziz Koka intoned softly.

"Any news from Abdur Rahman, has he returned from his expedition for the search of his father's murderer, Bir Singh Deo?"

"No, Your Majesty. Though, he remains wild and persistent in his search." Aziz Koka was lingering behind.

"Ah, the brave son of a brave father! He will never rest till his father's death is avenged." Akbar commented with a sudden vehemence.

Akbar was entering the gilded chamber of his harem, where most of the royal ladies were gathered to plead for prince Salim.

"Where is my dear aunt, Gulbadan Begum?" Akbar asked.

"She craves pardon, Your Majesty, for she is unwell and can't join us." Hamida Banu Begum intoned smoothly.

"And is Hakim Ali attending her as ordered?" Akbar began to pace.

"He had to go to Fathehpur Sikri, Your Majesty." Hamida Banu Begum responded gently. "One Raja is in danger of going blind, I hear. And the other doctors needed his services at the school of medicine for this delicate surgery."

"Dispatch orders for him to be summoned back to Agra, Miryam Makani, lest the emperor deprive him of his eyes!" Akbar kept pacing. "And who is attending my aunt, while the royal physician is gallivanting in Fatehpur Sikri?"

"Hakim Mirri and Fath Gilani are by her side, at all hours of the day or night, Your Majesty." Hamida Banu Begum sighed without restraint.

"Your Majesty. Prince Salim has been imprisoned in this palace for two whole weeks, now. He is wretched and remorseful." Salima commenced tremulously. "He has brought twelve thousand gold muhrs and seven hundred seventy elephants of the best breed, as gifts—" Her unvoiced plea was silenced by Akbar's sudden exclamation.

"Gifts, gifts! The gift of life most precious! Can anything compensate that loss? No! Not even a thousand kingdoms can breathe one spark of life into the bosom of my dearest of friends." Akbar exclaimed. "If I were guilty of an unjust act, I would rise in judgment against myself. What shall I say, then, of my sons, my kindred and others?"

"You judge your son unkindly, Your Majesty." Was Hamida Banu Begum's quick protest! "Prince Salim indeed is the victim of his follies, surrounded by parasites who claim to be his friends! He has a good heart, and he is devoted to you, Your Majesty. And he is not the murderer as you deem him to be. He merely wished to prevent Abul Fazl from seeing you. He did not command Bir Singh Deo to murder!"

"Nothing could have prevented Abul Fazl from seeing the emperor, even if the Himalayas themselves were to stand in his way, if he was alive." Akbar lamented aloud. "Seductions of our time, Miryam Makani! Yes, blame everything on time, with or without the men as parasites. My sons, the victims of *time* alone! Ruinous course of inebriation that all my sons have taken? One, already the supreme victim of religious drinking. My gentle Murad, my dearest, unforgotten and unforgettable son. And this eldest one! Now, mixing sedition with wine. And cruelty, too." His feet came to a sudden halt before Hira Begum. "And my beloved Hira. My dearest Mariam Uzzamani. Have you anything to say in defense of our beloved son?"

"I feel powerless against the rivers of your great anguish, Your Majesty." Hira Begum moaned. "Only your noble spirit can grant forgiveness to him. His hands are not stained with the blood of Abul Fazl. Bir Singh Deo alone is the murderer."

"Spoken like a noble mother, through her noblest of loves for her ignoble son!" Akbar exclaimed. "And the emperor had thought that all his children, by the sheer law of nature, would inherit his divine spirit which is believed by many to be the emperor's blessed boon." His feet were coming to a slow halt before Usha Begum. "Have you written to prince Daniyal, my sweet? He is drinking wine by the barrels. He stands charged of disobedience, if not of drunkenness and dissipation!"

"Prince Daniyal is most obedient to your commands, Your Majesty." Usha Begum murmured. "I have thought of a plan. He needs a sensible, loving bride, who can guide and check his excesses. Adil Shah's daughter is the bride, I have in mind. If you approve of this match, Your Majesty? He will be wedded as soon as he gets here."

"This marriage and alliance, the emperor approves most heartily, my dear. But, alas, no bevy of brides could cure his ocean-thirst for wine." One splinter of a prophecy escaped Akbar's lips. "Have brides cured prince Salim of his follies and excesses? Sedition and inebriation are his *masters*, and he is a slave to their tyranny. My son, constantly fed by the venom of his self-pity and self-love. Pouring tormenting lies into the sweet head of Man Bai, his ailing bride?"

"Your Majesty, you have endured the weight of many deaths with calm and fortitude. Drawing sustenance from your inner strength!" Hamida Banu Begum began tremulously. "One whole year! One long, mournful year, since Abul Fazl died. Cast away these robes of gloom and sorrow. Summon your strength back. Turn your thoughts to rule and conquest. How can this single tragedy crush your spirit thus?"

"This tragedy alone, dear Mamma, has not crushed my spirit, but the burden of tragedies as a whole." Akbar declared. "My spirit, as you call it, is crushed by the tragedy of evil in men's souls. My own remaining pure and blistered, gazing appalled into the sea of corruption in every heart. My strength within and without was fed by the mighty sons of Hind, by nature's wealth in devotion and fidelity? Todar Mall, my sturdy oak, died too soon. Faizi, my charming vine, was also cut off by the scissors of death. And Abul Fazl is no more! The White Pearl tarnished and blackened. Thrown into the bottomless deeps! Lost and irretrievable! My son, my own son, his murderer!"

"Once, you told me, Your Majesty, that even if I asked pardon for an enemy, you would forgive." Salima breathed chokingly. "Now, Your Majesty, may I ask pardon for your son?" Her voice was barely audible.

"Yes, my Love. My only Love! My Truth and my Soul! How can I not forgive, when divine truth shines in your eyes like beacons of light from the very heavens! This love, this light, this truth, for which I had hoped and had suffered to live all these years!" Akbar's eyes were gathering rills of pain. "My prince is pardoned."

"My son. Your Majesty. You are ill. The pain is shining in your very eyes." Hamida Banu Begum appealed apprehensively. "Let me summon Hakim Mirri.

"No, dear Mamma." Akbar laughed. "The emperor's body is a garden of delight, this very moment, where no ailments could ever visit. Only the sweet pain in my heart dares manifest its joy." He stole a glance at Salima. "You yourself look ill, Mamma! If we need any physician here, he should be summoned for your good health alone. But, right now, you need to summon prince Salim. He is your healing ointment."

All the emperor's wives were now gathered around him, hugging and kissing him. Prince Salim was brought in by his sister Aram Banu, and he prostrated most humbly.

"Get to your feet, Shaikhu Baba, and heed the emperor's words." Akbar commanded. "Look at Aram Banu! Treat this sister of yours with love and kindness, after I am dead and forgotten. She is most dear to me of all my sons and daughters."

"Your Majesty. May you enjoy a long, long life of health and prosperity!" Prince Salim protested quickly. His voice sincere and quivering.

"The emperor knows your ambition, Shaikhu Baba." Akbar indulged warmly. "Alas, that I know my sons too well! If you were assailed by your wish to covet the empire of Hind before the emperor's death, you should have killed me and spared Abul Fazl! I would have been grateful for that, even in my death, Shaikhu Baba."

"Your Majesty, I—" Prince Salim felt choked.

"No need to defend your sin and folly, Shaikhu Baba. You are forgiven. The Judgment rests in God's hands." Akbar's tone was kind and comforting. "But you must know, Shaikhu Baba! By this cruel folly of yours, you have driven the first nail of death inside my heart, if not in my coffin. My heart, it yearns for death. And I can feel death's presence quite near me. Soon, you will have your kingdom, and your crown, too."

"Your Majesty." Prince Salim fell at the emperor's feet once again. "I crave not your crown, or your kingdom, but your forgiveness. And your long life! Hoping, that I may prosper under the shadow of your love and judgment."

Akbar removed prince Salim's turban off gently and caressively, and replaced it with his own. Cradling his son's turban into his lap most attentively.

"You know what this signifies, Shaikhu Baba. That the emperor still holds you in favor, and that you are the heir to my throne." Akbar murmured to himself.

"Yes, Your Majesty! Glory of God is manifested in your very eyes." Prince Salim lifted his eyes up to his father, forcing back his tears.

"No need to flatter the old emperor, Shaikhu Baba." Akbar elicited one snort of mirth. "If you have witnessed the glory of God in my eyes, then this glory may go with you, if you reign justly. With love and compassion! With kindness and understanding."

"This day would be my talisman for justice and compassion, Your Majesty. I would not ever forget." Prince Salim murmured.

"Today, we always tend to forget, in the hope of tomorrow, Shaikhu Baba." Akbar commented softly.

"May I request a boon, Your Majesty?" Prince Salim pleaded suddenly. "May I request the gift of your Lone elephant, since your generosity has already cradled me in its loving arms?" He smiled charmingly.

"Lone elephant is yours, Shaikhu Baba. And my royal diadem would be bestowed on you shortly—that ornament of sovereignty." Akbar smiled.

"How can I voice my love and gratitude, Your Majesty! You have overwhelmed me." Prince Salim sang joyfully. "I have dreamed of owning this Lone elephant. You have made me so happy, Your Majesty. I would feel proud to ride this ferocious beast."

"On the thin fabric of our prides, we weave our silly dreams." Akbar murmured. "Just satisfy my curiosity, Shaikhu Baba. Why did you plot such a heinous crime so as to murder Abul Fazl? The emperor wishes to hear from your lips. Now, tell me truthfully, and with absolute sincerity. No lies!" He commanded.

"Your Majesty, he was no friend of mine." Was prince Salim's half stunned, half involuntary response! "He publicly and privately spoke against me, Your Majesty. Causing strife and discord! Your royal feelings were embittered against me due to the—"

"No more, no more, Shaikhu Baba." Was Akbar's wearied command. "Let me advise you on the matters of royal household, Shaikhu Baba. Treat all your wives with love and kindness. Especially, Man Bai! I hear, her health is not improving. What is the name of your newly-wedded bride? It has been a year, has it not?" He asked abruptly.

"Karamasi, Your Majesty." Was prince Salim's laconic response! "She is heavy with child." He added winsomely

"A beautiful name." Akbar muttered. "I should name a city by this name—" He paused. "Let me test your knowledge in government and governing, Shaikhu Baba. How many provinces do we have in our empire?" He asked.

"Fifteen, Your Majesty." Was prince Salim's quick response.

"Name them, my son. The emperor tends to forget in his old age." Akbar prompted testingly.

"Agra, Oudh, Ajmer, Bihar, Delhi, Kabul, Berar, Malwa, Multan, Lahore, Bengal, Khandesh, Ahmadabad, Allahabad, Ahmadnagar, Your Majesty." Prince Salim recounted with the fluency of a politician.

"Ah, Kabul! With Kashmir and Great Tibet, hosting the most fragrant of valleys. The emperor wishes to visit those valleys." Akbar pondered aloud. "More insurrections by that doomed infidel again, in Mewar. But you return to Allahabad, Shaikhu Baba. You will come to Agra, when we arrange for the wedding of prince Daniyal. Usha Begum is proposing an excellent match for him. When you visit us again, bring your Lone elephant with you. Let me see your skill in taming my favorite beast."

"Your Majesty, I might have an accident in taming the Lone elephant. And if he is still not tamed on the day of the auspicious wedding, and casts me down on the ground, it would serve as a bad omen." Prince Salim responded thoughtlessly.

"Don't cultivate ignorance and superstition, Shaikhu Baba. You are to rule the mighty empire of Hind." A quick reprimand broke forth on Akbar's lips.

"Let us celebrate this day of reconciliation with song and music." Hamida Banu Begum interceded, watching the hasty approach of Aziz Koka.

"Your Majesty." Aziz Koka curtsied low. "Gulbadan Begum is delirious. She is asking for you and Miryam Makani."

Akbar leaped to his feet with the alacrity of a young man. He was racing toward the chamber of his aunt, followed by Hamida Banu Begum and other ladies of the harem.

The blue, damasked chamber with ivory fringes was wafting the scent of candles and flowers. Akbar was standing at the foot of the bed, where Gulbadan Begum lay propped on her white pillows, gasping for breath. Hakim Mirri was feeling Gulbadan Begum's pulse most solemnly. Hamida Banu Begum was pressing her hand.

"Gulbadan, Rose, my dearest of friends. Open your eyes, love. Look, the emperor is here." Hamida Banu Begum was straining to catch her wordless expressions.

"I am weak and dying. May you live long." Gulbadan Begum's hand fell limp.

Hakim Mirri's eyes alone were announcing the verdict of death.

Since the death of Gulbadan, another year had curled up into the rivers of time with waves calm and turbulent. Prince Daniyal was to be wedded to his young bride, and this particular day was the final day of wedding celebrations. The betrothal had taken place in Ahmadnagar, from where the princess had journeyed forth to Agra.

One poet-scholar by the name of Ferishtah had accompanied the Princess. Akbar had found much solace in the company of this poet-scholar. Prince Salim was absent on this festive day of the wedding celebrations, for reasons known only to him and Salima. Somehow prince Salim's wife Karamasi was entering Akbar's thoughts. She had given birth to a daughter, and Akbar had named his grand-daughter, Bihar Banu.

That fool of a prince, gallivanting on some forested paths, or hunting somewhere, instead of thinking about attending the wedding of his brother.

Akbar, this morning, had sent Aziz Koka to fetch prince Salim from Allahabad to Agra. Aziz Koka had not returned, the emperor was just becoming aware with a sudden pang of regret. He was escaping the wedding festivities in the palace hall and seeking the refuge of his chamber where he was sure to find his beloved Salima.

Salima had not heard anyone enter her chamber, and was startled to her feet at the first note of the emperor's voice.

"You have been dancing to your heart's content, my sweet." Akbar began gently. "These mystic beats drain one of poise and energy. Quite an exhilarating experience, though." He laughed, watching her spring to her feet with the agility of a young girl.

"No, Your Majesty, not really." Salima protested. "I was dragged into dancing, and fled at the very first opportunity."

"The emperor only wishes to see the dance of love in your eyes, my love." Akbar sailed toward her. "Ah, love and truth, which I have been seeking all my life! And have found it at last! Love is, truth. My own beloved truth! All these years of searching and seeking, truth? Truth, wisdom, knowledge, and all those religious discussions, all pale before the gold of truth in your heart, my love. And before the flames of love in your eyes—oh, how blue and sparkling." He kissed her eyes and lips.

"Your Majesty. Your hands, your face, your whole body is burning with fever." Salima Begum's hands were caressing the emperor's cheeks. "Let me summon—"

"This is the fever of wait, my love." Akbar sealed her lips with a kiss. "Have you heard anything from our wayward prince?" He asked softly.

"No, Your Majesty." Salima murmured consolingly. "You should not suffer thus, Your Majesty. You know, why the prince is not here? Yet, he is kind and loving. Only the victim of his dark moods, these days, I suppose."

"The victim of inebriation, to be precise!" Akbar smiled, drifting toward the window. "Alas, the emperor knows too well. Yet, your love has sustained me through all those tragedies, or I would have gone mad with grief, despair and loneliness. Grief has left me. I despair no more. No, I am not suffering. Loneliness is still my companion though, when I am not with you. And sadly, that is the most part of all my living, breathing hours. Prince Salim, the royal hedonist! I know why he is not here? He is too drunk to perceive my urgent summons. I hear, he takes his wine mixed with opium. Craving intoxicated bliss, and disdaining the bliss in sobriety. And during one of those vile and drunken moods of his, he has acted most cruelly. He is charged of inflicting inhuman punishments, including the flaying of a young man before his very eyes. He knows that the emperor is informed of all the base and foul acts of his son. And now, my vile prince is shuddering with fright. Afraid, that the emperor would punish him. The emperor does not permit even to flay a sheep. How can our son be so cruel?"

Their eyes were locked. An eternity of pain and love suspended there like the calm oceans, but a discreet knock at the door had disrupted the blessed silence.

"Your Majesty." Aziz Koka greeted, and then he couldn't speak.

"Is prince Salim ill?" Akbar demurred aloud. "Speak, my brave brother?"

"No, Your Majesty. Prince Salim is in good health." Aziz Koka murmured.

"You are the messenger of some woeful news, the emperor can tell." Akbar sighed relief. His gaze intense and searching.

"The good news is, Your Majesty, that Karamasi Begum has blessed prince Salim with a royal daughter." Aziz Koka intoned evasively.

"You are going senile on the very rungs of your ripe years, my dear brother!" Akbar exclaimed impatiently. "That was a couple of months ago, and my royal grand-daughter was named, Bihar Banu."

"Pardon me, Your Majesty, Man Bai Begum has committed suicide." The words appeared to fall from Aziz Koka's lips like burning coals.

"By what means did she—" Akbar's anguished eyes were demanding answers.

"An overdose of opium, Your Majesty. She swallowed large quantities of opium, before she went to bed." Aziz Koka expounded.

"And where is my drunken son? The author of such tragedies?" Akbar asked.

"Prince Salim doesn't know, Your Majesty. He had gone hunting yesterday. Has not returned as yet." Was Aziz Koka's low response.

"Then the emperor himself would journey to Allahabad, and would put a noose of discipline around his royal neck." Akbar thundered, noticing Aram Banu fly into the room with the speed of a wild gust.

"Your Majesty, Miryam Makani has fainted in her room. She—" Aram Banu was clutching the emperor's arm and dragging him along, hastily and frantically.

The emperor had to swallow another morsel of grief before he could reach the chamber, where his mother lay resting under the sheets of eternal bliss. The tearful eyes of Hakim Ali were announcing the news of her death.

Another mournful year had flitted past in the funereal hush of its gloom and darkness. And when the emperor had thought he had purged his soul of all grief, a greater grief than the grief over his mother's death, had struck the mightiest of its blows. The news of prince Daniyal's death had come crashing on his head like an avalanche. The emperor was ailing. Seeking not the threshold to recovery, but the road to oblivion!

Five long months of hopeless, helpless pain after the death of his youngest son, and the emperor's heart was literally broken into splinters of anguish.

Right after the wedding celebrations, prince Daniyal with his young bride, had repaired to Burhanpur. As soon as he had reached Burhanpur, he had succumbed to his old passion in drinking. Aziz Koka was sent with a Farman from the emperor that the prince was no longer permitted to receive any supply of wine. It was stated that anyone violating that Farman would be sentenced to death.

After this Farman, none of Prince Daniyal's attendants could comply with his entreaties, holding the emperor's Farman with fear and dread. But one of prince Daniyal's devoted attendant, Murshid Quli, was moved to tears by his master's misery and despair. One evening, overwhelmed by prince Daniyal's incessant commands and entreaties, he himself had pleaded in a hopeless fashion.

How can I gratify your wishes, my prince, without incurring the risk of discovery?

To this, prince Daniyal had responded in a pitiful refrain.

At this moment, liquor to me is as much as life itself. Your life will be in no danger, and mine will be indebted to you for letting me live. Fill the barrel of my favorite gun, Jennauzah, with strong spirits, and bring it to me. And you will remain safe. No suspicion or discovery will fall on your head.

Prince Daniyal's request was granted fulfillment. For several days, he was content in receiving drinks concealed in the barrel of his favorite gun. Unfortunately, the drinks were gathering rust from the barrel, and these concoctions were to prove fatal to the delicate constitution of prince Daniyal. Within forty days of tremens and delirium, he had become the victim of death.

After the death of prince Daniyal, the mists of gloom and doom had made a permanent abode in the palace at Agra. Even now, as the emperor sat in the damasked chamber with his beloved Salima, he could see such mists floating and thickening. His only consoling thought this very moment as he sat luxuriating in the company of his Beloved, was that prince Salim had grown sober and disciplined. He was drinking moderately and with utmost caution. One more consoling thought was fanning his gloom, that prince Salim was blessed with two more sons. Karamasi was the mother of these twins, and Akbar had named his grandsons, Jahandar and Shahryar.

The empire of Hind with all its glory had lost its luster to the eyes of the emperor. Besides, his ill health could lend him neither peace, nor time, to keep the court intrigues in check, which had become to surface like the army of locusts. The emperor had favored prince Salim as the heir to his throne, investing him with his robe and diadem. But since prince Khusrau was still the emperor's favorite grandson, the viziers and courtiers were counting him as one of the contenders to the throne of Hind. Such rumors could not escape the emperor's notice, but then Salima was there, acting as a soothing interpreter to purge all canards of their sting and corruption.

"You have let grief and despair conquer you, Your Majesty, while you still remain a noble victor over the mighty empire of Hind." Salima commented thoughtfully. "Glory is yours too, and you can reclaim the vigor of your youth and health, if you could only let your sorrows breathe. They are being choked in the dark sea of your ever-grieving, ever-suffering soul." She added poetically.

"Glory! I had lost years ago, my love. When I was robbed of the precious jewels of my court! Birbal, Todar Mall, Fath Ullah, Tansen, Faizi, Abul Fazl, Bhagwan Das, Nizamuddin Ahmed, only Man Singh is left. All those precious, precious gems of my naurattan." Akbar responded warmly. "And my youth too, lost and irretrievable. It cannot be reclaimed, once that it is abandoned. The crumbs of glory, which are left, my sweet, shall also pass. Along with my grief and despair, when, I don't know?"

"Prince Salim has arranged an elephant fight for your entertainment alone, Your Majesty!" Salima declared evasively.

"The emperor knows, love." Akbar smiled tenderly. "Not for my entertainment alone, but for all to see, how his elephant defeats the brave elephant of prince Khusrau. Shaikhu Baba, still jealous of his son! Trying to prove to the world that he is the sole heir to the throne of Hind!" He demurred thoughtfully.

"Prince Salim wishes your audience, before this fight commences, Your Majesty. May I summon him?" Salima Begum requested winsomely.

"Yes, my sweet intercessor." Akbar smiled. "Though, he doesn't need any interceding. The emperor wishes to see him quite often, to make sure that he is not drunk. But wait a while. Two hours hence. This fight doesn't commence till—let me enjoy the peace and bliss of your dear, dear company."

Akbar sailed toward his Beloved. He cupped her face into his hands, and imprinted a soft kiss on her brow. He grazed his lips against her hair and then turned away abruptly. His look was still dreamy, as he began to pace abstractedly.

"This presage! I have this presage, that I won't have the bliss of being alone with you, for a long, long time? Not ever, perhaps." Akbar was thinking aloud.

"It's your grief speaking, Your Majesty, not you. My love alone, alas, has failed to absolve your grief." Was Salima's murmur of a response!

"Your love, my love, is my love and truth." Akbar murmured back. "It has sustained me this long. Surely, I would have been perished, resting in peace with my sweet Daniyal. Yes, dear heart, do summon Shaikhu Baba, I want to ask him something?"

"Your Majesty. Something concerning Man Bai's—" The word *suicide* was left unuttered on Salima's lips. Her hand reaching out for the gold rope!

Prince Salim, who was awaiting such summons rushed into this chamber in a flash, curtsying. Invited by Salima Begum to sit beside her, he sank into the cushiony depths with a sigh of relief and gratitude.

"Look into the emperor's eyes, Shaikhu Baba. Let me judge if you are sober enough to sit beside Salima Begum." Akbar challenged.

"I haven't had any drink since last night, Your Majesty." Prince Salim met the emperor's gaze with utter love and devotion. "Today is Sunday, Your Majesty. The blessed day of your birth, and I abstain from drinking on Sundays. This day, I hold in great esteem. Shunning ill thoughts, and entertaining noble visions."

"Your flatteries, Shaikhu Baba, are assuming the hum of a cataract. Sweet and soporific!" Akbar laughed. "Alas, that prince Murad and prince Daniyal couldn't summon enough will to restrain their passion for drinking." His look was intense and searching. "Do you have any fond memories of your brothers?" He asked abruptly.

"Quite a few, Your Majesty." Was prince Salim's cautious response! "Going, hunting with them was the most delightful of pleasures. They were both fond of shooting. Especially, prince Daniyal. He had named his favorite gun Jennauzah a few months before he—" He could not utter the word *died*.

"Yes, Jennauzah, meaning, bier." Akbar thought aloud. "Prince Daniyal. My youngest bloom of a son! Plucked out of the bower of his life, too soon. Didn't you receive a letter from him, just a few weeks before he died? What did he say?"

"Not much, Your Majesty. It was rather a brief missive." Prince Salim intoned reluctantly. "He wrote that he had named his favorite gun, Jennauzah, and that he had inscribed his couplet on this gun with his own hands."

"What was that couplet, did he say?" Was Akbar's eager query.

"In the pleasures of chase with thee, my soul breathes fresh and clear— tazwah

But who receives thy fatal mission, sinks lifeless on the bier—jennauzah."
Prince Salim recited obediently.

"I wanted to ask you something, Shaikhu Baba, I forget—" Akbar's gaze was shifting to Salima. Then returning to his son. "Oh, yes. Were you unkind to Man Bai? Unkind in such a way as to drive her insane with the desire to take her life?"

"No, Your Majesty." Prince Salim protested quickly. "I was devoted to her. And her devotion to me was such that she would have sacrificed a thousand sons and brothers for one hair of mine." He added passionately. "The grief and bitterness caused by the behavior of her son, and by the misconduct of her brother, Madho Singh, had made her the victim of such a cruel death."

"Ah, death! The emperor is wearied of it. Yet, waiting with aching heart to embrace its light and darkness." Akbar was watching his son with a gleam of curiosity. "What elephant you have chosen against the elephant of prince Khusrau?"

"Against his Apurva, my Grimbar is the bravest of all." Prince Salim murmured.

"Are preparations for the fight all complete?" Akbar got to his feet.

"Yes, Your Majesty. Spectators from all over Agra have been gathering on the banks of Jamna since last night. They will stay close to the fort of Agra to witness this great fight." Prince Salim's eyes were lit up with joy and pride. "I have trained Grimbar myself, Your Majesty. And I am proud to be its master."

"Yes." Akbar murmured. "Our little prides have the power to destroy everything which can lend us joy, love and peace. These little prides, stand in our way of progress and prosperity like the immovable rocks, blowing away our mighty efforts of goodwill and reconciliation down the abyss of shame and misery. Ponder upon this, Shaikhu Baba, while you order my groom to fetch the emperor's horse." He waved dismissal.

The scene below the Agra fort was one of a Roman Arena. The emperor was seated under the canopies of silks, with garlands of flowers. Prince Khurram, the emperor's next favorite grandson, was seated right beside him. The lower galleries were teeming with groups of viziers and courtiers. The snake charmers and the whirling dervishes were luring a crowd of young men to their side. But most of the eyes were turning to the commencement of the elephant fights with agog and anticipation.

Prince Salim, astride his white Arabian horse, was urging his elephant, Grimbar, to provoke prince Khusrau's Apurva to a quick fight. The emperor was praying for prince Khusrau's elephant to win. Though, his heart was thundering all of a sudden!

Grimbar was charging at Apurva, its snout moving with the hiss of a well-oiled whip. Apurva was being pummeled at the neck with maddening blows from Grimbar. Akbar was watching his elephant, ready to be brought into the arena as a referee, if the fight were to become unmanageable. Since Grimbar was going beyond the limits of its training to hurt Apurva, Ranthambhan was brought to the field to intervene. The followers of prince Salim were delirious with rage and excitement. They had begun to pelt Ranthambhan with stones, hooting and screaming.

Akbar, noticing this outrage, had sent prince Khurram to prince Salim as a messenger of his thundering commands.

"Tell your princely father, to discipline his mad devotees, and order them to cease this undignified behavior." Akbar was trying to stifle the pain in his stomach.

The emperor's message was carried on the wings of the wind, even before prince Khurram could reach his father. The pelting of the stones was truncated. Ranthambhan was distracted, and so was Apurva. Grimbar was declared the winner. Akbar's pain in the stomach was growing so intense, that he could barely breathe. His eyes were closing, and his head was drooping to one side. The sapphire in his turban was bright and dazzling, as if kindled with the fire of omens and prophecies.

The royal physicians were gathering around the emperor. The lips of the evening itself were gasping for breath, it seemed. Suddenly, a ripple of breeze was awakening, startled by the dwindling of sound and music.

The emperor had fainted!

The gilded litter was cradling the emperor in a peaceful swoon, while he was carried to his palace, guarded by friends and physicians. The grand show in the Moghul arena was disrupted, and the soldiers astride their horses on the sandy expanse of the Jamna River were watching the crowds dwindle and disperse.

The palace at Agra was once again the abode of doom and gloom. And this time, the emperor was its victim. Since his illness at the Moghul arena, the emperor had wakened to throes of physical torment he had not ever known before. Four weeks of diarrhea and internal bleeding had robbed him of his strength to defy the skills of his royal physicians, or to command them to cease their ministrations. For the past two weeks, the emperor had begun to gather inner strength, not of the body, but of the mind. He was able to command his viziers and courtiers to fetch his imperial robe and turban and his jeweled dagger, and to summon prince Salim before his presence.

This particular evening, the emperor had felt neither pain, nor delirium, and was endowed with a sense of subtle awareness. In this state of reprieve, he had discovered that he had lost his power of speech. All the viziers and courtiers were gathered in this tapestried chamber, as commanded by the emperor earlier this evening. Foremost among them was prince Salim, undeterred by the swarms of court intrigues, and pressed by the weight of his grief and penance. He was bending down to kiss the brow of his ailing father, his eyes gathering tears, as if he had read the emperor's wordless expression in his feverish eyes. Suddenly, the emperor's arm stirred, groping for direction, and his hand rested on prince Salim's head in one gesture of a caress and blessing.

The emperor's feverish eyes were fixed on his imperial robe and turban, and with a feeble gesture of his hand, he was instructing his viziers to invest his son with his own robe and turban. His gaze was turning to his jeweled dagger beside him, and his arm was rising in one last gesture of a command. This gesture was understood by his viziers, that the emperor wished his son to claim this dagger as the emblem of his power and sovereignty over Hind.

The viziers were quick to invest prince Salim with the emperor's imperial robe and turban, while he himself had girded the jeweled dagger at his waist. The emperor's eyes were moist, and falling shut. His lips were trembling, evoking one murmur of a prayer. The only audible words to be heard were, God, Allah.

Hakim Ali was feeling the emperor's pulse. He had lifted his gaze up to prince Salim, the flood of tears in his eyes announcing the death of the emperor.

The greatest of the Moghul emperors had died, his face as white as the white, satiny sheets. And the mournful hush in this imperial room was the only lament to proclaim to the world that Great Akbar was no more.

Bibliography

Amini, Iradj. *The Koh-i-noor Diamond*. Roli books, 1994.

Augustus, Frederick. *The Emperor Akbar* Vol. 1. Atlantic Publishers, 1983.

Berinstain, Valerie. *India and the Mughal Dynasty*. Discoveries Series. Harry N. Abrams Inc., 1976.

Beveridge, Annette, trans. *Humayun-Nama*. Sang-E-Meel Publications, 1987.

Burke, S. M. *Akbar: The Greatest Moghul*. Munshiram Manoharlal Publishers, 1989.

Early, Abraham. *The Lives and Times of the Great Moghals*. Viking, 1997.

Elliot, H. M. *Akbar Nama of Abul-Fazl*. Islamic Book Service, 1988.

———. *Memoirs of Jahangir*. Islamic Book Service, 1987.

Hansen, Waldmar. *The Peacock Throne*. Motilal Banarsidas, 1986.

Jarrett, Colonel H. S., trans. *The Ain-i-Akbari*. Vols 2 & 3. Atlantic Publishers, 1989.

Majumdar, R. C. *The History and Culture of Indian People*. Bhaharatiya Vidya Bhavan, 1994.

Raychaudhuri, Tapan. *Bengal Under Akbar and Jahangir*. Munshiram Manoharlal Publishers, 1969.

Rogers, Alexander, trans. *Tuzuk-i-Jahangiri*. Munshiram Manoharlal Publishers Pvt. Ltd., 1978.

Index

About the Author

Farzana Moon is a teacher and a bibliophile, a poet, historian, and playwright with a Masters in Education. She writes Sufi poetry, historical, biographical accounts of Moghul emperors, and plays based on stories from religion and folklore. She has written several books, including *Sufis and Mystics of the World* based on her lectures at Clark State Community College. Most of her Moghul sequels are published with the intent of exploring markets for documentaries. She is the author of *Holocaust of the East* published by Cambridge Scholars Publishing. *Answers from Mount Hira* is a biography of Prophet Muhammad, the first volume in a trilogy published by Dreamcatcher Books. She participated in author/panel discussions at Columbia University. A collection of her plays are archived at Ohio State University. Her most recently published book is *Irem of the Crimson Desert*. She is currently researching for a book about Bahadur Shah Zafar—the last of the Moghuls, adding another century and a half after the sixth Moghul emperor of India. Born and educated in Pakistan, Farzana is a US citizen. She is being considered for a Fulbright Scholarship to continue her research about Bahadur Shah Zafar in India.